For YOUR EYES Only

USA TODAY BESTSELLING AUTHOR

TIA LOUISE

For Kerissa and all my sexy book lovers who
always ask for more…
I love you!

PROLOGUE

Giana

O BSESSION KILLED MY MOTHER, BUT IT'S NOT HOW I WILL DIE. The detectives called it a *crime of passion*, but she would've hated that verdict. She adored passion and colors and beauty and music. She taught me to love these things. She taught me to sing and to sew and to dream…

"Your mother was a great beauty." Aunt Gratziela jerks my head as she attempts to pull a comb through my thick, gnarled curls, forcing a yelp from my lips. "You are not like your mother."

I don't cry. It's true, I'm not beautiful like my mother was, but I try to be strong like her.

My mother would walk through the streets of our small, coastal village in southern Italy with her silky brunette hair shining in the sun. Her skin was smooth as the delicately carved ivory plaques of Mary and the baby Jesus in the cathedral, and when she passed, the men would lean back, closing their eyes like they smelled fresh bread straight from the oven.

They would follow her along the narrow streets, hoping

to pick up something she dropped or to help her carry a heavy load—all to see her smile and perhaps even say *grazie*.

My olive skin was tanned brown by the sun, and my aunt would rub lotion on me saying I'd never attract a man with the way I looked. It only got worse as I got older, and she said I looked like a peasant with round hips and a full bust.

But I wasn't looking for a man.

When I was ten years old, a man took away the life I loved, a life of happiness in which my mother and I lived in a pretty little apartment overlooking the sea. A man killed my beautiful mother, and then he killed himself. And I was sent to live with my aunt.

My father died in a fishing accident before I was old enough to remember him. He gave me my love of dancing and running around the streets barefoot, which made my heels as rough and calloused as a donkey's hooves, as my aunt would say.

I started dancing when I was thirteen, and to everyone's (mostly my aunt's) surprise, I was very good at it (for a girl my size, she would say).

I wasn't as slim as a reed, but I could dance well enough to draw the attention of the city company. I was talented enough to be paired with a boy as light on his feet as I was, a boy who asked me to marry him and then broke up with me—but that came later.

The memories I cherish are the ones I spent with my mother, sleeping with the windows open so we could breathe the salty sea air. I would close my eyes and dream of lifting my arms and riding higher on the warm currents, my stubborn curls flowing straight in the cool breeze, the stars illuminating my skin from the inside like a goddess.

My mother once told me butterflies work very hard to become the beautiful, flying creatures that kiss all the flowers. She said their metamorphosis happens when they're not even expecting it.

She said caterpillars root in the dirt and leaves, dreaming

of nothing, when all the time, deep inside they have the power to become magnificently gorgeous creatures that can fly.

I wrinkled my small nose and asked if she was calling me a worm.

She laughed and hugged me close. "What do you love, Gia?" She threaded her fingers in my wild curls until they were smooth coils around my cheeks. "Follow what calls to you, and that's how you find your passion. Then spread your wings and fly."

Then she was gone, and I was left with no one who believed I was special.

She made it sound so easy—believe, work hard, fly. I didn't know metamorphosis was dangerous and cruel. I didn't know how easily everything could go wrong.

I only thought it created a beautiful butterfly.

I didn't know it also brought death.

CHAPTER 1

Trip

Ten years later

"YOU'RE OUT OF CONTROL, MOTHER." I EXHALE, STRAIGHTENING the lapel on my dark brown, Brioni suit.

Agitation itches beneath my virgin wool collar, but I don't let it show. I never let my irritation show. I study the Manhattan skyline through the oversized windows of our Upper East Side apartment and collect my thoughts.

At twenty-five, I'm well-connected and highly invested in the obscenely wealthy shadows of the city's real-estate, gaming, and nightclub scenes. I operate on the razor's edge of what's legal and what's, shall we say, *morally gray*.

Players from around the globe operate in my world, and high-priced lawyers use many words to construct the shady legality of our deals. The margins are thin. At any moment, someone's number could come up, in which they discover they owe more than they can repay.

Such things don't happen to me.

Remaining off the record, in the deep background, protects

me. I never stick my neck out for anyone. It's a world of poker players, and I've got the straightest face in the group—or should I say, the most detached smile.

"Don't speak to me that way." My mother acts offended, but she's not.

Turning from the window to the mini-bar, I pour a tumbler of vodka casually. "Forgive me. I wasn't trying to be rude. Would you like a drink?"

"Of course." She touches her hair lightly with her fingertips, preening like a goldfinch in her bright yellow Balenciaga caftan. "The very idea of you sleeping with my best friend, a woman twice your age. What would your father say?"

"He'd make some crack about my manhood." I glance at the bronze urn on the mantle holding his ashes. "He'd wonder aloud why I couldn't land a girl my own age or something like that."

William Robert Alexander II took great pride in tearing his only son and namesake to shreds. He'd focus his green eyes on me like a hawk, ready to rip through any exposed weakness or vulnerability. I hated him, but he taught me to be strong.

He sent me to the finest boarding schools his inherited wealth could buy. He made sure I got into Columbia, then when I realized I didn't need him, I quit wasting everyone's time and dropped out.

Naturally, he had many unkind things to say about that decision, and what he dubbed my failure to finish anything, as if he had any idea the deals I was closing. But I had stopped listening to that old bully a long time ago.

"Your father was *difficult*, but he took care of us financially. We can be thankful for that."

Did he? For starters, it wasn't his fortune to leave, not that it matters to me, and secondly, his finances always came with strings—or barbed hooks.

"I find other things to be thankful for." I hand her the drink.

She can live off the spoils of an unhappy marriage, pretending to be unaffected by years of emotional abuse, but I'm doing everything in my power to divorce myself from that man's legacy. I'm so close to being completely, utterly, independently wealthy. I just have to stay focused, then I'm cashing out, leaving the game.

"Still," she continues, "I don't know why you'd want to validate his low opinion of you by sleeping with that woman."

Taking a sip of my drink, I decide it's time to prick the air out of her precious gossip bubble. "I didn't sleep with Belinda Desayda-Rice."

Her eyes narrow, and I can tell she's trying to decide if I'm being honest. *Give me a break.* Of course, I didn't sleep with Belinda. I could murder Grish for putting me in this position. He's the one who can't keep his dick in his pants.

Greg Peters is one of my most trusted business partners— because we're the same age and equally hungry. He's from Moscow, so while *Grisha* is the Russian diminutive for Greg, I shorten it further to *Grish*.

Shaking her head, she sighs. "I confess, I wasn't sold on the story. Belinda isn't your style, and you've been friends with Debbie since you were a child. It would be too bizarre." My mother lifts the olive from her drink, chewing as she speaks. "But why would anyone spread such a lie? It must be a terrible strain for you, Trip dear."

I can think of several reasons Belinda would allow people to think I was her lover. For starters, it feeds her ego. It makes her look desirable if an ambitious twenty-something wants to fuck her, but more importantly, it distracts everyone from the fact she's actually sleeping with her daughter's boyfriend.

Fucking Grish. My clever Russian pal thinks he's scored a pair of queens, but he's got a seven and a two—a notoriously bad hand in poker.

"It'll blow over in a few days." I pause at the mirror to straighten my yellow silk tie.

My thick brown hair curls around my ears, and dark stubble

is on my cheeks. I need a trim and a shave, and I want to be anywhere but this goddamned city. I'm not in the mood for bullshit.

In that moment, I decide. "I'm going out of town for a few weeks. I'll check on our properties in West Palm…" *And my own business investments* while this drama dies out.

In south Florida my work is more colorful and a lot more relaxing.

"Sounds lovely." Mother walks over to give me air kisses. "I'm leaving for Saint Moritz on Monday, so before you go, would you be a dear?"

She smiles sweetly, which means she wants me to transfer money into her account. My father couldn't stop her from pursuing other interests (a.k.a., *other men*) after he died, so in his will, he put me in charge of her purse strings. Barbed hooks.

As long as she remains single, she's entitled to as much of the family estate as I am, but if she ever remarries, she's out. Our eyes meet, and I catch a flicker of apprehension in hers.

It fucking pisses me off.

My father put me in this position of power because he hoped it would turn me into him. It gnawed at him when I would watch him be a racist, elitist bastard and not laugh at his jokes. It infuriated him when I drank vodka instead of scotch. He called me names and said I thought I was better than him.

I didn't think it. I *knew* I was better than him, and the idea that he'd put me in a position to make my mother cower stirs an anger so deep in me it almost breaks my façade. Does she truly think she has to beg for what she deserves?

I suppose all those years of having to account for every penny created a mindset she can't break. My father was a nouveau-riche dipshit who didn't realize the truly wealthy never think about money.

My mother might drive me crazy with her frivolous behavior, but I've become protective of her as I've gotten older. I've learned how prolonged exposure to cruelty can change a person, and I only want her to be happy now.

"You can always have as much as you want." I slide my phone from the inside pocket of my blazer. Tapping the face, I quickly move ten thousand from the family endowment to her personal account. "Text me if that isn't enough."

Her brow relaxes, and she's about to speak when her phone interrupts us. One look at the face, and her entire expression lights up in a way I know all too well. Her boys are calling.

So much for that familial moment.

"Have to run, darling. Thanks." She gives me a little wave and starts down the hall before hesitating. "You're not spending the night here, are you?"

"No." The last thing I'm in the mood for is stumbling into one of my mother's threesomes.

"Have fun in Florida, and don't worry. I'm not upset with you." A smile curls her lips, and she's off again. "Whatever you did, I'm sure you had your reasons."

I don't bother pointing out *I did nothing*. She's gone, Chanel No. 5 lingering in her wake.

She's satisfied. I should be satisfied, but I'm tense. I want to get out of here.

Tracing the lines of our luxury apartment, I think of the years I've spent in this elegant prison. My family moved into the Andover, a historic, massive apartment building on Manhattan's Upper East Side, when I was in primary school.

I spent my days running through the halls and making friends with the other kids in the building, also offspring of ultra-rich, corrupt New York elites.

We spent summer days marching around the oversized fountain in the courtyard, stomping up the stairs, and screaming from the rooftops. We annoyed the older residents, the ones hanging on thanks to rent control, until they died.

Once you're in the Andover, you never leave.

Tapping on my phone, I order our family's private jet as I step into the hall, taking the marble stairs two at a time. My flight to south Florida won't be ready for another few hours, and my upstairs neighbors are as much like family as my own. Hell, possibly more.

They're the only ones who understand this shadow world that created us. They're the only ones who want to escape it as much as I do.

"Is it just me or has the gossip mill hit rock bottom?" Hana van Hamilton drapes her thin, dancer-body over the velvet sofa in her living room.

She's wearing light gray joggers and a matching, long-sleeved cashmere sweater, and her curly blonde hair is twisted up on her head.

"Since when did I become a topic of conversation?" I'm at the mini-bar pouring us both fresh vodkas. "I never kiss and tell. Even when it's interesting."

"Don't act so innocent." Her eyes sparkle, teasing me. "You slept with Belinda last year at the gala. Everyone said so."

Wincing, I shake my head. "I have never put my dick in that woman."

Her eyebrow arches, this girl who knows me better than anyone.

I pass her a drink, and she shrugs. "Either way, I think it should be illegal to sleep with the mother *and* the daughter. Ew."

Dropping onto the cushion beside her, I exhale heavily. "The law doesn't give a shit who we sleep with, *darling*, provided they're over eighteen. Hell, sometimes not even then."

She flinches, and I feel like an ass for adding that last bit. I know Hana's past injuries very well. Clearing my throat, I attempt to steer us back to lighter ground.

"The worst part was being cross-examined about my sex life by my mother." It takes all my self-control not to shudder. "She actually believed I did it."

Hana's glossy lips twist into a frown, and she slides her toes into my lap. "Your mother should know Belinda is not your style."

"That would require her to actually know me."

"Like I do?" She smiles, her dark blue eyes too big for her heart-shaped face.

Hana is a delicate beauty, but she's too much like my sister to be my lover.

We grew up together in this old place. She's fragile, and at almost twenty-one, she has survived more than she deserves. She tries to anesthetize her past with too many drugs and too much alcohol, and it gets her into risky situations. I do my best to protect her when we're out together. We trust each other implicitly, but Hana won't let anyone save her.

My brow furrows as I study her. "How are you doing?"

"Better than you." She gives me a teasing grin. "Look how stressed and annoyed you are. This is not the casual-cool Trip I know and love. Is juggling two women making you tired?"

"Not funny." I push off the sofa. "I'm sick of Grish dragging me into his love triangles. I want to make my money and be left alone."

"No one wants to be alone." Her voice turns quiet, and my lips tighten.

"I'm headed out of town for a little while. I need to find a place to relax while this shit dies down."

"It's not like you to run away."

"I'm not running. I need a break. You should do the same—don't you have family in one of the Carolinas?"

She shrugs. "Anywhere you go, your demons are right there waiting."

Impatience is driving me, but I hesitate. I won't be happy if I leave her this way. "Where's Blake?"

Hana's older sister Blake is strong and outspoken. She can't keep Hana away from the party scene, but she's a fighter. She's a better shield than none.

"Blake's got some modeling gig, and she doesn't like being here with Mama. All they do is fight."

"Why don't you see if she'll hang out with you while I'm away?"

"Blake doesn't like playing with me." Hana drinks more. "And she definitely doesn't approve of you."

Shaking my head, I shrug that off. "Blake only wants to protect you." She thinks I give Hana drugs, which I've *never* done. Debbie is the bad influence in this tight-knit circle. "When your trust fund matures, you can do anything you want. It's never too soon to think about the future."

"You definitely sound like Blake." Hana pushes off the couch.

I sound like a fucking high-school counselor. I want to kick my own ass. "Just a suggestion."

"Maybe I'll donate it all to a women's charity and work for UNICEF. I could be like Audrey Hepburn with the orphans."

That actually makes me laugh. "What would you do with orphans?"

"Teach them to survive."

"You are an expert at that." I push off the couch to stand. "Donations are fine. Just don't borrow any more money while I'm gone."

"I have IOUs all over town. What difference would one more make?" She laughs, but she has no idea the dangerous game she's playing.

Hana drifts through our world, drinking and taking whatever drug she's offered. She's like Alice in Wonderland, which makes me feel like the Mad Hatter, but I won't be here to lead her to the exit.

"I expect you to be alive when I get back."

Hopping over to where I stand, she hugs me. "You don't have to worry about me."

I wish that were true. "Things will get better. We just have to hold on until they do."

"Famous last words."

CHAPTER 2

Gia

"**Y**OUR HONOR, I DID *NOT* STEAL THE MERMAID TAIL." MY accent is a little too thick, and a nervous rasp is in my voice. I know it doesn't look good with me standing here, holding an iridescent rubber fishtail facing the head of hotel security in one of Palm Beach's ritziest resorts. "I'm not a thief. It was self-defense."

"You're not in court, Gia." My best friend Bianca steps forward to take the heavy costume from my hand. "You're in the Blue Coral Suite."

My chin quivers. "Please don't take me to jail."

"You're not going to jail," the man growls. "But you are leaving this resort."

It's so unfair to be punished for doing my job.

Let me explain…

First, the background: Bianca got me this job after the ballet company I moved to Miami to join (as prima ballerina!) went completely bust.

It's a long story that involves money laundering, adultery,

death threats, and pseudo-Evangelical Christians—but the end result is me stuck here in south Florida with no job, no money, no way to get home, and no work visa.

If it weren't for Bianca's couch, I'd be homeless.

That's how I ended up at the Whitecaps Resort as one of their "Happy Mermaids," holding hands with the babies, smiling, and wiggling my tail. It's an hourly job that doesn't require a bank, and the pay is very generous for what I do.

Bonus: The kids love me, and I love them.

Today, however, after a two-martini lunch, one of the dads also decided he loved the way I wiggled. After joining us in the pool, and basically crowding everyone, he started touching my hair and saying how my curls were "authentic mermaid." (What does that even mean?)

His wife sat fuming at me from her lounge chair, and when he put his hands on my clam shells, I belted him across the ears and high-tailed it out of there. (Mermaid-tailed?)

"Why didn't you call hotel security?" My best friend glares at me.

"I didn't know that was an option."

The entitled white men at this resort seem very much above the law. From what I gather, they can grab all the clam shells they want, whenever they want.

"You could've at least called me." Her voice is an urgent hiss.

The head of Whitecaps security frowns at me like he's heard enough. His team is right outside the door, ready to escort me off the property.

"I was trying to call you when you showed up at the door."

"Just give me the tail and go to my apartment. I'll catch a ride home with one of the other mermaids."

She's shaking her head, and I'm not sure why I feel guilty handing over the rubber costume. I was the one assaulted. Still, if she gets fired because I got groped, I'll feel like shit.

Four hours later, she still hasn't appeared. I'm with my former dance partner and fiancé Michele, who moved here along with me to join the defunct dance company. He wanted to have drinks at Roxy's, but I'm having coffee.

I actually prefer coffee, and as long as he's having alcohol, my drink is free.

"You do look like a mermaid with those curls and that tan." Michele is wearing a white satin shirt unbuttoned to the middle of his chest, a slim gold chain, and I'm pretty sure I detect eyeliner and mascara in the dim light of the bar.

"That's what he said." My tone is bitter. "You never said such things before we broke apart."

"Broke up. The American way to say it is broke *up*." He leans forward, his accent so thick, I roll my eyes.

"Like you know better than me." Glancing over my shoulder, I make sure no one's watching us. "You only want to be the center of attention."

The truth is, no one is watching us. In this part of south Florida, there are so many gay men, no one cares.

"You have to realize, *Mariposa*, we can be whoever we want to be in America. The ballet didn't work out, but we're on a journey to an even better life—like those butterflies you love."

"My life isn't better." Lifting the heavy mug, I take a sip of coffee to soothe the knot in my throat. "I came here to pursue my dream, and all it's gotten me is sleeping on a couch and being groped by a creeper."

"Maybe the caterpillar thinks his life is also good, but the universe knows better. The universe has bigger plans, spectacular plans!"

"This isn't spectacular, it's terrifying. I don't know what to expect next. I'm like Alice in the Wonderland."

Michele leans forward with a wink. "Then I'll be the Cheshire cat."

He flashes that dimpled grin all the girls love, and I lean back in my chair. "More like the queen of hearts."

"Yes!" He laughs loudly, taking another sip of piña colada as he points. "I'll be the queen."

My fiancé, the queen. Maybe I am too dumb to be outside of Santa Croce. I was engaged for a year to a gay man, and if we hadn't come here, I'd have married him.

"I'm the Dodo bird."

Michele almost does a spit take before covering his mouth and at least trying to act sympathetic. "You're still in the cocoon, Gia, but you'll come out of it. You're already showing signs of expression. You're a great beauty!"

"Don't make fun of me." Bending my knee, I slide my fingers across the butterfly tattoo on the top of my foot.

I always thought butterflies were good luck, but these days my life has turned decidedly *unlucky*.

He reaches out to cup my cheek. "You're not still angry with me, are you?"

My lips twist, and I haven't decided. "You lied to me, Misha. You made me believe you were in love with me, and you wanted to marry me."

"I am in love with you, and I did want to marry you." He pats the table. "*In Santa Croce.* Now we're in America, and we can live our truth."

"I was living my truth."

"Were you?" He narrows his eyes.

I thought I was.

When I met the dark-haired, dark-eyed boy with the dazzling grin who flew like Baryshnikov, I thought I'd found my fairytale prince. He was passionate and beautiful, and when he held me in his arms, new sensations simmered between my thighs.

I remember how I used to dream of our honeymoon

night, when we'd finally sleep together for the first time. I dreamed of us being lifelong dance partners, then husband and wife. I dreamed of us having a beautiful life together making art, making love, having babies.

Then we were offered the chance in America, and I didn't know how to dream any bigger.

Until we got here, and it all fell apart.

The company was a bust, and all of the dancers were unemployed. Most of them were American and could go back to where they started, but not us. It took every dime I could raise to get here.

As a student of the company and principal dancer, they were supposed to provide our room, board, everything we needed, and now I have nothing.

Then my fairytale prince turned out to be, well, a fairy.

"We can't stay with a student visa if we're not in school, and we can't work to earn the money to go home without a work visa." Michele leans back in his chair, extending his toned arms. "What choice do we have?"

"All that work and effort to get here only to turn and go right back." I grumble, still bitter about my shattered pumpkin of a happily ever after.

"So we work here illegally." Light sparkles in his eyes, and he's like a kid on Christmas morning. "Get paid in cash and don't get caught. Like a true *bandito*."

He laughs, and Bianca's voice cuts through my despair. "Somebody buy me a drink! I've got good news and bad news."

Michele flags down the waiter and orders our friend a frozen strawberry margarita. I'm happy to hear there's good news, but the mention of more bad news makes my head hurt. How much worse can my life possibly get?

"Start with the bad." Michele stands, kissing her cheek. "Things can only get better."

She takes the stool across from me. "We're not working as mermaids anymore."

A lead weight drops through my stomach, and heat floods my eyes. "Oh, Bianca, I got you fired, too? I'm so sorry." My heart beats like an ominous drum, and I'm so afraid. "What will we do now?"

"That's why we have the good news," she continues. "Franco got us a job that's going to make us more money than we can imagine."

Hesitating, I study the man strolling up behind her with his hands in his pockets and a smirk on his lips. Franco is attractive, with wavy, dark hair and a smooth, square jaw. I think he's originally from Cuba, but I've only spoken to him a few times.

He's always hanging around Bianca's place watching us, calculating. I'm not sure how I feel about this announcement. Something in his smile puts me on my guard. He's what my aunt would call *ragazzaccio*, a naughty boy.

"What is this new job?"

"Dancing." Bianca leans forward, tapping the tip of my nose with her finger before taking a long sip from her margarita. "No more sitting in a wading pool, turning into prunes in a stinky rubber costume for pennies. We're going to bring in the big bucks now doing what we love—and on our own terms."

I don't like the sound of this. Every good opportunity I've been offered in this country has taken a turn. I need to find an evil eye and wear it quickly. "What kind of dancing? Salsa?"

"It can be whatever type of dance you like. Not only that, we're moving out of my crummy apartment and into a condo overlooking the beach."

My eyebrows shoot up. "How? I don't have any money."

And I already feel like a remora sleeping on her couch and eating her food.

"You'll have plenty of money after we become cam girls."

"No." Michele straightens in his chair, and for the first time since we arrived on these shores, he turns macho. "Gia is not a cam girl."

"Just keep your shirt on." My friend holds out her hands.

"What's a cam girl?" I'm trying to catch up.

Michele lowers his chin, leveling his black eyes on mine. "It's a girl who performs in front of a camera. For money."

I'm still not following what he means. "Performs… Like dances?"

"Like strips."

An invisible hand squeezes my throat. "Oh, I don't know, Bianca…"

"First of all," my friend jumps in quickly, waving her hands, "it doesn't have to be nude. Franco said we have complete control over our act. We decide how much or how little to do or show, and best of all, we keep eighty percent of our income."

Michele shakes his head, pressing his full lips together. "It's stripping, and the only way you make money is by taking it all off and *doing things*."

"How do you know so much?" Bianca argues. "When Gypsy Rose Lee started dancing, everyone said she had to strip, but she didn't. She danced burlesque. She created a relationship with the audience, and she left them thinking they might be special and get more."

Franco crosses his muscled arms, his voice smooth. "Cam girls aren't necessarily strippers, but I do manage a strip club if you'd like to start there and build your audience."

I don't want to start there. I don't want to do any of this.

"That's where the next part of the equation enters," he continues. "If you can build a following, you can make even more money on our subscription service Private Eyes."

Bianca reaches across the table to squeeze my forearm.

"It's an amazing opportunity, Gia! Some of the girls make thousands of dollars a week! You came here to be a dancer, to live your dream. Let's dance!"

"I didn't dream of taking my clothes off." My voice is quiet.

Slipping off my stool, I slide my palm back and forth over my stomach as I shake my head. "I'm sorry. I don't want to poop on your parade or be the *downer Debbie*. I want to help you, Bianca, but this isn't my kind of thing. I'll have to see if I can find another way. I know how to sew costumes. Maybe I can get a job as a seamstress or…"

"Gia, wait." My friend jogs to catch up with me, and we walk out into the warm night.

The street here isn't as crazy as South Beach, but the road is wide with restaurants and clubs dotted along both sides. The palm trees are wrapped in twinkle lights, and the constant breeze from the nearby ocean lifts our hair off our shoulders.

Bianca loops her arm through mine, and we follow the road along the beach.

She's quiet for a bit before she speaks. "I didn't just take this on a whim. Franco has been talking to me about it for a while, and I've been talking to the girls who work for him. He has a good reputation. He really will let you perform however you want."

"So I can perform *Swan Lake* at his club?" I regret my words as soon as I say them. Bianca has only ever tried to help me.

"Maybe if you spiced it up a little?" She gives me a wink. "Make it modern?"

"Remove one feather at a time?"

"Something like that. I thought you could wear something sexy and move your body. You're very sensual when you dance. I think men would come from all over to be seduced by you."

I huff a laugh at her suggestion. "I've never even been with a man. I don't know how to seduce one."

"That's what makes you special. You have an innocent quality. I think men would pay to dream of possessing you."

"I don't think I want to be dreamed about that way." It makes me nervous.

She gives me a sly smile. "You've never caught a man watching you dance and suspected he had impure thoughts?"

Snorting a laugh, I shake my head. "I was too busy fantasizing about my gay fiancé."

"Take it from me, if you're engaged to a man for a year, and he would rather shop and eat and cuddle and dance than try to get in your pants, he's gay."

"Thanks, Captain Obvious. I know that now. I just thought maybe he was super religious."

"No man is that religious." She quickly returns to the subject at hand. "Just think about it Gia. You could sew your own costumes, and we could brainstorm outfits that get close but reveal nothing. All you have to do is dance. Can you imagine making ten thousand dollars a month?"

"No, and I think you're dreaming if you think I could ever earn that much money simply by dancing."

"You could try?" Her voice goes thoughtful, and we make the turn, headed back to the Roxy.

"I can't go back to Aunt Gratziela having done something like that. I'd be all the horrible things she always said I was."

"Your Aunt Gratziela is a cunty old bitch. You are kind and generous. You're a good friend and a beautiful girl."

"I can't let her be right about me."

"What if you wore a mask? Franco says they have very strict rules and very tight security. No one is allowed to touch you ever, and you can use a stage name. No one has to know who you are."

It's all too strange for me to comprehend. Pulling away, I shake my head. "I'm not ready to think about this, B. I'm tired, I was groped by a married man and nearly arrested, then I lost the job you helped me find. I need to go to sleep. Tomorrow, I'll try to find a job to replace the one I lost."

I turn towards the alley leading to Bianca's small, cinder-block apartment when she catches my wrist. "Promise me you'll keep an open mind about what I said, okay? This could be the answer to all our problems."

"I'll try."

Our eyes meet, and she shrugs. "Either way, we have to move. Perhaps when you meet the other girls and talk to them, you'll change your mind."

I'm not changing my mind.

CHAPTER 3

Trip

Ocean Drive is lit up like Mardi Gras with rainbow-neon lights and music and revelry blasting from every open door. The air is balmy for early spring, and I stroll up the concrete sidewalk with my hands in my pockets as the sea breeze pushes my hair around my ears.

I still need that trim, and I still could use a shave. My insides were just so fucking hot and twisted, I needed to get out of Manhattan as quickly as possible. The moment I got the text that our jet was ready, I threw my necessities into an overnight bag and took off for the airport.

Now I'm in jeans and a short-sleeved linen shirt, and I feel the tension melting away in the heat of pre-spring in the south. I want a drink, preferably straight alcohol.

Franco meets me, sliding through the doors of Salsa Mia, a neon-pink-lit dance and dinner club. The building next to it is neon blue, and the next one down is neon red. The entire row is the colors of the rainbow.

"You're in town early." His hands are in his pockets and

his nylon shirt ripples in the breeze. "I wasn't expecting you until tomorrow."

"Don't put yourself out. I'll crash at The Villa." Debbie's always going on about the former Versace mansion turned into a boutique hotel.

She's obsessed with the murdered designer. Personally, I think it's a bit macabre to walk up the white marble steps where he was gunned down twenty-five years ago.

"Fuck that. You're coming with me back to your place. I'll call and have the penthouse ready when we arrive."

"It's a two-hour drive." I groan, watching the lean bodies spilling out of the clubs onto the street. "I'd rather have a few drinks and walk to bed right here."

"You'll be glad when you're in your own place tomorrow morning." He grips my shoulder, pulling me close and slinging his arm around my neck.

It always takes a minute for me to remember how physical men are in South Beach. My instinct is to shrug him off, but I don't. I lean into the friendly gesture. God knows, I'm sick of being on my guard all the time.

"Can I at least have a drink before we hit the road?"

"You're the boss," he laughs, dragging me inside the Clevelander courtyard before releasing me and going straight to the bar.

Two tequila drinks later, I'm in the passenger seat of a gunmetal-gray, convertible Lamborghini, flying north on Interstate 95.

"I think I'm paying you too much," I joke, stretching my legs straight on the black leather passenger seat.

"You want a Lambo?" He grins at me from where he's driving. "Because I know a guy."

"A car in New York is about as useful as a screen door on a submarine."

He laughs, bearing down on the accelerator and letting the

engine eat as he swerves around the slower-moving vehicles. The top is up, but the speed at which we're moving is palpable.

"Doesn't matter. You can afford it. I'm telling you, investing in this business was the smartest move you've ever made. Profits have gone through the roof in the last two years. The Private Eyes girls are out-earning the cam girls three to one, and we get twenty percent off every account."

My eyebrows rise, and I shift, trying to make peace with this aspect of my business. Sure, I've worked in vice for years. I'm no saint. I'm perfectly fine separating overly wealthy, old, white men from large sums of their money either through slots, real estate side deals, or other forms of grift, but doping horses and selling women are two areas I avoid.

If it weren't for Grish assuring me this "subscription-based social media service" was legal and private, I'd have walked.

"Last month, we partnered with a group in India that helps maintain our largest accounts, replying to DMs and posting new videos."

"But the girls are still in control? They only do what they want?" I have a vague understanding of how the business operates.

"First, it's not just girls. It's male models, singers, dancers, fitness instructors…" He hesitates, tightening his fist on the wheel. "Speaking of dancers, we picked up two new girls last week. They're staying in the house."

"Whatever." I glance out the window with a wave. "Just be sure they're legal and cover their costs. No minors."

"Of course not. I didn't want you to be surprised is all. I'm trying to get them into the subscription side."

I'm not interested in what the girls do. I don't even visit the "house," which is actually an entire floor in a luxury West Palm highrise on the bay.

It sounds extravagant, but the sex trade in Florida is astonishingly lucrative. My group of investors is different—at my insistence. I'm not a pimp. I insist the women who work for us are safe, healthy, and have decent accommodations. It was my one requirement for going in on the deal.

Franco manages the details. Personally, I don't even know their names. When I visit this area, I come to relax, hit the links, check on my family's properties, and make sure everyone's following the rules. Drop-in visits only serve to keep people on their best behavior.

"You should stop by the club and catch a show. I think you'd be impressed, and it's good for morale to know the boss cares."

It takes all my strength to suppress a grimace.

Strippers don't interest me. Their performances have the opposite effect. Instead of being enthralled by their movements, my mind drifts to the forces that have driven them to such a state.

I wonder if they're taking off their clothes to make ends meet. I wonder if it's to save money for school or to support a dying relative. Perhaps I'm overthinking it.

Once I was informed some women strip to demonstrate their power over men. I'm not sure I buy it, but as someone who grew up with a complete asshole, I can respect wanting to hit back.

In fact, I support reclaiming what would be degradation and making money from it, but no matter how ecumenical I try to be, in the end, it all adds up to the same conclusion: I'm really just not into strippers.

"If I have a free night, I'll let you know."

Franco laughs at my tone, but I'm grateful to see we're exiting the interstate and turning towards the drawbridge that separates the mainland from the barrier island.

"It's so early. Let's make that free night tonight and stop by the club."

I turn my wrist, and see it's just after ten. "We should've stayed longer in South Beach."

While I don't care for women thrusting fake tits in my face for money, I definitely enjoy the sight of real women enjoying themselves on a dance floor, especially in tight skirts and low-cut blouses.

"Come on. I think we still have time to see Glitter Girl. She usually closes the night." My brow furrows, and he gives me a wink. "I think she might have something you'll like."

"Doubtful."

"That's what you say, but you're a straight man, right? Last time I checked?"

I'm not in the mood to argue, so I fall back on casual humor. "Sure. Let's go."

It's too early to crash, and it's been two hours since my last drink.

Franco follows the tree-lined streets of Worth Avenue, past the small shops and restaurants, taking a right and heading south into a tucked-away portion of the neighborhood.

He turns the car into the lot and parks, and I step out, glancing up at the unassuming, stucco walls of the Spanish-style cabaret tucked into a strip mall.

Two lion-head fountains are on each side of the entrance, and it's all very discreet and camouflaged. I suppose the old bluebloods don't want to have *Girls! Girls! Girls!* screaming in neon across the skyline. They left Miami for a reason, after all.

Inside, the mood is completely different. Laser lights flash across the smoke-filled dance floor. The crowd is mostly young men wearing jeans and black shirts with baseball caps, and the waitresses circulate through the space in fishnets and thongs with wavy hair hanging down their backs.

Loose laughter, provocative winks, and heavy tipping pass between them. The empty stage dominating the center of the room draws my attention away from the horny crowd.

"Grab a seat in the VIP section, and I'll get a waitress to

take care of us." Franco gestures to a roped-off area in the back corner.

He approaches two waitresses in little safari hats, and they give me curious looks before scurrying around to collect an ice bucket and trays. I nod to one who gives me a cautious smile before turning to make my way past the velvet rope.

I'm almost through when a tall, youngish man stumbles, almost falling on me in his haste. "Mr. Alexander?" He's breathing fast, and he scoops up my hand, shaking it roughly. "Damn, I can't believe this. They say you never come to the club."

Taking my hand back, I square my shoulders and face him. "I'm sorry, do I know you?"

"Hell, no." The guy leans back, passing his hand over his forehead to move his dark hair away from his face. "At least I don't think so. I'm nobody."

In my experience, someone identifying themselves as nobody is usually somebody. This guy is acting clumsy and innocent, but his black eyes are clever. My defenses are triggered, but I'm a great actor, too.

"Have a nice night, Nobody." I turn, but he stops me again.

"I'm Andre Bertonelli." He places a palm on his chest, straightening his shoulders. "Greg Peters hired me to keep up with your interests. I've studied your career since you graduated from Columbia—"

"I dropped out of Columbia after two years." Now I'm getting annoyed. "Greg hired you to follow me?"

"Not to follow you. I keep an eye on your interests."

"And stalk me it seems." I don't like the sound of this. "Andre, is it? You're fired. Effective immediately."

He starts to interrupt again, but Franco appears, scowling. "What are you doing here? VIP only, pal. Get lost." Franco holds an arm between us and ushers me through the velvet rope. "Sorry about that. Some people think the rules don't apply to them."

The guy gives me a sly wink before blending into the

crowd, and my jaw clenches. This is bullshit. Grish never told me anything about *Andre*. Franco is one of my most trusted employees, and he's never seen him before. Now I'm wondering what else I don't know.

It appears I've been disengaged for too long. I'm the boss in south Florida, and I'm not having bullshit like this. I intend to know everything before I leave here.

A waitress appears with bottle service just as the lights go down and a spotlight hits the mirrored stage. I take the glass of Cristal she poured, scanning the room for where my stalker went. I have no interest in watching an oiled woman with fake breasts grind on a pole in nothing but a G-string.

The music however isn't the usual club track. Instead of Megan Thee Stallion or Lizzo, a classic tune by Nancy Sinatra thrums through the darkened room, and all the men visibly come to attention.

I confess I've always liked this song, and my eyes are drawn to the stage where a petite woman with sexy, natural-looking curves marches onto the stage. Her dark hair is slicked back into a single, impossibly long braid, and she's brassy and bold.

She's dressed in a supple leather costume made up of a series of belts that run around her neck, waist, arms, and lower back. One strap rises between her legs, barely covering her hairless pussy. Another covers her full, round breasts, which appear refreshingly real—and amply gropable.

The best part of her costume is the fringed, assless chaps that end in stiletto boots. For what it's worth, her ass is golden and supple, peeking from the top of those fucking chaps, and *shit...* She knows how to move it. She rolls her torso like a trained dancer, the muscles in her narrow waist peeking out as every part of her silky body flexes and ripples in a way that would lead to a beheading in biblical times.

Who is this woman? I can't make out her face because the cowboy hat is pulled low on her forehead, and a black, Lone Ranger-style mask is over her eyes.

Instead of a pole, she uses two strips of fabric extending from the ceiling to climb and lift in the most fascinating ways.

She arches her back as she slowly turns, and the straps of leather covering her breasts loosen so that I almost catch a glimpse of her dark areolas, her hardened nipples. Her legs open in a V, and the strap sliding up her ass and pussy is so thin, I shift in my seat. *Fuck me.*

The men on the floor throw money at her feet, howling like ravenous wolves, and I've got a hard-on.

She's unbelievably sexy, and it only gets worse when the song cuts to the final, fast-paced measures, where the boots "start walking."

At this point, she rolls out of the fabric and her shoulders shimmy as she pulls strips of leather away from her costume, one at a time. When she pulls the last strip covering her breasts, she turns her back to us.

Her back is smooth and toned, and the bounce of her incredible tits is visible on each side of her body. She stretches her arms in a *V* as she lifts two giant, silver guns and pulls the triggers, showering the stage and everyone on the floor with glitter.

Perfect. The word appears in my mind.

The lights cut off, and we're plunged into black. We've seen absolutely nothing, and we all want to fuck her.

I do my best to calm my expression before the house lights come up. I'm hot around the collar, and I slide my palm over my erection, trying to relax. I've never considered myself a horndog, but that was *unexpected.*

When the interior lights rise, Franco's lips are curled in a knowing grin. "She's good, yes?"

"Very interesting." Clearing my throat, I take another sip of champagne. "What's her name?"

Franco's eyebrow arches, and he holds up both hands. "Glitter Girl does not want her identity made public."

His response irritates me more than it should—probably

thanks to the boner in my pants. "I'm her boss. I sign her paycheck."

"We pay the girls in cash as you well know."

Ah yes, for money laundering. "Right."

"You also made the rules. No forcing the girls to do anything they don't want to do. GG doesn't want anyone to know who she is. It's a condition of her dancing."

"I see." For a moment, I'm quietly furious.

Who dances that well and doesn't want to be famous? Who uses my own rules against me? This woman is playing with fire.

Then I realize if I'm the one who makes the rules, I can also be the one to explore why they might be broken, and who gets to decide.

I'm not in a hurry. Clearly, I need to take more time with my interests here. I'll know who she is, and I'll have a taste of this forbidden fruit.

CHAPTER 4

Gia

"**D**ID YOU HEAR HOW CRAZY THEY WENT FOR YOU TONIGHT?" Shula's voice is thinly veiled awe as I sit in front of the long mirror removing my makeup with trembling hands. "I can only dream of having men want me that much. You must've made a thousand dollars in tips."

My voice is wobbly, and I try to steady it. "It's a little unsettling to have that many men so… *eager.*"

"I would love it." She turns, holding her arms over her head. "Eat it up, boys!"

Shula isn't afraid of anything except not being popular. She's actually a sweet girl, one of the youngest dancers at the Rhino.

"You'll get yours, don't worry." Bianca slides up behind me, helping me take the bobby pins out of my hair.

"Oh, Gia." Shula turns to the side, holding out one of the straps. "I broke this again. Do you think you can help me?"

"You'll have to pin it for now." I massage cold cream on

my face to remove the layer of makeup I'm wearing. "I'll stitch it up tomorrow."

Shula's fake boobs are too big for her body, so she's constantly blowing straps. She's one of the first girls I met when Bianca and I moved into the condo—it's not a house. It's a blow-your-mind-it's-so-fancy condo on the beachfront in West Palm—and she was thrilled to learn I could sew.

She'd been paying the dry cleaner through the nose to take in and let out her costumes. Sewing relaxes me, so I do it for free.

While I sat at the machine repairing her outfit, Shula told me all the worse things I could do for money besides shimmy in a skimpy costume—some from her own personal experience.

It only took one sleepless night turning over everything everyone said to me, and I decided I owed it to Biance to try her idea. She gave me a couch to crash on, she found me job after job, it was the least I could do.

On top of that, she truly believes I can be a huge success at a strip club without showing a bit of nudity, and a big part of the reason I agreed to do it was to prove she was wrong. I never thought it would work. I expected to bomb.

Boy, was I wrong.

It's been a week, and the crowds keep getting bigger. Everyone wants to see the mysterious Glitter Girl.

I've been a dancer for a long, long time, but no matter how many times I perform at the Rhino, I come off the stage completely rattled by how insane the crowd goes when I finish.

My one consolation is Franco assures us the security here is top-notch. Still, I can't help thinking about my mother. I can't help thinking, *What the hell is going on?*

"I think it's because there's so much bad porn on the internet now." Bianca hands me a tissue to wipe my face. "You're elegant and gorgeous and a total mystery. It's irresistible."

"Maybe." Images of my mother crowd my mind, and I have to push them away. *I'm not my mother—just ask my aunt.*

Bianca continues unaffected. "Everyone loves a guessing game."

"They're hoping your mask slips as well as your top." Shula giggles, blowing an air kiss before heading to the stage, breasts fully out. "Maybe you can be like me."

I honestly don't know what's making me so popular. I simply go out there and move to the music. No lie, I'm waiting for the other shoe to drop and for it all to come crashing down.

Bianca is so excited. I really think she'd been planning this all along because she already had an idea for the music and the costumes. She wanted me to use the name *Puss in Boots* and to have signature boots for every performance, but I felt like that was too on the nose.

Instead, I took a bottle of glitter from her shelf, and it all clicked. *Glitter Girl.* I had these two glitter guns, and while I might be a virgin, I know how male anatomy works. Pulling the triggers, I shower everyone with glitter, the ultimate climax.

For whatever reason, the men love it, and it's how I end my dances—coming in glitter all over the stage. Now I just want to go home and hide.

"One of these days, you're not going to mind being a celebrity." Bianca smooths her fingers over the wild curls of my unbraided hair.

"If my aunt knew what I was doing…"

"Stop." She leans forward, hugging my shoulders. "You're not doing anything wrong."

"It's lust, and… I don't know what else she'd say, but it would be something bad."

"Jesus! You've never even slept with a guy. How can you be bad?"

"She'd find a way. She always finds a way, trust me."

Bianca shakes her head, standing straighter behind me. "We've talked about this. You're a dancer. You move your body to the music. No matter where you are or what you're doing, you can't help the effect you have on others."

"Yes, but it wasn't so focused on my *assets* before."

"How do you know? God gave you those assets. So you make a little money off 'em. So what?"

"I'm not sure that's what God had in mind." I scoop up a hoodie and pull it over the brown tank top that barely covers my boobs, then I shove an oversized pair of sunglasses over my eyes.

"How do you know? Maybe this is your blessing." She hesitates at the door. "Ready?"

Taking a deep breath, I nod, and we crash through the back door, walking quickly to the SUV that will take us to the condo.

A small crowd of people, mostly men, are waiting right outside the door taking photos and trying to capture my identity. My hood is on, and I lift the sides of my jacket over my face, ducking my head before diving into the Denali. Bianca is right behind me, slamming the door on the shouting crowd.

It's not a ridiculous number of people, not the strobing lights you'd see for somebody like Britney or J.Lo, but it gives me a whiff of what it would be like to be truly famous.

"It's worse every time." I stretch my back against the leather seat. "Can you imagine if they were following us everywhere?"

"It would suck." Bianca nods, and she pulls off the stiletto she's wearing. "It's kind of the best part of the subscription side. For a business based on exhibition, nobody knows who you are."

"What a weird world we're living in." Shaking my head, I'm still getting my mind around what we do. It all happened so fast. "Do you have to work tonight?"

She crosses her leg and rubs her foot. "I have a few chats, a few challenges."

Bianca doesn't dance. She's strictly on the subscription site, and even though she's starting out small, she's making decent money.

Franco said by starting me out as Glitter Girl, I'll be able to amp up my following through my dancing. He says my anonymity won't matter when I go live, and we can still make an insane amount of money by advertising at the club.

I wasn't sure I believed him until tonight. "Will you show me how it works tomorrow? Franco wants me to start soon."

"Of course." Bianca winks at me. "Franco's ready to make you a millionaire."

"He wants to make himself a millionaire."

"Still, you get eighty percent of what you earn—minus food and rent."

Chewing my lip, I look out the window. This isn't how I dreamed my life would be when I moved to Miami, but perhaps it's part of my metamorphosis like Michele said.

It doesn't have to be forever.

"Ready to learn?" Bianca bounces on my bed, rousing me from a dream of home.

I was dancing on the shore, tracing my pointed toes in the sand as the sun rose. My mom was smiling down and waving from the window of our small, upstairs apartment… *Best day ever.*

"Ugh… Go away!" I push her with my pillow, but she grabs it, pulling it out of my hand.

"It's after ten. If we don't do this now, I'm going to be busy with my own clients. Let's go, Gia!"

She goes to the window and whips back the curtains, and I pull the blanket over my head. "I don't want to go to school."

"You need to wash your face and decide what you want to wear to look for your special photos. These are the ones you'll only send to your fans, so they need to be a little racy. Maybe a sheer top or something super low-cut that will give a little peek when you lean forward?"

My brow furrows. One week ago I was fretting about

taking my clothes off and what my aunt would say if she found out. Then we moved into the "house" (condo), and we had a little girls' night where I met everyone, and we discussed my "problem." Then we started drinking champagne, and we all got excited.

I told them I could sew any costume. One of the girls pointed out we have access to a sewing machine and old costumes at the club that could be modified. Bianca and I started brainstorming shoes and wigs and masks and someone turned on dance music and I started to move, and everyone lost their shit over how good of a dancer I am.

I was like, duh! It's all I've ever done my whole life. It's why I came here—to be a real, professional ballet dancer. Not burlesque.

We were all *a lot* tipsy, and when Bianca shared my tragic backstory, I became the house project. All the girls are determined to straighten out my fucked-up fairytale and make my dreams come true...

And Glitter Girl was born.

And the rest is a hypersonic history.

And even though I'm not taking off my clothes, I'm sure the lust-inducing strip-tease I do would never pass Gratziela's smell test. I'm Salome, asking a horned-up King Herod for John the Baptist's head on a platter.

The thought makes my stomach feel like I've been on a fishing boat too long, but before I can get too queasy, my phone vibrates in my hand. Michele's photo is on the screen, and I smile in spite of myself. If anyone knows how to live brilliantly in spite of being an "abomination" (massive eye roll) it's my former fiancé.

"Hey, girl, hey." He's talking to me on FaceTime, and his square chin bobs as he walks. "Are you up for some brunch with your favorite guy?"

I haven't talked to Michele since the night I lost my job as a mermaid at Whitecaps. I'm not sure if he even knows what

I'm doing now, although he has an uncanny way of knowing everything everywhere all the time.

Wrinkling my nose at Bianca, I point to my phone. She can hear Michele through the line and she shrugs. "Whatever." She shakes her head. "You can learn another day."

"I'm just opening my eyes, but I'm down for brunch. Meet you in a few?"

Ten minutes later, we're walking down Frontage Road, headed to the Blue Pointe, which I've heard has the best seafood on the island. A week ago, I'd never be able to afford it, but Glitter Girl is flush with cash.

"You sure you want to go here?" Michele glances up at the classic white and nautical blue sign.

"I've been wanting to go here since the day we arrived in town." Leaning closer, I show him the wad of cash in my purse. "And I can pay for both of us now."

Michele's eyebrows rise. "Glad I dressed for the occasion."

He is handsome in jeans and a loose, button-up shirt. It's untucked and unbuttoned to the center of his hairless, muscled chest. I'm in a filmy sundress, and the host doesn't bat an eye, which is one of the perks of living on the coast. Pretty much all the dress codes are casual.

"Good morning, lover," I tease as I lift the elegant menu at my seat.

For whatever reason, my newfound, baby-fame has given me a sense of confidence I've never had before. The waiter takes our drink orders—coffee for me, and keep it coming, while Michele orders a Bloody Mary.

"I want oysters Rockefeller."

"Calamari and ceviche."

The waiter nods, disappearing, and I lift my coffee, taking a lingering sip as the hot liquid warms my insides. A little chill rolls down my spine, and I close my eyes. "Mmm… that's good."

Michele chuckles, sipping his tomatoey cocktail. "Only you can make drinking coffee look like a sexual experience."

My eyes blink open, and my cheeks feel hot. "I didn't think you noticed things like that."

"A beautiful woman having a coffee orgasm?"

Now my face is really red. "I wasn't doing that!"

"Sweet Gia, you've got to stop apologizing for being yourself."

Frowning, I think about how I've been apologizing for everything since I lost my mom and was sent to live with my aunt. I'm ashamed of my hair, my tanned skin, my bare feet, my soft body.

"You're right." Jutting my chin, I nod. "I'm going to work on that."

He laughs. "Good girl. Now, tell me where you got all this money? Did Bianca and Franco convince you to do those nudes, or did you start selling drugs?"

"I'm not selling drugs…"

My voice trails off, and he tilts his dark head to the side. "Are you really stripping?"

"Not technically."

"What does that mean?"

"I'm dancing at the Rhino, but I don't take off my clothes. I just sort-of, almost take them off, one by one, and at the end, I turn my back… if that makes sense."

His eyebrows rise, and a sly grin curls his lips. "I bet you're killing it. I've seen you dance."

Nodding, I lift my coffee. "I'm doing okay."

"And you're paying for our meal with cash? Can I order another Bloody Mary?"

"If you want one." I'm distracted, and he crosses his arms.

"Shit, Gia." He shakes his head, and sitting here across from him, knowing our past, I'm not sure how to take his response.

"Are you judging me?"

"No!" He holds up both hands. "No way. You're beauti-ful, and you have sex appeal in spades. Just look at those tits."

I immediately cross my arms over my chest, embarrass-ment rushing to my face again.

"Remember, no more apologies." He gives me a wink. "You're not doing anything wrong. If you've got it, flaunt it. Don't be embarrassed of your success."

I glance side to side, moving closer to the table and whisper-ing. "We can *never* let this get back to anyone in Santa Croce."

His dark head wobbles side to side like I'm being an old nag, but I move a little closer when I catch a glimpse of foun-dation at the corner of his jawline. Reaching across, I slide my finger over his neck.

"Are you wearing makeup?" I'm not surprised—when we were in productions, we had to wear stage makeup all the time, but if he got a job without me… "Are you performing?"

His chin jerks back, and he almost seems embarrassed. "What are you talking about?"

"What is this?" I hold up my finger. "What are you hid-ing from me?"

Inhaling slowly, he releases my hand and puts his elbows on the table. "I suppose it's time to confess my truth."

"You have *more* truth to confess?" I can't imagine what else he's hiding.

"I have a new job." Jealousy tightens my throat, and I want to cry. How can he get a legitimate job when I can't? "Meet Dickie Normous. I'm at the Palm Club every Thursday at nine. You should check out my show."

"Dickie Normous?"

"Say it again." His eyes twinkle, and I comply.

"I'm not getting it."

"Good lord, Gia, did you actually grow up in a convent? It's wordplay, a double entendre. Dick *enormous*."

It clicks, and a laugh hits me so hard, I cover my mouth.

Then I pinch my nose when I snort. "Why is that your stage name?"

"Everyone has a cheeky stage name in drag. It's part of my persona."

My eyes are saucers, and I lean forward again, whispering. "You're doing drag? Who do you impersonate?"

The waiter appears with our food, putting a platter of Oysters Rockefeller in front of me and a large plate of fried calamari with crispy potatoes and olives in front of him. I make him split the shrimp ceviche with me. It's too delicious.

Michele orders another Bloody Mary, and when the waiter leaves, I dive into the steaming shellfish grilled to perfection with parmesan cream and breadcrumbs.

Sliding the oyster into my mouth, I groan loudly. "It's so good!"

"Don't look now, but you're giving the old men boners."

I almost choke and kick him under the table. "Shut up!"

"Maybe you should incorporate eating oysters and drinking coffee into your act."

"Maybe I will." I jerk my chin, and he points at me.

"That's good. I like seeing you embrace your inner strength. I think this dancing thing is going to break you out of that cocoon after all."

Chewing my lip, I remember my earlier thoughts on this subject. "I think you might be right. I'm learning some things about myself—even if my job is sinful."

"Who said your job is sinful?"

"Everybody. Name one person who doesn't say stripping is dirty." I slide another perfectly grilled oyster into my mouth and shudder at how good it is. "We have to come here again."

"You listen to me, Giana Isabela, the bible is full of sex. Have you ever read the Song of Solomon? Or how about the descriptions of Bathsheba? Don't even get me started on David and Jonathan and that not-so-ambiguously gay romance."

I glance around again to see who might be listening. "Lower your voice, Misha."

"I'm done with being quiet. God made us and said we're good. It's us who fuck everything up and weigh each other down with our own shame and guilt. You and I are going to be loud and proud of who we are, starting today."

"I think I'll keep it down for now, if that's okay." I finish my oysters, but a feeling is stirring in my chest.

It tingles like a laugh caught behind my ribs, like a song wanting to burst free. I'm not sure why or when, but my wings are growing stronger, getting ready to unfurl.

"You sure they don't allow drag queens to live here?" Michele and I stand at the entrance of the high-rise where I live, looking up at the massive building. "I'm very neat and a lot of fun."

"Girls only," I tease, stepping forward to kiss his cheek. "But I can't wait to catch your show next week."

"I can't wait to catch yours."

"Oh, no." I hesitate, swallowing my embarrassment. "Not yet."

"Sweet Gia, you are a work in progress." He pulls me close. "I'll be ready when you are."

Bianca meets me at the door when I arrive at the condo. "What took so long? You're not going to believe what just happened."

"I was only gone an hour."

She pulls me into the room and shuts the door. "Franco texted me. William Alexander, the big boss, saw your show last night, and he wants to meet you. Isn't that amazing? The big boss wants to meet you!"

Lightning shoots through my chest, and I pull up so fast, I almost bump into Shula. "He saw me dance? He knows it was me? Nobody is supposed to know…"

"He doesn't know it was you." Shula slips an arm around my shoulders. "He only knows you make his dick hard."

"I don't like that." I step out of her embrace to follow my bestie into the kitchen. "Franco said he wouldn't tell anyone my identity. That was the deal. No one can know."

Bianca stands in front of the blender, dropping frozen fruit into the glass carafe. "Franco didn't tell him anything. He texted me. You can still say no." Her full lips twist. "If you want."

"If I start telling people who I am, it won't be long before everyone finds out, and then..."

"Your aunt isn't going to find out!" Bianca hits the button, and the loud grinding sound of ice in the blender rattles through the room.

I cover my ears with my hands and shout over the noise. "Tell him no. I'm not meeting anyone."

She gives the machine a few more pulses then pours her smoothie into a plastic cup. "What if you meet him first, without him knowing who you are, then decide."

"Why would I do that?"

"Because he's the big boss. If he's into you, that could be a really good thing for you."

"The last thing I want is to meet a guy who only wants to sleep with me."

"What makes you think that's all he wants?"

My eyes level on hers and she holds up both hands. "Okay, okay."

"You're going to teach me how to do Private Eyes, and then I'm not dancing anymore."

"I'll tell Franco what you said. That you have no interest in a super-rich billionaire, who I've heard is very charming and sexy, who wants to meet you."

"You know nothing about him."

"I know what I've heard." She arches an eyebrow, as she turns to go to her room, and I have a feeling she's not going to do what I asked.

CHAPTER 5

Trip

THE WARM SHOWER BEATS DOWN ON THE BACK OF MY NECK, AND one hand is braced against the wall. The other slides up and down my hard cock, and heat is rising in my pelvis, orgasm curling up my inner thighs.

With my eyes closed, I picture the back of her shoulders, the sides of her breasts bouncing with every strike of my hips against her ass. My cock is deep in her hot, slippery core. She moans, and I thrust harder, sliding my palm from her waist up the center of her back until my fingers thread in the back of her hair.

I wrap that long braid around my wrist and pull her up so her back is pressed against my chest. She feels so good, firm yet soft, tight yet pliant and grasping.

"Oh, fuck." My cock gets harder, and I slide my hand faster over the tip, picturing her full breasts bouncing as I fuck her harder.

She screams in ecstasy, and I come so hard, my back stiffens.

My head falls forward, and I let out a loud groan as I finish, leaning against the stone tile of the shower stall.

Fuck me, I'm obsessed with this woman, and I don't even know her name. I woke up with a hard-on tenting my sheets after she strutted through my dreams all night in those damn boots and fringed, assless chaps. *That ass…*

I grabbed my phone and sent Franco a text, *I'd like to meet Glitter Girl for lunch today.*

The words appear so calm on the screen. Text is the perfect shield for the need vibrating in my body, the desire swirling in my blood. I tossed my phone and immediately went to the shower to deal with my morning wood.

I'm still in my towel when I see a reply text from Franco on my phone. **She doesn't want to meet you.**

What the fuck? I'm ready to put my fist through the line and grab him by the neck. Instead I hit the call button.

"How can she say she doesn't want to meet me? Doesn't she know who I am?" I sound like a starving animal, a ravenous wolf.

I've got to get this shit under control.

"She's a stripper." Franco's tone is so condescending. I'm sure he's loving this. "I thought you didn't like strippers."

"I never said I didn't like them. I said they don't do it for me."

"I told you she was special."

She sounds a little too special if you ask me. "I want to meet her."

"Listen, GG's a sweet girl. She's very sheltered. She's only dancing so she can earn money to get home."

"Where's home?"

"I can't tell you that either," he laughs. "Look, I'm trying to get her to stay, but if you start crowding her, breaking your own rules, she's going to bolt."

I'm quiet, thinking about this. She doesn't know me, and I've always had a way with women. Franco's right. I have to come up with a better plan for capturing this luscious prey. I have to get my shit together and turn on the charm.

Women don't say no to me.

"I'll stop by the club tonight before the show and check on things. Make sure security's adequate. Last night was pretty chaotic in the parking lot."

"She won't be there. She's not performing tonight."

"You said it would help morale if I showed some interest in the club. I'm showing interest."

Also, it can't hurt to have the other girls saying nice things about me, piquing her curiosity.

He exhales deeply. "Whatever you say boss."

Baby powder laced with the pungent odor of sweat scents the air. The dressing room at the Rhino is as loud and busy as I'd expect the backstage of a strip club to be.

Girls rush in and out of small rooms, some wearing nothing but a G-string, some with sequined pasties on their nipples, all with heavy stage makeup and shimmer lotion or spray on their skin.

Even though Franco said she wouldn't be here, my eyes scan every face, searching for hers. I don't have a clear idea what hers looks like. Still, I feel like I would know her if I saw her. The back halls contain an assortment of blondes, brunettes, rainbow-colored wigs, and women of all shapes and skin tones. *What am I doing here?*

"Not much different than backstage at any other show." Franco holds out an arm, leading me down the narrow hall to where I assume the women exit to the stage.

"I wouldn't know." The long-sleeves of my white linen shirt are rolled to my forearms, and I'm in simple gray pants.

A handsome woman wearing nothing but a bright red

wig pushes past us, exhaling an "excuse me." Her bulbous tits bounce, and her tone is annoyed. We're clearly in her way as we step to either side of the hall so she can pass.

"Do you want to make a speech, or what did you have in mind?" Franco looks at me like this was my big idea, which I guess it was, but it was his suggestion.

"I don't think so. I just wanted to check on things."

"Come on," he smirks. "I'll introduce you."

We step into the large dressing room lined with lighted mirrors and an assortment of women in robes and feathers or nothing at all, and he taps on the wall. A few of the girls look at us with anticipation, while others groan and flop back in their chairs. Some don't even pause in their preparations.

"Oy! Listen up, I've got Trip Alexander here. He's the boss, and he just wanted to say a few words."

At that, everyone stops what they're doing and looks at me. Their expressions are either curious or worried, and I guess they're thinking I'm here to say I've sold the club or something.

"Right, hello." I clear my throat, and this feels like overkill. "Just wanted to say you're all doing a great job, and if you ever need anything or if any of the customers hassle you, let Franco know. We want you to feel safe here."

They all stare at me, and from this angle, I'm able to quickly study each face. Franco was right. None of these women have that strange allure that captures my attention and leaves me wanting more.

A skinny girl with heavy glitter on her oversized eyes steps forward and smiles, shaking my hand. Her fake tits are too large for her body, and her blonde hair is in two long ponytails tied high on each side of her head. I'm pretty sure the look she's going for is Manga schoolgirl.

"Thank you so much, Mr. Trip. I really appreciate the environment you've created at the Rhino. My last club was dirty and security sucked. I was groped several times by clients, and I felt very vulnerable."

That makes me cringe, but it also makes me feel a little better for at least providing an alternative.

I shake her hand, keeping my eyes on hers. "Excellent. That's what we're going for, ah…"

"I'm Shula." When she smiles, she seems way too young to be stripping.

"Shula. That's what we were going for." I release her hand, stepping back into the hall. "Good luck with your show tonight."

The other women return to their preparations, but Shula watches me leave the room like a curious kid, and it reminds me why I've stayed out of this business. She should be in school.

Franco is at my side as we walk towards the exit leading to the club. "That was fun." His tone is sarcastic.

"That was your idea." I don't add *asshole*. "Did it go as you expected?"

"Pretty much."

"That Shula's legal, right?"

"Of course she is."

Barely, I suspect.

Loud music greets us the minute we open the door, and two young women are standing right outside. They're holding drinks and laughing, and one has her hand over her nose and mouth.

"He totally recognized you," she says, flashing her eyes.

Her friend, who is not as tall and a bit curvier, shakes her head. "How could he?"

They both turn to face us, and my eyes lock on the smaller one's. She inhales a soft breath, and for a minute, I hesitate.

Her eyes are so dark brown, I can't see her pupils, yet they seem to sparkle, like she's lit from within. She has a sweet smile, high cheekbones, and a little dimple at the side of her full, glossy lips. Straight, white teeth and long, curly, curly hair. *Beguiling*.

With an internal shake, I force my eyes away from hers.

Maybe it's the south Florida sun or the humidity or the salt air, or maybe I'm not getting enough sex at home. Glitter Girl has my fucking hormones so amped up, I'm ready to bed everything in sight.

"Sorry." Her voice is soft and high with the touch of a sexy rasp.

"Hey, girls." Franco steps up, motioning between us. "Bianca, Giana, this is Trip Alexander, one of the club bosses."

"Nice to meet you. Are you dancers?" I study them both, searching.

"I'm an actress." Bianca, the taller one, tosses her sleek brown hair over her shoulder with a playful tease.

That just leaves… "Giana?"

"Oh, I… ah, I sew the costumes!" She blinks fast, looking from me to her two friends and back. "For the dancers. I'm a seamstress."

Pulling my chin back I nod. "Of course."

I hadn't considered where the girls got their costumes or how they tailored or repaired them.

Franco smirks like the arrogant Cuban he is. "Why don't you girls join us for a drink? We're in the VIP section."

Bianca takes his arm, and the two lead the way. I hang back with Giana, not sure if I should offer my arm or simply walk beside her. My mind is distracted by what happened here last night in that roped-off area, but even with the ghost of Glitter Girl clouding my judgment, I'm able to appreciate the beautiful woman standing in front of me.

"Are you from Florida, Giana?" I hesitate, offering her my arm.

"Everyone calls me Gia." She carefully slips her fingers onto my forearm, almost like we're walking in a cotillion. "I'm from Santa Croce."

"Italy?" I wasn't expecting that reply. "You're a long way from home. What brought you to the US?"

"I accepted a position at the Ballet Company of America, but then, well, it didn't work out."

"Shit, I heard about that. The BCA. It was a big news story." Some idiot developer married a trophy wife, and they both went off the rails, leading to an attempted murder—and the death of a lot of ballet dreams. "That must've been a disappointment."

"Yes, it was."

We're at the round booth in the back, and I watch as she steps away to sit by her friend. Curiously, I inspect her ass. *Nice.* It's perky and round beneath her skirt—not what you usually see on a ballerina. Her calves are sculpted, and I can judge from her exposed arms she's in great shape.

"Do you live in south Florida?" she asks before I have a chance to ask anything more.

"I live in New York, but I visit the area as much as possible. I have several businesses here."

"I see." She's so mature, her dark eyes sizing me up like she hasn't decided if she likes me.

It's intriguing. It makes me want to ask her more questions, but the lights go down. It's time for the floor show.

The waitresses in their safari hats place flutes of expensive champagne in front of each of us, and we turn our attention to the dancer strutting onto the stage in the spotlight. "My Type" by Saweetie blasts through the room, and Shula does an aggressive, grinding number, arching her back like a snake and getting in all the ravenous men's faces.

She struts proudly, her ponytails swinging as her tits bounce, and I avert my eyes to the neon-lit stem of my champagne flute. It's not a long song, and I lift the glass, taking a lingering drink.

When I lower it, I feel a pair of eyes on me. Gia is watching me curiously, and I give her a tight smile. Her expression is still uncertain, and I'm glad when the song ends and the lights rise again.

The audience howls and throws money, but the electricity of last night is missing—at least for me.

"You didn't like the show?" Gia leans closer, speaking louder.

"I'm not really a fan of strippers."

Her slim brows rise. "Then why are you here?"

Great question. "I just stopped in to check on things, security." Sliding out of the booth, I stand, motioning to Franco. "Have another round on me. I'm headed home."

"You sure?" Franco has his arm around Bianca, but Gia is sitting alone, her pretty dark eyes following me.

"I'll catch up with you later. Nice to meet you, ladies. Good luck with everything."

I don't suggest seeing them again, even as my eyes linger a bit too long on Gia's. She smiles, and I almost change my mind.

CHAPTER 6

Gia

"**H**E'S HANDSOME." I'M LYING ON MY BACK ON THE BED, HOLDING a small pillow in my hands and thinking about the elegant man we met at the club tonight.

"I told you!" Bianca has been bursting to say *I told you so* all night—when she wasn't flirting with Franco.

He was not what I expected. I thought "the boss" would be an overweight, sweaty, mafia type. One of those men with fat hands and hairy fingers pinched tight with gold rings.

Trip Alexander is sophisticated with wavy, dark hair that curls around his ears and an attractive scruff on his square jaw. His fingers are long and slim. The kind you'd want to slide along your cheek, into your hair, up your thighs, into your…

My pussy clenches, and I toss my pillow at my smirking friend. "Don't be a brat. He needs a haircut, but I like it."

She catches the pillow and tosses it back. "He needs some polish on his knob from the looks of things."

Rolling my eyes as I turn onto my stomach, I rest my face on my hand. "What kind of a name is Trip, anyway?"

"Rich, white nonsense. He's the third William in his family."

"How in the world do you know that?"

"I know things." She's in a lace teddy with a sheer robe on her shoulders, and she's getting ready for her nightly sessions.

Tonight, I'm watching her, and tomorrow, Franco's going to launch my site. He said I could cut back my performances at the club as soon as I'm up and running, provided I make enough to cover room and board.

Bianca thinks I'll make that in a day, but I'm not sure with the cost of real estate in West Palm.

"He'd never be interested in someone like me." Pushing off the bed, I go to the desk where a laptop is waiting.

"You're exactly what he's looking for. In fact, Franco said that's why he was at the club tonight. Apparently, he never goes to the Rhino." She straightens the blankets on the bed, preparing her camera and equipment. "He was looking for you."

"He was looking for her."

"Which is you. Now shut up, I'm starting."

Sitting in the desk chair, I watch as she transforms into an innocent baby-girl, curious and affectionate with her subscribers. Bianca goes farther than I plan to go. When one of her subscribers asks her to strip, she climbs onto her knees and slowly removes her robe, followed equally sensually by the top of her teddy.

She doesn't show more than her breasts. Instead, she gets on her knees and shows her butt in a G-string, then she rolls around on the bed stroking her breasts as she talks dirty and responds to their fantasies.

Resting my chin on my knee, I realize she wasn't lying when she told Trip she's an actress. All she's doing right now is acting, as far as I can tell, and I wonder if I'll actually be able to do this. Now that I'm seeing it, I think Glitter Girl might be easier—it's definitely quicker to do one dance and scoop up the cash.

Finally after a little more than an hour, she says goodnight to her last subscriber and shuts off her computer.

"That's it." She pulls on her robe and sits back against the headboard. "What do you think?"

"Are you tired?"

"A little, but it's really no big deal. I've spent that much time chatting with friends online."

"But you're not chatting. You're… acting, and that was a long performance."

"Still, I made more than eight hundred dollars in tips. That's about as much as you made last time you danced."

"I was done in four minutes."

She shrugs, climbing off the bed. "You're free to do whatever you want. Speaking of dancing, I have a great idea for your next performance."

Tuesday night, I'm back at the Rhino, making the dash from the side of the Denali to the back door. Bianca is with me, holding an umbrella this time, and I have enormous Jackie-O shades on my face.

Still, it seems like the crowd is growing thicker with every passing week.

A male voice cracks as it screams, "Glitter Girl! Glitter Girl! I love you!"

It's so strange, I actually look to see who's saying these ridiculous things, but before I catch a look, Bianca whips the metal door open and shoves me inside.

"Are you trying to blow your cover?" Her voice is sharper than usual.

I rub my eyes with the back of my hand as I take off the sunglasses. "How can anyone love me? They have no idea who I am."

"Which is exactly why they love you. You're whatever they

imagine." She takes my arm, dragging me to the dressing room. "We need to get started if we're going to get you covered up properly."

The costume she dreamed up is a crimson-satin bodysuit that's basically a series of bows I'll strategically untie as I dance. It's really gorgeous, and it was a bitch to sew so the ribbons would line up properly.

"It's perfect. Just like the one I saw online." She got the idea from a lingerie store, and she waits as I step into the G-string bottoms.

Two extra-large, flesh-colored triangular pasties cover my breasts. They're basically the size of a bikini top, and they'll be hidden by the two large strips of satin that crisscross and tie behind my neck.

We worked out a dance number in which I'll untie the series of bows, starting with the ones at the top of my calf-high leopard-print stripper heels. Next is the one holding the two large strips covering my ass, then the one around my waist, leading up to the one behind my neck.

It's inching closer to full nudity, and I'm thinking more about making this my last dance. I still haven't launched my subscription site, but I've been watching Bianca work hers.

She basically has the same core group of men she chats with each time, which makes it more like a relationship. I don't know if that's better or worse, but it makes her sessions less exhausting, she says.

It's not original content all the time. She's building on what happened in the session before. It feels strange to build relationships with people I don't know, people I'm using to help me raise money so I can go home and leave them. What other choice do I have?

"Try not to jerk your head, or this is all going to come tumbling down." Bianca pins my wild curls in an elaborate updo, then pulls a thin nylon cap over it.

"I am supposed to dance, right?"

"Your hair is so heavy. If you're going to keep doing this, you might consider a shorter cut."

"My hair doesn't respond well to shorter cuts." I reach up to help her fit the platinum-blonde wig over the cap. "We're going to need a bigger wig."

She snickers, handing me the black leather rabbit mask. "This will help."

I take it and fasten it around my head over the wig. It reminds me of something Halle Berry would wear as Catwoman, only I'm Glitter Girl.

Turning my head side to side, a tickle is in my stomach. "I love this look."

Bianca steps back inspecting her handiwork. "You look fierce."

I apply dark berry lipstick to my full lips, and electricity moves from my stomach higher into my chest as I wonder if he'll be here tonight, out in the darkness watching me, wanting me. Now I know where to focus all my energy.

For the first time in a long time, I've got stage butterflies. Excitement zips through my torso, and I'm having a hard time not smiling. I feel like I have to pee, but there's no way I'm getting out and back into this costume before I perform.

Bianca will never let me hear the end of it if she knows what I'm thinking.

Shula runs breathless and shimmering off the stage as we wait in the hall, and when she sees me, she stops dead in her tracks. "Holy shit! You look amazing!"

The smile I've been holding back bursts across my face. "Thanks."

"You're not going out there smiling, are you?" Red crosses her arms, eyes narrowed.

She's the oldest dancer at the club, and she got her name because she always wears a signature red wig. She's also grumpy as hell.

"This isn't my first time performing," I snap back, and she arches an eyebrow before turning and walking away.

People think I'm a pushover because I'm young, but they forget I was a ballerina for ten years, and at home, I had to contend with Aunt Gratziela. I'm tougher than I look.

"You got this?" Bianca puts her hands on my shoulders and looks me in the eyes.

"I got this." Glitter Girl is rising inside me, and I can feel her taking away my fear. "Is he out there?"

A beat falls between us, and Bianca doesn't breathe. I don't breathe. She leaves me for a moment and walks to the edge of the curtain, peeking out from the darkness into the now-lit house. It'll be dark when I perform, and with the spotlight in my face, I won't be able to see anyone in the crowd.

Her face gives nothing away as she walks back to where I'm standing, my breath shallow. Our eyes meet, and she nods. He's there.

He's watching.

"Let's go." I walk onto the stage.

Tonight we've planned my dance so I'll start on the stage, sitting backwards in a bent-wood chair with my arms stretched forward and my head bowed behind a thin, shimmering curtain. I'm dancing to "Open Your Heart" by Madonna, and as soon as the first beats of the drum strike, the curtain swirls away. I begin to move.

I know all the words to this song, and even if they don't exactly apply—I haven't been following Trip around, and he hasn't walked past and ignored me on the street—I'd be okay with him opening his heart to me.

I've imagined threading my fingers in the sides of his dark hair. I've thought of his scruff on my face, my shoulders, my inner thighs. I've pictured his full lips capturing mine in a possessive, dominating kiss.

I'm inexperienced, but I read romance books, and I have a vivid imagination. Now I'm on the stage dancing for his eyes only. I ignore the men howling like wolves. I can't see their drooling mouths. I can't see anything with the glare of the spotlight in my face, but I know where he's sitting.

Reaching my arms in his direction, I look down the line of my fingers. I skip away, turning as I lean forward, arching my back and sticking out my ass as I untie the first ribbon on my left boot.

I toss the scrap to the hungry men who mean nothing to me on the floor. Then I move to the next boot, repeating the process.

Energy hums on my skin, and I'm one with the music. I'll make them all want me. Moving higher, I untie the ribbon around my waist, twisting around and shaking my ass as I untie the next bow, allowing the fabric to fall away, leaving nothing but a G-string.

The roaring of the crowd grows louder, and I hear a voice yelling, "Glitter Girl!" Disregarding it, I continue the dance, strutting in my giant boots.

I wish I could see his face. Instead, I close my eyes and picture it in my head as I slide my hands up my body. I see the sly smile curling his lips, exposing straight white teeth. I picture those teeth clamping down on his full bottom lip, and heat warms my core.

Turning to the front again, I'm at the end. I skip to the side and bend forward, sliding my hands from my ankle to my thigh, to my waist, finally lifting my breasts. The last bow is tied behind my neck, and I'll release it as I turn away just slow enough to provide a teasing glimpse of my breasts.

It's time. The trumpets sound, Madonna is urging, and I do it. I pull the ribbon and start to turn. I'm midway through my spin when hands clutch at my feet. Someone is on the stage trying to grab me.

"Glitter Girl!" It's the male voice again, the one from before, only now it's hoarse and desperate. "I love you!"

He's screaming, reaching for me, and it knocks me off

balance. These needle-thin heels are not forgiving, but I'm used to dancing on pointe shoes. It's the only thing that keeps me upright. I roll forward onto my toes and finish my final spin without falling. Lifting my arms over my head, glitter confetti bursts from above and the curtain falls.

I showed a little more of my breasts than I intended, but that's why Bianca insisted on the oversized pasties—in case anything went wrong.

Technically, they saw nothing, but it was a close call.

I'm trembling from my near-fall. I can still feel the grasping hands on my feet, and I hear the scuffle of people on the other side of the thin shield. I don't wait around to find out what's going on in the room out front.

Bianca meets me at the door. "Holy shit, are you okay?" She quickly covers me with a robe, and we dash into my dressing room.

The girls crowd around me, offering sympathy and patting my shoulders as I pass. Shula follows us to my chair.

"It's okay." I sit, leaning down to unzip my boots. "I didn't fall."

"What an asshole!" Shula whisper-shouts, stomping around my space. "He grabbed your feet! Doesn't he know you could break your neck in those shoes?"

"Franco's handling it." Bianca's holding her phone. "He won't be back here again. He'll be lucky if the bouncers don't beat the shit out of him. If he'd hurt you or made you break an ankle…"

Leaning forward with my elbows on my knees, I breathe deeply. "I'm okay. Nothing happened. I caught it."

"Only because you know what you're doing." Bianca shakes her head.

Shula's big eyes are even bigger. "If that had been me, I'd have gone down right on my ass."

"I'm fine. Seriously." Sitting straighter, I reach for their hands, wanting to lighten the mood. "I guess it was a pretty good routine if it made them break the rules, yeah?"

"You were unbelievable," Shula gushes. "A true star."

Bianca levels her gaze on mine. She knows what I'm thinking. "If that didn't shake him up, nothing will."

What I don't add is he's not the only one shaken. With all my fantasizing onstage, I need to change my underwear.

CHAPTER 7

Trip

SHE'S ON FIRE. RUNNING MY HAND OVER MY MOUTH, I DO MY BEST to control my expression. It's impossible how gorgeous she is. She's pure sex, and then some asshole tried to grab her.

If it weren't for the velvet rope slowing me down, I'd have made it to the stage to beat the shit out of him with my bare fists before security dragged his sorry ass out.

She handled it like a pro. That asshole grabbed her foot, nearly pulling it from under her, and instead of falling, she went full *en pointe*. She rotated all the way onto the front of her shoes and spun as her top fell away, but not before we saw them.

Her tits are magnificent. Hell, her whole body is magnificent.

I'm sure it's because I'm an egotistical dick, but it felt like her entire dance was for me. I know it's impossible. I know how stage lighting works. The house is completely dark, and with the spotlight in her face, she can't see me. Still, she kept turning in my direction.

She would stretch her arms out to where I was sitting,

lowering her gaze to mine, then she would roll her shoulders, pulling her hands back as if drawing me to her luscious body.

She untied every ribbon in a position that gave me the best view of what was revealed. Her sexy ass bobbed up and down, and my erection ached in my pants as I watched the G-string sliding around her center. It's clear she's completely bare, and the way her costume is made, her pussy was practically exposed.

She turned and faced me, running her hands down her torso and between her thighs, up and down like she was masturbating, then she dropped her head back as if in ecstasy. *Fuck me.* I had to rub my palm over my dick outside my pants. Nothing eased the ache of wanting her.

Then she leaned forward, squeezing her tits together, causing that ribbon to loosen, and I could almost see everything. Franco didn't sit with me tonight. I was alone in the VIP section, and in that moment, I actually contemplated moving my hand inside my pants. No one could see me here in the darkness. No one would've known, but *shit.* I grabbed the reins on that insanity fast. I can't get arrested for indecent exposure. *What the fuck?*

It's like she had me hypnotized. I wanted to roar. I wanted to storm the stage, throwing all those other guys aside, and drag her out of here. I was a fucking cave man, wanting to drag her all the way back to my apartment and declare her *Mine.*

I was already out of my seat when that fucker dared to touch her. Now she's gone, and I stagger back to where I left my drink. A sheen of sweat is on my upper lip, and my brain is on fire. I need to fight or fuck—or go somewhere I can deal with this hard-on.

For a moment, I consider going backstage. I could easily excuse it as concern over her well-being. I told the dancers this was a safe place, and what happened to her broke our rules and violated her safety.

Franco's words drift through my head. *She doesn't want to*

meet you. Glancing down, I decide it's probably for the best. With the shape I'm in, I'd appear equally as threatening as the rest of these creeps. I know what women like, and it isn't meeting drooling assholes for the first time with tents in their pants.

So I cut out the side door and head to my car.

Hopping in the steel-gray Lamborghini Franco insisted on renting for me, I hesitate when I see a crowd surrounding the shiny, black SUV waiting at the back door. Easing my car forward, I catch a glimpse of two dark-haired women in hoodies and sunglasses as big as their faces dashing into it as camera flashes strobe in the night.

My stomach clenches, and my fingers tighten on the steering wheel. *It's her.*

The crowd of mostly men push forward on the SUV as it slowly drives out of the parking lot. They're like ravenous dogs, trying to follow her home, and I realize how smart she is to hide her identity.

Hunger burns in me. I'm dying to touch her. I know where she lives, but I'm not going there. I'm better than that. Fuck, if only my dick would get the message.

The back of her dark head presses against my shoulder, and her full lips are parted in an *O* of ecstasy. My hand slides down her flat stomach, joining hers between her thighs, and now I thread our fingers as I stroke her clit, increasing the pressure as I drive into her from behind.

She's hot and tight and so wet. I'm starting to come, even as I try to hold back, to make it last longer. I'm too desperate tonight; she's made me too feverish.

Looking down the front of her body, I watch her gorgeous tits, full and bouncing with every thrust. They're perfect, and the ribbons of her costume hang on each side. I untied them tonight, slowly, and as they fell away, I pulled her hard nipples into my mouth, sucking on them, squeezing them, lifting them in my hands.

Now I'm inside her, and we're riding all the way to heaven. Her orgasm mixes with mine, dripping from her pussy onto my thighs. We're coming together, and she bucks her ass against my pelvis. I kiss the side of her neck, moving my lips higher, behind her ear as I speak hot words to her.

"That's my good girl. Ride my dick. Come all over me…" My voice is ragged, and I groan loudly as I finish.

Her ass moves faster, drawing out every last drop, pulling me from base to tip, until my legs are trembling and weak. My knees give out, and we have to collapse forward.

Only, it's just my forearm pressing against the stone wall of my shower. I'm alone, holding my dick, wringing every last drop of orgasm from my body as her image slowly fades from my mind.

An angry growl replaces my moans. I want to hold her in my arms for real. I want to slide my fingers along her jaw and turn her mouth to mine so I can slip my tongue into her. I want to taste her. I want to possess her.

I can't go on like this. My hand is no substitute for the real thing.

In my robe, with my fourth vodka of the night in my hand, I quickly place the online order. It only takes a few moments, tapping on my phone face to be sure it's delivered by dawn. It's an expensive gesture, but it's worth it. I've got to get this ball rolling.

Sliding the device in my pocket, I step to the window and look out at the lights reflecting off the water. My condo faces the intracoastal waterway, and I gaze at the drawbridge with its old-fashioned, Spanish-style tower in the center. The blue water sparkles brilliantly.

Spring is the perfect time to be here. The air is cool, the humidity low, but it's still warm enough for the girls to wear slip dresses and the air to taste of salt and sin.

I take another sip of expensive, ice-cold liquor. It has to be my last or I'll feel like shit tomorrow. The tension has left my body. The fever is gone, and I've started the wheels turning. Placing the glass on the counter, I start for my bedroom when my phone buzzes.

I'm not in the mood to speak to anyone, but I check it to be sure there isn't a problem with my order. Hana's face is on the screen, and I slide my finger across to answer. We always answer.

"You're calling awfully late." I continue walking.

"Am I catching you at a bad time?" Her voice is tentative.

I hear street noise on her end, and I glance at the clock. It's after one. "No, I was just going to bed. You okay? Not walking up Fifth Avenue alone, I hope."

"Debbie's with me. She's been fighting with Grish all night. It seems she finally believes the rumors about her mother."

"Sounds like a terrific time to be hanging with those two." Sarcasm is thick in my tone, and I sit on the bed, stretching my back straight against the headboard.

"You know us so well." She's quiet, and it's not like Hana to call at this hour simply to chat.

As I'm deciding how to approach this, I hear a voice I recognize in the background. Odd—it's Blake's voice.

"Is Blake with you?" Hana's older sister despises the party scene—and pretty much our entire crowd.

Not that I blame her. We can be a bit much at times.

"Yeah…" She hesitates. "I kind of had a bad night last night. Debbie wanted to blow off some steam, and… I don't remember."

My brow furrows. I've been around for nights like that, and it can get way out of control. "Are you okay?"

I make a note to check Page Six for the inevitable photos. I only hope I don't see my friend passed out in an alley or looking like she's single-handedly trying to bring back heroin chic.

"When are you coming home? Blake didn't even know you were out of town."

Any time Hana has a bad night, Blake comes after me, even though I've told her repeatedly I don't give Hana drugs. "Blake wouldn't be with you if I were there."

"I think she's worried."

Inhaling slowly, I think about this. "Should she be?"

Female voices crowd the other end of the line. Debbie and Blake are talking, and I imagine they're back at the Andover deciding what to do next.

"Are you falling in love with Florida?" Hana's soft voice has the high timbre of a little girl, like Marilyn or Pam Anderson.

It hits me in the gut. "I'm taking care of business. Something unexpected came up."

"We should join you there. Debbie loves Miami. Did you go to Versace's mansion?"

"No, I came straight here." I think about my first night in town. It feels so long ago.

"Do you ever wonder what it's all for? Why we keep doing this day after day?"

I don't wonder. I know what I want, the freedom I'm working so hard to earn, but that's not what she wants to hear.

Instead, I lighten my tone, turning on the casual charm. "Deep questions for so late at night. Are you home?"

"Yeah," she exhales softly.

"I want you to go inside, go straight to your room, and get some sleep. Sleep til noon and then text me you did what I said, okay?"

"Night, Trip." The line goes dead before I can answer.

Lowering my hand to the bed, my mind drifts far away

from south Florida to another life waiting for me miles from here. It's a dangerous life, one of too many risks and too much money.

I'm mixed up with men who'd sell their own children to get what they want, but I plan to beat them at their own game. I plan to get out before it gets me.

Which begs the question, why the hell am I spending so much time here? West Palm has never been my focus. Scrubbing my fingers over my brow, I can't help thinking I should go home. What's happening here is a distraction.

I need to get my head together, but staying here pulls me so strong.

CHAPTER 8

Gia

'M CURLED UP IN MY SOFT BED, HUGGING MY PILLOW AND DREAMING of my handsome, elegant prince. All night I made love to Trip. I taunted him with my dances. I ran away, but he caught me. Okay, I let him catch me.

He put his hands around my waist, pulling my back to his chest. I reached up to thread my fingers in his soft, wavy hair. His beard scuffed the skin at the back of my neck, while his full lips traced a line up to my ears. Such an ecstatic combination—rough whiskers, warm kisses, wet tongue.

His hand slid between my thighs, finding the place right at the top, right in the center. He knew exactly how to touch me, firm circles, fingering and sliding back and forth. My nipples grew hard and tingly, longing for his mouth on them, his teeth.

When he plunged between my thighs, I could only imagine, but the orgasm that shook my body made me cry out. Turning my face, I buried my moan in my pillow. Bianca and I share a room, but luckily she likes to sleep with headphones. She claims we're all too loud at night.

As much as I tried not to be, I was too loud last night.

In my dreams, Trip took me places I've never been. He gave me so much pleasure. Now I'm stretching my arms over my head in the growing dawn, wishing there was some way I could see him again.

Even if I did, he'd think I was Gia the seamstress. How could I tell him I'm Glitter Girl? How would that change the way he thought of me? I'm sure it wouldn't matter either way. A man of his wealth and status would never be interested in someone like me.

The thought makes me frown. It definitely kills my fantasy after-glow. Tossing my sheets back, I get up and pull a robe over my shoulders. I want all the coffee, and then I want some re-tail therapy. I made so much in tips last night, I deserve a treat.

"Who sent them?" Shula's voice is whispered awe, and Dani, our housekeeper, is with her in the foyer, leaning over what looks like a potted plant wrapped in cellophane and thick ribbon.

"What's that?" I keep walking towards the kitchen, the scent of fresh-brewed java lighting up my insides. *Coffee…*

If I can't have the hot guy, at least I can have the hot bever-age. Shula gasps, and I hesitate, trying to decide if my curios-ity is stronger than my caffeine addiction. Caffeine is winning.

"Gia!" She jumps up with a shriek that makes my heart stutter and dashes over to me holding a little card. "It's for you!"

Wrinkling my nose, I pull my chin back. "What is?"

"Look!" She shoves the white card in my face. "It says Glitter Girl."

I take the card, tilting it so I can read the inscription. *Deepest apologies for the security lapse last night. I promise you it will not happen again. Sincerely, Trip Alexander*

My jaw drops, and Dani looks like a walking flower ar-rangement as she carries the massive bouquet of red roses to where I'm standing. "It's got to be at least five dozen."

"Five dozen roses!" My eyes are so wide, they're bugging

out of my head. Then she puts the crystal vase in my hands, and I almost drop it. "Holy crap! How much do they weigh?"

"A lot." Dani's voice is flat.

"You've got to write him back and thank him!" Shula is breathless with excitement, bobbing up and down on her toes at my side. "Maybe he'll ask you to dinner and you'll fall in love and he'll marry you like Richard Gere and Julia Roberts in *Pretty Woman!*"

"She's not a hooker." Dani shakes her head as she returns to breakfast preparations in the kitchen.

My head is spinning, and the softly clean perfume of the flowers surrounds me. I'm not sure what to do with them. All the butterflies have burst out of their cocoons at the same time, and they're rioting in my stomach. *He sent me roses…*

I slowly carry the massive arrangement to the round table in the center of the living room. "We can all enjoy them here."

"But they're for you." Shula's eyes are dreamy. "He's gorgeous and rich and elegant… And he's obsessed with you."

Chewing my lip, I think about Franco saying he wanted to meet me. I think about my dance last night, and how I did everything to make it just for him, to seduce him with my movements. Maybe I'm the one obsessed. I know who he is. He doesn't know who I am.

"Didn't you say his speech was about safety? He probably just feels bad."

No touching. That's the rule. Even if he wanted to, he couldn't touch me. Franco assured us it applies to everyone. *In the club.*

"I don't know. This is a lot more than a simple apology."

I study the beautiful bouquet then walk slowly to pour a mug of coffee. How am I going to handle this? She's right, it's a lot, and he wants to meet me. Only, if Trip is obsessed, it's with the tantalizing, mystery dancer, who taunts him with promises of wicked sex.

What would he think if the mask fell away, and he

discovered she's simply an innocent, small-town girl who's still a virgin? He wants the fantasy, but I'm only Gia.

My throat tightens at the thought. The room feels stuffy, and my head hurts. Returning to my room, I strip out of my pajamas and pull on leggings and a thin sweater that falls off my shoulder. I need retail therapy. *Stat.*

West Palm has amazing designer shops. It's one of the saving graces of moving here. Not that I've ever been able to set foot in any of them.

Until today.

I go straight to Carolina Herrera and close my eyes, smiling as I inhale the crisp-linen scent of luxury. A clerk puts a glass of champagne in my hand, and I stroll through the beautiful store admiring the elegantly tailored clothes. As a seamstress, I can't help noticing the stitching is impeccable.

Growing up in Italy, I would read about the fashion shows in Milan and dream of visiting the city for fashion week. It never happened, but I did see photos of the designer stores there. I would get the patterns and recreate them in my costumes.

Now I'm in one of those stores. Maybe it's a secret how I can afford to be here, but I'm here.

Pausing in front of an antique wardrobe filled with separates, I admire a skirt with an oversized poppy design in pinks and vibrant purples and greens on a navy background. The solid-navy top has long sleeves that are puffed at the shoulders. It's beautiful, but my breath inhales sharply when I turn and see *the dress.*

It's red crimson, the same as the ribbons on my costume last night. The bodice is form-fitted with a flared skirt like a mermaid, and the best part is the bust. It's composed of two small cups that rise up like clam shells to provide coverage.

"This." My voice is hushed, and a tickle is in my lower stomach when I imagine Trip seeing me in it.

He won't care who I am when his eyes land on "the girls" in this dress. It's incredible. *Does this mean I'm going to accept his offer and see him?*

"It's from this year's ready-to-wear collection." The store clerk smiles.

"May I try it on?" I'm almost afraid to ask, but she takes it off the rack at once.

"Size… eight?"

Blinking fast, I glance down at my bust. "Twelve?"

"Of course!" Her voice is bright. "I have two others you might like as well."

She escorts me to a room with quilted cream fabric on the walls. Soft chairs are arranged around the room and a small, round platform is positioned in front of a three-way mirror. I wish Bianca were here to share this experience.

First, I try on a white chiffon dress with a thin, black belt. It has small pleats along the collar, which is pinned tight around my neck, and it's too modest. I don't want to look like a baby. I'm a woman, and I'm coming out of the cocoon.

Up next, a bright yellow design reminds me of something Audrey Hepburn would wear. It's fitted all the way down to my knees, and a flared ruffle goes over the shoulder and down one side. It's fine, but my original selection, the whole reason for me being in this fitting room, is the clear winner.

I step into the red dress and straighten as the clerk zips up the back for me. With my spiral curls falling around my shoulders and those red cups just covering my full breasts, we both gasp.

"It's perfect." We speak at the same time.

I don't even look at the total when she rings me up. I pass over a stack of cash, thick because much of it is small bills, and she makes a little noise before giving me change. She probably thinks I am a hooker paying this way, but I don't care. I couldn't be happier.

Strolling down Worth Avenue, I step into the Lilly Pulitzer store. I'm not the biggest fan of her dizzying patterns and baby-doll styles. I want to look sophisticated, but I do take a beach coverup off the rack and buy it.

Finally, I'm in Valentino, which is as pink as Barbie's dream house. Walking through the store, I'm not sure how I feel about the intensity of this hue. Still, I can't resist a pair of candy-pink Mary Jane platforms.

Even if I never wear them out in public, Bianca and I can figure out a way to work them into my choreography.

My head is in the clouds, and I've forgotten all about the inferiority complex dragging me down when I left the house. I'm carrying designer bags full of gorgeous clothes. My chin is high, and I smile up at the towering palms when a low voice makes me yip.

"Giana?" I almost drop everything when I see him.

"Trip?"

"Sorry, I meant to say *Gia*." It's a baritone vibration I feel in my core, and my eyes devour him.

He's dressed casually in a long-sleeved shirt rolled up to reveal his tanned, lined forearms. The jeans he's wearing show off his lean physique, and he's so effortlessly handsome.

"What are you doing here?" My heart beats so fast, I might have to sit down.

"I live here." His full lips curl into a naughty grin. *Is everything he does sexy?*

"You do?" I look all around the shopping district. "I didn't realize…"

"I don't live *here*, on Worth Avenue. I live a few blocks down by the water. I was just out for a stroll, like you?"

He glances down at me in black leggings and a loose sweater. Black Birkenstock sandals are on my feet, and thank God my pedicure is fresh.

"Ahh, yes! I was just out for a walk, and… shopping." I lift the bags.

"Valentino? I didn't realize seamstresses were so well-heeled."

Pressing my lips together. I try to think… *How in the world can I explain this?* My mind is racing for something plausible. The key to hiding my identity is telling as few lies as possible, so I don't lose track. I'm already losing track.

"It's none of my business." He holds up both hands and takes a step away. "You owe me no explanations."

But I want to owe him explanations.

I take a step closer to stop his retreat. "It's my birthday." I blurt out the lie. "My family sent me money… to get myself a present."

He pauses, and his head tilts to the side. What do I do now? What if he sees my driver's license which shows my birthday isn't for three more months?

Now why would that happen? He's not going to card me. I need to get it together.

"In that case, happy birthday. May I buy you a coffee? I know a little bakery that has the best Cuban coffee in Palm Beach."

"Yes!" I answer too fast, and I feel the warmth coloring my cheeks. *Sophistication, Gia.* "I mean, I adore Cuban coffee. All coffee, really."

"I'm sure it's not as good as what you'd get in Italy." We start to walk.

"No…" I smile, forcing my shoulders to relax, the line between my eyebrows to loosen. "But I've found some close seconds. Maybe you'll introduce me to another?"

We walk to a small shop on the corner. It has white tile floors and dark-brown painted pastry cases. It has a vintage feel, and Trip orders two café Cubanos. I step to the side admiring the croissants and pastiletos behind the glass. Pastiletos are Cuban puff pastries, filled with guava jelly or cream cheese.

"Do you live around here?" He hands me the paper cup, and I take a sniff, exhaling a little sigh at the delicious aroma.

"Mm-hmm…" When I look up, his eyes are fixed on me curiously. "Sorry. What?"

"I asked if you live around here."

"Oh!" Jumping, I can't let him know I live in the condo he owns. That will really lead to questions I'm not ready to answer. *Shit.* It's nearly impossible to have a normal conversation with so much to hide. "No. I mean, I live around here, but I walked here."

"Okay." He starts for the door, and my eyes slide down to his toned ass in those jeans. *Hot.*

Clearing my throat, I tear my gaze from his body. "Do you have family here?"

We're out on the sidewalk, and he shifts uncomfortably. "No, my family is in New York, or what's left of it."

"What do you mean?"

"It's only my mother and me. My father died a few years ago."

"Oh, I'm so sorry."

"Don't be. He was not a nice man."

I want to ask why he wasn't nice. I want to ask how he died. I want to know everything about Trip's family and his life in New York, but I have to take it easy.

Shifting gears, I think about the city. "I'd love to visit New York. It seems like a magical place." I exhale a soft giggle. "I'd probably be hit by a car, walking around looking up at the skyscrapers all the time."

Amusement is in his eyes, and a touch of warmth. "You're cute, you know that?"

It's like a splash of cold water in my face. "Puppies are cute."

It comes out sharper than I intend, and he course-corrects fast. "Forgive me." He holds up a palm. "I wasn't trying to insult you."

"No, I'm sorry. Of course you weren't insulting me. I shouldn't have said that."

An awkward silence falls between us, and I'm completely deflated. I don't want him to think of me as *cute*, but he won't think of me at all if I'm a snappy brat. I have to be cool, elegant like he is, like the girls in New York.

I wish I had more coffee. Cuban coffee is basically an espresso shot, and I prefer to linger over my favorite, hot beverage.

Sneaking a glance at him, I notice his eyes are lowered. He's watching my feet. "Cute tattoo. Is that a monarch butterfly?"

Pausing, I look down, tilting my foot side to side. "Yeah." I smile, doing my best to sound sweet, welcoming. "It reminds me of my mother. She liked to talk about butterflies and metamorphosis."

"Are you close to your mother?"

"I was, but she died."

"I'm sorry." Then he exhales a laugh. "I can't seem to say the right thing today."

"You didn't say anything wrong. I'm the one who nearly took your head off for a compliment." Crossing his arms, he narrows his eyes at me, but I continue carefully. "I don't know how to say everything in English. I don't know the perfect words, so I speak from my heart and hope my feelings translate."

"You're very expressive." His voice is gentler now. My stomach squeezes, and I think he's stealing little pieces of my heart. "Maybe we could start over?"

"How do we do that?"

"Here." He lifts his hand, palm open, and I slide mine over it. "How do you do, Miss Rossi? Lovely day for a stroll."

He gives me a little wink. Another little piece of my heart.

"How do you do, Mr. Alexander? It is nice out today." Especially with him standing here, holding my hand.

He releases me, and loss filters through my stomach.

"Are you on your way home now? I'll give you a lift, make sure you get there safely."

"I'm not sure anywhere is safe with you."

"Smart girl." He chuckles. "Seriously, though, I'll give you a ride."

I can't accept his offer as much as I want to. "It's okay. I'm not going straight home. I, ahh… have to visit a friend."

"Anyone I know?"

"Do we know the same people?"

"I know Franco… your friend Bianca. One of the girls from the club?"

"No, just a friend of mine from home."

"Boyfriend?"

It's my turn to study him. *Does he care?* "No."

"Again, none of my business." Taking my hand again, he lifts it to his lips for a brief kiss. I feel it all the way to my shoulders, my chest, my stolen heart. "Happy birthday, Gia. Perhaps we'll cross paths again."

"I'd like that." My voice is soft, and I can't let him slip away. "Would you like my number?"

It's his turn to hesitate, and what the hell have I done? If he says no, I'll literally die on the spot. If he says yes and never calls, I'll die slowly, staring at my phone twenty-four hours a day.

"Sure." He slides a phone from his pocket and unlocks it. "Enter your digits."

The image on the front of his phone is a cityscape at night. "Gorgeous," I note before quickly tapping in my number.

"I've always liked it. It's the view from my apartment in New York."

"Right." Again, I'm reminded how rich he is, how far apart our worlds are.

I give his phone back, and I'm lost in thought when my phone buzzes. Studying the screen, I try to figure out who I know with a 212 area code. "Now you have mine."

My lips part, and I look up at him. "Thanks."

That grin curves his lips again, and he's looking at me like he wants to say something. God, I hope it's not that I'm cute.

When he turns to take a call, I quickly save his number as *Mio Marito*, or *Hubby* in Italian. My cheeks flush, and I tuck my phone in my pocket, grinning as I trot to catch up with him.

CHAPTER 9

Trip

I DON'T KNOW WHAT TO MAKE OF THE BEAUTIFUL GIRL STANDING IN front of me. She's bright and open like a sunflower, lighting up the world. Her sweetness is intoxicating, and when she speaks, her accent is adorable. Every word is laced with honey, and I'm the bee ready to consume her.

I'm a selfish prick, more like it. Gia knows nothing of my life in New York, the dirty deals and the underworld I'm entangled in. I'm not here for romance. Still, if I were… I could hardly keep my eyes off her curves in those leggings and that loose sweater.

I'm a sucker for naturally voluptuous women, obviously, ones with tiny waists and full tits and ass. Hourglass perfection. Now I've got two of them occupying space in my mind, sweet Gia and sinful Glitter Girl. One is a flight of fantasy, unreal, distant, disinterested, but the other is the real thing.

Gia looks at me like the man I want to be, honest and real. Curiosity, fascination, at times, I think even hunger is in the depths of her brown gaze.

And I need to get my head out of my ass.

Standing in the street, I tell her goodbye, deciding that's the end of it. Seeing Gia again would be a colossal mistake. She's trying to get back to Italy, and even if she weren't, an innocent little seamstress like her has no business getting mixed up with a guy like me.

She should be with a good, upstanding citizen. A man who does something useful like bake bread or make shoes. *Make shoes*? What the hell kind of fable am I casting her in? And why the hell does the thought of her with that fictional cobbler make me want to break things?

I don't recognize myself these days. I've always been in complete control of everything and everyone, most of all myself. I've never been on edge like this, my blood hot at all times.

Walking up the palm-lined boulevard between the designer shops to my penthouse condo overlooking the intracoastal waterway, I think about our morning, what I learned about Gia.

It's her birthday. She was carrying shopping bags from Carolina Herrera and Valentino. I smile at her expensive taste, then I stop in my tracks. My brow furrows. *Expensive taste…*

If her family can afford to send her thousands of dollars for clothes from top designer stores, why is she trying to earn money to get home?

She said her mother is dead. She wouldn't let me drive her home or tell me where she lives.

Pulling out my phone, I scroll to Franco's number and hit call. "What's up, boss?" His voice is groggy, like he's just waking up.

Squinting up at the bell tower, I see it's almost noon. Instead of charging right into my suspicions, I start with the most pressing issue. "Any word on the guy from last night?"

"Nobody seems to know who he is." Franco groans, and it sounds like he's walking. "The waitresses said he paid for everything in cash, and he ran after the bouncers pulled him off her. They lost him."

"I want his name, description, everything we have at the door. He's not allowed in the club again."

"Already done." The sound of water running makes me think he's making coffee. "It would help if we had a photo. Not everybody saw him."

I don't like it. "If he's stupid enough to show up again, I want him detained. I want to know who he is, and I want him handled."

"Consider it done."

The line falls quiet, and the only noise is coffee preparations. My mind drifts to Gia… she loves coffee of all kinds.

"Hey, tell me what you know about these girls, Bianca and Gia."

More silence. The sharp slam of a cabinet closing and things moving around fills the space between us.

The longer he doesn't respond, the angrier I grow. "Franco?"

"I'm thinking." His tone is impatient. "Gia said she's a seamstress? Did she tell you how she got here?"

"She came to join the Ballet Company of America is what she said."

"Yeah, that's right. That place was a clusterfuck. They even made one of those documentaries about it."

"I'm concerned it's all a lie, a cover story."

Silence.

A few seconds pass, and Franco slowly says, "Why would you think that?"

"I ran into Gia today on Worth Avenue. She said it was her birthday, and she had shopping bags from Valentino and Carolina Herrera… very expensive stores."

"She got presents for her birthday? So what?" Franco is being so dim-witted, I wonder why I trust him to manage my business at all.

"Why would a poor girl trying to get home to her family spend the cost of an international plane ticket on designer dresses? Hell, she could buy three plane tickets for the price of one Valentino dress."

More silence. "It's true."

"I offered to give her a ride home, and she declined. She wouldn't tell me where she lived."

"Is that so?" He doesn't sound as concerned as I am, which worries me.

"Is Gia being trafficked?"

Franco explodes in a coughing fit, and I hold the phone away from my ear. *What the fuck?* I give him several seconds to get it together.

When he's no longer coughing, I put the phone to my ear again. "You okay?"

"I don't think Gia's being sex trafficked."

"I didn't say *sex* trafficked. She's a seamstress. She could be here against her will, forced to make clothes in a sweatshop. Hell, I don't know what all these assholes do."

"That's a pretty big accusation you're making."

"How well do you know her?" Silence again. It lasts too long, so I continue. "How well do you know Bianca for that matter? When did you meet her?"

"I've known Bianca long enough." He pauses, and I hear him drinking. "I don't think they're being trafficked. I would know."

"Her situation doesn't make sense. Get your guys to look into it. See what they find out and let me know."

"You're the boss." He's respectful, but I don't like his dismissiveness.

In my line of work, you never allow suspicious situations to go unchecked.

"Keep me posted." I disconnect, annoyed by his lack of interest.

Criminal enterprises take hold because regular people don't believe it can happen in their neighborhood. It can.

My walking pace increased while I was speaking to Franco,

probably because my adrenaline was pumping. Now I'm back at my building, taking the elevator to the top floor, the penthouse.

I don't know what it is about that girl, but she stirs something in me I can't deny. I want to be sure she's safe. Her wild curls and sparkling black eyes, her dimpled grin all filter through my memory, and my stomach warms. I smile.

Alone. In my living room. *Smiling.*

Even if Franco isn't convinced something's up, I have her number. What the hell am I waiting for? Opening my phone, I tap out a quick text. ***You should have a birthday dinner, and I know just the place.***

It takes a minute for her to reply, but her answer is perfect. ***Are you asking me to dinner?***

Yes, silly girl. I don't text that. Instead, I reply, ***Tonight, HMF at The Breakers, 7. Send me your address, and I'll pick you up.***

I wait, watching the gray dots bounce, and I anticipate her reply before it even appears. ***I'll meet you there.***

My molars grind. Still, I have no grounds to push against this, so I tease. ***I'll have a white rose.***

I'll be wearing red.

Sliding my phone in the breast pocket of my jacket, I gaze out the window at the water below. From this height, it looks calm and still, nothing disturbing it. Only on the shore do you see the crashing waves, feel the strength of the current wanting to pull you down.

My phone buzzes, and I'm taken from my thoughts. Furrowing my brow, I lift the device, wondering if Gia is going to say more, change her mind, cancel.

It's Hana, and I exhale, nodding at the message. ***I did what you said.***

Quickly, I tap back. ***Feel better?***

Gray dots float, and I watch a gull lifted on an updraft. ***Some. Still need a vacation. You're smart to get away.***

It's not like Hana to be so open. She's usually a complete mystery—or her memory really is for shit. She has a habit of developing convenient amnesia when situations get out of control or dangerous, or she's done something she doesn't want to (or can't) explain. I've never been able to tell if it's the truth or her version of my poker face.

Sounds like I made the right call, I reply, thinking of the mess I left at home.

More gray dots. *Make good choices*.

Her sign-off makes me chuckle, and I can't resist. *Don't do drugs.*

She doesn't reply, not that I expected her to. It'll take more than a text to get her to behave.

Pulling my shirt over my head, I have time to get some exercise before dinner, and the workout facilities in this building are first rate.

I spend an hour and a half on torque fitness, pull-ups, push-ups, and rowing, and I'm heading to the top floor a sweaty mess but with the edge off my appetites. I only have time for a quick shower and to towel-dry my hair, which is still too long. Rubbing my hand on my jaw, I decide just to trim the beard, make it neat, then I slip into my Armani suit.

HMF is named after the Breakers resort's founder, Henry M. Flagler. It's located in the massive ballroom of the hundred-year-old resort, and it's a local favorite—for locals with money, of course. The south Florida bluebloods flock to this area, which is why our business is concentrated here. More old white men to relieve of their excess income.

Dress code is cocktail chic, the atmosphere is light jazz, and the expectations are high. No one steps out of line at the Breakers unless he or she wants to be escorted off the property and possibly to jail.

I check in at the gate and park the silver Lambo in the circle lot. Strolling up the red-brick pavement to the rambling, four-story resort, I chose this place for its Italian-inspired design, massive arches, and interiors. I hoped it would make her feel at home.

I don't like meeting her. I would much rather escort her through the courtyards, past the grand ballroom, and into the restaurant overlooking the Atlantic. Still, I can work around that part, since the grounds are dotted with wrought-iron benches where I can easily wait for her to arrive.

I'll order a drink, take a seat, and respect her wishes.

Vodka in hand, I watch the oversized fountain surrounded by twinkle-lit palm trees as black SUVs glide up the brick-paved circular drive to deposit wealthy visitors at the front door.

Tonight, I'll get to the bottom of what's going on with her. No more mysteries. No more secrets.

CHAPTER 10

Gia

THE MUSIC SWELLS, AND I'M *EN POINTE* IN BLACK BOOTY SHORTS OVER a white leotard. Radiohead's *Reckoner* blasts through the speakers, and I swivel my hips extending both arms overhead before falling forward then rolling up through my shoulders.

My hair is secured in a ponytail, and I'm lost in the driving cymbals, the light guitar strumming. Curving my arm forward, I lean into the sway of the music. Bending down, I swoop up through my hip and kick my leg straight up to my ear before falling forward, another arc from my waist, as I rise and spin.

I'm one with the music. I'm shoulders, hips, arms, hands swaying to the waves of the ocean. Scampering across the length of the large room, I stop on point and extend both arms overhead then fall back.

When Misha danced with me, we'd do this choreography as mirrors of one another. Every spin and arc of my arms and hips, he would do the same. We were in perfect sync. It was our audition piece for the Ballet Company of America.

Now I dance alone.

The music fades away, and I drift to the floor. My arms and legs are wilted, and I'm in mermaid pose, leaning my head forward as I fold into myself.

Loud clapping startles me, and I lift my head to see Bianca walking into the empty room on the bottom floor of our high-rise. It's attached to the fitness center, and I think it's intended for yoga classes or group fitness. Mirrors line the walls, and the wood floor is padded. It's perfect for dancing.

"What are you doing down here by yourself?" She walks over to where I'm sitting, now with my legs crossed.

"Oh, you know." I shrug. "What I love."

Her lips press into a tight smile and she sits on the floor beside me. "Sorry it didn't work out for you. You're an amazing dancer."

"Spilt milk." I push off the floor, walking over to where I left my water bottle.

"Have you thought about applying to the Miami City Ballet? I've heard good things about them."

"Not accepting applications at this time." I recite the notice on their website as I return to where she's sitting. I sit on the floor again and untie the laces on my pointe shoes and slip them off my feet with a groan. "I'm out of shape."

"I don't know how you're ever in shape for those shoes." I rub my toes as she watches me, and a curious light is in her eyes.

"What?"

"I heard you met someone in town today."

I sit straighter. "How did you hear about that?"

"Franco." My brow furrows, and she continues. "Apparently Mr. Alexander is worried about you. He said you won't tell him where you live, and you were shopping at Valentino? Not the first choice for a poor little seamstress saving every penny to get home to Italy."

Heat floods my cheeks. "I don't think I played it up that much."

"Maybe not, but now he thinks you're mixed up in the Miami underworld. He's worried you're being trafficked."

"What the... *Trafficked?*"

"It's not that far-fetched. Large city, access to an international port, undocumented immigrants. How does he know you're not slaving away in a sweatshop sewing designer jeans for ten cents an hour, being kept by some evil mob boss who dresses you in designer clothes?"

My nose curls. "Good lord, is that how I come across? I have a student visa."

"You're still acting suspicious, and he's a rich white man determined to save you."

"I said it was my birthday." Propping my elbow on my bent knee, I collapse my face in my hand. "I'm lying so much. I hate it."

"So tell him the truth!"

"I've thought about it."

"But?"

We stand, and I collect my shoes and my bag, sliding my feet into flip-flops for the walk upstairs. "Don't make fun of me."

"Have I ever made fun of you?"

"I want him to like me for me, and maybe if he does like me, he won't care about Glitter Girl anymore."

"But you are Glitter Girl."

"Not really. She's a character, a fantasy. A mask."

The elevator opens, and we have the small space to ourselves. Bianca presses the button for the twelfth floor. "Maybe... But she's a part of you. You wouldn't be able to do what you do if she weren't. What if she's a bridge helping you get where you want to be?"

The bell dings, and we cross the short foyer to the door of our condo. I think about Bianca's words. When I'm on stage at the Rhino, I zone out and let my persona take control. I let the sexy music and the costumes and the wigs and masks transform me, and I do what I imagine she would do. I'm fearless because of her… Or is Bianca right? Does she help me see who I really am?

"What's going on in that head, Gia?"

I file away these thoughts for later. "He asked me to dinner tonight. You're going to flip out when you see the dress I bought at Carolina Herrera. It is so gorgeous. I'm going to wear it. And I got some shoes at Valentino we've got to use in the show. They're Barbie pink platforms, and they are amazing."

"You're giving me a fashion show?" She puts her arm around my shoulders. "Lead the way!"

At six-thirty, I'm standing in front of the full-length mirror in our bedroom, and my heart is beating out of my chest.

The dress looks even better with my hair and makeup done. Bianca helped me blow out my curls so they're hanging in large waves down my bare back, and she patted a light shimmer powder on the top of my cleavage and shoulders.

I look like a woman, and I feel like a nervous wreck.

Touching the large, smooth wave hanging down to my breast, I try to hide my trembling fingers. "No telling what my hair will do when the humidity hits it."

"You look amazing, and the humidity is low." She's standing behind me, smoothing her hands down the back of my waves. "He's going to swallow his tongue when he sees you in this."

"Gross. I hope not." I want his tongue right where it belongs—unless it's where I've fantasized it being.

Heat tickles my inner thighs as I imagine him placing his lips there, moving higher, touching my most sensitive places with his mouth. I've never done it, but I've heard stories.

"Your boobs are unbelievable in this top. Glitter Girl's got nothing on you tonight."

Everything she says makes my heart beat faster. I'm excited and nervous and thrilled and…

"You are not taking an Uber in this." Bianca's voice turns mother-hen-ish. "I'll drive you."

"And how will I get home? I'll have to Uber back."

Her eyebrow arches. "If he doesn't carry you straight to bed after dinner—hell, before dinner—he's not the man I think he is."

"Bianca!" Butterflies swirl in my stomach. "Just because a man buys me dinner, it doesn't mean I have to put out."

She snorts. "That's my girl. Make him beg for it."

Another butterfly swirl. "I don't think he's the begging type."

"Every man will be the begging type when you walk in tonight."

My eyes drift to the clock, and I pick up the small clutch containing my phone, a lipstick, and a hundred dollars in cash. "Ready?"

"Are you?" She cuts her eyes, and I shake my head.

"As I'll ever be."

We make the short drive to the luxury resort I've only read about. It's a hundred years old and one of those places super-rich people go—like the really super-rich old people, the ones who've had billions of dollars since the country was young.

Bianca tells the guard she's dropping me off for dinner, and he opens the gate.

"They're not letting just anybody in here," she teases and drives her pale yellow Hyundai slowly towards the large fountain in the middle of the circle drive.

The massive Italian Renaissance-style hotel rises, dramatically lit behind it.

"I should've had a drink." I feel very small all of a sudden. "I can hardly breathe."

"Hey, look at me." She grabs my hand, and I do as she says. "You look amazing. You *are* amazing, and you're going to have fun tonight. Now, deep breath. Summon Glitter Girl. Pretend you're about to go on stage for a big performance."

We inhale, exhale, and I feel fractionally better. "Thanks."

"Break a leg." She gives my hand a squeeze before releasing it. My door opens, and a doorman reaches down to help me exit the vehicle. "Call me if you decide you're not going to put out," she says too loudly, and my face turns purple.

I laugh. "She has an inappropriate sense of humor."

"Of course." He smiles, like he hears stuff like that every night at the Breakers, which I'm sure he does not.

He probably thinks I'm a hooker now. First, I'm being sex trafficked, now I'm a hooker—when in reality I'm only a stripper. Correction, *burlesque dancer*. What is happening to my life?

The valet leads me as far as the arch-and-column lined front walk, but before I take the first step, a white rose appears followed by the man who takes my breath away.

"Trip." I take the short-stemmed white rose from his fingers.

"Hello, Gia." His low voice is like a caress, and when he leans closer, he pauses. "May I kiss your cheek?"

"Of course." *Such a gentleman.*

My eyes close at the touch of his velvet lips against my skin accented by the scruff of his beard. Heat rushes from my chest to my stomach.

His are more green than brown, and when they meet mine, my knees go liquid. "You're stunning in that dress."

"Thank you."

He lifts my hand, putting it in the crook of his arm. "Let me guess… Valentino?"

My nose wrinkles, and I shake my head. "Carolina Herrera, but you were close."

"Fifty-fifty chance. It's definitely not Lily Pulitzer."

We pass through the arched entrance into a long, gilded lobby with what looks like twenty-foot ceilings. It's all marble columns and ornate archways and floor-to-ceiling windows looking out onto a courtyard with yet another, massive fountain.

Round tables are positioned down the center of the walkway, and each has an enormous flower arrangement containing either lilies or roses, scenting the air with their fresh perfume. I feel like a princess entering a castle.

"It's modeled after the Palazzo Carrega in Genoa." Trip leads me up a short flight of steps to where the restaurant is located.

"Is the bar made of glass?"

"It's an aquarium. It has live fish in it." My eyes widen, and he grins. "Very small ones."

He stops to face me, and his eyes drift from my hair to my shoulders to my breasts then quickly to mine again. "You really are beautiful tonight. Did I tell you happy birthday?"

"Earlier." I feel giddy… and perhaps a little powerful.

I've knocked him off balance, and while he fumbles his way to control, he steals another piece of my heart in the process.

"Good." He nods, shifting into business mode. "I'll see if our table is ready."

I step to the unique bar while he walks to the hostess stand, and sure enough, a brightly colored fish swims past, beneath my fingers. It's lit from the inside and filled with aquarium rocks, water plants, and small coral.

A curl slips over my shoulder as I look down, and I straighten, sensing eyes on me. Glancing around the semi-crowded bar, I don't recognize anyone. Trip catches my eye as he returns to where I'm waiting.

He's so handsome in his gray tailored suit and patterned tie. He walks with the casual confidence of money and privilege, and it's so clear he's used to getting what he wants.

I want to thread my fingers in his hair. It's swept back from his face, just brushing his ears and collar, and I imagine it's soft, unlike my coarse, wild curls. I liked having his lips on my cheek. I'd like to have them other places as well, and I lift the fragrant white rose to my nose.

Our eyes meet, and the dimple in his left cheek appears. "That was a very naughty look, Miss Rossi. How old are you today?"

"You're not supposed to ask a woman how old she is."

"I'm a bad boy. Haven't you heard?"

"I haven't, but I'm starting to believe it."

"You'd better. Now tell me how old you are."

"Twenty-two." It's true, even though it's not my birthday.

"Hm." His lips press together, and I can't read his expression.

"Too young or too old?"

"I'd say you're just right, although you're too young for that dress."

"What does that mean?" I lift my chin defiantly.

He leans closer, tracing his finger from my chin to the line of my jaw. The clean citrus of his cologne fills my nose, and his voice drops to a slight growl. "It's very motivational."

His finger traces down to my neck, and heat rises in my core. My lips part, and I almost exhale a whimper. His eyes flicker down, and my breasts feel too full for the small cups holding them. I want him to touch me.

"Mr. Alexander?" A chipper female voice interrupts us, and that hand goes into the pocket of his suit pants as he turns away. "Right this way."

We start to move, and I remember to breathe.

"*Very* motivational," he whispers close to my ear, again taking my hand and putting it in the crook of his arm as we follow the hostess to our table.

We take our seats in high-backed, satin-upholstered chairs, and Trip orders a bottle of red wine, a Barolo.

"I've never been in one of these restaurants." We're surrounded by velvet and satin, and linen menus with raised lettering in folders at each of our plates. "It's so elegant."

"It's what the old guard demands, but don't be intimidated. They're just like you and me."

"No they're not." *Not like me, at least.*

He leans back in his chair, lifting his hand to his chin as he studies me. His eyes simmer, and I shift in my seat.

Leaning forward, I tease him. "That's a very naughty look, Mr. Alexander."

"You have no idea." His eyes flicker to my breasts pressing against my bodice, and I straighten in my chair.

"I think we should get to know each other better." I slide the taupe dinner napkin across my lap, glancing down.

"That's just what I had in mind."

The waiter interrupts us with the wine service. A ruby-red vintage is uncorked and poured, sampled then served. Trip orders the swordfish for himself, and I have the Chilean sea bass, although I can't imagine eating a bite. My stomach is full of those butterflies, and they're swirling like I'm on fire, faster every time he gives me one of those sinful grins.

Fingering the base of my wine glass, I wonder if I can pick it up without my hand shaking. He takes a sip, and with his eyes diverted, I quickly do the same. Sharp, dry cherry is on my tongue with a hint of pepper.

"That's nice." I nod, placing it on the table.

"I'm glad you like it. Are you familiar with wine?"

"Not really. Barolo is Italian, though. I had it once at a ballet opening." Shaking my head, I glance down causing a wavy lock of hair to slip over my shoulder. "My family could only ever afford Chianti."

His eyes drift to my hair. "You straightened your curls."

"It's more formal this way."

"It is elegant, but I prefer it wild."

"Do you?"

His eyebrows flicker, and I press my lips together before taking another sip of wine. The warmth of the alcohol is helping me relax, helping me play along, and my fingers don't tremble as I raise the glass this time.

He does the same, and I get the ball rolling. "So what do you do for fun? Any hobbies?"

"I don't know that I have actual hobbies. I can do a few card tricks. The summer I turned twelve, I taught myself to juggle."

"You're kidding? You can juggle?"

"It was a very boring summer."

"I can't imagine being bored in New York City."

"You'd be surprised. There's a lot to do, but after a while, you've done it all." His words settle between us, heavy with meaning, but his smile redirects the mood. "What about you? What's your hobby?"

"Dance."

"Of course. Anything else? Baking, knife throwing?"

A short laugh huffs through my lips. "My mother taught me to make biscotti, but I never could seem to get the hang of knife throwing."

"It's all in the wrist." He winks as the waiter places our food in front of us.

Fresh cracked pepper, more wine, and the server disappears. My stomach is way more relaxed after my glass of wine, and I take a bite of fish.

It's rich and buttery, and I exhale a groan. "So good."

His eyes fix on mine, and my nipples tighten in my dress. Michele's comment about how I respond to delicious flavors flashes in my memory. *Orgasmic.* I wouldn't say my fish is pure sex, but the look Trip's giving me definitely is.

"Do you like your swordfish?" My voice wobbles, so I clear my throat and try again. "Is it good?"

"Clearly not as good as yours."

My cheeks flush, and I take another bite, stifling my response to the taste.

He does the same then lifts his wine glass, leaning back in his chair again. My eyes lift, and his playful expression is gone.

"Were you brought to this country against your will?" He watches my face.

"What?" I exhale a laugh. I didn't expect him to go there, especially not after that heated look. "I told you I came here to join the BCA."

"Gia?"

"Trip?" I imitate his tone.

"That's not an answer to my question."

"No, I was not brought here against my will. Good lord."

His brow quirks, and I can't tell if he believes me. "But you're not in a rush to get back to Italy."

"Well, I mean, I am, but maybe I can wait and see what happens here. I've got a job, I'm making a little money…" *Understatement of the year.* "Bianca and I are good roommates, and I don't know. I thought I might try to stay, maybe audition for another company when the time comes."

"I see." He relaxes a bit more, and his playful side returns. "What was your first job? Have you always been a seamstress?"

"That's two questions." I sip more wine. "No, I have not always been a seamstress. I think my first job was…" I wrinkle my nose, glancing up to the ceiling. "Babysitting?"

He watches me with that look again—like he thinks I'm amusing, but he also wants to do dirty things to me. It makes me shift in my chair. "What about you?"

"I have never had to babysit anyone. Correction, I've never had to babysit children."

"So you babysit adults?"

Looking away, this time he shifts in his chair. "My business is boring dinner conversation." He's deflecting, and I'm about to call him on it when he surprises me. "How do you feel about tickling?"

"Tickling!" That makes me laugh. "While we're on the subject."

"You can tell a lot about a person from their answer. For example, if you like to tickle others, you're clearly a sadist."

That makes me laugh more. "Is that so?"

"Definitely. Sick fucks, ticklers. Whereas if you prefer *being* tickled, you're adventurous." Another dirty look.

"I can't stand being tickled."

He nods slowly, taking another sip of wine, and the waiter appears to remove our dinner plates.

"Two chocolate soufflés," he says to the fellow.

"Oh, no!" I wave my hand. "I can't eat another bite."

"One chocolate soufflé, two spoons." He stops the guy. "And a coffee."

That makes me smile. He remembered how much I adore coffee.

"You can't miss the chocolate soufflé here. It's decadent."

"One bite," I concede.

"So no tickling? Not even a little feather on the arch of your foot?"

"I can't stand it." Shivering, I shake my head.

His expression turns naughty. "What if the person doing the tickling promised to stop whenever you said?"

The tilt of his lips, the shimmer in his eyes, makes me think we're not talking about tickling anymore. Or maybe we are, but not in the childish, chase-you-around-the-playground way.

"So I take it you enjoy tickling. Does that make you a sadist?" My voice is quiet, and I'm speaking like I have experience with such things. "Do I need a safe word when we're together?"

"Most definitely."

"In that case," I cut my eyes up to his. "I might be willing to try… with someone I trust, of course."

"Good girl." His voice is low, and pleasure unfurls in my stomach, like I got all the answers correct on a pop quiz.

I'm not sure how I feel about my body's response to him, but I'm pretty sure I'd be willing to try anything he asked me. I've never been so adventurous with a man, not even Michele.

It's like the night I danced for Trip as Glitter Girl, I felt like we had some kind of special chemistry. He's holding the forbidden fruit with a naughty grin, and I want to bite it so badly.

The waiter places the chocolate soufflé in the center of the table and produces two coffee cups.

"None for me, thanks," Trip turns his cup over in the saucer.

The waiter pours mine, and I add a dash of cream.

"No sugar?"

"Not if I'm having dessert."

"I see." Trip breaks the crusty top of the dark brown soufflé and scoops a small bite. "Taste."

Pressing my lips together, I meet his eyes before leaning forward to take the bite. His lips part as the spoon passes between mine, mirroring my movements, and when the rich, dark chocolate coats my tongue, bliss surges to my brain.

"Oh my God," I moan, unable to hold it in, and I see his teeth close, almost as if he clenches them.

Almost as if he's fighting for control.

He slides the spoon away, and I lift my eyes to his. I'm still leaning forward slightly. My hands are on the table, and my breasts press against them, lifting in a daring way.

Trip's eyes flick from my mouth to my body, and tension crackles in the air between us. My panties are wet, and he puts the spoon on the ramekin.

"You've had your bite." He stands, holding out his hand.

"You don't want any?" I look up at him.

"I have something better in mind."

CHAPTER 11

Trip

GIA IS A TANTALIZING MIX OF CONTRADICTIONS. SHE'S WIDE-EYED and innocent, talking about sewing costumes and being a dancer. Then she shows up for our date in that dress, like a vixen from hell.

Fuck me, I almost sprung a boner when she stepped out of that silly Hyundai. Then she somehow made the doorman grin, and I was ready to storm over and punch him in the face.

I didn't, of course. I waited and presented her with the white rose I picked up at the gift shop.

Every sex noise she made at dinner added fuel to the heat below my belt. My fingers curled against the need to stand and toss her over my shoulder, carry her to the nearest guest room and fuck her senseless. Instead, I controlled myself, while our chat about tickling enhanced the growing library of dirty things I want to do to her.

First I want to kiss her.

We're outside the resort, strolling the breezeway between the restaurant and the main building. A light breeze is in the air, and our fingers are entwined. Her long hair wraps around her arms, and those luscious breasts ripple with each step.

I can't take it anymore. Catching both her hands, I turn her so her back is to the wall in a shadowy alcove. She inhales a soft gasp, and my dick responds.

"What are we doing?"

"I'd like to kiss you, Gia." I sound like a desperate man, and I can't think of the last time I had to ask for a kiss. "May I?"

Large brown eyes meet mine, and my stomach clenches. It's my last warning to turn back. My brain knows, even if my dick doesn't give a shit, kissing Gia is going to change me whether I want it to or not.

"Okay…" Her tongue slips out to wet her full bottom lip, and I exhale a groan.

She's fucking perfect. Leaning forward, I cup her face with both hands, sliding my thumbs along her cheeks. Her lips are so full, like ripe fruit.

Bending down, I slide my lips over hers, back and forth. Kissing her is a rare delicacy I want to savor, to remember. A whimper escapes her throat, and I seal our mouths together, plunging my tongue in to find hers.

Opening her wider, our tongues curl and dance. She tastes like fine wine and dark chocolate, and my dick is so hard. She clutches the front of my suit coat, and she dips as if her knees weaken.

One of my hands moves from her face to wrap around her waist, holding her up against the wall as I trace my mouth to her cheek, to her ear. "I've never wanted to kiss someone so much."

She exhales a sigh, and her fingers thread in my hair. "Do it again."

With pleasure.

Covering her mouth with mine, this time I don't have to part her lips. She rises to meet me, sliding her tongue next to mine and moaning like I'm the fucking chocolate soufflé.

"Fuck, I want to be inside you." My voice is feral.

Leaning down, I place my lips on the top of her breast. I want to lift it out and devour her. I want to slide the zipper down and consume her. I want to pull her nipples with my lips and lift and knead them as I drive my cock into her slippery core.

"Oh, God," she gasps. "Trip…"

Hesitation is in her voice, and I fight to grab the reins on my raging libido. It's too soon, I know. We've only seen each other a few times, only had dinner once. Straightening, I press my fist against the wall, panting like I've run a marathon.

"I'm sorry." My voice is rough. "I wasn't trying to pressure you."

"You didn't." Her voice is equally breathless. "I want this, it's just…"

"It's too soon."

"No, I mean, I suppose it is, but it's more than that." Dark eyes flicker over my shoulder, scanning the space around us.

Is that what's worrying her? "We're pretty hidden here."

"It's not that." Her cheeks turn a pretty shade of pink. "I'm not very experienced with things like this."

Bending my elbow, I place my forearm on the wall, bringing our faces closer together.

"They say practice makes perfect." I smile, gauging her response. "Unless you'd rather not."

She blinks quickly, still with that adorable flush on her cheeks. My eyes lower, and her succulent breasts rise and fall with her pants in a way that's unfairly tempting.

"I'm familiar with the concept of practice." My eyes flash to hers, and her full lips are parted. "What did you have in mind?"

"So many things, sweet Gia." Leaning closer, I trace my nose along the shell of her ear. "I wonder if every part of you is as delicious as your sweet mouth."

Turning my face, I capture her lips again, pulling them with mine before parting them, sliding my tongue with hers, tasting her hunger, coaxing another broken whimper from her throat.

Her slender hands still grip the front of my coat, and her gasp sounds like a beg. "One way to find out."

With a glance over my shoulder, I drop to one knee in front of her, placing my hand on her calf before sliding it lightly up the inside of her leg, lifting her dress.

"Your skin is so soft." Tilting my head, I look up to her face.

Her dark eyes are hooded as she watches me, her breasts press seductively against the strapless top faster as my hand rises higher. When I reach the apex of her thighs, she gasps.

"Oh, God." Her fingers clutch my shoulder, and she presses her other hand against her flat stomach.

"Still with me?" She nods quickly, and a lock of dark hair falls across her cheek. It makes me chuckle. "I'm going to make you come so hard."

My index finger is against her pussy, and I move my hand back and forth against it, between her legs, circling her clit with my thumb.

"So wet already." I reach down to unfasten my belt so I can ease the pressure on my throbbing dick. "Let me see you, juicy little peach."

Pulling the tiny scrap of lace to the side, her body is completely bare. *Did she prep for me?* I lift her leg over my shoulder, as I pull her thong out of the way. She has the softest skin. As I draw closer, I scent her light musk, the faintest hint of the ocean. My mouth waters, and I drag my tongue up the seam of her pussy, swirling it forcefully around her clit.

"Oh, fuck…" Her body jerks, and I do it again, pleased that she's so responsive.

She's right on the edge, and I can sense the blood humming in her veins. We're electric.

Moving my lips to the crease of her thigh, I kiss her leg, tracing higher to her belly, and she squirms, exhaling soft moans.

"It feels so good," she whimpers.

"Such a sensitive girl." I move my hand so I can tease her opening with my thumb before returning to finish what I've started.

My mouth is on her pussy again, my beard scraping her soft skin as I lick, suck, devour. At the same time, I taunt her, inserting my thumb and pumping in and out, mimicking the movements of my cock as her juices coat my hand.

"Oh, God… oh, God… that's it…" Her hand moves from my shoulder, driving into my hair.

Her response is so intense, I want to make her scream.

Another lick, another plunge of my thumb. I lift my eyes to see her face, and she's a goddess. Glossy lips parted, her eyes squeeze shut, and her hips nearly fly out of my hand as she comes with a sudden buck, a shuddering moan.

"Fuck fuck fuck…" Her fingers clench over and over in my hair in time with her orgasm.

I circle my tongue again and again, and her ass jumps. Her thighs quiver. She's pulling me closer, and she tenses like she's touched electricity. A hand rises to her breast over the dress, and her fingers curl against the shell of fabric as if she wants to rip it free.

My dick leaks at the intensity of her orgasm, at the thought of her touching her breasts while I make her come. I want to take her somewhere and see what she'll do with my cock inside her.

With a parting kiss to her sweet pussy, I remain on my knees a moment longer. Sliding both hands to her outer thighs, I move them higher to her soft ass, kneading the smooth cheeks as her breathing slowly returns to normal.

"You okay?" Reaching into my pocket, I take out a handkerchief. "Need this?"

She takes it, seemingly embarrassed as she turns to clean the orgasm from her inner thighs. "I'm sorry… I told you I'm not very experienced."

Rising to my feet, I place my hands on her shoulders. "Why are you apologizing? Do you know how fucking hot you were just now?"

She looks down, moving her hands over her skirt, straightening the fabric. "I made a mess on your face."

Catching her chin, I lift her eyes to mine. She only glances, blinking away quickly, so I give her a gentle shake. "Look at me." Another blink, and worried, dark eyes meet mine. "If you're not making a mess, somebody's doing it wrong. What happened just now was incredible."

The rosy flush paints her skin, and a shy smile curls her lips. "It really was." Her eyes roll around. "Amazing."

A fist of childish joy hits me in the stomach, and I have the strange urge to laugh. Is this happiness? When is the last time I felt this way? I'm playful and high, thinking I gave her something she'd never had before. I want to know what else she's been missing.

So I can give it to her.

Releasing her chin, I lean down to kiss her again, pulling her full lips with mine before parting them, sliding our tongues together. Again, she's right with me, rising onto her toes and kissing me eagerly, pulling me closer by my lapels. She's as hungry as I am, and my dick can't get any harder.

"That does it." I look around us, trying to judge how busy they are. "Come with me."

Taking her hand, I lead her along the stone walkway to a small courtyard with a blue-tiled fountain and white wrought-iron benches.

"Wait right here. I'm going to get us a room for the night."

Her eyes widen. "A room?"

Pulling her to me by the waist, I kiss her neck, leaning lower to kiss the top of her pillow breast. "I'm only just getting started with you, beautiful."

"But, don't you think… You think they'll have a vacancy?"

"This place has more than five hundred rooms. I'm sure

they'll have one for us." Lifting her hand, I grin as I press her knuckles to my lips. "I'll order champagne. Give me five minutes."

Hesitating before I step inside the lobby, my eyes drink in her graceful form in that gorgeous dress standing in front of the fountain. She's breathtaking.

Her eyes meet mine, and my chest shifts. I don't remember the last time I felt this way, like I don't give a shit about all the personal baggage I'm juggling back home. Nothing matters except this night and her in my arms.

"I need a deluxe guest room for the night. No bags." I slide my black AMEX across the counter.

The agent arches an eyebrow. "Do you have a reservation, sir?"

I'm sure he's looking at my disheveled hair, lack of a tie, and is it possible to see I gave the sexiest woman I've ever seen the orgasm of her life on the patio just now?

The thought makes me smother a laugh. "I do not. My ahh… fiancée and I had dinner, and we decided to stay over for the night."

"I see." He glances skeptically. "One moment, and I'll check if anything's available on such short notice."

"Perfect, and send up a bottle of champagne while you're at it."

He glances at me then runs the card. In an instant, his demeanor flips. "Mr. Alexander, my apologies. I have you set up in the ahh… Yes! In the Royal Poinciana Suite with an ocean view and a *complimentary* bottle of wine. Can I get you anything else, sir?"

So he knows who I am now? At least he has the decency to make up for his cool reception.

I decide to let this guy off the hook. See how Gia is changing me? I could give him shit, possibly have him fired, but why would I do that? A fancy place like this can't have hookups going on all the time.

Only some of the time.

"Thank you." Leaning forward, I read his name badge. "Lewis. Thank you."

"My pleasure, sir, and let me know if I can get you anything else tonight. It will be my personal pleasure."

Snatching the door card, I nod. "I will."

I take off in a sprint, pissed it took longer to get the room than I anticipated and hating that I left Gia alone for so long. When I reach the passage to the small courtyard with the blue fountain, I slow my pace, straightening my suit and smoothing a hand over my hair. I don't want to look like a raging bull.

Tonight is going to be epic. After what just happened, the spectacular way she came on my face, I'm ready to see what else we can do. I wonder if I can get her to make that sound she made for the chocolate soufflé while she's riding my dick. The thought sends the blood racing to my cock, and I'm not using my hand to relieve the pressure tonight.

It's been a long time, and it's going to be a long night.

I step around the corner, ready to feast my eyes on her beauty, when I stop short. An older woman with a walker is sitting in front of the fountain gazing up at the relief sculpture behind the flow. I quickly scan the area, but no one else is here.

Dashing into the courtyard, I look up and down the open breezeway.

Empty.

Where are you? I tap on my phone face, quickly hitting send.

I jog up a little further to the oversized fountain in the circle drive, but I only see SUV drivers chatting with doormen.

Turning on my heel, I'm ready to charge in the opposite direction when my phone buzzes in my pocket. I take it out quickly and my shoulders drop.

I felt dizzy. Bianca picked me up. I'm so sorry. Thank you for an amazing dinner.

Holding my phone, I read her words over again as my brow tightens. *Dizzy?* What the fuck?

Stopping at the first outdoor chair I encounter, I sit and quickly tap out a response. **Are you okay?**

Gray dots, then, **I'll be fine. Just need to rest. Thank you so much for dinner.**

Sorry? Thank you for dinner? Seriously? After that orgasm? She left me… But why?

I enjoyed our dinner as well. Rest. I don't know what else to say.

Did things move too fast? She'd had a few glasses of wine, but she wasn't drunk. She was definitely willing. Tearing through my memory, she did hesitate one time, but when I offered to stop, she told me to keep going. Our final kiss, she devoured me.

What the fuck just happened here?

CHAPTER 12

Gia

I PANICKED.

I've never felt this way in my life. The way he touched me, the way he kissed me. I've masturbated, of course, but I've never had an orgasm that intense in my life. I think he reset my brain.

Oral sex was not what I expected. It was more—*way* more. *Holy shit* more. And I have no clue how to do that to him, how to make him feel that way.

Walking fast to the circle drive, I slide my hands up and down my crossed arms. Embarrassment burns in my cheeks. I came on his mouth like a freaking geyser. I didn't know it was possible for me to get that wet. What else do I not know about myself? His lips were freaking glossy, and the burning look in his eye when he said he wanted to get a room…

I panicked.

Trip is used to experienced women, daring women, women who know exactly how their pussies will respond to the touch of a man's tongue. He's used to women who would wear the dress I have on tonight with confidence, who'd know how to take it off with maximum effectiveness.

I don't know what the fuck I'm doing. I'm a silly little inexperienced girl playing dress-up. I imagined I'd summon Glitter Girl, and she would carry me through whatever he proposed we do. Then the wine started to wear off. Then I remembered who I really am.

I'm Gia the virgin in over her head trying to impress a man who is way out of her league.

Bianca's yellow Hyundai appears like a tiny rescue boat surging up the long, red-brick drive to save me, and as soon as she stops, I bunch my skirt and jump inside. "Thanks for picking me up."

"I didn't expect to hear from you." Bianca glances at me, then shakes her head. "Or maybe I did. How'd it go?"

The way he kissed me floods my memory. The way he made me feel, his mouth on my body, his hands, his fingers… *his thumb.* My core clenches at the memory of that pumping tease, and a phantom thrill floods my stomach. *Is that what a cock feels like?*

Pressing my head against the headrest, I groan. "It was amazing."

"Then why did you call me?"

I lift my hands and scrub them against my eyes. "I didn't know what to do. It was all moving so fast, and I was still reeling from what happened. I've never felt that way. *Never.*"

"What way?" She tilts her head to the side, and my eyes slide to meet hers. "What does that look mean? Did you sleep with him?"

"No…"

"But you did something. What did you do?"

"We were walking, and he kissed me, and then he went down on one knee, and he… *French* kissed me." I nod towards my crotch. "I think my brain melted."

"Wait." She holds a palm at me. "Are you saying he freaking

licked your pussy? What the hell are you doing in this car? I'm turning around."

She takes her foot off the gas, and I panic. "Don't you dare!"

"The man goes down on you, gives you the Big O, and you called me? What's the freaking problem, Gia?" Her voice rises.

"The problem is I don't know what I'm doing!" My voice rises to meet hers. "He has expectations, and this is *not* like dancing. I know how to dance. I know *nothing* about this."

"It's actually a lot like dancing." She shakes her head. "You probably know more than you think. Haven't you ever watched porn?"

"Porn isn't real." Shame burns in my face as I realize it's like me—a lie.

"No, but at least it can be educational. It gives you an idea of what goes where."

I think about the things we said at dinner. I've never been with a man like him, exciting and daring. "I don't want him to be disappointed."

"So you ran." Bianca's voice is quiet.

We're back at the condo, and she slowly enters the parking garage. The green light washes out my skin, making me look as sick as I feel. How did I go from soaring through the galaxy on unbelievable waves of pleasure to plunging to the depths of the ocean so fast?

My phone buzzes with a text, and my stomach sinks when I see *Mio Marito* on the face asking where I am. *Hubby...* "He's going to be so mad at me."

"Maybe not," she exhales. "He'll definitely be frustrated. I'm sure he has the worst case of blue balls, but if he's a good guy, he won't be mad."

I text back saying I got dizzy, which isn't far from the truth. The mountain of lies came crashing down on my head, and I was completely disoriented. His reply is kind, which makes me feel even worse. He tells me to rest.

I follow Bianca into our room and take off the beautiful dress, feeling a little like Cinderella. I had the perfect evening. I flew to the highest heights, and then the spell broke.

"It's probably a good thing you came home tonight. Franco's got you all set for the soft launch tomorrow. He wants you to do a live welcome video and answer any DMs that come through."

"We're doing it tomorrow?"

"You said you were ready to stop dancing. Franco thinks you can dance once more this week then maybe a farewell number if you want and introduce your subscription side. It should be enough to launch Glitter Girl online."

"He still wants me to dance tomorrow night?"

"You're on the schedule, but they haven't found that guy."

I think about dancing again. Would Trip still be in the audience after our date? Does it make sense for me to be upset if he is, when it's me he's watching?

My head hurts, and I climb between the sheets, pulling the blanket over my shoulder in an effort to hide from my twisted life.

"Hey." Bianca sits on the side of my bed, rubbing my shoulder. "It's normal to get cold feet before your first time. Sex is a big step."

"Add to it all these things I'm doing. I'm playing a game, and I'm in over my head."

"What if you're not playing?"

Pulling the blanket down, I study her face. "What does that mean?"

"You chose that dress for tonight. You danced for him as Glitter Girl. What if you're just doing you, and you're afraid to own it?"

I don't have an answer. I feel like I'm being honest, not afraid. I've been here before, at the edge of this cliff, looking down and not being able to see the bottom. I'm not the type to leap without knowing what's in the water below. Is that fear or intelligence?

"What happens if I do me, and it all blows up in my face?"

"You have to take that risk if you're going to get what you want."

Metamorphosis.

Turning over again, I think about stepping out of the cocoon, learning to fly. I want to jump, and I want to do it with him… And I want to do it without a mask.

The cat mask is firmly in place over the platinum blonde wig, and I'm on the bed in the room I share with Bianca.

My costume is the same crimson-ribbon bodysuit from the last time I danced, only I'm supposed to do something special for the subscribers, so I've untied the top.

"What if you lean forward onto your elbows?" Bianca is behind the camera directing. "Are you comfortable with that?"

"Like this?" I roll onto my stomach, leaning forward so my bare breasts flatten against my forearms. "Can you see my nipples?"

"Not from this angle." She turns to the laptop. "It looks hot. I think this pose and hearing you speak will be special enough."

We spent the morning brainstorming how to maintain my near-nude persona while pushing it as close to the edge as possible.

"Ready to go live?"

My heart beats faster, but I nod, holding the remote in my hand. "Let's go."

The screen counts down from three, and like a whisper, I'm live on the platform, waiting to greet my first paying visitor. "What if no one shows up?"

Bianca holds a finger to her lips, shaking her head and

pointing to the laptop then her ear. I guess she's telling me they can hear what I'm saying, which I already know. I also know no one is on my livestream yet.

A popping noise tells me someone is here, and @Number1Fan appears with the comment, **Hello, Glitter Girl**.

I smile brightly. "Hi, Number 1…" I use a breathy, sweet voice and blink my eyes slowly. "Is that what I should call you?"

@Number1Fan: **Makes sense to me.**

"I guess it does, since you're my first." I exhale a giggle, like I just realized I made a sex joke. *Duh*. "Welcome to my livestream! Thank you for being here. I'll just wait a few moments in case anyone else decides to join us."

Arching my back a little, I can see my areolas are just visible and a ding sounds, meaning I've gotten a tip. Glancing up, I see it's $100, and I blink fast. "Thank you…ahh…Wow. Who do I thank?"

A stream of hearts flies up the screen, and I see several additional users have joined the audience with usernames like "BigBoi" and "Horndog" and "WillHungus." The only original one is "Anmlvr," and I'm not sure if that stands for animal lover or anime lover. Whatever.

Another ding, and it's another $100 tip. Another ding is $150. It's like a contest to see who can out-tip the other. I'm having a hard time keeping track of which ding goes where, and I look up at Bianca in a panic. *What do I do now?*

She points to her exaggerated smile, and I quickly smile, looking at the screen again. "My goodness, looks like everyone arrived at the same time!" Another breathy, babydoll giggle. "Thank you all! Thank you for being here and for your love. As I was saying, welcome to my livestream. I'm excited to launch my brand-new channel and to get to know you all better."

The hearts are nonstop as well as the dings.

"You're all so generous!" I make my voice go high at the end. "Do you have any questions for me? I have time for…" My eyes cut to Bianca and she holds up one hand, fingers spread. "Five questions from my favorite fans."

A stream of questions glides up the screen, ranging from **Do you have a boyfriend?** to **Show us your tits**, which feels more like a heckle. A question from my Number 1 fan catches my eye.

"These are coming fast, so let me see… Several of them are the same question, and no, I do not have a boyfriend." *I have hopes*, I think, as I emit another squeaky giggle. I'm starting to hate this live video. "Number1 and several of you asked if I'm dancing tonight, and the answer is…" I roll my eyes around like I'm thinking, giving Bianca a quick glance. She gives me two thumbs up. "Yes!"

The screen explodes like a volcano of red hearts, and more dings. "Let's see, Bigboi asks if I'll be doing live dances on this channel… Um…" I look at Bianca, and she's shaking her head. "This channel is for private chats and pictures. My dancing is only at the Rhino."

Questions fly by at a dizzying pace. "Phew! This isn't as easy as it looks. I'm still learning, so be gentle with me." I use my Marilyn voice, and the screen explodes with approval.

It's like I'm playing a video game with bunch of horny cheerleaders.

"Yes, private chats will be available for purchase, and one more… My goodness! So many of you want to see my breasts. But you know how shy I am. Let me see what I can do."

Lowering my chest to the mattress, I slide my fingers over my breasts and sit up in a dramatic fashion, covering my nipples with my palms. The computer lights up like a slot machine in Vegas, and I just hit the jackpot. If hearts were coins, I'd need two buckets.

"For my very special fans. Thank you for stopping by this afternoon. I hope you have a glittery day! Til next time!" Bianca reaches forward to tap the key to end the live video, and I smile until I'm sure I'm no longer live.

She pushes the laptop closed for good measure, and my shoulders drop along with my overly bright smile. "Wow." I groan. "That was intense!"

"You are such an introvert. How is it even possible? You should have an adrenaline rush right now. That was an incredible soft launch! You had at least fifty users, and Franco didn't even advertise. That means they were on the site searching for you, ready to pay to see you live."

"Is that weird?" Standing, I release my breasts and scoop up a tank to pull over my head. "It feels very stalker-ish."

"Someone tipped you $500—that means he's been on the site long enough to be above the tip limit."

"Who gave me that much?"

"Your Number 1 fan, of course."

My nose wrinkles. "He seemed normal, I guess. I told him I'd be dancing tonight, so I guess I'm locked in now."

"Don't be nervous. Franco doubled security, and they've got all the bouncers on alert. Nobody will get near you tonight."

Nodding, I chew my fingernail, thinking how this new channel has given a whole new set of people access to me, and I just flashed my tits for them. "Yeah, I'm not dancing anymore after this week. I'll let Franco know."

Bianca nods, smoothing her hand down the back of my hair. "I think that's smart. From the looks of things, you're going to make more money online than you can spend."

"And nobody can touch me." The words leave my lips as an afterthought.

My phone buzzes in my hand, and when I see *Mio Marito* on the face, my heart jumps. **Feeling better?**

A smile stretches my cheeks, and I want to kiss him again. I quickly tap a reply. **Much better, thank you. So happy to hear from you.**

Gray dots float, and my mind drifts to last night. I want to tell him all the reasons I had to leave. Would he understand? Would he be angry?

It hadn't even entered my mind last night that he's my *boss*. It all happened so fast, from the drink to the coffee to dinner. He doesn't know he's my boss, which adds an additional layer of potential anger. Would the boss date a dancer?

On top of that potential landmine, I can't tell if he's the type of man who would be put off by my occupation. He's rich, powerful, elite. Do men like him date strippers?

I need to learn his feelings on this matter somehow. Maybe Franco can tell me? My chest is so tight at the thought he might not understand, or worse, be disgusted and walk away. I feel ill.

Shall we try again tonight? Dinner at 8?

My lips twist, and I realize I'll be at the Rhino getting ready to dance. ***I can't tonight. I'm so sorry. Tomorrow?***

Tomorrow I can tell him face to face all the things I should have told him before that first kiss. That incredible, amazing kiss I'll never forget.

It takes a little longer for him to reply, and my heart sinks. I want to see him again so much. If only I hadn't said I'd dance tonight. I don't want to do anything but be with him—at the same time, a realization unfurls in my stomach. He didn't want to see Glitter Girl tonight. He wanted to see me. Warmth surges through my chest. I want to squeal, and his text appears.

Tomorrow, 8. I'll pick you up, and you can tell me who beat me out for tonight.

"No one," I say in a smiley, dreamy, oh-so happy tone, falling back and hugging my pillow to my chest. "No one could ever beat you, *Marito*."

Of course, he can't hear me, so I simply reply, ***I can't wait.***

CHAPTER 13

Trip

"**G**LITTER GIRL IS DANCING TONIGHT." FRANCO'S VOICE ON THE phone is somewhere between a smirk and a challenge.

"Make sure she doesn't get groped." I walk over to the mini-bar in my suite. "I'd like to keep at least one of my promises to these girls."

"Already lost interest? I thought you'd want to be there."

"Not tonight." For some reason, no longer care about the fantasy-girl with the, granted, dream physique. Okay, it's Gia. The reason is Gia. "I've got something else going on."

Franco's voice turns serious. "It's actually more of a re-quest. We still haven't found the guy who went after her, and you're one of the few people who knows what he looks like."

Do I? "It's been a few days, Franco, I'm not sure I remember him." Also, I'm not interested in going to the Rhino anymore.

"You'll remember better than someone who's never seen him at all. I could really use your help tonight. We tell the girls their safety is our top priority."

Fuck. Exhaling, I pinch the bridge of my nose. He's

throwing my words in my face, my dumb speech. "Sure," I nod. "I'll be there."

"See you in a few."

Ending the call, I look at the phone in my hands for several minutes, wondering if I should tell Gia what I'm doing tonight and why.

I dismiss the thought as fast as it appears. We've only gone to dinner once. I'm not sure if buying her coffee counts for anything. I guess we did have that drink at the club...

Still, telling her what my plans are and why sounds like boyfriend shit. It's also something I've never even done on the few occasions when I *did* have a girlfriend.

I do what I want to do and when.

Yet I feel unsettled. *Dammit.* I knew when I kissed her this would happen...

The Rhino is unusually crowded when I enter through the side door. Not interested in mingling with the patrons, I go straight to my usual seat in the VIP section. A waitress brings me a vodka neat, and Franco steps out from the office. When he sees me, he lifts his chin, speaking briefly to a bouncer and crossing behind the mob of what looks like predominantly drunk frat-boys on the main floor.

"Thanks for coming out." He steps through the velvet rope and sits beside me at the table. "Not having a photo puts us at a real disadvantage tonight, especially with this crowd."

"Is it a south-Florida holiday I don't know about? It's too early for the world cup."

"I think it's the spillover from the soft launch today." My brow furrows, and he explains. "We're transitioning Glitter Girl to the subscription-only site. She did a little welcome livestream this afternoon and said she'd be dancing tonight. It went viral."

I only have a surface understanding of what he's referencing. I know about our subscription site, and I've heard several of our girls make significant amounts of money performing behind the paywall—of which we take a twenty percent cut plus monthly room and board.

"So she's not going to dance live anymore?"

"It's what she wants." Franco shrugs. "Probably safer for her anyway."

Again, I'm impressed with this girl's foresight. At the same time, "How will that affect our business here?"

"Eh… Shula's building a following, and there's always an appetite for live shows. We'll see a dip, but I doubt it'll last long."

Nodding, I take a sip of my drink. "And if she makes more money behind the paywall, so do we."

"Exactly." He pushes off his legs. "I'm going to pass through the bar. If you see anything suspicious, signal me or DJ there in the corner. He was working the last time she danced."

He gestures to a tall, beefy man who looks like he could be a professional wrestler.

"Will do." I lift my drink and study the face of my phone, wondering what Gia is doing right now.

She only said she couldn't meet me, and I didn't want to be the guy who has to know every detail of her schedule. I'm not sure what guy I'm even trying to be these days. I'm not moving to Palm Beach. Why am I hanging around, trying to start a relationship with her?

Something about her has a grip on me. My mind drifts to last night at the restaurant, her fresh face and sweet smile, how quickly I could make her blush. She's young, from a small town, her dead mother taught her to make biscotti. She dreams of visiting New York like a little kid.

She tastes like fine wine and chocolate… and she makes the most exquisite noises when she comes on my face. She'd be willing to let me tickle her. My lips curl with a grin, and heat moves from my stomach to my cock.

Yes, it's clear why I'm hanging around here, even if I did push her outside her comfort zone last night. She's playful and curious, and I like testing her limits.

The lights lower, and the mood in the room visibly shifts. The crowd on the floor turns to the stage and seems to sway like a gang of hungry dogs preparing to be fed.

I quickly scan the perimeter, gratified that Franco has doubled the number of bouncers near the stage. He's taking this situation as seriously as I would.

A spotlight flashes, and the other girl Shula struts out, doing her usual shimmy dance to the song "U Can't Touch This" by MC Hammer. *Clever*. I exhale a short laugh, and my eyes return to my phone. Even with my sweet Gia as a distraction, I'm keeping track of my dealings in New York.

Grish used my connection to Hana and Blake to figure out their late father had access to stables out of town. My friend is enmeshed in the race-world's horse-doping scene, and he's got a lot of money on the line. I've told him I don't fuck around with horses. Still, by virtue of our association, if things go south, he could pull me down with him.

Last thing I want is to get any of his shit on me.

I don't see anything new in the trades. Trainers are gearing up for Triple-Crown season, and the Belmont Gala is a little more than a month away. Everyone will be in attendance at that event. I'll have to head back for it as well or my people will wonder. It's a black-tie affair, and Hana and Blake's mother always organizes it. All the top brass make a point of showing up.

The lights change, and my eyes rise to watch Shula collecting her tips, shaking her bare ass as she struts off the stage, waving and blowing kisses. Checking my watch, it's after nine, which means Glitter Girl is up next. My stomach tightens, and I wonder if I'll have the same reaction to seeing her. Objectively, she's a beautiful woman, and her movements are undeniably seductive. It would only be human for me to respond to her, nothing more.

Shifting in my chair, I move my gaze to the crowd of mostly men growing more restless as her time gets closer. They know the rules—*No touching*. Still, the tension is growing strong.

It's not going to get out of control in here, and if it does, we're ready to shut it down. I glance at the door leading back-stage, and another big guy steps out, crossing his arms and lowering his brow. *Perfect*.

As the lights dim, I scan the crowd once more, focusing on the faces at the very edge of the stage. They all look the same to me—entitled, bloated, drunk-eyed assholes with fists full of dollars, who wouldn't be here if they spent time devel-oping real relationships.

Like I have room to talk, I think sardonically. I haven't spent time on a real relationship in years.

A woman's voice blasts across the speaker, and the strum of violins launch the rhythm of "Scandalous" by Mis-Teeq. I barely have time to wonder how long it's been since I've heard that song when she struts out in an ultra-sheer, bubble-gum pink costume, and the entire room erupts into deafening whoots and cat-calls.

She's not wearing a dress. It's more like long strips of sheer fabric that lift and curl all around her, blown back by fans that have lowered from the ceiling. Two see-through lengths of fabric billow around her chest, attached to pasties covering her nipples, but leaving every other part of her round breasts completely exposed.

Her navel is bare, and a belly-dancer's large pink gem cov-ers it. Her costume somehow covers her pussy, although when she turns, her ass is completely exposed with only sheer pink strips rippling around the sides.

She isn't wearing fishnets or any other hosiery, and her legs and body glow as if she's been dusted with some kind of iridescent powder. Her hair is loose in giant waves that billow around her face, and her lips are glossy pink. *Fuck*, she's practically naked and unbelievably gorgeous. I growl in my throat as my hand tightens on my phone, as I try to deny the rush of blood to my dick.

Tonight, she isn't using a pole or curtains or any props. She struts across the stage on matching pink platform shoes, moving her body in a way that exudes professional training. She's not a stripper, she's a dancer, bending forward and using her arms to arch and rock her body up straight.

Her stomach flexes as she stretches higher, then she drops down, spreading her knees wide apart and mouthing the words to the song, a piece of hair caught on her full bottom lip. My jaw clenches as I see the men sway closer to the stage, but she's up again, her eyes lifting to where I'm sitting.

She can't see me. I know she isn't dancing for me, but she reaches her arms in my direction and circles her waist, undulating her hips like a hula dancer, like Elvis simulating sex, then turning her back and whipping her head to look over her shoulder straight at me. *Fuck*.

As always, her face is covered by a mask. I'm not sure if all that dark hair swirling around her is real, but either way, it's incredible. Rising out of my chair, I walk slowly out of the VIP section, closer to the edge of the raised area.

Her movements beckon me like a spell. She rolls her hands as if she's drawing me, and she snaps her hips, bouncing her tits and ass, like she would if she were riding my body. My throat is dry, and she's the water that can quench it.

No touching… the words blast in my mind like an alarm, and glancing down, I see him.

That fucker is there in the same black hoodie obscuring his face, right at the edge of the stage, his hand poised to grab her. Her eyes are on me. She's completely unaware as she does her steps, planting her foot directly in his range.

"It's him!" My shout is lost in the frenzy of the crowd.

He has both hands around her foot this time, and he's not

letting her go. Glitter Girl stops dancing, but she doesn't fall. She struggles, trying to get her foot out of his grasp.

Squaring my shoulders, I plunge into the sweaty crowd of drunk males with hard-ons. Some of them are cheering him on, while others are holding back their friends. We're one second from a riot when a bouncer bursts onto the stage from the dressing room to help her.

I've just reached the motherfucker when I hear him chanting softly, eerily, through gritted teeth. *"Mine."*

Her pink platform is ripped from her foot, and he drops to the floor, crawling away through the chaos of legs.

"He's down!" I shout, but Franco shakes his head, unable to hear me.

"Are you okay?" The deep voice of the bouncer helping Glitter Girl draws my attention, and my ears tighten when she speaks.

"I'm okay." Her voice is soft, slightly high with a faint rasp. I recognize the sound.

Turning, my eyes flash to her face, but the spotlight blinds me. I have to be wrong, but then my eyes land on her now-bare foot. A butterfly tattoo. *What the fuck?*

Heat burns in my throat, and anger roars to life in my chest. What the hell is going on here?

Automatically, my hand shoots out, and I catch her foot, holding it tightly in my grip so I can see the tattoo closer. There's no mistaking it.

"Oh!" she yelps, dropping again to one knee and placing her fingers over mine in an attempt to pry them off her.

Our eyes meet, and hers go wide when she sees me. "Trip..."

"Gia?" The mask can't hide her from me anymore, and it all snaps into place.

"Doesn't matter if you're the boss," the big guy growls, his hand closing around my wrist like a vise. "No touching!"

She blinks rapidly, her eyes never leaving mine. Her full

lips part, and I release her, taking a step back into the crowd. What the ever-loving *fuck* is going on here?

For a beat, I watch as Gia runs off the stage with the big guy hulking behind her. Then I shake myself out of it. I'm ready to hoist myself onto the platform to follow after them and demand she tell me why the hell she hid this. Nobody fucks around with me, and she's got some serious explaining to do.

Little miss innocent, shy and demure, running away from me last night only to turn up dancing in my club, taking off her clothes for strangers? If she thinks she's playing me for a fool, she's got another thing coming.

I'm one foot on the stage, ready to go after her when the first fist flies. Next thing I know, I'm pulled down in the middle of a bar fight, and there's no negotiating with this mob. These drunk assholes are full of adrenaline and testosterone, and the object of their lust is gone.

A meaty hand grips my shoulder, and I dodge the fist that flies past and hits the guy beside me. Making a quick calculation, I drop to my hands and knees, seeing what our hooded assailant already saw. The best way out of this is on my knees.

CHAPTER 14

Gia

As soon as I enter the backstage area, I'm swept under a blanket and rushed to the exit.

"Wait!" I struggle and try to get out of the grip of the giant bouncer practically lifting me off my feet. "Put me down!"

No one listens to me, and I'm carried out of the club into the waiting SUV at the back entrance. I land on the seat, nearly bouncing off it onto my ass, and the door is slammed fast before we jolt into motion.

"Holy shit, Gia! Are you okay?" Bianca is in the seat behind me leaning forward. "It's a freaking riot in there!"

I'm shaking all over, but my mind isn't on the men throwing punches. All I can see is Trip staring at me with a mixture of confusion and fury in his hazel-green eyes. My stomach is in knots, and I want to get out of this fucking truck and get back in there and explain to him.

Only I don't know where to begin explaining all of this.

"I need to go back!"

Bianca only laughs. "You'll be lucky if you ever go back

to the Rhino. That performance literally brought the house down."

"It wasn't my fault." My voice is defeated as I look out the window at the streetlights illuminating the dark night, as we speed away.

Everything was going so well. Franco told us he'd doubled security, just in case the guy who grabbed me tried to do it again. Bianca said it was also because the livestream had been so successful, we had a lot of new customers at the club.

A mixture of excitement and jealousy twisted in my stomach when I peeked out and saw Trip in the audience. Then Bianca told me Franco asked him to come since he was one of the few people who had been on-site the last time I'd danced. He knew what my attacker looked like and could help spot him.

I felt a little better, and when it was time to do the new dance, I wanted it to be like before. I closed my eyes and imagined all my moves were between the two of us, and it was only him and me—except this time, I wasn't working off my imagination. This time I had actual memories of his lips against mine, his hands on my body.

Tonight, I'd danced with authenticity… and it blew up like Mount Vesuvius. Then Trip saw it was me. My chin drops, and I shiver at the memory of his anger and confusion.

"You're right," Bianca fusses as we pull into the parking garage at the apartment building. "Everything was going great until that guy grabbed your foot again. Asshole. He ruined everything."

It's true. I might have actually gotten away with keeping it all a secret… Until tomorrow, when I'd planned to come clean. Pulling out my phone, my fingers tremble as I type a short text. **We need to talk.**

I've just hit send when the doors open, and DJ the bouncer reaches for me. "Franco said to be sure you both get inside the condo safely."

My phone is clutched in my hand, and I'm waiting for any acknowledgment or text reply from Trip. Nothing comes.

I go to my bathroom, wash my face, shower and scrub the shimmer off my body. Closing my eyes under the warm spray, I allow hot tears to fall. I can still feel the hands grabbing at my feet, and fear shudders in my chest.

Leaning down, I use the loofah to try and scrub the sensation off my feet. This entire situation has gotten completely out of control, and I can't bear the thought of losing the one good thing to happen here. It wasn't supposed to be like this.

When I danced for Trip, I communicated all my feelings for him through my movements. My heart was so full, and I pictured holding him, his hands on my body. I imagined us together, skin against skin, moving like waves through the thrusts and the swirls.

Bianca helped me design my costume to match my brand-new Valentino Mary Janes, and it all came together like fire. My hair was big Barbie waves, and my makeup was sixties chic. It was one of my favorite creations, a look I'll copy again, except…

"He stole my shoe!" I yelp in the shower.

We fucking rushed out of the Rhino, I didn't get a single tip, I possibly lost my chance with Trip, and that motherfucker stole my shoe!

"Gia? You okay?" Bianca's voice echoes in the bathroom.

Slamming off the water, I grab a thick towel off the hook. "He stole my Valentino!"

"Oh." She nods, slanting her mouth to the side. "He's probably making it his trophy or whatever those assholes do with the stuff they steal."

"That was a twelve-hundred-dollar pair of shoes." I wrap the towel around my body, storming out of the shower to face her. "Nobody's going to sell me one shoe to replace it!"

Bianca presses her lips together, blinking a few times. "That's all you got out of what happened tonight?"

My fists are on my hips. "No, but it's the icing on the shitty cake."

Wrapping her arm around my shoulders, she leads me into the bedroom. "I get that it's a violation, but you made three times that in tips on the soft launch. I think you're going to be able to replace the shoe."

Growling, I take a turban off my dresser. "I guess."

I check my phone again, but still no reply. Sadness pushes harder against my chest as I lean forward to wrap my curly hair so it'll dry while I sleep. I put the towel on my chair and step into my underwear, pulling a tank top over my head.

"Do you think you can sleep?" Bianca sits beside me on the bed. "I was going to meet up with Franco for drinks. You could come with me?"

"I don't want to go anywhere." My voice is quiet.

If Trip won't speak to me, I only want to hide under the covers and cry.

"It wasn't your fault." She leans forward to kiss my cheek.

I only wish I could believe that.

I'm so pitiful, I can't help myself. Falling asleep, I send one last text, **Please talk to me.**

"Something's different about you, *Mariposa*." Michele wraps an arm around my shoulders, as we walk from his apartment to the café. "You look like a woman with secrets."

"What happens when the caterpillar isn't completely honest and gets all tangled up in the cocoon, and it ruins everything?"

"I've never heard of that happening."

"It happened to me."

He slides his hand down my arm, lacing our fingers as he drags me into the small coffee shop. "You're alive and well, so there's still hope, yes?"

"I don't know."

He leaves me to order us two coffees, and I step to the side. After a long night of waking myself every few hours to check my phone, I finally got up and called my ex-fiancé. After dancing together for five years and being engaged for one, I figure he's the closest friend I have besides Bianca. He's also a male, so even if he's on the other team, I hope he can give me some perspective on what I've done—and how to fix it.

"Americano, Americano, Americano," he croons, placing the white cup in my hand.

"Thank you." I lift the cup to my lips and sip, allowing the warm caffeine to soothe my soul.

"Now tell me what happened." We're walking along the boulevard through the center of the shopping district.

Sky-high palm trees line the street, their skinny trunks reaching to the sky, and I blurt it. "I'm not a virgin anymore."

His eyebrows shoot to his hairline. "You had sex? With who?" Then his brow immediately furrows. "Was he a gentleman? I'm a bit protective of who my girl sleeps with."

"I'm not your girl." I push his shoulder.

"You're the only girl I've ever almost married. Now tell me what happened. Did he hurt you?"

"Mm…" I take another sip, thinking. "I didn't actually do the penetration part."

"Gia." Dark eyes narrow at me. "If there was no penetration, you're still a virgin."

"That's a very male thing to say. You wouldn't call two lesbians in a relationship virgins, would you?" He frowns, and I continue. "I read a book that said we should find a new definition for virginity, and it should be based on your first *fulfilling* sexual experience, but I don't know if that's going to catch on."

"Giana Rossi." Michele stops walking. "Did you take a dick or not?"

"Oh my God, shut up!" I grab his arm, pulling him away from the early-morning crowd now watching us curiously.

An old woman wrinkles her nose at us, and he blows her a kiss. "Good morning, Mamma."

I drag him farther down to a somewhat secluded park bench. "Here. Sit. I need your help."

"It sounds like you do, claiming you're not a virgin when your hymen is right where it's always been."

Exhaling, my shoulders drop, and I look at my cup. "I met this amazing man. He's handsome and rich and elegant, and he actually wanted to be with me." Blinking up at him, I point to my chest. "With me."

"Why does this surprise you? You're a beautiful woman. I would have been honored to be your husband in Amalfi."

"We're not talking about that. I would have lived a long, sexually frustrated life."

"Who says you would've been sexually frustrated?" He holds out his hands. "I would've taken care of my wife."

I catch his fingers, pulling them down. "I don't want that. I don't want a husband who settles for me because he can't have what he really wants. I don't want to be a consolation prize."

"You are so much more than a consolation prize." His voice is warm, but I know it doesn't hold the meaning I need.

Shaking my head, I continue walking. "Back to this man. We had an amazing dinner. He made me feel like no one ever has." I exhale heavily. "Now he won't speak to me."

"Why not?"

My chin dips, and I study my fingers. "He has so many reasons. I'm not sure exactly which one is the problem."

Pushing off the bench, I start to walk again. Maybe talking to Misha is a bad idea. How could he ever understand what Trip is feeling? Even if Trip weren't my boss, even if I hadn't hidden my true identity from him, how could he tolerate watching me dance like that for other men?

Michele is with me again, catching my wrist. "Tell me one of his reasons."

Squinting up at him, I watch his face closely as I ask, "If

we were together, and you weren't gay, would you care if I were a stripper?"

To his credit, he doesn't flinch. "I wouldn't like it. I would be worried about your safety. But if I loved you, it wouldn't be enough to break that love."

It's entirely too soon for love to be on the table when it comes to Trip Alexander.

"Would it matter to you that I was a virgin?"

A teasing smile splits his cheeks, and his green eyes sparkle. "But I thought you were no longer a virgin."

Damn him for being so good-looking. I'd never have let him string me along for a year if he weren't. Oh, hell, or maybe I would have.

"Answer the question."

His expression grows serious, and he nods, his dark brow lowering. "I never wanted to take that from you, not if there was a chance you might find a man who would love you better."

"Better than you?"

We face each other, and a familial warmth is between us, this friend who holds so much of my history. "You always have a special place for your first. He is someone you'll never forget, so if it can be special, it should be very special."

Taking his arm, I lean my head against his shoulder. "You've always been so good to me, Misha. Thank you."

"Mariposa," he coos, moving as if to place his lips to my head.

We're not paying attention to the path ahead, when a steel-gray Lamborghini screeches to a stop on the shoulder in front of us. It's so sudden and unexpected, I jump in place.

The door opens, and my heart flies to my throat when I see who's storming out of the vehicle. Trip slams his door too hard, stalking towards us with fire in his eyes.

Even angry. He's also gorgeous as fuck (Maybe even moreso because he's angry?) in a blue blazer over a cream-linen dress shirt. He's wearing jeans and loafers, and the possession radiating from his face makes me shiver.

His eyes level on mine, the green smoldering like fire. "Who's this guy?"

I'm ready to fall at his feet and kiss those damn loafers, but before I can say a word, Michele steps forward projecting a machismo he never shows.

"Who are you?" His chest is puffed up, and my jaw drops.

"Trip Alexander." They're standing too close, and if they fight, I swear…

"Michele Santorino."

"He's my friend." I pull Michele's arm so I can step between them.

The men don't break eye contact.

"Your friend?" Trip studies Michele as if he's not sure whether to believe this.

"Yes, her friend." Michele's hand goes to my waist like it used to when we would dance.

I'm momentarily comforted by the protective gesture, but it evaporates when Trip's expression cools.

"I see." He takes a step back, passing an elegant hand over his mouth, and my heart twists painfully in my chest.

I want to take his hand, thread our fingers and lead him away from here, walk out to the beach and explain.

"If Gia has a problem, she comes to me," Michele continues. "Are you a problem?"

His hazel eyes land on mine, like a stab to the chest. Then a casual smile drifts across his lips. He shakes his head like he's finished here. "Not me."

An invisible wall rises between us, making me panicky and desperate. I want to run after him, but Michele slides his hand over my forearm, holding me back.

"She'll be with me tonight at the Palm Club. Ask for Dickie Normous, and they'll show you to my table."

Trip gives us one last glance, noticing Michele's hand on my arm. "Good to know."

He walks to his car, stepping inside without another word, and drives away. My shoulders fall, and I collapse onto a nearby bench, pulling my knees up and resting my forehead on them.

Hot tears are in my eyes. "I'll never see him again."

"I like that guy." Misha is smiling, and I lift my face to scowl at him. "What?" He has the nerve to act confused.

"What was all that macho-protector act? 'She comes to me,'" I mimic his voice. "Like you're some mafia don."

"Men don't like easy things. Is he the one you were telling me about?" I don't answer, trying not to cry. "You'll see him again."

"How can you even say that?"

"Have you ever heard of *The Alchemist*?" I shake my head, and he explains. "You're pursuing your dream. The universe is conspiring to help you. Trust it."

"After all that's happened?" I shake my head. "I can't trust anything anymore, especially not the universe."

"You can always trust your dream."

If only I could believe that.

CHAPTER 15

Trip

I'M ONE OF THE RICHEST OF MANHATTAN'S SOCIAL ELITE, EXPERIENCED in vice and well-acquainted with the underworld, and a stripper brought me to my knees. Grinding my teeth, I left the rioting club and drove straight to the condo *I own* to confront Gia.

DJ the bouncer met me in the parking garage. Placing a meaty fist in the center of my chest he held me back.

"Franco said no one sees the girls tonight."

Anger burned hot in my throat, fueled by her obvious text, **We need to talk.** I didn't even respond. I'd say what I needed to say to her in person.

"I pay Franco and you, now get out of my way."

DJ squared his shoulders and looked down on me with one word. "No."

My jaw had been clenched as well as my fists, and I imagine I looked like hell on wheels. "I will have your motherfucking head—"

"Listen." The Dwayne-Johnson-sized bodyguard caught

my elbow in a hand the size of a baseball glove. "I don't know what's going on with you two, but I know it's something that will benefit from a night's sleep. Trust me. I've fucked up a lot of relationships in my time."

"I'm sure you've had your share of fuckups, but I am not you. I'm here to see Giana, and you're going to get out of my way."

He lowered his caveman brow. "I'm not letting you in, boss. You made the rules, and that's the end of it."

It's a peculiar place to be when you want to murder some-one for following your own instructions. As it is, I am the most controlled person I know. A bead of sweat rolled down my back, but I straightened my coat, gave that asshole a cool smile, and walked to my car. Clearly, I wasn't going to fight my way past him.

This morning, looking at my phone, I saw her last text from hours of no reply, *Please talk to me.*

My stomach twisted at the plea in her words. I had every intention of talking to her. I needed answers, and I was ready to get them.

Hopping in my car, I sped down Worth Avenue in the di-rection of the condo, when right out in broad daylight, I saw her walking hand in hand with Mr. Tall, Dark, and Handsome. What the fuck? How much do I not know about this woman?

Slowing my speed, my eyes drank in her perfection. Dressed in a bright coral shorts outfit, her shapely dancer legs flexed seductively with every step. A belt cinched in the mid-dle accentuated her narrow waist, and the top was a plunging V-neck that allowed a peep at the curve of her breast.

She was so damn sexy standing at his side, smiling and laughing up at him. He smiled back at her, dimpled with straight, white teeth. He put his hands on her, and rage burned in my chest.

Without thinking, I whipped my car to the shoulder and

threw it into park. Red flooded my vision as I stepped out, going straight to confront them.

He dared say *I* was the problem? That *he* took care of her? Where the fuck was this brigade of bodyguards when I had my face in her pussy two nights ago?

Oversized, dark sunglasses made it impossible for me to read her expression, but her full lips were glossy nude and parted. She was fucking kissable with her hand on his arm and the other holding a paper cup of coffee.

I hated this guy acting like he was her protector.

That's my job.

My internal response shook me, and I had to fall back. I summoned my inner cool, fumbling everywhere for my poker face until I found it.

What is this girl doing to me? I don't lose control. I don't play games. She thinks she's got me wrapped around her finger. She thinks she can lie to me, lead me around, make me beg, but she'd better think again.

I don't beg.

The Palm Club reminds me of Vegas. The entrance is a gigantic neon palm tree with lights blinking from the base, changing colors up the trunks and out through the fronds. Rainbow neon lines the exterior façade, with tracing flashes leading patrons all the way to the entrance.

I step through the glass door, and an oversized bouncer with a clipboard stands in my path. "Name?"

My jaw tightens, and I'd hoped it wouldn't come to this. With a cringe, I utter the name, "Dickie Normous."

The bouncer's thick brow relaxes. "Oh, sure." He chuckles, stepping to the side and opening the door.

Possessive anger vibrates in my body, driving me here, into

this club, walking through this dark hallway. When I saw her with him this morning, I'd told myself it was over, I was done with pursuing her. I was out. *Not a problem.*

Yet here I am.

I don't know what I'll find at the end of this hall, but if she's wrapped in his embrace, if he shows any indication of ownership, I'm walking. I'm no simp.

The hall opens to a rowdy, disco-themed club full of men dressed in speedos, walking around with trays of Day-Glo test tubes.

A shimmering, sea-green curtain is drawn across the dance floor, and fake smoke and laser lights shine through the haze, rising to the roof. Generic house music pumps like a heartbeat, and a little guy in bondage attire runs back and forth on the bar, shaking his ass in people's faces as they laugh and slap it.

It's a predominantly male clientele, and at first I'm confused. Is this the right Palm Club? It has to be. The doorman knew the name to let me in.

"Hey, handsome." An attractive young man in a halter top pauses at my side. "You here with anyone?"

My brow furrows, and I hesitate. His interest doesn't bother me, but I'm not sure what I've walked into. "I'm technically alone, but perhaps you can help me."

"Gladly." He sidles closer with a conspiratorial grin.

"Where's Dickie Normous?"

"Another one." He rolls his eyes, flicking his wrist over and checking his smartwatch. The house lights lower, and he looks to the stage. "Is your timing always so perfect?"

I look around as well to see the shimmering curtain on the dance floor start to sway. The house music switches, rising louder with synthetic violins followed by thumping bass, drums, and an explosion of "Vogue" by Madonna.

The curtain sweeps away to reveal a trio of slim male bodies covered in leather bodysuits. They're all swinging long, straight black wigs that extend almost to the floor, and their faces are fully made up with exaggerated eyes and lips.

Leading the pack, in the center, performing an athletic dance is Michele Santorino. He's lip syncing with The Material Girl and moving hands around his heavily made-up face. The three of them fall into precise choreography, and it hits me. He's a drag queen.

What the hell?

Male bodies surge past me to crowd the stage, and they're cheering and dancing all around, swept up in the show. Tearing my eyes from the performance, I quickly scan the perimeter, searching every leather booth for her.

Our eyes meet, and electricity crackles between us. She's standing near the wall, dressed in a white, strapless pantsuit. The top is a plunging V, highlighting her cleavage, and her wild curls are thick around her shoulders. Her lips are berry red. She's wearing oversized gold hoop earrings, and the effect is edgy, sophisticated, and fabulous.

My demeanor cools, my poker face snapping into place. Too much has happened in the past twenty-four hours, and if this is another game, I'm calling her bluff. Sliding my hands into my pockets, I lift my chin in a challenge. *Show your cards, sweetheart.*

With that, I turn and head for the exit.

"Trip!" Her voice is behind me, growing closer, but I don't stop. "Trip, wait!"

The bouncer makes some crack about leaving so soon as I push through the glass double doors. A fresh, cool breeze sweeps up the street, and I cross to the wide sidewalk that runs alongside the intracoastal waterway.

Another slam against the glass doors tells me she's outside the club as well, and the rapid click of her heels on concrete gains on me as I slow my pace. Adrenaline vibrates in my chest. I want her to catch up with me. I'm ready for this reckoning.

Stopping at the edge of the boardwalk, I look out at the

black water, tipped silver by the full moon. She stops at my side, looking out at the water. Her breath is quicker from walking fast, and with a glance to the side, I see her beautiful breasts rising and falling rapidly beneath that strapless top. The moon highlights her skin, and my jaw grinds. Why is she so damn gorgeous?

Calming my voice, I turn to her. "He's gay."

She nods, pulling her lips together. "If it makes you feel any better, I was engaged to him for a year."

"Engaged?" I'm not sure if this new information makes me feel better.

"Misha was my dance partner in Italy. We came here together, and when everything went down, well, he… came out." Shaking her dark head, a hint of a smile curls her lips. "Bianca said I should've known when we were engaged a year, and he never touched me."

That makes me feel better. "Bianca is right. Especially someone like you."

Her smile grows tentatively bigger. "Someone like me?"

Her eyes are so round and full in the moonlight. Her cheeks are pink, and her lips are shiny and kissable. *Someone exactly like her.*

"You lied to me. Why? Were you trying to make me look weak or show how you had some power over me?"

"I would never do anything to make you feel weak." Her voice is low, that little rasp taunting me.

My gaze travels around her face, searching for any sign of deception. Her expression is sincere, without guile, the same as the night we had dinner, the night she told me about her childhood. *What is this contradiction?*

"You started a riot last night."

Her eyes fall to my hands in my pockets. Stepping closer, she slides her fingers over the skin of my exposed wrist. Her touch stokes the fire simmering in my blood, the fire she started the first time I saw her dance.

"Did I start the riot? Or did the guy who broke the rules?" Her dark eyes blink up to mine. "Or the second guy who broke the rules?"

Clearing my throat, I slip my hand out of my pocket, and she immediately slides her palm down so it's flush with mine. Our fingers lace together, and the feeling of her bare skin against mine rocks my shield.

I lower my gaze to her slim hand in mine, a beautiful shade of olive. "When you left me at the Breakers, I was afraid I'd come on too strong. I thought you were an innocent seamstress. Now I don't know what to think."

"No one has ever touched me the way you did that night." Her eyes flicker down. "I liked it. I liked it so much, it made me afraid, and I ran."

It's hard for me to believe her words after all I've seen. "Don't play games with me Gia." It comes out as more of a growl.

She reaches up, placing her hand on my chest, round eyes holding mine. "I don't know how to play games like that. I want to be with you. I want to know you all the way better. I want you to know me. Is it too late? Have I spoiled everything?"

Her fingers curl in my jacket, and she moves closer, stretching her chin higher. The delicate scent of honeysuckle wraps around us. It's intoxicating, and I want to kiss her. I've been on fire for her so long, and now she's here in my arms begging for me. I don't have enough answers, but I can't deny this need.

"Gia…" Anger tightens my fists, gathering the fabric at her waist and pulling her closer.

Her hand slides up to touch my cheek. "Take out your frustration on me."

Jerking her closer, my lips brush hers as I warn, "You don't know what you're asking."

"Show me."

Our mouths seal and open, and our tongues curl together. A soft moan scrapes from her throat, and my hands move from gripping the fabric at her waist to sliding around her, pulling her to me forcefully.

Her hands are on my neck, her fingers in my hair, and our mouths move quickly, grasping, nipping. We're ravenous, kissing cheeks, chins, lips. I slide my hands over her round ass, this ass I've watched twist and grind for me on the stage.

She draws closer, flattening her breasts against my chest. She taunted me when she danced, sliding her hands over them and reaching for me, knowing it was me watching her when I had no idea who she was.

Her rapid breathing pushes them above her top. My cock hardens in my pants with the memories of her movements, of her moans when she comes.

Tracing my teeth along her jaw, I groan in her ear. "Let's go."

I've got to get her back to my place before I take her right here in the sand. She holds my arm, matching my pace and keeping herself close to my side as we retrace our steps to where I parked.

I hold the door, and she pauses, touching my cheek and brushing her lips over mine before stepping into the car.

My head is on fire, and I'm not seeing straight as I jog around to climb into the driver's seat. Stabbing the starter, I whip the wheel, pulling us into the traffic and lowering the pedal to the floor to quickly cover the distance to my apartment.

Her hand is on my leg, and my jaw tightens. We don't speak. The noise of wind through a small crack in the window roars in the interior space, matching the roar in my ears. I'm not sure how I can drive. Her fingers slide higher, moving her palm back and forth on my inner thigh, her fingers tracing the line of my erection through my pants.

"Gia…" It's a warning growl, but she doesn't stop.

She curls her fingers, scratching her nails along the fabric, teasing every hardened ridge, forcing more blood to rush below my belt. I'm ready to nail her to the wall when we reach my parking garage. I almost lean on the horn when the arm doesn't immediately open.

Entering the garage, I quickly pull around to my designated space, slamming the car in park and flinging open my door. I'm on fire as I circle the car, and she's already out, closing the space to meet me. My hands plunge in the sides of her hair, and I pull her face to mine for another hit of her sweet lips.

A high whimper, almost a squeal comes from her throat, and she holds my wrists, fighting to keep up with the movement of my mouth, the invasion of my tongue claiming hers. Dragging her down the short walk, we enter the private elevator, and I swipe my card before turning her back to the wall.

My hands are on her waist, tugging down the fabric of her top. It slips lower, revealing the beige top of her strapless bra, but it won't release.

"Dammit, you've teased me too long." I'm hoarse with desire, and she whimpers, moving her fingers down my shirt, quickly unfastening my buttons.

"No more teasing." She presses her open mouth to the skin of my chest, and I groan as her tongue touches me.

She slides her mouth higher, to my neck, and I've got to get her out of this fucking pantsuit.

The bell dings, and I catch her wrist, dragging her across the short foyer, through the door of my penthouse apartment. We're inside, and I drop my keys on the floor.

She turns, sweeping her hair aside and urging me breathlessly. "Unzip me."

My fingers fumble with the gold zipper, but I manage to drag it down. The top falls away, and I pull her to me, sliding my hands from her flat stomach up to her full breasts. Her hands are between us, and with a flick, her bra falls away.

"Fuck me," I groan as I wrap my palms over her hardened nipples, kneading her gorgeous tits as her head falls back on my shoulder.

I've dreamed of these so many nights. I've jerked off in

the shower with images of my mouth on them, my hands, my cock.

"So good," she hisses, arching her back against my bare chest and pushing her clothes to the floor. "I want your hands all over me."

I want my hands all over her. My mouth is on her shoulder, moving higher to her neck, behind her ear as I continue to pinch and tease her nipples.

My shirt is open, and I step back, catching her wrist and leading her to my bedroom. She's a vision in nothing but a thong and heels, full breasts bouncing as she walks, ass flexing.

"Fuck me," I groan, fumbling with my belt and jamming my zipper down.

Shoving the pants to the floor, I go to the nightstand to pull out the entire box of condoms. It's going to be a long night.

When I turn to face her, the breath hisses from my lungs. She's standing, breathing heavily, her hair flowing, watching me with her lips parted. Reaching down, I slide my palm over the slickness leaking from my dick as my eyes travel down her hips to her bare pussy partially covered by the smallest scrap of lace.

My face was there last time we were together. She flooded me with orgasm then ran away, only to taunt me from the stage, knowing what she'd done. A sinister grin curls my lips as I watch her panting, waiting to see what I'll do next.

Closing the space between us, I cup her breast with my hand, circling the tight nipple with my thumb. Then I bring my hand to her chin, sliding my thumb between her pillow lips into her mouth.

Blinking, she slides her tongue against my finger before closing her lips around it, locking her eyes on mine and sucking. It's all I needed to know.

"Get on your knees."

CHAPTER 16

Gia

I AM G*LITTER* G*IRL*.

Glitter Girl is me.

Energy thrums against my skin as I stand fully nude except for the micro thong covering the front of my pussy. Trip's eyes are drunk with lust, and I feel beautiful, powerful. I've never been completely bare in front of a man, and I want it to be for him, for his eyes only.

The only item of clothing he wears is the shirt I unbuttoned in the elevator. The salt from his skin is still on my tongue. His cock is thick and turgid, long and veiny. A shiny drop is on the tip, and I can't tear my eyes off him. I've never seen a hard, angry dick up close and personal before.

He touches my breasts again, and I swallow a moan as he lifts and pinches my nipples. Each touch is possessive and lusty, and I want him to savor my body. Last time we were together, I got a little taste of what he can do to me. I want more.

Now his hand is on my jaw. His thumb is in my mouth, and

I remember Bianca's words. My body knows what to do. It *is* like dancing, a primitive dance I was born knowing.

Curling my tongue around the thick digit, I slide it up and down, thinking how it will make him feel if I do the same on that part of him straining for release.

"Get on your knees," he rasps, and I immediately comply.

A fluffy rug is at the foot of the bed, and I place my palms on his muscular thighs. His body is lean but tautly lined, and his chest is lightly dusted with hair. Leaning closer, I slide my hands closer, wrapping my fingers around his thick shaft.

I have watched porn, and even if it is fantasy and exaggeration, I have a general idea of what I'm doing and what seems to evoke the loudest moans. Licking out my tongue, I focus on the tip, sucking lightly as I trace my nails lightly under his balls.

"Fuck," he groans, threading his fingers in the side of my hair.

A thrill tickles low in my belly, and wetness slides through my core. I'm doing it right. I'm making him feel the way he made me feel, and the encouragement drives me on. Curling my fingers around the shaft, I slowly pull it to my lips as I suck him further into my throat.

Another deep groan, and his grip on my head curls and tightens. I'm bobbing my mouth faster, dropping my jaw and moving my hands to his ass. Lifting my eyes, he's watching me, lips parted, eyes glassy with need.

"You're amazing," he hisses as I lean back, focusing on the tip as my hands return to pumping his shaft.

"I want to make you come." I can do this. I am the object of his desire.

Reaching down, he lifts me to my feet, holding me by the elbows before pulling me against his chest. Our mouths seal together for another demanding, pussy-drenching kiss. His tongue slides against mine, and he bites the seam of my lips before pulling away.

"Get on the bed."

Turning, I'm ready to do as he says when I notice it's an

all-white duvet with a thin, black stripe embroidered around the edge. It seems very fine and expensive.

When I hesitate, he frowns, seeming angry. "What?"

"We should get a towel—"

"You think I give a shit about the sheets? They'll wash."

"It's not that, I…" My stomach pinches, and I don't want to stop this. I want all of him, rough and angry and possessive.

He grips my arm, turning me to face him. "What is it?"

Inhaling slowly, I don't know why it's so difficult to say. "I'm afraid there might be blood. You see, i—it's my first time."

Silence fills the air between us. His eyes narrow, and I pull my lip between my teeth. I know his trust is shaken, but I want to be completely honest with everything going forward.

"You're lying." His tone is flinty, but he releases my arm. "You're trying to run away again."

He takes a step as if he'll leave, as if he'll take that massive cock to the shower and deal with it alone, without me.

"I'm not. I don't want to run. I want this to be with you. I only…" I gesture to his pristine king-sized bed. "I don't want to ruin your sheets."

Closing the space between us, he catches my upper arms in his angry hands. "Fuck the sheets. You honestly expect me to believe you've never slept with a man with the way you dance?"

Our faces are close, and I'm breathing fast, my breasts rising and falling against his skin, the fine hairs on his chest tickling my nipples. A heartbeat throbs in my pussy, and I want his dick to soothe that ache.

"Every time I danced, I thought of you. I imagined what it would be like to have your body next to mine, inside me." My voice is soft but strong, cautious but confident. "Didn't you know?"

The anger in his hazel eyes wavers. His gaze holds mine for another beat, then he blinks. "You're not real."

Reaching up, I carefully slide my fingers along his neck,

threading them in the side of his soft hair. "You're not real. I thought I'd lost everything, then I found you."

Turning fast, his mouth is on mine again, his arm around my back. I feel him rip the sheets away before sliding me back onto the bed, higher so we're in the center. I'm lying on my back with him between my thighs, and his mouth moves to my jaw, down to my neck, biting and sucking the soft skin.

Firm hands are on my ribs, sliding up to lift my breasts, squeeze them. His torso is a delicious weight on my stomach, my thighs, and I drag my hands up his shoulders, pulling him against me.

Moving down, he pauses to kiss the side of my breast, moving his mouth over one nipple, pausing for a nibble, to the valley beneath and up to the other, biting and sucking.

"Yes," I moan, threading my fingers in his hair. It's so good.

With every appreciative kiss, every nibble and bite, my back arches. Sensations pulse through my blood. My nipples are so hard, my toes are pointed, and wetness leaks from my core to my ass.

Now his lips are on my navel, his tongue circling and kissing.

He rises up on his elbows, gazing at my bare pussy. "This little scrap of lace is in my way."

"Rip it off," I beg, and his eyes flicker to mine. "Please…"

I'm squirming beneath him, and he curls his fingers over the fabric. A sharp jerk is followed by a little sting. I gasp an *Oh*, and his mouth is on me.

The first stroke of his tongue, warm and wet against my clit, has me rising off the bed with a scream. His palm is flat against my stomach, and this time as he licks, drawing me frantically closer, racing to that burning orgasm, he inserts two fingers, three, stretching and circling my slippery core.

"This might make it hurt less." His mouth is against the seam of my thigh.

"I don't care," I gasp, tugging his hair, needing him to get back to my pulsing clit.

His beard scratches my skin as he grins, and it provokes my first jerk of orgasm. "Oh… oh, yes," I moan as his mouth returns to finish what he started.

Sucking and licking, my eyes are closed, and I'm lost in the waves pulsing through my thighs, radiating down to my toes, up to my brain. His fingers are gone, and I hear the noise of foil ripping.

His tongue flickers back and forth, and I break with a scream, shudders rippling through my stomach, moving through my legs. He slides his tongue around two more times, two more ecstatic bursts move my hips, and he quickly kisses my navel, wrapping his forearms under my knees and spreading me wide.

"Deep breath," he orders before his mouth covers mine, and *fuck fuck fuck*… Pleasure, meet pain.

He slides fully inside me and holds, groaning deeply. "Gia, fuck me." It's more like the rumble of an earthquake.

The earthquake is inside me. My orgasm slams against the sea wall of tearing pain, and I gasp a wavering moan. "Oh, God."

My fingers curl against his shoulders, and his mouth is at my ear, lips soft as he kisses me, as he whispers hotly, "Relax, baby. The hard part is over."

The sensation of fullness clouds my mind. He releases my legs, sliding his palms behind my knees before moving them up my thighs to cup my ass.

Wrapping my legs around him, I do relax my fingers, flattening my palms against his skin and moving them higher to hold his shoulders as my body adjusts to this completely new experience.

"I've got to move." His voice is strained as he kisses my neck, hot breath at my ear.

Nodding quickly, I turn to meet his eyes. Our gaze meets and holds, and desire blazes through my stomach. *My first.* And his hips begin to rock.

"Oh," I whisper at the sensation of his hard cock moving rhythmically against my clenching core.

"You're so beautiful," he whispers, kissing my lips briefly, moving higher to kiss my brow.

His rhythm picks up speed and intense focus fills his gaze. My back arches as my eyes flutter closed. The movements trigger something deep inside me. The friction stirs a need I didn't know I had. The pain is gone, and in its place is a growing urgency.

Longing for something I've never felt simmers low in my stomach, encouraged by the movement of his hips, the hoarse groans in his chest. Strong hands clutch and grip my curves. Our bodies slide together, slick with sweat and moving in time.

We're dancing. My hands are on his shoulders, and his are on my waist. His chest is at my lips, and I place my open mouth against his skin. Salt is on my tongue as I trace it along the line of muscle in his shoulder.

"Gia," he groans, bending down to capture my mouth in another ravenous kiss. "You feel so good."

My hips begin to rock, matching his time, and warmth spreads across my pelvis. "So good," I murmur, learning his choreography, groaning as his cock hits a place inside me that radiates pleasure up my spine. "Yes… Yes… Keep doing that." I'm grasping, pulling his shoulders.

"That's it," he gasps, kissing my mouth and seeming to let go.

Was he waiting for me? His hands go to my hips, and his shoulders bow. His cock moves deeper, hitting me in a way that has me clawing at his skin.

"Come for me, Gia," he growls, biting the top of my shoulder, sending orgasm sparkles shimmering in my pelvis.

"Don't stop," I beg.

We're arms and mouths, grasping and moaning. He's driving me higher, and a bead of sweat rolls down his cheek. I lean forward to lick it away, and he covers my mouth as he bears down two, three, four, more times until the growing bubble in my stomach fractures into a million sparkles of light.

"Come," he orders, and with a loud moan, my insides clench and draw him into me.

He groans long and loud, and his body stiffens. His pelvis holds, and I feel the movement of his cock as his orgasm spills into me, filling the condom.

He shudders, groaning again, and I'm wrapped around him like a vine, arms and legs clinging for dear life. This is incredible, something I've never experienced in my life.

We're holding, breathing hard. It takes me a moment to come back, to remember where I am, blinking slowly at the room around us.

Still inside me, Trip leans heavily on his elbow, putting his forehead in his hand. A smile pulls at my cheeks, and I reach out to thread my finger in a damp curl at the side of his neck.

Turning his head, he looks into my eyes, and emotion races from my heart to my throat. I swallow hard, fighting the sudden urge to cry. It was all so amazing and primitive and beautiful. For the first time, I understand the phrase "two become one," and I know what we just shared is something I'll never experience again, not even with him.

"Thank you," I whisper. Maybe it's stupid and childish, but I don't know what else to say.

For a first time, I can't imagine it could be any better than that. It was legendary.

He shakes his head, blinking his eyes away, and making me wonder if he's feeling the same emotions as me. My fingers are still in his hair, tracing that damp curl like it's the most treasured thing.

Reaching for my hand, he pulls it to his mouth. He places his lips against my palm, inhaling deeply before kissing my shoulder softly, his scratchy beard against my skin. Inhaling the clean citrus scent of his hair, I trace my thumb over his brow and he kisses my hand again.

Lifting his chin, he studies me, then with a rough voice, he asks, "What are you doing to me?"

CHAPTER 17

Trip

GIA SITS IN THE MIDDLE OF MY BED, WRAPPED IN MY DRESS SHIRT, her long curls bound in a messy bun on top of her head, smiling adorably as I hold a cube of cheese to her full lips.

"We got everything late. I grew up watching badly dubbed *Friends*," she explains while chewing. Then she mimics that fucking obnoxious line. "We were on a break!"

"God, I hated that show," I groan, taking a sip of my wine.

After that tremendous fuck, we were both hungry. Gia said she didn't want to go out, so I ordered a charcuterie board and a bottle of sparkling wine.

I didn't believe she was a virgin. I didn't believe any of her shit after last night. Now, sitting in my black boxer briefs, I watch her eat an oversized grape and wonder from which realm of heaven she dropped, and what the fuck I did to deserve her.

When I realized it actually *was* her first time, all I cared about was making it good for her. If I was going to be a memory in her life forever, I wanted it to be something that would make her smile and not cringe or hold up as a cautionary tale.

Our consummation was not cringe, and it was far from a cautionary tale, unless the tale is about losing track of one's goals. Perhaps it was because I'd fantasized about her too many times or maybe it was simple chemistry, or I'd been alone too long…

What happened between us was different. I was feverish with need, burning from the inside out, and sinking into her body was like a sip of cooling water. Only it was far from cool. It was hot as fuck, and I'm filing this away for later reflection.

Once I had a grip, I carried her to the bathroom to clean her gently, and she placed her hand on my cheek. She kissed me sweetly, smiling into my eyes. She looked at me like no one ever has, like I was precious to her. It made my stomach twist, and I simultaneously wanted to run away and pull her closer, protect her from anything that would try to hurt her. *Mine.* The word was on a neon sign flashing in my brain.

It freaked me out, so I ordered food, and now she's wrapped in my shirt in the middle of my bed, stripping away the last of my defenses.

I'm fucked.

"No!" She pushes my arm. "How can you hate the friends?"

"Very easily." I pop a roll of thin-sliced prosciutto into my mouth. "Ross is an asinine wimp, Chandler is a hyperactive dork, Monica gave me the itch. The only tolerable characters were Joey and Phoebe. Oh, and Rachel."

"Oh, and Rachel." She rolls her eyes, shaking her curls as she sips her wine. "All the boys love Rachel."

"She had the most believable character arc, although that apartment in Greenwich Village was a total fabrication. There's no way they could afford to live there."

"I like the way that sounds." Her dark eyes glow, and she's sexy as fuck leaning back on my pillows with only a few buttons holding my shirt closed over her glorious tits. "Greenwich Village. Is it really a village?"

"In a way." I lean on my arm beside her, sliding a loose

curl behind her ear. "Your friend Michele would fit in very well there."

She nods, drinking more. "What was your favorite movie as a little boy?"

"Transformers." Her nose curls, and I shrug. "I was a kid. Meghan Fox made my dick hard."

"I like when your dick is hard." She leans closer, letting the front of my shirt fall open.

"Good thing." Setting my glass aside, I reach for her waist, pulling her onto my lap so she can feel my semi. "Are you sore?"

"A little." Placing her hand on the headboard behind me, she slides her lips along my cheek. "Not so much I'd turn you away."

The faintest scent of honeysuckle lingers in her hair, and I reach up to hold her face, kissing her lips. I set her wine glass to the side and pull her forward so her cheek is against my chest. Wrapping my arms around her, I'd never hurt her, physically or otherwise.

"What was your favorite movie as a little girl?" Tracing my fingers down her back, I love the feel of her warm body, soft against mine with only thin linen between us.

"*Bridget Jones's Diary.*"

"What?" My brow furrows, and I look down at her. "How old were you?"

"Eleven. It was on my aunt's television, and I watched it over and over. I liked the part where the men were fighting. And the part where her butt hits the camera."

She breaks into sweet laughter that ripples through her body. Her bare stomach touches mine, and my chest tightens. Emotion filters through my arms, which are wrapped around her, and I drop my head back against the headboard. *What is this feeling?*

"I liked that movie." My throat is dry, and I reach for another sip of wine. "She had great tits in that bunny costume… and a pretty decent ass."

"You love tits and ass."

"And that's a problem because…"

"You're like the player, Daniel Cleaver."

I set the wine glass aside, thinking about my carefully cultivated persona. I suppose it is similar to Hugh Grant's character in that film. "Only on the outside." My voice quiets. "Only for protection. When it comes to you, I'm entirely Mark Darcy. I like you just as you are."

Her cheek lifts against my skin with her smile, and she turns her face to kiss my chest. "Why do you say it's for protection? What does that mean?"

"Hmm…" Pressing my lips together, my mind travels back to New York, which currently feels galaxies away from this cozy nook where we're hidden. "The men in my world believe they're better than everyone. They make decisions that change the world—sometimes literally. It's important never to let anyone see you have feelings… or they use them against you."

She's quiet, and I lift a curl from her shoulder, studying the way it wraps and clings to my finger. It reminds me of the way her body wrapped and clung to mine moments ago when we made love.

They use them against you… My own words drift through my mind, a warning whisper. I shouldn't allow these feelings for her. I'm cultivating a weakness, a vulnerability.

Not only that, I'm her fucking boss. She's my employee— at least for now. I'm not supposed to be touching her… which is probably what makes it all the more irresistible. No touching? *Watch this.*

"I'm sorry they're like that." Her voice is quiet, and I push away my dark, angry thoughts.

"Didn't mean to bring down the mood." I exhale, shifting my position. "Should I tell you a funny story? One summer when I was a kid, I pretended I was fluent in French, and our doorman Rusty gave me a shopping list for one of the temporary residents. Everything I bought her was wrong. Everyone was pissed."

Gia blinks up at me. "You should have confessed."

"I thought I could figure out the words." I shrug. "It felt like a challenge."

"Now you can look them up on your phone."

"It's true." It gives me an idea.

Taking out my phone, I pull up Instagram and start tapping.

"What are you doing?" She arches higher. "Searching for Italian words? I can tell you."

"I'm searching for your Instagram account."

"Oh." She pushes up fully, sitting back on her feet.

The bun in her hair is loose from lying in my arms, and it falls beside her neck. She's facing me in my thin shirt with her nipples pointing at me, coils of dark spirals on her shoulder. For a moment, I'm distracted by her beauty.

"You have an Instagram, don't you?"

"I did." She shoves a curl behind her ear. "I haven't looked at it since I came here."

"Giana Rossi?" Another nod, and I tap on an account that can only be hers.

Photo after photo of Gia in perfectly executed ballet poses fill my screen. In one, she's on pointe, one arm over her head with the swirl of a chiffon dress in an arc behind her. In another, she's facing forward, one leg straight below and the other straight overhead with a stiff peacock skirt circling her middle.

"These are incredible." She's mesmerizing in her form and grace and strength.

The last one is a photo of her and Michele smiling and holding a letter. He's doing a thumbs up, and the ocean is brilliantly blue behind them. It's dated three months ago.

"You stopped posting."

"It hurts to look at them now." Her chin drops. "Dancing

was my whole world. I thought it would carry me to a better life, then it all fell apart."

Blinking to her pretty face, I set the phone aside. "Palm Beach isn't the end."

"I just had so much hope, and I was left with no job, no way to get home, no way to make money. If it hadn't been for Bianca and Franco…" Her dark eyes blink to mine. "And you… I'd be on the street."

"You seem pretty resourceful. I bet you'd have found a way." Holding out my hand, she hesitates only a moment before placing hers in mine. I pull her to my chest once more, cupping my hand under her chin and lifting her mouth so I can kiss her. "Sometimes we have to let go of our expectations and see where life takes us."

"Where is it taking you?" Her voice is soft.

"Right now? I have no idea, but I'm going with it." *God help me.*

Her smile is shy but coy. Little vixen. "You're not offended by what I do?"

My beautiful girl. She has no idea. "I'm only just learning all the things you'll do."

CHAPTER 18

Gia

My arms are stretched above me, and a silk scarf covers my eyes. Electricity crackles in the air, and my breath comes in short pants. We went from looking at pictures of me dancing to warm kisses that turned hungry.

His cock grew hard and long in his boxers, and I wanted to play like we had before. I wanted to put it in my mouth. Instead, that naughty grin curled his lips, and now I'm lying on my back, wearing nothing but his thin shirt, blindfolded, with my hands bound in his necktie and hooked on the headboard above.

"What's the safe word?" His lips are at my ear, whiskers scuffing my skin.

"Bowtie." My skin hums, adrenalized and expectant.

"That's right." His voice is rough, and his hand goes to my stomach, sliding aggressively up my torso until it reaches my breasts.

My stomach twists, and he disappears. The room is quiet, and for a moment, I don't know what to do. *Did he leave me?* Is he going to punish me for playing with him before, for dancing for him, taunting him when I knew he was my boss? When I knew it was forbidden?

The scratch of his beard on my inner thigh makes me jump. A sharp squeal bursts from my throat.

"Don't be afraid, little butterfly. I want to hear you scream." Warm hands slide up the sides of my legs, and he places open-mouthed kisses in the middle of my thigh, moving higher.

Tremors shake my stomach, aftershocks of the earthquake he set off before, but he doesn't go where I think. He moves away again.

"What are you doing?" I'm blind and curious, straining for his next touch.

Silence, and then the faintest flickers, like plucks of an insect's feet. I think of a spider. "Oh! Oh, no!" Fear rages through my insides, and I'm kicking my feet fast in the sheets. "What is that? A spider? Get it off, please!"

The tiny touches disappear, and he's at my ear, quieting me. "Shh, baby, shh... It's not a spider. It's a feather." He runs a velvety frond across my neck, letting the spidery tendrils fall along my skin. "I purchased a few things after our dinner I think you might like."

"A feather..." I exhale a laugh, relief pulsing in my veins and tightening my nipples.

How is it possible for fear to turn to arousal so fast? The memory of our dinner date and the dirty way we played afterward prickles in my brain.

"Are you going to use it on the arches of my feet?"

He scoots around behind me, sitting with his back to the headboard and pulling me onto his lap. "I was thinking of something a little more sensitive."

My back reclines against his chest, and my head is on his shoulder. Slowly, he unbuttons the shirt I'm wearing, leaving me bound, blind, and exposed.

"You are so beautiful." His warm breath skates over the

skin behind my ear, and my core clenches. "Your nipples are so hard. If I put my fingers between your legs, would you be wet for me?"

A soft noise escapes on a breath, and I nod. "Yes."

"Good girl." His large hand cups my jaw, turning my face to his mouth for a possessive kiss. "I'm going to use you now."

His cock is hard against my lower back, and a strangled noise is my only reply. The feather tickles across my stomach, moving lower between my thighs, to my bare pussy. It's the softest touch, but it's teasing, promising.

"How does that feel?" His mouth is beside my ear, biting me gently, making me moan.

"It's… different."

"I think it's too soft. You need something stronger."

My brow furrows, and he slips out from behind me. The noise of drawers opening and closing, and the distinct sound of a foil wrapper, a condom. He's back, lifting me onto his lap, only now his boxers are gone. His hard dick is against my ass, and something is in his hand.

"What do you think of this?" Reaching down, he places his palm against my inner thigh, and buzzing zips against my skin.

I jump, straining against the tie. "What is that?"

Soft lips touch the side of my neck. "It's a bullet vibrator. It's on the lowest setting. Do you like it?"

He moves it up my leg, drawing closer to my bare slit, and my throat tightens.

I'm breathing faster, and my voice rushes out on a breath. "It tickles."

"Have you ever used a vibrator?" Shaking my head no, my entire focus is on his buzzing palm, now circling my lower stomach. "This should be interesting then."

"Oh, God…" He slides it lower, over my pubic bone, hovering just above my clit as my heart beats faster.

"Ready?" A wicked smile is in his voice, and he doesn't wait for my answer.

His hand covers my pussy, and a burst of vibration sizzles against my most sensitive place. It's like a shock straight to my spine, up to my brain. It's an orgasm building on overdrive, growing stronger by the second.

My knees lift, my toes curl, my back arches. My lips part, and I let out a noise like a cat. Then it's gone. I'm gasping, confused, sensations radiating out through my thighs.

"Oh…" I didn't finish. I'm right at the edge, and the absence of vibration is almost as painful as the presence.

"You like it?" Trip's beard scuffs my sensitive skin, and I'm overwhelmed.

"What?" It's practically a sob. "You're torturing me."

"The technical term is *edging*, but it's a little like torture." Warm lips cover the base of my neck, opening to allow his tongue to touch me as his hand returns, buzzing against my inner thigh. "Feels so good when you finally come."

Gasping again, my entire body tenses. My legs tremble wildly as he slowly moves higher, his touch growing lighter. My stomach flutters, and my core clenches repeatedly when he reaches the seam of my thigh. With the lightest pass, he grazes my clit, and a yelp jumps from my throat.

He grazes me again, and I rise off his lap, clenching my thighs.

A deep groan rumbles in his throat. "I need to feel this."

He slides his empty palm firmly over my pussy, flattening his fingers against my skin, then gently slapping my hypercharged clit several times.

I cry out, my knees jumping with every slap. "What are you doing?"

I've never heard of these things. His hand smooths over me again, easing the spasms, then he dips two fingers into my core. A satisfied hum rumbles in his chest.

"So wet." The tip of his cock replaces his fingers, and his hand moves to my stomach. "Ride me, beautiful girl. I want your messy come all over me."

His command is almost a relief. Pushing against him, I open greedily, taking his rigid cock fully into my core with a moan. I'm still a little sore, but the need provoked by his torture drives me.

His hand goes to my leg once more, and the vibration is steady and firm, moving higher. I'm clenching faster, bucking and pulling on his dick as he groans against my neck. "Fuck yeah."

Another soft skim of vibration against my clit, and I wail. My thighs close over his hand, and I'm shaking, thrusting my ass against his pelvis, riding his cock like my life depends on it. I can't take much more of this, yet at the same time, I don't want it to end.

"Last time." His voice is strained, and his empty hand rises to cover my breast, squeezing and pulling my nipple while the vibrating hand moves down my stomach, lower, winding me tighter the closer it gets.

Until it's there.

Relentless vibration arches my back. My eyes squeeze tight, and I strain higher as the shockwaves of orgasm activate every muscle in my body. I writhe against him, and with my hands bound and my eyes blind. He groans loudly, but my entire focus is on his dick, pumping hard and fast as I come, screaming.

When the pleasure turns painful, and I can't take it anymore, I gasp, "Bowtie."

The vibration disappears. I hear the small device fall to the floor, and he embraces me, holding as his cock pulses inside me, my breathing mixed with his orgasmic groans.

As his breath slowly comes down, he reaches overhead, loosening the tie around my wrists. I push the blindfold off my eyes, and we roll so I'm on my stomach. He's behind me, still buried to the hilt. Soft lips cover my back with kisses as he rubs my shoulders.

My arms are bent, hands beneath my cheek, and a smile curls my lips as he massages my arms, my shoulders. Moving away, he quickly disposes of the condom before returning to soothe and kiss me.

"You are amazing." Another warm kiss to my cheek. "Spectacular."

"Hmm…" is all I can say. I'm boneless, so relaxed, and a little sleepy.

"Did you like that?"

Nodding my head, I push against the mattress to roll over in his arms. He's beside me, looking down with a smile, sliding my hair off my face.

"I think you broke me."

That makes him laugh. "Not even close. We're just getting started."

Lifting my chin, I wriggle an arm out of his embrace, reaching for the table on my side of the bed. He watches me with a curious smile as I take my phone, swiping and tapping several times.

Once it's open, I go to my Instagram and hold it over us to snap a photo. I inspect it closely to be sure nothing is exposed. It's actually perfect. He's not smiling, but his eyes are full of warmth.

We're wrapped in white sheets, both of us with messy sex-hair. My lips are swollen and pink from so much kissing, and I'm smiling like I haven't smiled since the day I got that letter in Amalfi.

No filter. I caption it, then hit post.

Shula greets me when I walk through the door of the condo. "Gia!" She puts a hand dramatically on her chest. "You are absolutely *glowing!*"

"You're late." Bianca meets me at the door, far less dramatically. "You have three important DMs needing your attention *now.*"

"Oh, Gia." Shula makes a sad face. "Can Private Eyes wait? I ripped a strap last night on my very best top. I wanted to wear it tonight."

She holds out a sequined bikini top (no cups, of course).

"Another one?" I study the network of straps designed to lift her breasts while leaving nothing to the imagination.

"I was dashing around backstage, and it got caught on a hanger." Her collagen-infused lips press into as much of a frown as possible.

"Okay." I take the top from her. "I'm only answering DMs. It's not like I'm dancing. I'm sure I can sew as I… type?" Our eyes meet, and we both start to laugh. "Maybe not."

"Gia!" She throws her arms around me.

I hug her back. "I'm sure I can fix this by tonight. Don't worry."

"Come on!" Bianca has me by the elbow, leading me through the living room to our bedroom, where the laptop awaits.

My head is in the clouds after last night, and I haven't stopped smiling all day. With every step, I'm reminded I lost my virginity *fully* last night, and the orgasms… The thought makes me sniff a laugh.

"What is wrong with you?" Bianca hisses. "Are you on drugs?"

"If sex is a drug." I lean forward, covering my mouth with my hand.

We fell asleep entwined after that ecstatic tickle-torture session—*edging*, sorry. I didn't know it was possible to feel so good. I thought I was losing my mind.

Usually, I can't sleep well if someone is too close to me, but last night, I wrapped around him like a soft pretzel, our faces a breath apart. I've never slept so well in my life.

In fact, I slept so well, I didn't open my eyes until almost noon. He was fully dressed but met me at his bedside with a perfect cappuccino when I opened my eyes. God, his smile, the warmth in his gaze, the coffee. It's all so amazing.

He brought me home with the promise we'd be together again tonight. Only… I have another idea brewing in my mind. He likes torturing me. Maybe I can torture him a little as well.

"I thought we had a service to answer our DMs on Private Eyes." I stretch out on my double bed in the room I share with Bianca.

I didn't know my muscles would be sore after a night of orgasms.

"We do, but for big tippers, you personally answer. It keeps them coming back."

Rolling onto my stomach, I rest my head on my hand. "What kind of big tippers?"

"One thousand, seven-fifty…" Her eyebrow arches, and my lips part.

"You're kidding. Someone tipped me a thousand dollars?"

"Yes. Now get on there and make him feel like the only man in your world."

The suggestion sours my stomach. My upper lip curls, and I don't like this job now. I don't like lying. I don't like pretending I care for someone for money. I feel like a prostitute, especially when I only care for one man… who happens to have a lot of money, but I wouldn't give a shit if he were a poor fisherman.

Bianca studies my face, shaking her head. "Gia!" Her tone is scolding. "You're only acting. They know you're acting. Stop overthinking it!"

I don't think I'm overthinking it. Blinking down to the computer screen, I pull up the first direct message. Of course, it's from my Number1Fan.

I heard you had a scare the other night. I'm sorry.

Glancing up at Bianca, I'm not sure how to proceed. "Will they be waiting for my answer? This was posted last night at eleven."

"Just answer, and if they're there, keep talking." Her tone

is annoyed, like I should know this. "If not, they'll respond when they see it."

Twisting my lips, I peck out a reply. *It was a little scary, but I trust my bodyguards.*

It's the truth. I was alarmed by the man's hands on my feet. It was different this time from the first time. The first time, it seemed like he only wanted to touch me. This time, it felt more like he wasn't letting go. He was chanting something… It was so loud, I couldn't understand him.

Still, I knew DJ had me, and now I know Trip was there as well, ready to punch that guy's lights out. Rolling onto my side, I exhale a smile at the memory. My brave protector who gives me so many orgasms. Who cares if he's my boss?

"Is Trip still my boss if I'm only on Private Eyes?"

Bianca's gaze flickers to me. "I guess technically, no. You're more of a contract worker if you're not dancing. Although, we are living in his house. I'd have to double check with Franco."

With a sigh, I flip over onto my stomach to the other two DMs waiting. The second is from a user named BigBoi. I remember him from my soft launch.

Would you be put off by a man who cries in sad movies? My wife says I'm weak.

That makes me frown. I want my man to be sensitive, and I would never make fun of him for crying in a sad movie.

Thinking about this, I reply, *What movie was it? I cry in movies all the time. Maybe we can cry together.*

The last DM is from a username I don't recognize. AnmLvr, which I assume stands for *animal lover*, or *anime lover*? It says, *I found a dead kitten in the woods, and I kept it in my basement for a long time. Should I tell anyone?*

Oh, great. My lip curls, and I look over at Bianca filing her fingernails. "How do I reply if I get one that's very strange?"

She puts the file down and crosses the room to where I'm holding the laptop. Her green eyes quickly scan the screen.

"Ew, Jesus." Pulling her chin back, she faces me. "And he tipped you a thousand."

"A crazy rich guy? That's kind of a cliché. Should I give him the number of the crisis hotline?" I point to his username and shrug. "Or maybe he's really disturbed by the death of a little animal?"

"More like he's a serial killer." She stands, rubbing her hands up and down her bare arms. "I'll ask Franco to put a double firewall on your account so no one can hack your personal data."

"Hack my data?" Now my arms prickle with nerves. "What the hell? Does that happen?"

"I heard it happened to a girl in Tampa, but pfft, you know Tampa. They're pretty lax."

My eyes blink wide. "I don't know Tampa! What happened to her?"

"I don't remember. Just give him a neutral reply, something sweet. If anyone's phishing, we'll catch them." Then she points. "Literally!"

Doing my best to imagine this person really loves animals, I answer sincerely. *I'm sorry you saw this tragedy. Maybe bury the poor little thing and sing a song or read a poem. Show him you cared.*

It seems like a kind, neutral response. Non-judgmental.

My laptop has been silent since I sent the first message, but Bianca says I need to wait a little longer to be sure they don't come back within ten minutes of answering.

I can only think of one person I want to be messaging. Resting my head on my hand, I take out my phone and pull up the Instagram post I made at 2 a.m. I love his square jaw, his intense hazel eyes—more green than brown. His longish hair is messy around his head, and when I remember what he did to me, my core clenches.

I can't resist sending him a text. *So I'm sleeping with the Big Boss now?*

Again, I don't know how long to wait for a reply. Luckily, it doesn't take too long.

I guess I have to fire DJ—or fire me.

The tease in his text makes me laugh. My stomach is bubbly, and I feel like a swoony teenager with a crush.

Perhaps I should find another job?

Gray dots precede his reply. *I do like breaking rules, but I don't like sharing.*

The implication of ownership floods my veins with warmth. Still, I'm not one to lose my independence so easily.

Bianca warned me some admirers might get too attached.

I'm taunting him, and my heart beats a little faster as I wait for his reply.

Just leave those assholes to me.

A laugh bursts through my lips, and a ding on my laptop draws my attention. I quickly text, **Hold please**, and hit send.

Dropping my phone, I pull up the DM on my computer. "My Number 1 fan is back," I sing-song under my breath.

Bianca glances at me from the desk. "He's a big fish. You'll want to keep him on the line."

"This doesn't feel icky to you?"

"We're providing a service, Gia."

I quickly scan his message, and my throat grows tight. *I read an article that said I might be chatting with a teenage boy in India. How do I know this is really Glitter Girl?*

Chewing my lip, it's a valid question, but I can only reply with the truth. *I am Glitter Girl, but I don't know how to prove it.*

The cursor blinks and then begins to move. *Tell me something only she would know.*

Wrinkling my nose, I think about this request. How would he know something only I would know? My eyes circle the room, and I think about my last performance at The Rhino. *The last time I danced, a man stole my favorite shoe right off my foot.*

The cursor blinks, and I have no idea if he'll accept that answer. My internal defiance says if he doesn't like it, he can chat with someone else. Then the nerves hit, and I'm afraid I'll lose my biggest tipper.

His reply is not what I expected. *What kind of shoe was it?*

I'm not sure if he's testing me, so I answer fast. *Pink Valentino Mary Jane.*

Size?

My brow furrows, and again, I type a quick reply. *Seven medium.*

A new chat window pops up on my screen, and BigBoi is back. *You're welcome to cry on my shoulder any time. Just don't tell my wife.*

Ew! I groan loudly. "Why am I doing this again?"

Bianca doesn't even look up. "Because you make more money in a day than you would in a month—two months—as a housekeeper or a seamstress. Because it allows you to live in this awesome condo. Because it's going to help you get home."

My lips twist, and I realize I'm not as excited about getting home as I used to be. I still don't have a work visa. One of the ways we've kept it a secret is The Rhino pays me in cash, and we used PayPal to set up my Private Eyes account. I'm not sure if working online through a service based in the UK is a technicality that would save me from deportation, but hopefully I'll never have to worry about it.

"Can I stop now?" I give Bianca puppy eyes.

She looks up at the clock. "You've been online for an hour." With a shrug, she returns to her nails. "If you want to stop you can. It's long enough, but you might offend them."

I'm already slapping my laptop closed. Bending my knees, I rest my forehead on my hands. Three weeks ago, all I could think about was getting back to Italy. Now, the thought of leaving makes my stomach hurt.

I can't go on this way, but what choice do I have?

CHAPTER 19
Trip

"**S**OMEONE'S TRYING TO FIND HER." FRANCO STANDS AT HIS laptop, frowning severely. "They're using a bot to ping every password on the Private Eyes site."

"Fuck. Who would do that?" My brow furrows.

"I have a guess."

"You think that guy has the resources for that?"

"Only one way to find out. Our security team is trying to isolate it, so we can trace the location."

My phone pings, and I glance to see a text from Grish. *Call me*.

Grinding my jaw, I slide the phone in my inside pocket, but I can't keep ignoring his texts.

It's been a week since our first night together. A glorious week—a week of breakfast in bed and late-night suppers and orgasms and thinking crazy-big dreams.

It's another week I shouldn't be away from Manhattan, but it's a week I wouldn't have missed for my life.

God, Gia is amazing. I love getting out of bed in the morning to find her in my kitchen making coffee. I'll go to where she's standing, move her hair off her shoulder and bury my face in the scent of honeysuckle on her skin. Her shoulder rises and she giggles, and my stomach tightens like a fucking drum.

Thursday night, she made spaghetti for me. Authentic, hand-rolled, spaghetti with crushed tomato and basil sauce. I've never tasted anything so good—not even at the finest restaurants in New York. I found a bottle of expensive red wine. It was heaven, but the best part was watching her with her hair tied up on her head, barefoot in a wrap dress with a plunging V-neck, pulling the long strands of noodles out of the pot. She would hold them over her mouth, and my dick would stand at attention.

Franco found out I was sleeping with her in the most mundane way. He came by my apartment to drop off the new building contracts and saw her in my bed.

His black eyes met mine, ice cold, and for the first time since I've been old enough to care, I couldn't meet his critical gaze.

Fuck him. I know what I'm doing.

I'm sleeping with one of our dancers. I'm crossing every line. I'm being unprofessional and undisciplined, and what happens if things don't work out? The thought tightens my throat. I can't let her go.

Now he's standing in front of me telling me someone is stalking her?

"Who's trying to find her?" My tone is less controlled than I'd prefer.

I'm not the same person with her. In New York, I'm an unreadable wall. If anyone gets too close or threatens me, I slip the mask in place. Poker face.

Gia has blown the fucking lid off that.

"If I knew who it was, I wouldn't say *someone*." He doesn't look up from the email on his screen, and I'm pissed he has this power now, this knowledge.

It's not a lot of power, but it's enough to make him annoying as fuck.

"Gia has to be safe." Not only for her or for me, but for all the girls.

If one of them is threatened, they all are. Anyone could get to them.

"She's trying to get on the schedule again." Franco lifts his hands, as if it's beyond his control. "I think it's a bad idea. You saw what happened the last time she danced."

Gia not dancing has made things less complicated for us. I like it that way. I don't like that she's trying to get back on the stage without telling me.

"I thought she was strictly Private Eyes now."

"Is that your excuse for sleeping with her?" His tone is challenging.

An invisible hand tightens on my throat. I want to snap back with *I don't need an excuse*, but he's right. I'm dipping my quill in the company ink, and it's not a good precedent.

Instead, I answer calmly. "What do you want me to do?"

"I'm sorry, are you asking me what you should do now? At this point in the game?"

That's it. I'm ready to pop him in the mouth. Franco. My best manager—the guy I trust with all my south Florida businesses. I actually want to punch him like I'm some goddamn animal.

Pinching the bridge of my nose, I exhale slowly, searching for wherever I left my control. "Look. It's not like I came here expecting to meet her. It happened."

"And what? You're going to build a life with Gia? You're going to commit to her? Take her to New York? She doesn't even have a work visa. She came here as a student, and when that went to shit, she couldn't get home."

It hits me like a pan of ice water in the face. "She's working with no visa?"

"We pay her in cash like all the girls." Franco's dark brow

lowers. "Because we use the club to launder money. Which laws are we worried about now?"

Still, I don't like the thought of her doing illegal things. We'd be punished—maybe, depending on how quickly we could move—but she could face jail time, a big fine, permanent deportation. If I helped her, that would pull her into my world, which in turn, would put a target on her back. *God dammit.*

"Who knows about her status?"

"Me, Bianca, and Gia. And now you."

"Keep it that way." My tone is level. Calm washes over me, like it always does when I'm confronting a challenge. It's a learned response. "I'll handle it on this side. You handle it in there."

I point to the computer, and he shakes his head. "I always do."

My jaw tightens, and I straighten my coat before leaving the Rhino. I've been putting this off for too long. Now Gia and I have to talk.

"Oh, God, yes..." Her voice is a soft gasp. "Right there... That's it... Harder!"

We're in the kitchen of my penthouse apartment, and she's gripping the edge of my custom-made mahogany bar. Her short skirt is flipped over her backside, and I'm buried balls deep, rhythmically thrusting my pelvis against her soft ass as we rise higher to the stars.

"Fuck, you feel so good," I groan, leaning forward.

My hands slide in the top of her wrap dress, unwrapping it. She's not wearing a bra, and I can grope and squeeze her bouncing tits. Jesus, I love her body. My mouth goes to the top of her shoulder, and I'm biting at her skin, pulling her closer, holding her so I can fuck her harder.

Her back arches, and she makes loud noises, gasps, high-pitched whimpers, indecipherable chanting, and I'm moving faster, chasing down that mind-altering high. Her hand circles fast over her clit, and with a mewl, her core breaks into spasms, clenching and pulling me as she comes on my cock.

Orgasm radiates through my pelvis, pulsing through my dick. It's like standing beneath a waterfall, waves of warm release pounding over me. Again and again, my orgasm comes. I encircle her waist with my arms, and I hold her back to my chest. I hug her so close. She's the only thing keeping me upright as we groan, as our trembling breaths slow, as we blink our eyes open, dazed and regaining our bearings.

That's when it hits me as hard as an anvil. I can't let her go.

She's this rare treasure I've found here, near the ocean, like a gift from the sea. She's mine, only mine. Everything we do is ours alone, and it's glowing and perfect.

I was her first. All I've ever heard is that being someone's first makes them needy and tiresome. She's none of those things. I can't get enough of her body, so fresh and eager to learn, so hungry for me. She touches me with wonder, looks at me with wonder. It makes me want to protect her, never let anyone disappoint her or make her cry.

"Gia." Holding the condom, I slide out and quickly dispose of it.

Reaching for her, I pull her to me again, needing to feel her against my chest. Needing her to seep into all the cracks life has beat into me. She makes me whole.

Fuck Franco. Fuck Manhattan. Fuck being the boss. Only Gia and I matter.

A happy little smile is on her face, and she carefully unbuttons my dress shirt. I didn't even take my clothes off when I got home and saw her in the kitchen in that same cooking dress, barefoot, with her hair all up on her head. Hunger took over, and I had to have her.

Now her hair has fallen around her shoulders. Her top is

unwrapped and when she has my chest bare, she pulls me into a hug with a contented sigh. We're skin against skin, and my eyes squeeze shut. I turn my face so my nose is buried in her curly hair, in her sweet scent.

She's something I've never had in my life. Being with her is a place I didn't know to look for, because I didn't know it existed. Who says we can't be together? Who says this is forbidden? Fuck them.

Then Franco's words come drifting back.

"I don't want you dancing at the Rhino anymore."

"What?" Her voice is high, and her body stiffens in my embrace. "What are you talking about?"

Releasing me, she steps back, adjusting her dress so it's wrapped tightly around her body again, as if she's preparing for a fight.

"It's not safe for you at the club." My tone remains steady. "You know what happened last time. I don't want you putting yourself in danger again."

"Are you firing me?" Anger flashes in her dark eyes, and I'm annoyed and proud of her.

I'm pretty confident she's as invested in what we have here as I am, but she won't let me order her around.

"I'm not firing you." Although, I haven't completely made up my mind it isn't the best course of action.

"And I'm not giving up my independence to be with you."

"Come here." I step forward, catching her arms. She half-heartedly resists before allowing me to wrap her in my embrace. "I'm not asking you to give up anything. I want you to be safe. We still haven't found that guy who grabbed your foot."

"You didn't stop Glitter Girl from dancing when you hadn't found him the first time."

"I didn't know it was you."

"So now you think you can tell me what to do?"

"Yes."

Her brow furrows furiously. "What gives you the right?"

You're mine.

I don't say that. Instead, I opt for the obvious answer, "I'm your boss."

"But I have something special planned." Her lips are pouty, and I want to kiss her. "One last dance."

"No." I'm shaking my head. "You're doing the subscription side now. You don't need it anymore."

She slides her hands to my neck, lifting her pretty eyes to meet mine. "One last time. I want to know you're there, to know you know it's me. I want to dance with you watching, unable to touch me. I want you there with all those men going wild, knowing it's my last dance, and when it's over, only you can have me."

As she speaks, her voice softens, seduction enters her tone, that little rasp, and even though we just fucked hard, my dick twitches. This beautiful, dangerous girl, jeopardizing everything.

"Gia," I groan, and she leans in closer.

Rising on her toes, she traces her lips along the side of my neck. "Please let me, sir?"

How the fuck can I say no to that?

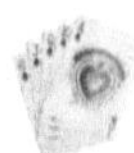

This is a bad idea.

I've circled the perimeter five times, checking for uncovered ways in or out. Franco has tripled security, even hiring guys from one of the neighboring clubs.

We managed to capture "hoodie guy" on the security cameras last time, but the image isn't very clear. The black hood obscures his face, and all we know is he's tall, slim, and somehow manages to elude us. I remember last time he dropped and crawled through the fighting crowd—hell, I did the same, and it wasn't a bad escape route.

This time we're prepared for everything.

Hoodies are not the preferred wardrobe of our patrons. Most of them are in flat-brimmed caps and skin-tight tees that show off their overdeveloped muscles and tribal bands. They're practically the same guy over and over.

Our troublemaker should stand out, and we'll be ready when he does. Ready to nail him if he makes a move.

I'm sitting in the VIP section, and as much as I urged everyone to keep tonight's performance on the QT, the place is packed. It seems all of Palm Beach knows Glitter Girl is back, and even if they're not fans of strip clubs, the notoriety of her last performance made the rumor mill. Someone also leaked it's her farewell dance.

My chest is tight as I take another drink from my second vodka of the night.

Otherwise, it's a regular night at The Rhino. Shula warms up the crowd with her standard, no-holds-barred dance to "First Class" by Jack Harlow. Her costume is a too-small flight attendant's dress, and her oversized tits bounce, her duck lips blow kisses, she bats fluffy lashes as she twirls and shakes her ass-length hair extensions to the song.

As unappealing as her cartoon-character persona is to me, she's got a decent-sized following. I have to hand it to Franco. He knows this business better than I do. Gia, or Glitter Girl, might be packing the house tonight, but Shula will pick up the slack when she takes her final bow tonight.

I'll be glad for her to pass the reins. This entire setup makes me uneasy. The standing-room-only crowd is one wrong move from a fight, and I don't like Gia being the center of attention, the target of their lust.

Shula, by contrast, seems to be exactly where she wants to be. She skips and blows kisses, lifts and shakes her boobs, and holds out her hands to the rain of bills falling all around her. The song winds down, and she has cash fanning from all possible elastics on her body.

The stage manager appears to quickly help her sweep the dollars thrown on the stage into bags she can take backstage. She blows kisses and skips away on white platform tennis-boots.

Tension grows in my chest with the end of her dance. The house music kicks on, and the crowd seems to ripple to the thumping 808 drumbeat.

I don't know anything about her dance tonight—other than she wanted to do it just for me. She wouldn't let me see her costume or even know her music.

I'm on my third vodka drink, but as the time gets closer, I'm on my feet. The packed crowd on the floor stomps in time to the music, ready to start the show. Scanning over their heads, I see DJ at the door leading to the dressing rooms. I make eye contact with Franco, who gives me a nod.

We're ready.

The house lights dim, and a roar filters through the crowd. I drop into the chair positioned in front of the railing, and I can't deny the bubble of pride growing in my stomach. She's right, none of us are allowed to touch, but she'll be in my bed tonight.

Smoke machines flood the stage with fake smoke, and ne-on-green laser lights shoot through the crowd, floor to ceiling. The music belches out in an aggressive, grinding rhythm. It begins with the intro to "Pony" by Ginuwine, but two measures in, just as the spotlight hits, Britney Spears's "Toxic" mixes on top of it.

The curtain is gone, and standing in the center of the stage in a sheer bodysuit with only specks of rhinestones from neck to torso (matching the one Britney wore in the video), is my girl.

Shouts fill the house, and she moves her hips, dancing in a jerky fashion to the stripper back-beat of "Pony" while lip synching the words to "Toxic." A metallic face mask appears to be painted on, and it's impossible to take my eyes off her.

Rhinestone clusters cover her nipples, but her breasts bounce and move with every step of her performance. The bottom is a thong, so her luscious ass is completely exposed—except for specks of rhinestones glued to her skin.

Her curls are blown out and styled in oversized 1960s-inspired waves. The fans again drop down from the ceiling, so nonstop wind sweeps it all back. A bent-wood chair is her only prop, and she works it hard.

She takes a seat and leans over backwards, popping her head to look directly at me. My stomach tightens. Single diamonds are placed on the tops of her cheeks, in the cupid's bow of her mouth, and her full lips are high gloss.

Turning her back, she moves her hips and ass in a circular motion that summons muscle memory. My dick is wide awake and hard as a rock. Following every turn, she whips her head and looks straight in my direction.

I'm breathing fast, my lungs heaving in and out. I want her so much right now. I want to push all these assholes aside and tell everyone she's mine, only mine. They can look, but only one man in this room can have her. *Me.*

She straddles the chair, grinding her hips, then she bends her knees and starts to thrust. It's the last straw. In that body-suit with her bare pussy and naked ass practically exposed, I shove into the crowd.

My eyes never leave her face, and I see when she sees I've lost control. Her full lips press together before breaking into a huge smile, revealing her straight white teeth. She doesn't stop dancing, circling her ass and whipping her hair around.

I'm pushing men aside, throwing them out of the way in my fever to get to her. She lifts a hand to her mouth, holding it over her lips and blowing an invisible kiss to me. Her nose wrinkles, and she skips around the stage as if she's waiting, taunting me to come and get her.

Reason has left my mind. Concern about how I look or what the other employees will think has left my mind. The rules never made it to my mind.

A guy twice my size stumbles into my path. He's clearly

drunk, and I grab him by the collar, roughly jamming him into his friend.

My dick has grown two sizes, and it's calling the shots. The only thing that will give me relief is getting to Gia and taking her out of here, back to my place where we can finish this.

When I finally reach the edge of the stage, her eyes are fixed on mine, and her dance changes. Before it was showy and wide, directed at me, but open to the whole crowd. Now that I'm directly in front of her, she narrows her moves.

Her wingspan is only open to me, and she dances in the square facing me, even dropping to her knees to give me a better view of her beautiful body.

The song continues loudly, but she's on all fours now, crawling to where I stand with my mouth dry from panting like a wolf. The crowd slams into me, doing their best to get to her, but her eyes are locked on mine.

She reaches out a rhinestone-speckled arm directly in my face, and purrs, "Touch me."

I'm standing in front of her, doing my best to stay calm, not even worried about the tent in my pants. I'll deal with that later. Only one thing exists in this moment, this sex goddess on the stage who gave herself to me, holding out her arms and asking me to take her.

The men around me sway like waves on the ocean held back by nothing but the invisible rule of *no touching*, waiting to see if I'll break the only law keeping us in check. Bouncers draw close, making the space seem smaller.

"Take me…" Her arms are outstretched, and my hand rises from my side.

I'm ready to do as she asks. The song is ending, and I'm ready to claim what's mine for the whole audience to see.

"Stop." DJ appears behind her ordering me, ready to carry her offstage. "No touching the dancers."

"I don't dance here anymore." Her voice is loud, and it's all I need.

Placing both my hands on the glossy stage, I hoist myself onto it, brushing off my suit as I stand. She stands in front of me, looking up with a glossy smile, her beautiful tits rising up and down with her breathless pants.

Her entire body sparkles, and I don't think it's just the rhinestones. She's illuminated from within. Lifting my hand, I slide the back of my fingertips over her cheek. She closes her eyes, leaning her face into my touch. I bend down and lift her into my arms before turning to face the crowd.

For the most part, the men cheer, some laugh, and a few make booing sounds. Gia kicks her feet and waves as she blows kisses, telling them goodbye, and I turn, ready to carry her through the dressing room door, through the backstage area, to my car, to my place.

She wraps her arms around my neck, hugging her head under my chin, and I lean down to kiss her forehead. I'm the victor claiming his spoils, when my sight lands on him lurking in the corner, cold eyes glittering.

He's not wearing a hoodie tonight, but I recognize him all the same. I don't know how I never saw it before. I guess the hood obscured his features? There's no mistaking Andre, my shadow, watching me with daggers in his eyes.

His fists are clenched, and I hug Gia closer, as the desire burning inside me turns to defiance. What I did here broke the rules. It made a big show of ownership, and it opened her up to everything I want to keep away from her.

Still, even as I dare him to touch her, I know we're not hidden in Palm Beach. I know the man watching me now wouldn't hesitate to use this information to keep me in line, to bend me to their will.

I've been dodging Grish's texts and calls, but now it's time to get back on the grid.

CHAPTER 20

Gia

STANDING IN TRIP'S OVERSIZED, STONE SHOWER, I CLOSE MY EYES as three rainfall shower heads spray me from above and both sides. It feels so good, massaging my muscles and energizing me for him.

Tonight was better than I ever could have imagined. I was powerful. I was the fully emerged butterfly. Tonight was our hard launch as a couple—we let the world know Trip and I are together. I'm no longer dancing, and I've chosen the man of my dreams.

When he lifted me in his arms and carried me off the stage, I felt like a true Cinderella. I'd found my prince at last.

He brought me back to his penthouse apartment, where we've spent most of the last week practically inseparable, then with a kiss, he said he'd be right back. I didn't question it. Walking through the gorgeous, empty apartment, I got an idea.

First, I left one shoe in the entrance hallway. The next a few feet along. I stopped just inside the kitchen and unfastened the delicate chain holding up the silky hose speckled with tiny rhinestones and left them in a glittering puddle.

A few steps more, I peeled the taupe mask from my face and left it on the table. At his bedroom door, I shimmied out of the nude leotard with clusters of rhinestones in critical locations. It came out exactly as I hoped, and I'm obsessed with this costume.

Still, I left it at his bedroom door, and with nothing left to remove, I went to the shower to wash the stage makeup and shimmering body paint off my skin.

I've just finished rubbing the last of the makeup off me when I turn to see him standing in the doorway, watching me, and a thrill races to my core.

Reaching out, I push the glass door open. He looks like a model in his suit pants, no blazer. His light green dress shirt is unbuttoned at the neck and rolled at the sleeves to expose his heavy, silver watch. One hand is in his pocket, and a grin curls the side of his sexy mouth.

My stomach trembles, and I'm not sure what to say. I want him to join me, but for some reason, he's holding back, watching.

Sliding my tongue out to touch my bottom lip, I massage my hands over my stomach, sliding them higher. "Do you like what you see?"

"Very much." His eyes slide from my mouth down to my breasts and lower, making my body weak. "I could watch you all night."

Turning my back, I look over my shoulder at him. "You can do more than watch. Care to join me?"

The dimple in his cheek appears through his dark scruff, and he takes the hand out of his pocket, methodically unbuttoning his shirt. Chewing my lip, my blood starts to heat as I watch him strip off his clothes.

His shirt is gone, and I admire the lines in his chest dusted lightly with hair. The muscles in his stomach flex, and the lines in his hips drop in a V into his dark gray pants. He unzips them, allowing them to fall, then he reaches down to fist his erection, slowly pumping it up and down.

Desire clenches my core, and I take the hand-held shower attachment out of its holder, switching it on to pulsing mode. Watching him tug his cock, I lower the sprayer down my stomach to my bare pussy and begin to circle it over my clit.

I'm so hot already, the first pass makes my stomach jerk, and I exhale a moan. His eyes flash, and I turn to face the wall, placing my arm on the stone surface and arching my back as I spread my feet wider.

The sprayer is between my legs, and I rock on it, simulating our movements when he's fucking me from behind.

"Fucking hell." The heat of his body is at my backside, and his rough hands slide over my wet skin, moving straight to my breasts as his lips press against my neck.

Electricity races through me, and I have to move the sprayer away before I come. His hands grope me hungrily, and I moan louder, dropping my head back on his shoulder. I love his obsession with my body. I've never felt so desired and sexy. It makes me want to do anything he says.

"You make my dick so hard," he groans in my ear. "I want to fuck you raw like an animal."

A sizzle races from my hard nipples, made harder by his fingers pinching and twisting them, to my slippery core, growing wetter with every dirty word.

I'm breathless as I rock my ass against his cock. "Okay."

"You want that?" He bites the side of my ear, and his large hand covers mine holding the shower attachment. "You want me to hold you down? Fuck you mercilessly, not letting you up until I've spent my load inside you?"

As he speaks, he returns the water jets to my clit, circling slowly.

"Yes," I gasp as the tendrils of orgasm radiate through my thighs, heat tingling in my core only his cock can soothe.

"You want me to push you over the couch, face first, and spank your ass as I thrust into you again and again?" More circling of the water jets, and I rise onto my toes.

"Yes... God, yes."

"What if I make you swallow my cock, then fuck your mouth like the dirty girl you are?"

"Oh, God!" My orgasm crests, and he presses me against the wall, driving his iron rod roughly into my clenching depths.

One hand grips my hips, and I reach down to take the spray attachment from him, to continue what he started as he grips me with both hands, slamming into me from behind.

He's impossibly hard, relentlessly thrusting, and it feels so fucking good. When my orgasm turns from pleasure to pain, I drop the attachment, curling my fingers against the glass with my eyes squeezed shut.

His beard brushes against my shoulder, and I moan as he hits my G-spot, sparking another round of orgasm radiating in my core. "Fuck, Gia, fuck me..."

My palms flatten on the glass, and I push back, sending him deeper, so he hits that magical spot again and again.

We're moaning and fucking in time. He groans so loud as he breaks, pulsing and filling me, holding me steady as he stumbles forward, bracing his hand on the wall in front of me. His body is pressed against my back, and my face is turned. Our mouths unite, and we kiss ravenously, tongues licking and sliding together.

Our breathing calms, our fingers thread, and he slides out, turning my back to the wall so he can pull me fully against his chest as he kisses the line of my brow, to my temple, and down to my lips again for another, consuming kiss.

"You're so perfect," he murmurs, dragging his lips along the top of my cheek. "So utterly, fucking perfect."

Happiness burns in my stomach. Our gazes mingle, and for the first time, I realize I'm in love with this man. It's terrifying and amazing, and his brow furrows just before his eyes close, just before he puts a hand on the back of my head and draws me into his chest again.

"Gia," he whispers. "Sweet Gia."

I don't know whether to be thrilled or afraid. I only know I love him, and I never want to leave his side.

A large platter of assorted meats, cheeses, fruits, and vegetables is arranged artfully on the bar with crackers and crusty bread in bowls. I'm sitting beside it on the bar wrapped in his scotch-plaid flannel robe with my bare feet in a barstool. A glass of sparkling wine is in my hand, and Trip walks through the apartment collecting my trail of clothing.

Lifting his hand, he holds up one of my pink Valentino Mary Janes by a finger. "You bought another pair?"

Shaking my head, I nibble a slice of pear. "It appeared at the house today with a note from my number one fan. He got it for me somehow."

Trip's brow furrows. "Who is your number one fan?"

Shrugging, I dip my nose in the collar of his robe so I can take a deep breath of his clean, citrus cologne. I think I might steal this garment so I can wear it all the time.

"I've never met him, but he's one of my biggest tippers on Private Eyes. He wanted me to prove he was chatting with the actual Glitter Girl and not some teenage boy in India. So I told him about the stolen shoe, and he sent me a new one."

"He sent you a new pair?"

"No, just the one." I laugh as I pick up a piece of goat cheese and put it in my mouth. "I think it was sweet."

Trip's expression says he doesn't agree. "How does he know where you live?"

Taking another sip of my wine, I think. "I don't know. I

just assumed he sent it to the main address and Franco or one of the guys brought it over."

He places the pink platforms on the table then stacks my sparkling costume on top, still not smiling. Kicking out my feet, I hop off the bar and close the space between us, wrapping my arms around his waist and pressing my cheek to his bare back.

"I'll ask Franco about it tomorrow. Let's don't worry about it tonight."

Large hands cover mine on his waist, and he slides his hands up and down my forearms. "I don't want you going back to that condo. I want you to stay here with me."

My heart beats a little faster, and I tilt my head to the side, resting my chin on him. "Are you asking me to move in with you?"

"I'm not asking." His hand closes on my forearm, and he pulls me around to stand in front of him, putting his other hand under my chin and forcing my eyes to meet his stormy green ones. "You're staying with me until I'm sure you're safe. I'll send for your clothes. I don't want you out of my sight."

My lips twist, and I kind of like this overprotective vibe he's giving. "I think I'm safe in the condo. We have on-site security."

"Yes, but there's eight of you and one guard. When you're here, it's one to one."

Rising onto my toes, I kiss his lips lightly. "I like the one-on-one attention I get here." I grin, sliding my nose along his jaw, but he's still wound so tight. "Are you angry?"

His eyes blink to mine again, and finally his brow relaxes. His shoulders loosen with an exhale, and he pulls me into another hug.

"Never with you." He traces his fingers in my hair before kissing my brow. We stay that way a few seconds, and his voice turns wistful. "We know so little about each other... so many things you should know about me and can't."

Dread pinches my stomach. I don't like his tone or the distance his words create. Stepping back, I thread our fingers and lead him to the bar laden with food and drink.

"Here." I pour him a glass of sparkling wine. "Have a drink, and we can talk. Maybe you can tell me something I shouldn't know."

He takes the wine with a brief smile, sitting on a bar-stool. "What should I not tell you?"

"I know." I climb onto the bar to sit in front of him, facing him as I lift my glass of wine. "Tell me about the first time you had sex."

"Is that something you shouldn't know?"

"I don't know, but you were my first. It's only fair."

He chuckles, taking a sip of wine. "Is that so?"

"I think it is." I tilt my head to the side, smiling with all my fresh, new love for him fizzing in my veins.

"One of my mother's friends was bored—or maybe she thought I was developing nicely. I never knew. She cornered me in the guest bathroom and..." His eyes flicker to mine. "She made a pass."

I almost do a spit-take. "She felt you up?"

His eyebrow arches. "It was more of a grab, followed by an assessment of my size."

"How old were you?"

"Fifteen."

"You were Mrs. Robinson-ed?"

"Pretty sure Dustin Hoffman was a college graduate in that film. I was in high school."

Crinkling my nose, I pick up a slice of cheese and bite half, giving him the other half. He pulls it into his mouth, and I lean forward to kiss him. "I'm sorry that happened to you. Were you scared?"

"No, Gia. I was not scared." He chuckles seductively.

"I was a horny fifteen-year-old. I was very interested in sex. Probably too interested. I went pretty quick, but she didn't complain. I think she got off on the thrill of seducing me. It didn't get cringy until later."

"Pregnancy scare?"

"Jesus, no." He slides his hand up the outside of my calf, and a little thrill moves through my stomach. I love his affectionate touches. "We hooked up a few more times after that. She'd corner me in a coat closet at a party or in the wine cellar. It was always fast and dirty, but I thought she actually had feelings for me."

Pain twists in my chest, and I lean forward to thread my fingers in the side of his soft hair. "You got attached?"

His lips tighten, and he thinks a moment. "I definitely liked the fact that I was having sex pretty regularly, but I wasn't attached. I only thought we had a connection, something more meaningful."

"What happened?"

"We were at the Belmont Gala—it's this massive event every year all our families attend. I asked her to dance, and she glared at me like she didn't know who I was. Then she simply walked away."

Setting my glass aside, I slide down onto his lap. Initially he hesitates, but I wrap my arms around his neck. I press my body to his and hold him, closing my eyes and imagining my love flowing in to heal that old wound.

"I'm sorry she did that to you. You must've been so embarrassed."

He sets his glass on the bar and wraps me in his arms, sliding his hand up my back and into my hair. "I learned a valuable lesson, which led me to make a very important decision."

"What's that?"

"I decided I'd never let them make me feel worthless again. It was the start of my journey to independence."

Lifting my head, I give him a smile. "So it turned out to be a good thing?"

With a wince, he takes another sip of wine. "Maybe."

"But you have so much money now." I push out of his arms, returning to my seat on the bar in front of him. "Surely you can tell that old cow to suck it if you want."

"I could definitely do that." His voice is quiet. "I could do a lot of things. I made a lot of choices to get to where I am, and I never cared about the consequences. Until now."

Stillness falls between us. A deep stillness that drives me to tell him the critical point in my life, the point where everything changed.

"My mother was murdered by a man who said he loved her."

Trip's body stiffens, and he pulls his chin back. "What the fuck? How did... Was it your father?"

"No, my father died when I was very small. He was a fisherman, and an accident happened on his boat when they were out to sea. I barely remember him." My voice quiets. No one ever talked about my dad. "For a long time, it was just my mother and me, living together in a one-bedroom apartment overlooking our small village. I could look out the window at night and watch the moon drifting over the ocean. I thought we were so happy."

He twines one of my curls around his fingers. "She taught you to make biscotti."

Nodding, the mist warms my eyes. "See, we do know things about each other."

"You said you thought you were happy. But you weren't?" His voice is warm, like he understands.

"She was always smiling. She would walk through the village, and the men would take notice."

"I imagine you look just like her." Both hands are on my calves now, and that familiar heat sparkles between us.

"Maybe a little. She was slim and willowy. Her hair was

smooth and flowing. If we look alike, it would be in subtle ways."

"So what happened?"

"This man, Matteo, was obsessed with her. He would follow her through the streets, saying he couldn't live without her. He would stop her in the alley on the way home. He would try to make her want him. He said if he couldn't have her, no one could." Pain stabs my chest, even after all these years. I'm a little girl again, sitting at the window, looking out at the moon, waiting for my beautiful mamma to come home so we could curl up together and sleep. "One night she went out and never returned. He was so obsessed, he killed her. Then when he saw what he'd done, he took his own life."

"Jesus," Trip hisses. "And you?"

"I was sent to live with my father's sister, my aunt Gratziela."

"Gratziela's a pretty name."

Puffing air through my lips, I shake my head. "Her favorite hobby was telling me how ugly I was. How my body was thick like a peasant's, and my hair was wild like a gypsy's. She made me so ashamed." Tapping my finger along Trip's jaw, I lean forward. "Then I discovered I could dance."

"Is that cunt still alive?" The smoldering rage in his tone burns my misery away.

"She is, and I would love for her to meet you."

"I'm not sure I could be a gentleman to someone who hurt you like that, especially after all you lost."

Cupping his face in my hands, I lean forward to kiss his lips. "I hope you meet her one day so she can see what I've found."

Trip stands out of the stool in front of me, catching my waist, and pulling me off the bar. "I'm obsessed with you, Giana, and I promise I will never hurt you. I promise to do everything in my power to keep you safe. Always."

My emotional response to his words sneaks up and hits

me so hard. A lump forms in my throat, and I blink quickly, doing my best to swallow it down.

I never expected him. I wasn't prepared for him. He appeared in my workplace, looking like the best thing in the world. Then he stole my heart. He taught me to love. He changed my life.

Now he's making me promises, and I don't know how to put the brakes on this. I don't know how to slow down my racing heart. All I know how to do is reach up and put my arms around him, to allow the robe to fall open, revealing my nude body, and to luxuriate in his warm hands finding their way to the most sensitive parts of my body.

All I know how to do is give him all of me.

CHAPTER 21

Trip

"**W**HERE THE FUCK HAVE YOU BEEN?" GRISH'S VOICE GROWLS at me through the speakers in my car. "Things are getting tense here, and where are you? Partying in Miami?"

Effortlessly, without even having to think, I'm back to casual cool. He's flying off the handle, and I'm Teflon. I think it's triggered by the tone of his voice.

"Jealous much?" I chuckle.

"Fuck you, Trip. When are you coming back to the city?"

"Possibly never. I forgot how relaxing Palm Beach is. Did you know it's sea turtle nesting season here?"

Grish's cynical laugh rolls through the line, and I remember why I like this guy. As pissed as he is at me, he can still manage to laugh. Because he knows as well as I do, in the end, it's all bullshit.

The fact he's freaked out, however, has me on edge.

"I can just see it now." The hint of a Russian accent laces his words. He's been in the states a while, but he'll never lose that accent. "The ice-cold asshole melted by baby sea turtles trying to escape the big, bad hawks. Did you find a heart tumbling in the surf?"

"Nah, I'll leave that for the tourists." Sliding my hand along the leather steering wheel, I cruise up the beach highway. "I'm just here for the party, remember?"

All levity leaves his tone. "Simon Petrovich is coming to town. Do you know who that is?"

"I do not." My tone is indifferent.

"He's someone you never, *never* want to fuck with. He's an oligarch. Tell me you know what that is."

"I know it's someone with enough money he shouldn't care about us."

"He cares about anyone who threatens his power. He cares about his money and who owes him, which means he's coming for Hana."

The mention of Hana cramps my stomach. Still… "What does this have to do with me? I have no dealings with this man."

"Only because I shielded you."

"More like you used me." Don't get me wrong. I like Grish, but I have no illusions about our friendship. "By the way, who the fuck is Andre Bertonelli, and why do you have him shadowing me?"

Silence fills the car, and when he answers, he sounds genuinely confused. "I don't know anyone named Andre. Why would you think that?"

"He said he was keeping tabs on me for you. You're saying he was lying?"

"I'm saying I don't know anyone by that name." He exhales a laugh. "And I don't like you enough to keep tabs on you."

"Why am I having trouble believing you?"

"Probably because you've been out of town too long."

My brow furrows, and I think about him lurking in the shadows at The Rhino, touching Gia. Touching what's mine.

"Why would he lie about something I could disprove so easily?

"Maybe he didn't think you'd ask me. Maybe he didn't think you'd believe me if I said it was a lie." Impatience enters his tone. "Is that where we are now?"

My jaw tightens, and I consider this. Grish is a major-league criminal and a cold-hearted asshole. He says we're the same, but he's the champion of the freeze. Still, he's always been straight with me. I've always known I can trust him. There's no honor among thieves, but we're not thieves. We're survivors.

"No."

"Good." He hesitates, thinking. "He's probably one of Simon's men."

"Why would a Russian oligarch I've never heard of have someone shadowing me?"

"Because you're a mystery? Because you're enmeshed in the Manhattan elite, and he's searching for a weakness?"

Shock flashes in my chest, and I momentarily lose track of what he's saying. All I can think about is my beautiful Gia.

"...I need you back here yesterday. Simon is calling everyone to New York for a meeting. I need you there at my side."

"I don't work for Simon Petrovich. I have no reason to meet him."

"Remember the deal we did with Shadow of the Moon?"

"I had nothing to do with that. I don't trade in horse doping."

"You introduced me to Charles van Hamilton. It was his horse. You're in this."

Charles van Hamilton is a name I don't like hearing. He's Blake and Hana's father, and he was a royal fuck-up. He lost all his money gambling, and then he started spending money he didn't have. Then he used his youngest daughter as a marker. Then he turned up dead.

"You're my wingman, Trip. I need you to have my back. You're one of the few people these guys are hesitant to kill."

"That's not encouraging." They can still hurt me, and now Andre knows how. Pain leaches through my stomach, and I take the next turn before exhaling. "I can't come back to Manhattan right now. I'm in the middle of something here."

"Franco can handle it. Come back for a few days to stand at my side when I face this guy. You owe me that much."

"I don't owe you anything. We're free agents."

"No one is a free agent in this town. If you turn your back on me now, when I need you the most, it'll damage our relationship."

Fuck. "You're not threatening me, Gregory."

"Listen, if you're worried about this Andre character, you can confront him here. If he's one of Simon's guys, he'll come when he's called like a good dog."

Tightening my jaw, he has a point. If he's right.

"Give me a few hours to see what I can set up. I'm not leaving if I don't feel like things are under control here."

"I'll see you tomorrow."

The line goes dead, and my fists tighten on the steering wheel. *Fuck fuck fuck.*

"Why can't I go with you to Manhattan?" The way Gia says *Manhattan* with her cute Italian accent makes me want to say fuck them all. I'm never leaving her.

If only my life were that simple.

"Not this time, angel." I'm packing a small bag that will fit easily in an overhead compartment. I can't believe I'm flying commercial, but it's the only way I can get there and back in the timeframe I want.

"But I want to meet your friends. I want to see the city."

"I know, and we'll have time for that one day." *I hope.* "I'm just making a quick trip. I'll be back before you miss me."

"I miss you already." Her glossy lips pout, and I reach for her, pulling her petite, luscious body to mine.

"I'll miss you, too. I'll be thinking about you the whole time, and I'll text you every night."

"You'll text me," she sniffs. "I'll still be out of your sight."

She's using my words against me. The reason I wanted her to move into my place was so I could have her in my sight at all times. I kiss the top of her head.

"Franco has strict orders to keep you safe. If I didn't trust him, I wouldn't go." Hooking my finger under her chin, I kiss her pillow lips. "Don't worry, my beautiful girl. You are always on my mind."

It's not a lie.

"Isn't that what Elvis said to Priscilla?" Her eyebrow arches.

"*Were*. There's a big difference in *were* and *are*."

"English is so tricky." She shakes her head, but I catch her arm, pulling her to me for one final embrace

"Gia." I inhale the honeysuckle in her hair. "You are the only one on my mind."

She doesn't come with me to the airport. She's checking on her Private Eyes account, and I have Franco, DJ, and another bouncer named Kip watching over her at all times.

Still, as I take my seat in first class on the nonstop flight to Manhattan, I can't help feeling like I'm leaving my heart in south Florida. I can't help noting I've never felt this way before. I've never cared about leaving anywhere or anyone—in fact, I'm typically all too ready to move on to the next place.

Not this time.

This time it's different… and that worries me.

Three hours later, I'm touching down at LaGuardia, retrieving my bag from the overhead bin and walking out to meet my car. I'll be at the Andover by ten. As soon as my phone makes connection, it lights up.

One text is from Grish, saying to let him know as soon as I land. I'll let him know when I get to the apartment building.

The next is from my girl, and the surge in my chest at the mere sight of her words rattles me.

I used to dream of dancing in New York as Clara in the Nutcracker. She sent this an hour after my flight took off.

As I wait for the car, I quickly tap back, *You'd be amazing, but I think you'd be happier in Miami. More fun.*

I hit send and check in with the limo driver. I don't know him, and it'll take almost an hour to get to my apartment. Settling into the back of the ride, I retrieve a tumbler from the mini bar and pour myself a vodka and soda.

If I have to be here, it's time to check in with friends. *Just landed at LGA. Quick visit to town. You around?* I hit send, wondering if she's home, and how long it'll take for a response.

Gray dots float at once, and Hana's text appears on my screen. *Finally! Debbie wanted to check out this new place, the Beatbox, but we'll wait for you if you want to join?*

Twisting my wrist, I check the time. It's after one, and I won't get to the apartment until almost two. *Carry on without me*, I reply. *We'll catch up tomorrow.*

I can see she's answering, and as I wait, I get one more text from my girl. *Your bed is very big without you in it.*

Sliding my finger over the face, I think about her alone in my bed. *Wish I were there to make it feel smaller.*

Hana's reply interrupts our conversation. *You're getting old, chairman. See you tomorrow.*

Tomorrow, I reply.

Only, tomorrow turns into tonight when I arrive at my mother's apartment to find she has company. I hear the moans and turn on the landing, heading back out and up the flight of stairs.

I really need to get my own place, I text Hana.

Her reply is almost as annoying as my welcome home. *Oh, your mom came back early.*

Thanks for the heads up. I'm not smiling.

Gray dots, then her reply. **We're a block away. Crash at our place.**

I always do, I think, sliding the loose sconce above their door to the side, I retrieve the hidden key and unlock the door. I return the key before entering the empty van Hamilton apartment. Their mother is in St. Moritz—which is where Cheryl should be.

I go straight to the minibar and pour another vodka.

"Bestie, you're home!" Hana's high, soft voice reaches me before she does, arms open wide.

"I might as well be," I grumble, returning her hug.

"I'm sorry." She makes a pouty face. "Someone posted a photo of your mom getting snuggly with her ski instructor on Instagram, and it caused friction with her boys in New York. She flew back yesterday to smooth their ruffled feathers."

"I almost caught the live show."

She giggles, and I take another sip of my vodka to drown the growl in my chest.

"Debbie distracted me or I'd have told you."

"Shut up, beesh, I did not!" Debbie yells from the kitchen, and it sounds like her mouth is full. She sticks her head around the corner and blinks a thick black eyelash at me. "Hello, lover-boy, I'm making sugar cookies. Want one?"

"No." My reply is flat, and Hana snorts a laugh. I squint, leaning closer to her face. "What did you take tonight?"

Her eyes go wide, and she holds a finger over her mouth. "Shh!"

"Trip, what a surprise." Blake breezes into the living room. "Back on our couch?"

"Trust me, I'm as happy about it as you are." *As in, not at all.*

Hana's older sister is dressed in a white velour track suit that shows off her full breasts and round ass, and her dark hair is pulled up on top of her head.

While Hana is waifish and dresses like circa-1990s Kate Moss in black tanks and jeans or a little black dress with pale lips and eternally smudged eyeliner, Blake is modern and curvy and always impeccably styled.

Debbie is somewhere in between. Her wild, strawberry-blonde hair is thickened by extensions, her makeup is simply a bold red lip, and she always wears Versace. When Grish starts acting up, she pretends to be sleeping with me, which I find annoying, but it keeps my mother from throwing eligible young socialites at me. So I've allowed it.

"I'm so happy you're back." Hana bounces on her toes, kissing my cheek before skipping in the direction of the kitchen where her friend is baking. "Let's do lunch tomorrow, okay?"

"Sure. I have some business with Grish if I'm not here when you wake up." Which I expect will be closer to dinnertime.

"It is late?" Blake tucks her bag under her arm, glancing at the clock. "Or is it early? I'm sure you know where to get whatever you need?"

"I don't need much." She nods, and I stop her. "Tell me, B, why don't you ever go to St. Moritz with the moms?"

She studies me then shakes her head. "For a minute, I thought you were serious. You know those women make me itch."

"You never date." I slide my blazer off my shoulders. "You know what they say about all work and no play."

"Hana plays enough for the both of us. As for dating, when you find a good man in our crowd, let me know. I'm not holding my breath. Or wasting my time."

Can't argue with that, still. "One of these days, you'll have to let down your guard or you'll end up alone."

"If I need dating advice, dear Trip, I'll be sure and ask for it."

I hold up both hands in surrender, and she breezes down the hallway in the direction of her bedroom.

Hana and Debbie are giggling and speaking in low voices in the kitchen, and the scent of sugar cookies drifts through the air. In the past, I would've gone in there with them, but tonight my mind is far away with Gia. I miss her, and I'm not looking forward to the meeting I'm attending with Grish tomorrow.

I step out of my shoes and place my jacket on the back of a chair, then I wrap a fleece blanket around my shoulders and prepare to sleep on their generous, leather couch. It isn't the welcome home I'd imagined, but perhaps it should've been.

It's a reminder of why I'm working so hard to get out of here. Blake's right, this is no place for roots.

CHAPTER 22

Trip

Gibson's is a cigar bar in the basement of a storefront in the Financial District. I don't know who the actual owner is, but Grish has managed it as long as I've been here.

Whoever pays the bills clearly slips an extra thousand or so to the chief of police, because smoking is banned in all bars and restaurants in New York City. But in Gibson's, with its wine-colored leather furniture, carpeted walls, and heavy velvet curtains, the air is thick with spicy cigar smoke.

Frank Sinatra croons over the house speakers, and the counters are lined with whiskey and bourbon and assorted spirits. The atmosphere is something out of a mafia movie, and hidden behind the curtains are round, leather booths where all varieties of dirty deals are made.

I usually hang around the brass-studded, wooden bar while women in high-fashion, skimpy cocktail dresses drift through the room carrying glasses of champagne in their slim hands. Their hair is perfect, their makeup on point, and it's hard to tell which are escorts for hire and which are socialites looking to hook up.

At this time of evening, the club is closed to the public. Members only. The beefy guy at the door nods for us to enter, and when we descend the stairs, a new crowd of well-dressed, eastern-European types are standing at the bar. I assume they're Russian, as we've all been summoned by Simon, but they could be Romanian, Czech, Ukrainian, or even from Belarus.

"That's him." Grish's voice is low, and he nods to a small-ish man sitting in one of the round booths as if he's holding court. "Stay with me. I'll do my best to keep you out of the conversation."

I'm about to tell him I'm not afraid of these guys when my eyes land on Andre standing at the bar, and my insides flash. He smirks, and my surprise turns into fire burning at the base of my throat.

Grish gives no indication he recognizes any of the men at the bar, and I decide he was telling the truth about Andre. This guy is tracking me for Simon, the small man with blond hair and cold blue eyes. The one who doesn't smile, and looks like he orders hits as easily as he orders shots of vodka.

"Gregory, good of you to join us." His greeting is cordial enough, if it weren't for the lack of emotion on his face and the fact Grish was ordered to appear. "You've gotten into some trouble, it seems."

Grish tugs on the front of his dark brown suit coat before sitting on the edge of the booth. Grish is slim with blond hair and eyes black as coal. His smile reveals a few too many teeth, and the combination gives him the appearance of evil.

Some say he's sneaky, but I know Greg Peters doesn't need to sneak. He has thugs right where he needs them at all times. He might not be up to this guy's level, but he's working hard to get there.

"I did nothing wrong." My friend's voice is flat, but his cadence is slightly faster than usual. "It was the vet your men chose. I didn't approve him. I'd never worked with him before, and he used the wrong dosage."

"He has paid for his mistake. You, however, have not."

I've never seen Grish sweat. I've never seen him be anything but steely calm. Unlike me, his demeanor is based on menace. I prefer to have a little fun, laugh at the bullies. It pisses them off when I smile instead of fighting or cowering, but it also loosens them up.

Trust me, being underestimated is extremely useful when you run with criminals.

"I've managed your businesses for five years, and I've made them profitable. I've been a loyal soldier." Grish's tone is barely restrained rage. "This is the thanks I get? One strike, and I'm out?"

The smile that curls Simon Petrovich's mouth makes his thin lips disappear. It makes me want to fade into the thick velvet surrounding the table. I know the hidden rooms in this place, and it feels like a good time to hide.

"Are you attempting to tell me what to do?"

"I'm asking why loyalty isn't valued anymore."

"Loyalty. Perhaps you simply need a reminder not to get too cocky. Nothing you have cannot be taken from you. Including your life." His eyes slide from Grish to me to the big guy sitting beside him in the booth. "Luckily for you, you still have use to me."

"Is that a threat?" Greg's jaw is clenched as he says the words, and his hand moves from the table to his lap.

Every muscle in my body tenses. He doesn't usually carry a gun, but considering our errand tonight, that practice might have changed. Simon doesn't even flinch.

His cold eyes instead move to me. "Who is this? I don't recall saying you could bring a friend."

My shoulders relax, and I smile. "Mr. Petrovich, I'm William Alexander the third. Call me Trip." Holding out a hand, I lean forward to shake.

His eyes briefly drop to my gesture before returning to mine. I straighten, sliding my unshaken hand down the front of my dark gray suit coat.

"Perhaps you would be more comfortable at the bar while we finish here." It's not a request.

I give an easy nod. "I'm a bit parched now that you mention it. See you in a minute, Grish."

I'll get the full story from him later, and I actually would like to go to the bar. I've got some business with Andre, who's still watching us with that stupid smirk and glittering brown eyes.

"Vodka, neat." The bartender immediately sets to work on my order, and I turn to Andre. "Funny seeing you here."

"We come when we're called, don't we, Mr. Alexander?" His accent is thick, and his voice is deeper now, unlike in Palm Beach.

Now I'm wondering if all the shit he pulled at The Rhino was an act, but why? Was he trying to send me a message? Was he trying to show I couldn't stop him from touching what was mine, even with all the security we used? I don't like it.

I also don't like his implication that I'm on Simon's call list.

"The only person who called me was Greg Peters, and the only reason he called is because he's apparently on the hook for a lot of money."

"Too bad. The boss invested millions in Shadow of the Moon, and he lost it all. Not to mention, the horse can't run or breed now. He's worthless."

I lift the vodka and take a drink. "Put him out to pasture."

"We're making what we can on dog food and glue."

My stomach turns. These people have no souls. They use animals the same way they use people, and when their usefulness is done, they cut up the corpse and sell it for parts.

"I told you in Florida, you're fired. I'm not on Petrovich's payroll. Why are you keeping tabs on me?"

"You might not be on his payroll, but you are in this."

Andre polishes off his vodka drink, giving me an evil grin. "I'm simply keeping track of the things you cherish, things you wouldn't want damaged or destroyed."

Fury erupts in my chest, and my poker face is gone. He was there for Gia's last performance, and he watched me carry her off the stage. He knows what I cherish.

Slamming the glass on the polished bar, I step to him, my voice a barely contained growl. "You touch one hair on her head, and I'll make sure you die slowly, one piece at a time."

His eyes flash, and he nods, grinning wider. "Sounds like for both our sakes, you'd better stay in line."

My blood flames hotter with every heartbeat, and the back of my neck sweats. I'm ready to get out of here, to get back to south Florida before this guy does.

Grish stands at that moment and gives me the signal to go. I shoot the rest of my vodka, doing my best to recover my calm disposition. I thank the bartender, leave a tip, and turn my back on Andre without another word. He won't leave New York as long as Simon is here, and I need Grish to tell me how much longer that will be.

We're on the street, and my friend fills me in. "He's giving me three weeks to come up with the money. I need to meet up with Ivan and the other guys to see where we can put our hands on some quick cash. You coming with me?"

"No." I shake my head. "I've done enough for one night. I'm headed back to the Andover, then I'm returning to West Palm."

Famous last words.

I haven't been to The Vogue in two years, and I don't particularly want to be here tonight. However, when I got back to the apartment, ready to change my return flight to Florida to now,

Hana stopped me, saying we should go out since I stood her up for our lunch date.

I noted she wasn't awake at what is universally considered *lunchtime* (not even close). Instead, I pulled up the flight schedules on my phone, searching every possible airline. I was willing to fly coach, but when I saw I wasn't getting out of the city tonight, I relented to her begging. At least I know Andre isn't going anywhere tonight.

Debbie claimed to be feeling under the weather, so it's the rare occasion where Blake, Hana, and I are out together, just the three of us. Blake is dressed in a light brown tank and jeans, and she keeps checking her phone while she nurses a glass of white wine. She's only here to keep an eye on her sister, something she's been doing more and more, from what I understand.

Hana's on her third cosmo. She's dressed in a flesh-colored sheath dress with tiny sparkles all over it. If she had any curves at all, it would remind me of Gia's last dance, but Hana still has her ballerina figure, even though she abruptly quit dancing at thirteen and started partying.

I'm pretty sure it had something to do with her mother's accountant Victor, who took over running the family finances after her father died. That creep was always sniffing around the sisters, trying to touch them. If I'd been a little older… hell, I don't know. I was only fifteen and managing my own adult "admirer."

"What's so interesting in south Florida all of a sudden, anyway?" Hana shimmies over to where I'm sitting, phone in hand.

"You'd be surprised." I'm nursing a vodka neat while keeping tabs on what's happening at Gibson's.

One of the doormen is a friend, and he promised to text if the Russians cleared out tonight. Actually, I slipped him a hundred, and he's keeping me apprised on anything that happens there tonight. So far it's been pretty quiet.

I've been so preoccupied, I haven't checked in with Gia. I also haven't heard from her. I'd be worried if I didn't know

Andre is still at Gibson's and Franco promised he'd keep her safe, although I'm not sure Franco's ready for this level of thuggery.

I'm not sure I am.

"Did you meet somebody?" Hana perches on the arm of my chair, and my eyes drift to the dance floor then up to her as I consider her question.

"No." The fewer people who know about Gia, the better.

I'm not worried so much about Hana spreading gossip, but she might say something to Debbie. Then everyone would know. Hell, Debbie would probably say I had broken her heart and gotten engaged.

Hesitating over this, I realize the thought of being engaged to Gia makes me calm. It's a life I could see myself living happily for the rest of my days. My stomach twists with dread as I realize Andre is right. I'll do anything to protect her, and he knows it.

"Yes, what *are* your interests in Miami?" Blake turns her attention to me. "I swear, I have no idea what you do anymore since you dropped out of Columbia."

Blake and I were both enrolled at that prestigious university here in town. I realized halfway through my degree I didn't need it. I have enough connections to make my own deals in this city.

I think for Blake, a college degree set her apart from the other party girls. She despises that scene, and she's smart enough to stay out of it.

Still, for whatever reason, she feels responsible for what happens to our fragile, China doll, and it keeps her hanging around, even though her massive trust fund would allow her to live wherever she wanted.

"China Girl," I say, holding up a crisp twenty to Hana. "And anything else you want."

"Yes!" She immediately snatches the bill and dashes off in the direction of the jukebox.

"Is it classified information?" Blake is watching me with those intense, gray-blue eyes.

"I have a few investments in West Palm." I'm not interested in Blake knowing my business, so I quickly turn the questions around. "Are you still modeling?"

"Of course not." She slides her smooth dark hair behind her shoulder. "I only did that to cover the bills until I turned twenty-one."

Twenty-one would be when her trust fund matured. I lift my chin in understanding.

Blake and I have a tenuous relationship. She doesn't trust me, and I've never given her a reason to. We could be friends. She made certain choices to remain independent, and now I'm making my own. She's smart, but I don't need a fucking guilt trip.

Her eyes drift down to her buzzing phone, and when she picks it up, her brow furrows as if she's confused by what she's seeing. Then her thumb begins tapping on the screen.

"Not bad news, I hope?" I've grown up with these girls, so I know everyone they know.

She doesn't answer, and I see from the light flickering, her phone screen is loading a video site. I take another drink of vodka as her lips tighten. She swipes her finger up the phone face then slams it down on her clutch on the table, eyes searching the room.

"Where did Hana go?" she snaps.

I don't care for her tone, but I let it pass. "I sent her to the jukebox. House music is better if it's mixed with other genres."

"We need to leave. Now." She stands, and I lower my foot to the floor. "I'm calling the car. You can stay if you want."

I stand beside her, chuckling as I polish off my drink. "Are you kidding? I didn't want to come here in the first place."

Hana bounces up looking a little glassy-eyed. "Are we dancing?" Her voice is high, artificially happy.

Hana will break your heart if you let her.

"We're going home." Blake's voice is stern, and her sister's smile turns upside down.

"No!" she cries. "I just played a bunch of fun songs. We have to wait for them."

"We can listen to them in the car." Blake picks up Hana's wrap and drapes it around her shoulders. "I've got a migraine."

Hana looks to me with her pleading face, and I shrug. "Can't argue with a migraine. They're a bitch from what I hear."

Her shoulders fall with her exhale. "I hate when everybody gets sick the night I want to dance."

Sliding my arm around her narrow waist, I pull her in for a side hug. "I'll play your songs in the car. What's up first?"

"China Girl." She's still pouting, but I'm searching for the song on my phone.

We spend the short drive uptown listening to Bowie. It's a rainy night, and the wet pavement shines black while the streetlamps bathe them in gold. It's beautiful, but when you step out, it smells like a wet dog.

The limo pulls up to the Andover, and Blake opens the door as we slow to a stop. She's clearly pissed and ready to get inside, but she freezes in place when she steps out of the car.

"What the hell?" Her voice is soft.

Leaning forward, I see the flashing red and blue lights streaking the sky and the buildings around us. My first thought is *police raid*, but they wouldn't raid the Andover. One of the older tenants must've had a heart attack or someone's stuck in an elevator.

Hana bolts out of the car without looking and bumps into her sister. "Oops! Sorry, Blake."

She giggles, clearly buzzed, and I put a hand on her hip, moving her to the side so I can exit the town car. A crowd is forming, which means whatever it is just happened.

Police officers are creating a perimeter, holding up their hands to back people up, and TMZ and the rest of the media are already on the scene, jumping out of vans or racing up on bikes with their cameras ready.

I don't see any damaged cars, so it's not a wreck. An officer stretching yellow crime tape draws my attention, and that's when I see the dark lump lying on the sidewalk in front of our building.

A clump of black-uniformed cops are talking nearby, but the blood drains from my face when I look closer. A thick, strawberry-blonde braid is not completely covered by the black tarp they've haphazardly spread over the victim.

Thin, pale arms and bare legs are spread and bent in odd angles, but the thing I don't want to recognize, what makes ice filter through my chest, is the gold and black robe with the distinct Versace pattern surrounding the body.

"Debbie?" Blake's voice cracks as we all realize it's our friend.

She's lying face up in the gutter, on the steps of our beautiful building, broken with dark red liquid seeping from her mouth and nose.

No. A growl, tightens my jaw, and I push past the girls. "What the fuck?"

I bolt to where the police are forming a line no one can cross, doing my best to get to her.

"It's a crime scene, sir. You have to stay back." I don't even look at the officer's face as he grips my shoulders, moving me away.

A uniformed woman does a better job of covering Debbie's body, but I hear Hana behind me. "I don't understand... What's happening?"

Blake has her sister, turning her from the grizzly sight. Lying on the sidewalk between me and them is a fluffy, white Louboutin slipper with Debbie's initials stitched in black cursive across the band. An invisible hand tightens around my throat, and I try not to imagine how it flew off her foot as she fell to her death.

More police cars arrive and an ambulance, and there's nothing I can do to help her now. I go to where the sisters are making their way into our apartment building.

Hana looks from me to her sister. "Why is it a crime scene?"

"It's illegal to kill yourself in Manhattan." My voice is mirthless, almost sarcastic, because we all know our friend didn't kill herself.

I'm the only one who might know why this happened, but I can't be sure. What I am sure of is I need a drink right now.

I'm pretty confident none of us sleep. As the sun rises and the breakfast cart arrives, Hana replaces me on the couch, gold facial strips under her red-rimmed eyes.

"It had to be an accident." Her voice is shaky from crying. "She just bought a closet full of designer dresses during fashion week. We were talking about all the parties we would attend at Cannes."

A copy of the Times is on the cart, and when I lift it, my jaw clenches at the headline. "*Debbie Does Death*? Seriously?"

The story is below the fold, still, that idiotic headline is plastered over three columns along with an unflattering photo of Debbie at a bar on one of her worse nights.

"I guess that's what passes for clever these days." Blake walks to where I'm standing, then turns away from the news.

She goes to the window, looking out at our view of Central Park.

It's a practice I understand. Sometimes looking down at all the people on the street, knowing there are hundreds of neighborhoods in this city where none of this happens, where people live good, happy lives, have children, grow old. Somehow it puts all our bullshit in the appropriate little box where it belongs.

I return the paper to the cart, which also holds three plated omelets with sausage. Assorted breads and fruit are in baskets beside carafes of coffee and juice—as if any of us has an appetite.

Uncrossing her arms, Blake goes to the bar, taking a bottle of expensive vodka from the small refrigerator and pouring two fingers, neat.

"Would you make one for me, Blake?" Hana holds out her hand.

"Me, too."

Blake's lips tighten, but she prepares two more drinks. "Has anyone told her mother?"

"I'm sure the authorities will find her." Belinda is the least of my concerns.

Blake levels her gaze on me. "Shouldn't you check on your own mother?"

"God, no." My mother only cares about two things, and they're both probably in her bed.

I'm rebooking my flight home when the door bursts open, and my stomach roils. Natasha Sidoro bursts into the room with her undreaged minion Rainey at her side.

"O, em, gee, Blake! Did she really throw herself off the balcony in nothing but her Louboutin slippers?" Natasha is annoying as fuck.

She's a scheming little climber vying to take over running Gibson's and who knows what else. She thinks she can join the ranks of the criminal underworld. I have no idea what Rainey wants.

Blake quickly kills that rumor. "She was wearing her Versace robe."

"She was always such a drama queen." Rainey's tone is bored.

Hana stands, lifting her chin. "I'm going to my room. It's stuffy in here."

"Perhaps you should try coffee for breakfast," Natasha quips, and I want to throw her out myself.

The girls discuss the possibility of suicide, as if we all don't know better. Debbie was a party girl, but she was always in control. I need to find Grish. I need to know if Simon did this. I need to know if Grish had any warning it was going to happen.

I need to know how much danger I've placed Gia in.

"How well do we truly know anyone anymore?" Natasha laments as if she cares.

Blake asks before I have the chance, "Where's Greg?"

"Oh, you know Grisha." Natasha waves her hand, plucking a strawberry off the breakfast cart. "He's not one for big family gatherings."

"It's not a family gathering. It's a wake," Blake notes coldly. "He's supposed to be her boyfriend."

"Will they have a funeral?" I polish off my vodka and do my best to pretend I don't care. I need these girls to think I'm far removed from what just happened, which unfortunately, might not be true. "Their family tradition is cremation."

"Is that a tradition?" Rainey snorts a laugh, and Blake's eyes narrow.

Blake is barely containing her disgust with these two, but I need to find out what they know. Natasha always sticks close to Grish at Gibson's. She was probably there last night, and I need to connect the dots. Where was he?

Blake leaves the room, going to the small table in the foyer, as Natasha and Rainey continue to conjecture, making snarky comments and plucking items off the breakfast cart like vultures on a carcass.

When Blake returns, she's holding an ivory linen envelope. "Why don't you all go home?"

It's all I need to make my exit.

I place my empty tumbler on the table and pause. I'm ready to get out of here, but I don't like leaving my friends this way. "Let me know if you need anything."

"I don't need anything." Blake's posture is straight, and I glance at what she's holding.

As previously noted, Blake is smart. She's very capable of ensuring her safety and taking Hana with her. Hana will do whatever her sister says. It appears she has a plan, and so do I.

Turning, I wrap my arms around Natasha and Rainey as if I'm ready to get plastered. As if I have no feelings, no involvement, no worries. It's my mask.

"Come, girls. Time for an Irish wake."

CHAPTER 23

Trip

WE TAKE A CAB TO GRISH'S LOFT IN SOHO, A THIRD-FLOOR WALK-up on Prince Street.

He's not home when we arrive, so we let ourselves in. Natasha has a key to his apartment, which I find unusual, but Rainey acts like is the sort of thing that happens every day.

I file that detail away for later. I don't give a shit if Grish is fucking Natasha or Rainey or both of them. It's not my concern. My focus is on finding out what really happened to Debbie and who is involved—and how bad of a situation I'm in.

The loft is a single, long room divided into thirds by exposed brick half-walls. The front is the kitchen-dining area, and the middle is a living room with the bedroom all the way in the back by the picture window overlooking the street below.

Natasha goes to the kitchen and takes down a bottle of Mamont, which I know is his favorite Russian vodka, a very expensive brand. She pours two tumblers. Rainey apparently isn't underage drinking for once.

"Where's Grish?" I tilt the tumbler side to side, doing my best to keep up my careless, detached vibe.

Natasha walks around, pulling a book out of the built-in bookcases. "He said he'd be here soon. I texted him on the drive over."

"Does he know about Debbie?" Rainey's voice is small and hushed, like it's a secret.

"I'm sure he read the paper today." Nat's head tilts to the side. "Yeah, he wouldn't have read the paper. Maybe he saw it on his phone? I don't know."

I'm not particularly interested in being the one to break the news his girlfriend is dead, but we're here now. The best I can hope for is to pump the girls for information, not that I expect them to have any.

"For a proper Irish wake," I act like I'm thinking about it, "we all have to share our fondest memory of the deceased. What's your best memory of Debbie?"

Natasha's face scrunches as she thinks, but Rainey rushes right in.

"One time, when I was getting out of a cab, the driver's foot must've slipped off the brake or something because it started to move on me. I almost fell, but Debbie ran in front of the cab and beat on the hood. She yelled at him for being an asshole." Rainey's chin dropped. "I don't think she even knew who I was. She was just cool like that."

"She was probably high." Natasha's tone is dismissive. "Debbie loved to play the role of the tough girl when she was stoned."

She rolls her eyes, another mental note. I didn't know Natasha paid so much attention to Debbie's behavior. I wonder if it had anything to do with Grish. I feel like a window has been opened, perhaps a clue I've ignored in the past.

I'm not ignoring it now.

"Did you have a fond memory of Debbie, Nat?" My tone is teasing, and her face blanches at my suggestion.

I never liked Natasha. Now I think she's a shallow, self-centered cunt, who possibly knows more than she's saying.

"Debbie was a drug addict with a big mouth." Natasha levels her eyes on me, and I think she knows I'm fishing for clues and isn't intimidated. "She was entitled. She had no qualifications to do anything, and I'm not surprised she finally looked herself in the mirror and realized the world was better off without her."

"Nat!" Rainey gasps, crossing herself. "How can you say something like that?"

"Very easily and with very little remorse. Debbie was a thorn in my side for too long."

I'm ready to dig deeper into this, but the door opens, and Grish steps inside quickly. I catch the panicked expression on his face the half-second before he realizes we're all here.

The moment he sees us, his mask of cold indifference snaps into place.

"To what do I owe the pleasure of this visit?" He slides his hand down the front of the same brown blazer he was wearing when I left him last night. *Interesting.*

He hasn't been home since we parted ways.

"Oh, Grisha!" Rainey closes the space between them, walking straight into his arms and burying her face in his chest. She sniffles like a little girl, before finishing. "You don't know? You really don't know?"

My friend's body stiffens, and he catches Rainey by the upper arms, moving her off him. "What do you think I don't know?"

Rainey's chin wobbles, and she pulls her bottom lip under her teeth with a sharp inhale. "It's Debbie. She's dead."

Grish's eyes slide closed, and his chin drops. "I heard she was dead."

Walking slowly to the kitchen, he pours himself a tumbler of vodka. I don't miss the look he exchanges with Natasha as he passes. She shrugs and walks away, through the living room area into the bedroom, stopping at the window overlooking the street below.

I turn to Grish. "Do you know how it happened?"

"How would I know that?" His black eyes glitter.

"You don't seem as upset as I'd expect."

"How the fuck would you know, Trip? You've never loved anything."

My gaze drops, and all I can think about is Gia. He has no idea, and I need to keep it that way. Her mere association with me is enough to put a target on her back… or her forehead. Or the middle of her chest.

All three possibilities nearly drive me to my knees, but I hold it together.

Grish, however, doesn't miss a thing. "You'd better get rid of whatever that is fast if you know what's good for you."

"I don't know what you're talking about." I exhale a laugh, taking another drink of my vodka.

He lets it go, but Rainey is watching, making me uncomfortable. She always acts like an air-headed little minion, but I have a feeling it's a cover. We all have our masks, and she knows more than she lets on.

Hell, maybe I'm just paranoid. Rainey isn't old enough to be part of this gang. She can't even drink without a fake ID. I need to get Grish alone.

Before I do, however. "I need the john."

He motions to the living room. "You know where it is."

I place my empty tumbler on the table and make my way to the small, closet restroom, closing the door and turning on the tap. There's no fan or anything, so I flush the toilet to hide the noise as I slide to the floor.

I can't act anymore. My insides are tight and twisting tighter. Grish is acting tough, but fear was in his eyes when he walked through that door. I saw it.

Pressing the heels of my palms against my eyes, I fight this onslaught of emotion. Debbie was my friend. We grew up together, and even if she drove me crazy, I can't get that image of her on the concrete out of my head.

She was thrown to her death, and all I can hear is Andre's warning about the things I cherish.

Breathing deeply, I struggle for control, but it's slipping through my fingers.

Anxiety has a tight grip on my throat. I think about everything Andre has done over the last few weeks, from demonstrating how easily he could get to Gia in the club to returning her stolen shoe at the condo. He wants me to know he can get to her wherever she is.

Gia's Number 1 fan is my Number 1 nightmare. I won't let him hurt her, but there's no way I can be with her at all times. I have only one solution, and every time I think about it, my stomach revolts.

A tap on the door precedes Rainey's small voice. "You okay in there?"

Twisting my wrist, I check my watch and push to standing. A glance in the mirror affirms my mask is back in place, and I turn off the water.

"Sorry," I step out. "I just realized I have to go."

"Go?" Grish's brow furrows, and he watches as I collect my overcoat.

"I'll be back tomorrow—possibly the next day. I just have one loose thread to cut."

Our eyes meet, and I'm pretty sure he understands.

I leave them without another word.

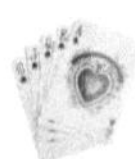

Leaning forward in my first-class seat, racing to the southern tip of the country, my life drains from my limbs in the face of what I must do. There's no way around it.

It's my fault. I dared to reach for happiness. I recklessly

grabbed it with both hands when I had no right to touch. It was forbidden, but I broke the rules.

My choices put me here. The life I've made for myself dictates I must be alone. Happiness, relationships, love, they're the price I pay to be who I am, to have what I have. Grish knew it. I know it. Never give them something they can use against you.

I selfishly put her in danger, and there's only one way to get her out, to keep her safe.

It's time to do what's right, to play the hardest hand I've been dealt. I should have tapped out when I had the chance, but I didn't. Now I only hope I'm convincing enough to make it work.

They have to believe me. Everyone has to believe me.

It's the only way to save her life.

CHAPTER 24

Gia

AN OLD SONG IS TRAPPED IN MY HEAD AS I BREEZE THROUGH TRIP'S penthouse apartment. It's an old song about stupidly saying *I love you*, and I've been humming, floating on clouds of happiness, a silly grin on my face, since I got his text that he's flying home early.

Stupid or not, tonight, I'm going to say it.

I bought five-dollar bouquets of fresh flowers, which I've arranged in every room. I've got my homemade marinara sauce simmering on the stove. The entire apartment smells delicious, and I've hand-rolled pasta and sent it through the machine that cuts it into perfect spaghetti. To think in the past, we did this by hand.

I remember how much he loved it the last time I made it for him. And yes, after only three days, I've missed him so much, I've turned into a complete, utterly smitten girlfriend, racking my brains to remember every single thing he loves.

My hair is piled high on my head, my red wrap dress is loose on my body, and I'm not wearing a bra—all things I know lead to lots of orgasms for me. I exhale a laugh as I lift the lid to give the sauce a stir and a taste.

Okay, so maybe I'm doing all this for me, too.

Lifting my phone, I check the time and read our last text exchange again. It's two days old, but it still gives me a thrill.

He'd sent me the question, *What's your favorite sexual position?*

I'd only taken as long as my fingers needed to reply, *You on top, holding me down.* Then I had a second thought. *Or behind me, filling me up.*

His eggplant emoji reply still makes me laugh, but what he said next made me wet and helped me decide on what to wear tonight. *I like your red wrap dress. I like sliding my hands inside and unwrapping you like a present.*

My chest squeezes, and I go to the bedroom. Taking my honeysuckle cologne from the dresser, I put a drop behind my ears, in the bend of my arm, between my breasts.

Closing my eyes, I dream of his smile, his rough hands, and aggressive kisses. Heat sizzles beneath my skin, and I slide my palms over my flat stomach, wishing they were his, sad he won't be here for at least another hour.

Returning to the kitchen, I switch on the streaming music and lift the lid on the pot again, giving it a stir. I uncork a bottle of red wine and pour myself a glass. I check my Private Eyes account, but I'm all caught up on my messages. I'm caught up on everything.

It's been a busy week with several new accounts. I'm on track to make six figures this month, which I still can't believe. Bianca says I'm a natural, but she's doing pretty well herself, and she never danced.

I've gotten used to the rhythm of the job, and I actually look forward to chatting with a few of the guys. They're sweet, and they only want affirmation, a friend. Anmlvr turned out to be a sensitive soul whose heart breaks whenever he sees a wounded bird or roadkill. I'm pretty confident he's not a serial killer, although I think he could save money by going to therapy rather than talking to me about it.

My Number 1 fan has been strangely silent this week, and I think BigBoi must've gotten busted by his wife, which suits me just fine. I don't like chatting with married men.

I take a long sip of wine, wishing time would hurry up, wondering if I should go over and visit with Bianca, when a sharp rap on the door makes me jump a foot in the air. I'm not expecting anyone.

Walking slowly, I stop at the black wooden barrier and cautiously ask, "Who is it?"

"Gia, open up."

It's Franco, and my shoulders drop as I exhale in relief, quickly turning the bolt. "Hey—"

"I just got off the phone with Trip." Franco enters without any greeting, and my heart beats a little faster. "He asked me to drop off this envelope."

He places a large brown envelope on the table and glances around the room. His dark brow is furrowed, and he seems angry. Or maybe he's worried?

"Is everything okay?" My voice is hesitant, and his dark eyes land on mine.

Something is in his expression I don't like. "Do you have all your things with you here?"

"Yes… I mean, I think so. Bianca might have a few things at the condo, but for the most part—"

"Trip wants you to pack everything in your suitcase. Now."

I'm confused. "I just unpacked my suitcase. Does he want me to move again?"

Franco's jaw tightens, but he doesn't answer. My stomach is in knots when he starts for the door, still not answering.

"Franco!" I hurry after him. "Did something happen?"

He hesitates before leaving. "He'll explain when he gets here. Just do what I said. Lock this door behind me."

With that, he leaves me alone and confused. I turn the

bolt then go to where I left my glass of wine. Taking another sip, I look at the brown envelope bearing Trip's name and consider opening it.

My stomach shivers, and I don't want to invade his privacy. I want to be a good roommate, a good girlfriend, a dream he never wants to lose. Carrying my wine to the bedroom, I hesitate a moment, thinking about this sudden turn of events. Trip didn't seem angry when we were texting, and he never said a word about packing. *What does this mean?*

Slowly, I pull my large suitcase out of the closet where I stashed it and lay it open on the bed. I'll take my time, and if it's something fun, I can always finish fast. Maybe he's taking me on a vacation to get away from whatever he's worried about here.

I can tell him I haven't had any more contact from my Number 1 fan, and maybe that will put his mind at ease. Either way, we can't leave tonight. I made spaghetti. His favorite.

At least packing slowly makes the time pass quickly. I'm skipping into the kitchen in my bare feet again to check the sauce when I hear the bolt move in the door. I let out a little yelp, and my insides squeeze and zip as I replace the lid and slide my hands over my hair, the front of my dress.

It opens, and there he is, as always impeccably dressed in a dark gray suit, collar unbuttoned, hair too long, scruff on his cheeks, taking my breath away.

"Welcome home, Mr. Alexander." My voice has that faint rasp I get when I'm excited or nervous.

Our eyes meet, and his flash with the desire I know so well. It warms my blood, and I close the space between us quickly, wrapping my arms around his neck and pressing my lips to his.

The first thing I notice is he doesn't kiss me back. His lips don't open; there's no hungry devouring. Instead, his hand goes to my waist, and he hesitates briefly before moving me away.

"Giana." His voice is all business, not the way he usually speaks to me, and he leaves his small suitcase just inside the door as he enters the apartment. "Did Franco come here?"

"He did." My voice wobbles, but I do my best to be up-beat. "He was very cryptic. He left an envelope and told me to pack all my things."

"Did you?"

"I started."

Silently, he lifts the brown envelope off the table and opens it, taking out another long envelope like they used to give for airplane tickets. He lowers the parcel to the table, takes a beat, then turns to face me.

"What do you have left to pack?" His eyes are level, the warmth I'm so used to seeing in them extinguished.

"Oh, a few toiletries and shoes. I had just finished moving all my things into your closet." I'm still trying to keep my voice optimistic, but I'm faltering.

"Who told you to do that?" His icy tone makes me nervous.

"You did?"

"I never told you to unpack."

"But you told me to move in here."

"Now it's time for you to go."

My brow furrows. "Go where?"

"You're returning to Italy. Tonight. I have your airline ticket here."

Cold filters through my veins. Panic rises in my neck. *I'm returning to Italy? Just me?*"

"I'm not going with you."

All the air leaves the room. "Did something happen?"

"Yes." His lips curl with a smile that doesn't reach his eyes.

Silence falls between us, and I'm afraid to ask. "What... happened?"

"I discovered you were performing without a work visa. You put my entire business at risk, every single job, all of it. I could've been raided, shut down permanently for hiring an illegal alien."

"But it wasn't your fault." Panic shivers in me. "You didn't know."

"That's right. I never would have jeopardized everything for a *stripper*."

My lips part as the word slices through me like a knife.

"You lied to me, and now it's time for you to go." He turns, striding to his bedroom where my partially packed suitcase is on the bed.

I'm blinking fast, but the tears are coming too quickly for me to stop them. My nose is hot, and I'm trying to see, trying to wipe the moisture from my face. When I reach the room, he's throwing the rest of my things in the open case.

"But what about Bianca? I have to tell her goodbye…"

He doesn't respond. He doesn't even look at me. He continues moving fast, not bothering to fold anything or arrange it in any way.

I'm having trouble breathing as I watch my costumes, my dresses, *slam, slam, slam*, one after the other he throws my things into the suitcase. Then he storms into the bathroom.

Carefully, I creep to the bed, arranging my dresses with trembling fingers. I can't see for the tears burning in my eyes. *Why is he doing this?*

"Put on your shoes," he orders. "You can't walk around like a barefoot peasant at the airport."

Everything he says is a hit to the stomach, a slap to the face.

"Trip, I'm so sorry." I go to where he's standing, trying to wrap my arms around his rigid, unyielding shoulders. "You're right. I should have told you. I was wrong, and I'm so sorry. Please forgive me. Please don't send me away."

Strong hands grasp my arms, removing them from his body. "You knew this would end one day."

"I did?" My voice cracks. "I thought we would go to New York. I thought I would get a job there, dance with the company, pursue my dream."

"What gave you that idea?"

My throat is so dry, I can't answer.

"I don't want *you*." He shakes his head, a cruel smile on

his face. "It was never about you. It was the fantasy, the chase. It was about fucking *Glitter Girl.*"

"I don't believe that!"

He turns, slamming my suitcase closed and zipping it. "Believe it."

"But…" I'm broken, a child begging. "I love you."

For the flash of a second, I think I see him yield. It's gone so fast, I must've imagined it.

He only growls. "Put. On. Your. Shoes."

With those words, my heart dies. Like a dying star, it pulls everything inside me as it collapses. The butterflies are dead. The dreams are ashes. My lungs struggle to expand. My fingers are numb as I put on my sandals, fasten the buckles.

He rolls my suitcase out of the bedroom, not even waiting for me, all the way to the door, passing it to a large man I've never seen before.

"Marco will drive you to the airport, and he'll watch you board the plane." He hands me the brown envelope. "Defy him, and I'll have you forcibly deported."

He's not taking me to the airport. He's throwing me out like garbage.

Oh, God, it's all happening so fast, my head is spinning, my chest is hollow. I can't find my bearings. I can't find anything to hold onto. I'm in the path of a roaring tornado, and it's ripping my world to shreds, destroying everything, tearing it up by the roots and slamming it to the ground.

No…

God, no…

I have to hold on. I have to walk out of here with something, the last shred of my dignity. I'm a dancer, after all. I've spent years training my body to move, even through the worst physical pain, even on bleeding and blistered feet.

Summoning all the strength I have left in the world, I force myself to stand straighter, to face him through the tears, through the invisible nails clawing at my neck.

"You promised you'd never hurt me."

His brow arches, and he exhales a laugh. "I've promised a lot of women a lot of things. Goodbye, Gia."

I collect my phone and my purse off the small table inside the door. "Goodbye, Mr. Alexander."

I hold my shoulders straight as I follow Marco out the door. Devastation might be tearing me apart, but I won't let him see it.

I'll make it to the elevator. I'll make it to the car. I'll make it all the way to the airplane, and maybe I'll even make it to Santa Croce before I break down.

I have to. It's my only choice.

CHAPTER 25

Trip

AT THE CLICK OF THE DOOR LATCH, I COLLAPSE AGAINST THE WALL. Her honeysuckle scent lingers in the air, and I clutch my mouth. Diving into the half bathroom across the hall, I'm on my knees, barely getting the lid open before I vomit in the toilet.

"Fuck." I cough, my body heaving like I've consumed poison.

Her beautiful eyes… they were glazed with tears. Her beautiful face was so pale. I hurt her. God, I hurt her so bad.

With my forehead on my arm, I can't move as I heave up the shards of glass tearing my insides to shreds. Then I do something I haven't done in a long, long time.

I break.

Tears burn my eyes as I fall against the wall. "Fuck… fuck."

My muscles contract as if trying to expel the evil inside me.

She was wearing her red wrap dress. The one I told her I love. The air is scented with her marinara sauce, her spaghetti dish I love. She greeted me at the door with so much hope in her eyes.

I struck her like a snake, poisoning her world. I was the fire coming to burn her to the ground.

I'll always see her precious body shuddering with every word I spoke. They were violent, invisible blows, each one beating her down more.

Then she killed me. She looked up at me with her round eyes full of tears and spoke the only words that could make me stop. *I love you.*

Leaning forward, I dry heave into the toilet. The muscles in my torso flex and fight, forcing my stomach to spasm. Coughing, I clutch the bridge of my nose.

There's nothing left in me.

Even if I had no choice. Even if I had to save her life…

I can't.

Pushing myself off the floor, I stagger into the kitchen. A crystal vase of roses is on the table. A sauce pot is on the stove, a bottle of red wine, her lipstick on the rim of the glass. I reach out to touch it, stopping just before…

I turn off the fire under the burners, then I go to the kitchen, digging out an unopened bottle of Mamont vodka. Grish gave it to me some time ago. I don't know why I saved it—probably for the night I kicked my own guts out. The night I destroyed the only woman I've ever loved. The only woman I'll ever love.

I love you. Her broken voice, her tear-flooded eyes.

The primal yell broils up from my stomach, tensing all my muscles as I grab the plates in front of me and slam them against the wall. Going to the table, I lift the vase of red roses and throw it across the room. It shatters against the fireplace like an explosion, but it's not enough. I want to tear the place to the ground.

Shards of glass cover the hardwood floors, crunching under the soles of my stupidly expensive loafers as I go to my bedroom. Open spaces are in my closet where her clothes briefly hung. They're like gaping holes, empty sockets. I can't look at them.

Where did I leave the vodka? I return to the kitchen to retrieve the bottle, breaking the seal and taking a sip. I try to chug it, but it only burns, making me cough. Fuck not being a fucking alcoholic. I still try again, coughing hard, drinking more.

Sitting on the foot of the bed, I see her butterfly tee tucked under the pillow where she slept. Lifting it, I hold the piece of fabric to my nose and inhale deeply her warm scent of honeysuckle.

With the bottle in my hand, I slide down to sit on the wooden floor, holding the cotton shirt over my hot, wet eyes, over my nose, so I can breathe it in like oxygen.

Between breaths, I drink vodka, until after what seems like a long time, my phone buzzes with a text from Marco. **She's gone.**

My world ends. My stupidly expensive, guilded world with all the money I was determined to make by any means necessary. What does it matter, now that it has taken everything I love?

I take another, longer sip.

Then another.

A guy with a sledgehammer is banging on an anvil.

No, it's faster than that.

A guy with a jackhammer is breaking up the pavement.

My eyes squeeze, and I push off the floor. A near-empty bottle of vodka rolls away from me, and I hold the side of the bed as I stand. Someone is beating on my door with a vengeance.

I'm not sure I'm even dressed as I shuffle from my

bedroom, studying the destruction of my living room, broken glass covering the floor.

Down the narrow hallway, a muffled voice is outside yelling. I go to it, leaning forward to look through the peephole. It's Bianca.

Frowning, I turn the bolt, but before I can even open the door, it pushes me against the wall.

"You fucking bastard." She's too loud, and the light from the hallway is too bright. "You cruel, fucking bastard."

Holding up a hand, I cover my eyes. The last thing I remember is turning off my gas stove, thank God. "What time is it?"

"Time for you to tell me what happened, you ungrateful monster." Bianca is loud. "I brought her to you. I told her you were a good man, a caring boss. I vouched for you."

"Your mistake," I growl through my cotton-mouth.

"Don't give me that shit. Gia was an innocent girl, a *good* girl, and you treated her like trash."

I know. I don't answer.

She pushes past me, headed to the living room. "You say she jeopardized your business? She brought more money into your club than anyone ever did. She had talent. Correction, she has talent. *You* are the trash who needs to be thrown out. I hope you burn for what you did to her. I hope…"

I don't know why she stops. She's right. Every word from her mouth is a whip I would use to beat myself, tear my own flesh, if I could. Instead, all I can do is take it.

Silence stretches between us. She pauses at my couch, studying the wreckage. "What happened here? Did you do this to her? Did you hit her?"

"No." My voice is sandpaper. "She had already gone."

Reaching out, I brace my hand on the side of the bar, doing my best to stay upright. She needs to get out of here. Where the fuck is Franco?

"What are you holding?" She closes the space between us,

taking Gia's shirt from my grip. "It's hers. You smell like a distillery. What are you hiding? What's really going on?"

Fuck. If I could tell Bianca, I would've told Gia. If there were any way around this, I would've taken it.

"Nothing." I clear my throat, doing my best to shake the heartbreak I failed to drown in vodka. "You're right. I don't deserve her. So I sent her away."

Bianca's dark brow furrows, and she frowns in my face. "I don't believe you. Why do you look like shit? You destroyed your apartment? Why?"

"Stop." I snatch the shirt from her hands. I'm never letting that scrap of fabric out of my grip. "I don't have to explain myself to you. I'm the boss."

"Not anymore. I came to let you know I quit, and most of the girls are quitting too. They heard what you did to Gia, and they don't want to work for you anymore."

Running my hand over my face, I inhale as I nod. That's good. I need them all to hear what I did. I need them to talk about it, to get the word all the way to Manhattan. We're finished, violently and definitively.

"If it makes any difference, I'm going back to New York. I intend to sell my interest in The Rhino and Private Eyes, everything. You can keep your jobs. None of you will see me again."

I decide on the spot to divest completely. I'll sell this condo, our property in West Palm. South Florida can rot as far as I care. I'm never coming here again.

Bianca crosses her arms, her eyes never leaving me. "You're not a monster. You care about our safety. You never took advantage of us. You asked Gia out thinking she was only a seamstress."

"Show yourself out." Straightening, I pass her, going to my room.

She follows me. "I know you're lying."

Without another word, I close my bedroom door in her face and turn the lock. I go to the shower, switching it on full blast and stripping out of my clothes. As I stand in the hot blast, I struggle to regain my bearings, to refocus on what I have to do going forward.

I clean up, put on a fresh suit of clothes, and when I emerge from the bathroom, the living room is swept and cleaned. The kitchen is also cleaned with the pots on the drying rack and the food gone. A note is on my counter.

Snatching it up, I read, *Your plate is in the refrigerator. I took the rest with me to the house. I believe in you. Don't let me down. —Bianca*

Crumpling the paper into a ball, I drop it in the trash before going to the door. Taking the small suitcase from where I left it, I head out again, back to New York.

I'm at Gibson's the next night, nursing a hangover and a vodka. "Perhaps it's time I start drinking like the old guys."

"I thought you were already doing that." Ivan slaps me on the back, and I frown at him. I don't like this guy.

"If you're going to be an alcoholic, do it now, while you're young." Grish's tone is flat. A cigarette is dangling in his long fingers, and I have yet to see him grieve. "Then you can do rehab and avoid turning into a cliché."

"And that would be?"

"The abusive old man who ends up losing everything."

Another grimace. I've already lost everything. I already feel like an abuser for the words I spoke to Gia. I scrub my forehead with my hand. *I did it to protect her.* I keep repeating the phrase, but it gives me no comfort.

"What's the latest on our situation?" Grish turns to Ivan, and I take another sip, pretending I'm not interested in their dealings, like I have a choice.

"Honeypot isn't responding," Ivan grumbles.

"Make her respond." Grish's tone is ice. "If I go down, you go with me. All of you. I can't shield you from the ground."

Ivan shifts in his chair under my friend's glare. "I can't believe Simon would take you out. What would be the point of that?"

Ivan is doing his best to kiss ass. He's such a fucking amateur. I drink more vodka, wondering how I'm caught up in this mess. These idiots are not part of my long-term plan, and yet here I am, having to keep tabs on them, and make sure no one has put a mark on me.

My phone buzzes, and I pull it from my pocket. A text from Franco is on the face. **Gia resigned. How should I handle her earnings from PE?**

Tapping quickly, I reply, **Send them to her.**

I wait, watching the gray dots float, drinking more vodka, tapping my glass for a refill, which comes quickly.

His reply takes a while, and then it's questions about Venmo vs. PayPal because of her visa status, and how much should he hold out for room and board, considering she was staying with me, and... *what the fuck?*

I frown, typing my reply. **I don't care. Send her all of it the easiest way possible. Don't hold anything out.**

I want her to be taken care of. I want her to have everything she needs. I want her to be happy.

I love you... Her voice is in my head. I take a longer drink, finishing my second tumbler of vodka, thinking one good thing about being drunk is it silences the relentless ache in my chest, that fucking pain I can't escape when I'm sober.

Grish slides his gaze to me. "What's going on with you?"

"Nothing." I shake my head, my tone grim. *Nothing anymore.*

His eyes narrow, and he sits back in his chair, sliding his fingers down the sides of his mouth. He thinks he has me figured out, but he doesn't know shit about me. Nobody does.

Pushing out of my chair, I only sway a bit. "I'm calling it. Good luck with the honeypot, whatever the fuck that means."

Grish is on his feet, gripping my shoulder. "I'm going to let this pass because of your friend—"

"My friend… You mean your *girlfriend*?" I don't know why I'm picking a fight with him.

I'm miserable, and he is clueless as to why. I should be glad—it means Gia's safe.

"Fuck you, Trip." Grish growls. "You know how it was with Debbie. I'm letting this pass, but you get your shit together. I need you."

"You need me." My tone is sardonic.

His jaw tightens, and he can fuck right off. Only, I can't walk away from this group of gangsters. I've lost control of my level of involvement, thanks to this prick. If I separate from them now, I won't know what's coming, and I can't let that happen. I have to know if she's in danger because I carried her off that stage. Who's the fucking amateur now?

Clearing my throat, I get it together. "Give me a night. I'll be better tomorrow."

The tension in his body eases, and he nods. "You're not going anywhere?"

"I'm not going anywhere." Fuck that pain trying to come back. I wish I had another drink. "I'm not going anywhere."

CHAPTER 26

Gia

I MADE IT THROUGH THE CAR RIDE.

I made it through the flight.

I made it all the way to Santa Croce, but when my aunt met me at the door of her house, when the door opened, my shoulders broke. Confronting this woman who'd lived to remind me of my shortcomings added the last bit of weight to the load of failure.

"So, you're back." Her tone is as harsh as her black eyes and unsmiling face.

It's too heavy. The breath I've been holding whooshes out of my lungs, and I almost fall to my knees.

Instead, she catches me up in strong arms, holding me against her firm chest in an embrace I don't see coming.

"Come inside. Family takes care of family." She speaks to me in Italian, and her words give me a modicum of hope.

A sob jerks my chest, but I struggle for control. This isn't the relationship I have with my aunt.

"I'm sorry." I wipe my eyes, also speaking in Italian. "I

don't mean to impose on you or take advantage of our relationship. If you would only let me spend the night, I'll find my own place tomorrow—I have money."

"You'll stay here with your family." Aunt Gratziela grips my arm and drags me into her small house. "Those Americans lied to you. You should not have been treated that way."

My validated truth unleashes a torrent of tears, and I shudder, holding her arms and crying all the pain I've held in my chest for fourteen hours. They did lie to me, and I believed them so much. *I believed him.*

Her husband, my uncle Pietro, quietly rolls the suitcase in after us. In all the years I lived here, I've never heard him speak more than five words at a time. My aunt has him firmly under her thumb.

"I don't want to be a burden."

"I won't have you out on the street like a beggar, shaming our family."

There it is. This generous display is so I won't embarrass her.

I hate being under obligation to this woman, but I don't have a choice. "Thank you."

"Sit down, Giana." My aunt leads me into the kitchen. "Would you like a coffee or a chianti?"

It's a fair question, and checking the time, it's late. "Chianti, please."

She nods, pouring two glasses of the deep red table wine. "I thought you would be home sooner, but Bianca said she was taking care of you. Still, how well can she take care of you when she's not even married herself?"

I take a sip of the wine, wondering how soon I can get out of this place. My head hurts, and I'm tired, and I'm not letting her off the hook for years of calling me names and comparing me to other girls. Yet I wonder, without her nonstop belittling, would I have been strong enough to make it back here?

"Bianca helped me get a few jobs, but I couldn't stay without a work visa." That's all she needs to know.

I know damn well how she'd respond to Glitter Girl.

"Ah, yes." My aunt lifts her chin, taking a sip of her own wine. "So what will you do now? I heard Michele is staying in Florida."

Michele. I swallow the bitter laugh that almost slipped from my lips. My erstwhile fiancé would be the answer to all my problems in her small mind. *Marry this one off, and get her off my hands.*

Somehow, I have to cover why I don't need her help or a job. I only need a place to crash until I can get my affairs in order. Franco texted the amount he's sending to my Venmo account (in U.S. dollars, no less), and it's enough to live on for at least nine months, possibly longer if I'm frugal.

"I'll get a job as a seamstress." I might actually like that.

"Yes, you have always been good at sewing." She stands, taking our glasses, even though I haven't finished mine. "You'll stay here in your old room until then. Now go to bed."

She's still trying to be the boss. If I were less tired, I'd tell her I'm not staying here any longer than absolutely necessary. As it is, I'm grateful to have a place to sleep, even if it is marred by memories of anger and struggle.

Tomorrow, I'll go to the bank and open an account, then I'll seek out a realtor who can help me purchase my mother's old one-bedroom apartment overlooking the sea. It's the one thing I want most right now. The one thing I'm allowed to want.

I enter the small, light-blue room. The single bed is very small compared to how I lived in Florida. It's familiar, but I never made this my home. Only a few things indicate I ever occupied this space—a butterfly snowglobe, the patch I was stitching when my mother died, my dance scrapbook.

Pushing through the sheets, all the pain comes crashing

down on me again. I can't stop seeing his cold eyes, hearing his emotionless voice telling me to go. It was all a lie.

I don't believe him. Pain twists my chest, and I take out my phone. Opening my Instagram, fresh tears heat my eyes when I see us together in the bed. The warmth in his eyes is unmistakable.

"Why is he doing this?" Sadness echoes in the empty place where my heart once beat.

A tear falls on my cheek, soft as a butterfly kiss. Why is he tearing apart what we had when it was so very beautiful? I know he loved me. I don't know why he's lying.

I'm not ashamed to mourn the loss of my dreams, because I'll never find new ones as beautiful as the ones I lost.

Four weeks later

From the small balcony of my mother's old apartment, you can see the sapphire blue waters of the Adriatic Sea. The breeze blows light, salty air through the open windows, and my linen curtains lift and fall gently.

"I like what you've done with the place." Michele has come home to wait for his work visa, and my aunt is both shocked and pleased he's staying with me.

His long hair is highlighted gold from being in the sun, and he has it tied up in a man-bun. His pink linen shirt is cuffed at the elbows, and he looks handsome, happy. Gratziela probably thinks we'll be engaged again before long, and when we're not, when he goes back to Florida, she'll have certain opinions about that as well.

"My mother never had money to decorate." I pour boiling water over the coffee grounds at the top of my carafe.

"Any questions about how you earned it?" He turns,

strolling to where I stand at the kitchen counter, frothing the warm milk.

"I told them I got a settlement from the ballet company, so if anyone asks, you did, too."

"Of course. In the meantime, what are you doing these days? How can you stand to be back here? Are you dying to return to Florida?"

"No." Palm Beach is forever damaged in my memory, although I do miss Bianca and Shula. "I like being home, in this place. It's peaceful, and I can look out at the ocean and heal."

The dark coffee is poured into large mugs, and I spoon the frothy foam on top, making a little heart design in the milk.

Stepping around behind me, he massages my shoulders as I sip the comforting beverage. "You never told me what happened, why you left."

"Because I don't know what happened." After so many weeks, a wobble still enters my voice.

I pass him a cappuccino, and his eyebrows rise. "You could be a barista."

"And ruin the thing I love?" Curling my nose, I shake my head. "I'm glad you came for a visit. I do miss you and Bianca and Shula."

"So that leaves *what* are you doing now?"

"Oh, I take in sewing jobs for the dry cleaner in town, and my aunt suggested I apply for a teaching position at our old company. That was a hard no." My voice turns quiet. "I'll never dance again."

Sympathy fills his eyes, but I shake my head. I don't want to go there.

Quick as a blink, he shifts gears. "What the hell do you do for the *dry cleaner?*"

"Minor garment repairs, replacing zippers, you'd be surprised. Last week I had to reattach the lace on a Valentino dress. It was gorgeous."

"Did you take a photo?"

"You know I did." I grin, hopping over to grab my phone and pulling up my photos.

He takes it, and while he studies the gorgeous red dress, I take another sip of coffee. "I have enough money. I don't need to do anything, but I like to sew. It reminds me of my mother." Standing at the window, I think about those old days. "Before I started dancing, I thought I might move to Milan and try to be a fashion designer or work at one of the houses. I designed all our costumes for The Rhino."

Handing my phone to me again, the picture of Trip and me is on the face. "I'm going to walk down and get a bottle of wine, then we're going to talk."

"Misha, please don't."

He holds up a hand, shaking his head. "As my former fiancée, I have a vested interest in your happiness. We're going to make a plan."

With that, he's out the door, and I exhale heavily, turning to the window again. He has to understand I don't want to make plans or pretend my heart isn't broken. He has to let me heal.

Our relationship came on quickly, but it was intense and real. It had fire and passion, and it's going to take time to get over it, to believe I'll find another person who'll make me feel that way again.

The door creaks as it slowly opens, drawing my attention. "That was fast, did you forget something? Oh!" My heart flies to my neck, and I jump up, going around behind my chair. "Can I help you?"

Standing in the doorway, staring intensely at me, is a tall man with dark hair and glittering black eyes. "Hello, Giana."

"How do you know my name?" My heart beats painfully fast. "Have we met?"

"Not face to face, but you know me." He takes another step closer, entering my apartment. "I'm your number one fan."

His voice is creepily friendly, and fear squeezes the breath from my lungs. My eyes flicker around the small apartment, searching for anything I can use as a weapon. A blanket is on my bed, and a picture is on the wall. I have a candle, but it's not lit.

"What are you doing here?" My voice rasps. "You weren't supposed to know where I lived."

"Trust me, it wasn't easy, but I have connections, technology." He takes another slow step towards me. "You left without saying goodbye. That hurt."

"I-I'm sorry. I didn't have a choice." Silently, I pray Michele will hurry, come back... *Come back.*

"Is he paying you to stay here? To *hide* from me?"

"I don't know who you're talking about." A glass vase of flowers is on the table in front of me, and I step closer to it, doing my best not to indicate my intentions. "No one is paying me, and I'm definitely not hiding."

"You know who I mean. *Trip Alexander.*" Anger rises in his voice. "The man who carried you off the stage. Is he keeping you here?"

"We broke up." I'm closer to the vase. "He never wants to see me again."

The man's eyes narrow, and he blinks at me, taking another step closer. "I don't believe you. Why would he do that?"

"He... he said I jeopardized his business. It's over." I'm close enough to slide my hands forward and grab the vase, but can I hit him hard enough from this angle?

Dark eyes shoot down to my hands, and he lifts the vase quickly. "I'll just put this out of the way for now." He carries it to the counter. "If he's not paying you, how do you afford to live here, in this apartment by the sea?"

"It was my mother's place. I was able to buy it with the money I made from Private Eyes."

"Ah..." Another sinister grin. "So *I* helped you buy it? You're welcome."

"You'd better go. My fiancé will be back any minute, and he's very protective of me."

"The drag queen?" His eyes narrow. "Don't play games with me, Giana. He's not your fiancé."

"He was, and he'll make you pay if you hurt me."

The man begins pacing, driving his fingers into the sides of his hair. "I'm not here to hurt you, don't you understand? I love you."

Cramps fill my stomach as memories of my mother, of the man who was obsessed with her, the man who killed her, crowd my brain.

Inhaling slowly, I do my best to remain calm. "Let's start over. I can't call you Number 1 anymore. What's your name?"

Worried eyes meet mine. "Andre Bertonelli."

"It's nice to meet you, Andre." I take a cautious step to the right, in the direction of the framed picture on the wall. "Why did you come here? Do you want something from me?"

He stops pacing and looks at me. "I need money. I hoped you could help me."

"Okay." I nod carefully. "I can give back the money you gave me if that will help you. Then you can go back to Florida?"

"No… That was a gift. I only wanted *his* money." His face twists. "I'll have to find another way."

"Another way to do what?"

"To get out."

I'm confused, but I'm also curious. "Why do you want Trip's money? Did he hurt you?"

"He can only hurt me if he forces my hand." His words form a lead weight in my stomach. "I'm the only one who knows about you, and if I can get out, I won't have to do anything. I don't want to do that."

Goose bumps break out on my arms, and I cross them, rubbing my palms up and down my skin. "What would you have to do?"

"Goodbye, Giana. I hope you don't see me again."

He dashes out the door, and I run around the table, chasing

after him. "Wait! Andre, tell me what's happening!" I'm at the top of the stairs when I run slap into Michele. "Oh, shit!"

"Hey, slow down." He grabs my shoulders, catching me before I fall. "Where are you going so fast?"

"Did you see the man who just left here? Tall with dark hair, olive skin?"

"You just described every man in the village." I'm shaking all over as Michele leads me back into the apartment. "What happened? You look like you've seen a ghost."

"A man was just here asking about Trip. He said he needed money." Shaking my head, I turn over everything he said in my mind. "He was... unhinged."

"Did he try to hurt you?"

"No... it was very strange. He wasn't here to hurt me."

He can only hurt me if he forces my hand. Looking down, I try to make sense of what he said. Something is happening, and I can't imagine what it could be.

"I'm afraid, Misha."

He puts his arm around my shoulder, hugging me close. "Good thing I'm stuck here for the duration . I'll stay with you."

Rubbing my fingers over my forehead, I can only think of one way to get answers. Picking up the phone, I dial Bianca's number.

CHAPTER 27

Trip

S IX WEEKS HAVE PASSED SINCE DEBBIE "COMMITTED SUICIDE"—A cover story I don't believe for one minute. Six weeks since Grish was given his ultimatum from Simon Petrovich, the all-powerful oligarch.

Six weeks of me growing increasingly furious at the fucked-up web in which my friend and former business partner is entangled. The web in which he's entangled me, which is now threatening everything I've worked for and love.

I've done my best to follow the money, to connect the dots, to track down the motives and the key players—so I can get out of this bullshit, lethal game.

Shortly after our meeting, Petrovich's Master List went missing. He actually kept a *hand-written* record of all the people who worked for him, how much money they controlled, and their locations. Naturally everyone is salivating to get their hands on it—for blackmail purposes, leverage, money.

Overnight, Grish's ticket to salvation changed from paying back the millions he owed to finding that book. Then Grish told me who'd stolen it, none other than Andre Bertonelli, my Number 1 nightmare.

I went back to being Grish's right-hand man with one focus on both our minds—finding Andre. My reasons were known only to me.

Andre was the only one who knew about Gia, and if he was motivated enough to steal something that valuable from the scary big boss, he'd squeal like a pig when they caught him and start cutting off his fingers, one by one.

We followed the trail to Hamiltown, a hamlet on the South Carolina coast named for Blake and Hana's family (because they own the town). We found the sisters staying in their great uncle's big-assed mansion, which is complete with extensive grounds and horses.

I noticed Grish was very familiar with the place—like he'd been there before—and I realized this was where Shadow of the Moon was stashed. It all made sense. Blake's father the fuckup kept that racehorse here, and this was where all the shit went down.

We tore the place apart, but we never found Andre or the book. What we did find was Blake being guarded by Hutch Winston, an oversized, former military brute and his buddy Scar, an even bigger, scary wolf-like dude with tattoos covering some pretty gnarly burn scars on his arms and chest.

Blake said her uncle hired them without her knowledge, but the whole setup was suspicious, like the old man knew somebody was coming for him. Honestly, I was relieved my friends were protected. One less thing for me to worry about.

Grish and I stayed until it was clearly a dead end, then we came back to the city. Blake came with us, and when I found out why, I was pissed as hell.

It's a story for another day, but suffice to say, Ivan the dick-head had been blackmailing her to help Grish raise that fucking payback money. Now that the payback is off, Ivan has gotten greedy and won't leave her alone.

I plan to handle his bullshit, but for now, we're regrouping at Gibson's.

Grish holds an unlit cigarette between his fingers, the muscle in his jaw ticking rapidly. "I've got to find that ledger," he growls. "I've got to get Simon off my back."

I'm nursing a vodka, thinking about finding Andre.

"So, Trip…" Natasha rounds Grish's shoulder to stand in front of me. "I heard an interesting story about you."

Rainey trots up behind her like a good little puppy. I turn, resting my elbow on the polished wood, to face this underworld climber.

"What about me could possibly interest you?" My careless smile is firmly in place.

"My thoughts exactly." Natasha can't resist a dig. "Then I heard you got serious with one of the strippers at your West Palm club."

Surprise flashes in my chest. The last thing I need is another person knowing about Gia, especially one with criminal ambitions, but I hold my expression steady. "Gossip loves to travel, doesn't it?"

"You dated a stripper?" Rainey's green eyes widen. "So that's what was so interesting in Florida."

Grish's attention turns to me as well. "I thought we had rules against sampling the merchandise."

"Rules are made to be broken." Like he has any say in what I do.

"So the famously aloof Trip Alexander has a weakness after all." Natasha crosses her arms.

"I have a dick." My tone is flat. I need to kill this story before it takes hold. "She was a good lay. Nothing more."

"That's not what I heard. I heard you got *very* involved."

Taking a beat, I study Natasha in her designer black dress. Her hair is styled in a high ponytail, and she's wearing too much eyeliner. She thinks she has something on me, something she can use at a later date. Maybe she does have leadership potential, but she's not ready to lock horns with me.

"You know I don't date girls our age."

"So you weren't living together?" Her eyebrow arches.

Exhaling a laugh, I fall back on casual indifference. "She slept over a few times—made it easier to fuck her when I wanted. But she got too attached. I had to send her packing."

"Heartless bastard." Grish grins into his drink, approval in his tone. "Give Trip enough vodka, and he'll sleep with anyone."

Pointing at him, I lift my glass. "Almost anyone."

I finish all the vodka in my tumbler, but it doesn't kill the pain of this conversation. Discussing her is like knives stabbing my insides.

Natasha's eyes narrow, and she wanders back to where she left her drink. I'm wondering who the fuck she's been talking to and what she's after—besides leverage.

"Attachments can be dangerous." Rainey's voice is quiet, and she watches me like she knows something. *Who is this girl?*

Doesn't matter. I've got to find Andre. His continued absence has me on edge.

"This is where I leave you." I slap Grish on the shoulder. "Don't do anything I wouldn't do."

I'm out the door with my phone in my hand, dialing Franco's number.

"Trip?" His voice greets me from the other end of the line. "Wasn't expecting to hear from you. Everything okay?"

"Yeah… Have you heard from Gia lately? How's she doing?"

"Seriously? You're asking me about Gia?"

"I'm not fucking around, Franco. Andre is missing, and I need to know she's safe." I need to know what my next move will be.

"Bianca talks to her pretty regularly. I can ask her if she's heard anything."

"Do that and tell me as soon as you know."

"You okay? DJ is in the city this weekend. I can text him if you need backup."

"I'm good." My protection isn't important. Only one thing matters to me at this point. "I want Gia to be safe."

"I'll call Bianca and text you back."

"Thanks, Franco."

Disconnecting, I tap out a quick text to Ivan the bastard. *Meet me at The Vogue in twenty.* I'll handle his blackmail shit, then I'm out of here. Let them come and find me.

It's open mic night at The Vogue, which I despise. Thankfully, this should be quick. I can't imagine Ivan fighting with me. He knows who I am.

I'm at a table in the VIP section with a fresh drink in my hand when he saunters up in his uniform—jeans and a flat-brimmed ball cap with his denim jacket around his arms like a cape.

He's such a fucking low-rent gangster wannabe. The idea this douche has my friends on the ropes offends me. At least Grish and I know how to dress like professionals.

"What up, T?" He holds out his palm like he expects me to slap it.

Like I'm an animal.

"I heard you're blackmailing a friend of mine." I cut right to the chase. The less time I'm with this idiot, the fewer brain cells I'll lose.

"Yo, I'm blackmailing a lot of folks." He laughs, rolling his blue eyes. "You'll have to, like, be more specific than that."

What I really want is to slap that fake accent out of his mouth. He speaks like he's got some level of street cred, and I'm pretty sure he's from suburban Ohio.

"Blake van Hamilton. You have a porn video of her sister. I want it."

"Oh, yeah?" His eyebrows rise, and he nods. "You into that? She's all fucked up, and this old dude is licking her pussy. It's sick."

Anger rises hot under my collar, and I'm ready to grab him by the neck. The only thing holding me back is it won't get me what I want.

"I'm not interested in the content. I want the video gone. I want any backup copies gone, and I want your personal guarantee it will never reappear." Leaning closer, I level my eyes on his. "If it ever does, I will see that you're *handled*."

He holds up both hands. "Yo, I didn't know she was your girl, man. Grish said he needed dough, and I just had this on hand. No worries. I got you. Consider it gone."

"And you'll return the money you took from her sister. Grish doesn't need it."

That gets me some pushback. "Ay, man, that's my only payday this month. I got to cover my tab."

"Send it to this account. Now."

His jaw is set, and I know this clown would be a problem for me down the line if I had any plans to hang around this shithole, which I don't. He leans forward, lazily tapping on his phone as I watch, sipping my vodka.

My phone buzzes in the breast pocket of my rust-brown blazer. I lift it out to see the money is in the dummy account, from which I'll forward to Blake once it's no longer pending.

"That it?" His expression is as flat as the brim on his hat, and I notice his fake accent is gone.

"Pleasure doing business with you. Remember this next time you go after one of my friends."

He pushes the air with his hand, turning and leaving the bar.

The band rips into a loud guitar song I don't recognize, and

I linger only as long as it takes to finish my drink. Avoiding the line at the door, I slip out the side exit into the alley.

I'm about to text Blake to let her know I got her money and the blackmailer off her back, when he grabs me.

Like a fucking monster, he comes up from behind, a six-foot-four tower of scarred muscle covered in ink, lifting me by the neck and pinning me against the wall.

"Fuck," I grunt as heat floods my eyes.

He's crushing my windpipe. Gritting my teeth, I clutch his wrist, doing my best to break his hold on my throat. It's no use. This motherfucker is twice my size in every way.

"Let go." I try to kick him in the nuts.

He growls something about me double-crossing Hana, and I realize he thinks I'm working with Ivan.

The only thing that saves me is Hutch walking up slowly. "Let him speak."

Scar's grip relaxes, and I drop to my ass on the dirty pavement, my back against the alley wall. They're towering over me, and I shake my head.

"I'm not blackmailing Blake."

They don't believe me. I don't really care, but it's the only way out of this alley. It takes showing them my texts to get them to relent.

Scar walks away, but as I slowly rise to my feet, I narrow my eyes at Hutch. Blake has decided this small-town detective, former military man, is good enough for her.

I wonder…

"How would you feel about a little three-way split? I could skim it right off the top, and you could still be a hero."

He turns into a column of fire in front of me, grabbing me by the front of my shirt. "Didn't you get enough or are you asking for more?"

Calm settles through my limbs, and I decide she's probably right. "That was a test. Just making sure you're good enough for my friend."

He releases me, and I watch as he saunters away, following his partner up the dark alley in the direction of the street. My phone buzzes again, and I pull it from my jacket. I'd hoped it would be Franco, but it's Grish.

Andre is dead.

Everything falls quiet, like I'm waking from a fever dream. My chest tightens, and I can't believe it's over that easily. I need to know how. I want proof he's gone, and he didn't tell what he knows.

Quickly tapping, I reply, **I'm headed to your place for the details.**

My throat hurts from being nearly strangled to death. The bodyguards are good at their jobs, and I'm glad to know my friends are covered if anything were to happen to me.

What I don't expect when I arrive at the loft, is to find Blake there, holding a gun. Hutch steps up behind me as I enter the room.

"Well, hello." I chuckle. "Still don't trust me?"

"Not on your life," he growls.

"Why did you bring him?" Grish snaps at me, sounding rattled.

I can't believe he thinks Blake would actually shoot him. I mean, she has reasons, but Blake doesn't know how to handle a gun.

Going to the cabinet, I attempt to cut the tension in the room. "Why yes, I will have that drink, thanks."

We're all old friends here. No reason to pull guns on one another. Turning, I catch Grish sliding his hand inside the small bookcase in the corner. *Fuck.* The vodka is on my lips when I realize he's actually going for it.

"Get back, bitch," Grish lunges at her, slapping her hard.

Blake's gun hand swings wide, and I see the flash of light as a loud *BLAST!* echoes in the room. I'm hit in the chest so hard, I'm thrown against the wall.

The glass I was holding slams against the cabinet, and I'm on my ass, pushing into a sitting position. I can't inhale all the way, and looking down, I see a small, black halo on the front of my white shirt. *Fuck, Is that a bullet hole?*

The question forms in my mind as the pain explodes through my chest. The spot starts to grow larger, red and sticky.

"Stay down," Hutch orders, but I don't think he's talking to me.

I couldn't get up if I tried.

He's fighting with Grish, but my vision is clouding. My old pal hits the floor beside me, but I can't help him. I'm too weak as I watch my life drain out of me in a thick, bright-red stream.

"Trip?" Blake's voice breaks, but Hutch lifts her off the floor and carries her away.

The door closes, and the room falls silent.

Grish is unconscious at my side, and I'm bleeding out fast. *Shit.*

Blinking my eyes takes effort. Looking around the room, I don't have the strength to reach for my phone. Dammit, I'm not going to escape this time.

I always said I didn't care if I died. Now I realize I can't die this way. I can't leave things how they are. I have to see her one more time. I have to explain.

I need to tell her why I hurt her like I did, tell her how sorry I am. How I started dying the day I sent her away.

Closing my eyes, I remember the first time I saw her. I fell in love with her pretty brown eyes, wide and shining, open and innocent. She was so beautiful. How could I not fall in love with her? I didn't deserve the gift that was her.

With my final breath, I speak her name. My beautiful Gia. *I love you.*

CHAPTER 28

Gia

"So you're good?" Bianca's voice is insistent. "You haven't had any strange visitors?"

"I'm fine, B! I'm sewing, hanging out with Michele… It's all good." I hate lying to her, but I don't want her to worry. She's too far away to help me anyway.

Glancing towards the window, I remember Andre standing in my door a week ago, his eyes desperate and scary. What would Trip say if he knew Andre came here? Would he care?

Exhaling heavily, I have to stop thinking about it. Trip doesn't want me, and I have to put him behind me and move on with my life.

"I'm glad Michele is with you. Tell him everyone is asking for him."

"I will. Is that all you needed?"

"Yeah, I just needed to hear your voice." Her tone is gentle now. "I miss you, Gia. We all do."

My lips tighten, and I inhale slowly. "I miss you, too. Tell the girls I said hey."

"Maybe you can come visit sometime soon?"

"Maybe."

We say goodbye, and I slide my phone in my pocket. Michele is out, and I'm supposed to be finishing up a dress for the dry cleaner.

It's a beautiful, gray Prada dress made of nylon gabardine. It's backless with a halter top and a skinny belt at the waist. The full skirt has been torn at the stitching, and I'm carefully aligning the pleats, reattaching it under the belt, pretending I'm in the fashion house, preparing for fall Fashion Week.

I carry the dress onto the small balcony overlooking the sea. The breeze is in my hair, and as I stitch, the memories flood my mind. For a little while, I was a princess. I wore beautiful clothes and lived in a beautiful place. I made love to a prince.

I think about our first date at that elegant resort. I was so nervous in my fancy Carolina Herrera gown. I'd never worn anything designer. I'd never felt beautiful.

Trip was so handsome in his suit, his hair long and cheeks scruffy. I remember the dimple when he'd smile. He was so naughty. He made me feel so many new things.

Pressing my lips together, I remember his mouth on my inner thighs, between my legs, that orgasm… Oh, God… Will I ever feel that way again? Mist heats my eyes, and I prick my finger with the needle.

"Shit!" I hiss, hooking the needle in the skirt so I can fetch a bandage. "No bleeding on the designer dress."

I've just entered the room when Michele bursts through the door, eyes wide. "He's been shot!"

My heart jumps, and I quickly place the dress on a chair. "What are you talking about? Who?"

Shuffling noises come from the stairwell, and I hurry to the door. DJ's face appears, red with strain, and my heart stops when I see the man he's carrying.

"Trip?" I can barely breathe as I grip the banister. His face is so pale. His eyes are closed, and he looks like he might die. "Oh my God! Bring him inside. Hurry!"

DJ and Michele work together to get him through the door and onto my queen-sized bed near the open window.

"What is he doing here?" My stomach cramps, and I sit beside him, placing my hand on his shoulder.

"I'm okay," Trip groans as the stocky bouncer adjusts him to a sitting position.

His face is so pale, and with his beard shaved, a sheen of sweat is visible on his upper lip. His hair is a little shorter, but it still curls at his collar, behind his ears. My fingers ache to touch it, and despite it all, my heart burns like I've found a long-lost treasure.

I have to grab the reins on that response.

"He's lucky to be alive," DJ tells me. "He was shot right in the chest, missed his heart by a fraction."

"But I don't understand. Shouldn't he be in a hospital?"

"He should be, but when the doctor said he might not live, he demanded I bring him here immediately. We flew all night."

Trip starts to cough, and his face ghosts as if he's in excruciating pain. "Fuck." He reaches for my hand, holding it tightly, waiting… After what feels like an eternity, he glances at the two men hovering over us, his voice weak. "Can you give us a minute?"

DJ immediately heads for the door, but Michele doesn't move. His brow lowers, and darkness enters his scowl. "I'm not leaving him alone with Gia. He's done enough damage."

I take my hand from Trip's and go to where my friend stands ready to protect me. "It's okay, Misha. I don't think he can hurt me in this condition, and you'll be right outside if I need you, yes?"

His eyes meet mine, and he hesitates. "Right outside the door."

I nod. "Thank you."

The two men step outside, and I turn to face Trip, pale

and hunched on the side of the bed. His shirt is unbuttoned to the center of his chest, and I can see the wide, white bandage wrapped around his torso.

Longing surges in me like a rising tide, and I want to wrap my arms around him. I want to stroke his forehead, kiss him, nurse him back to health, but I hold still.

"Why are you here?" My voice is calm. In fact, I'm surprised how controlled I sound.

His chin drops, and his brow furrows. "I needed to see you one more time. I needed to tell you I'm sorry." He pauses, fingers tightening on the duvet covering my bed. Another cough, another low groan.

I hurry forward, holding out my hand. "Please let me get you something. Pain medication?"

"No." His voice is like sandpaper. "Just let me say this, and I'll go."

He inhales slowly then takes my hand.

My heart drops at how cold he is. "I don't think you should go anywhere."

"I've done a lot of bad things, Gia, but hurting you is the worst thing I've ever done." He pauses for breath. "You deserve better. You deserve to be cherished."

His hazel eyes lift to mine, and they're brimming with so much emotion, I inhale sharply. "Trip—"

"Don't say you forgive me." His voice is weak. I've never heard him weak, only strong. "I just wanted to tell you I'm sorry, so very sorry."

With extreme effort, he rises to his feet, reaching for the back of the chair and starting for the door. He only makes it one step before another cough wracks his body, and he grasps the wood with both hands, clearly in agony.

"DJ!" I yell, going to him and wrapping my arms around his waist.

I duck my head under his arm and turn him towards the

bed. "I won't say I forgive you, and we will have this conversation, but first you must lie down."

The door flies open, and the big guy is with me again, helping me guide Trip to the bed.

"Where are we taking him?" DJ looks down at me.

I look over at Michele. "Turn back the blankets. He'll stay here for now."

"The bullet glanced off his rib and exited through his back. The doctor said it was a lucky strike, but he's not out of the woods yet. If he survives the next twenty-four hours, he'll make it." DJ tells me once we have Trip tucked in my bed, "He gave him a 50-50 chance."

My throat closes, and I fight the tears flooding my eyes. As much as he hurt me, I don't want him to die. I can't imagine a world without him in it.

The stout bouncer takes out two prescription bottles. "This one's an antibiotic to prevent the wound from getting infected. These are narcotic pain pills, but the damn fool won't take them. He said he's not getting hooked on drugs. He just keeps pouring vodka down his throat. Like that'll do him any good."

I grab my bag off the chair, digging in it for money. "Michele, go out and get more vodka."

"I don't like this." Michele scowls. "He needs to be in a hospital, not dying here in this room."

I cover my face with my hands, pushing against the fear twisting in my chest. Trip is out cold.

DJ puts a hand on my shoulder. "He's strong. He fought to hang on all the way across the ocean so he could see you one more time. The doctor said if he makes it, he'll be able to move around in a week, but it can take six for a full recovery."

"Six weeks." I study him lying in my bed, thinking there's no way to hide him in this little town. "Is he safe here? Is whoever did this looking for him?"

"I don't know." DJ shakes his head. "Franco told me to

stay with him, so if you're letting him stay here, I'll find a place nearby."

Misha catches my elbow, tugging me to the other side of the room. "Don't do it, Gia. This man does not deserve your pity."

I hurt so much, and I know Michele is right. I know my silly heart can't be trusted around him. Still… "I can't turn him away like this, Misha. It wouldn't be right."

"So send him to a hospital."

"Where whoever shot him can come back and finish the job?" It's hard to breathe at the thought. "He has to stay here. DJ will help us."

My ex-fiancé grits his teeth. "You know that's not what worries me."

"I won't get attached." I squeeze his arm. "Trust me. I remember what he did. We'll get him back on his feet, then I'll show him the door."

"I'm holding you to that."

"I'm counting on you to hold me to it. Now help me find DJ a place to stay. We can't all fit in this little apartment."

With Trip settled and sleeping in my bed, they head out to secure a place for DJ and to buy more vodka. Crossing my arms over my stomach, I swallow the pain racking my insides at seeing him here, hurt, needing my help.

The words he said are on repeat in my brain. *I had to see you one more time… You deserve to be cherished… I'm so very sorry.* He believed he was going to die, so he came here, to me.

"Stop it, Gia." I tighten my jaw.

Michele is right. Having him here is playing with fire, and I have to be strong. He hurt me, and I'm not jumping back into his arms simply because he appeared on my doorstep nearly dead.

CHAPTER 29

Trip

I'M NOT DEAD.

Paradoxically, I did not die, yet I woke up in heaven.

Franco sent DJ to find me in New York using my phone's locator service. I didn't know he was tracking me that way, and if I had, I probably wouldn't have allowed it.

I found all this out as I was dying in the passengers side of DJ's SUV, while he drove wildly to the nearest emergency department. Franco argued it's the best way to ensure my security. He also ordered me not to die, like I had a choice.

DJ had been in the street outside Grish's loft when he heard the shots fired and ran in as Hutch and Blake were running out, saving me from pretty much immediate death.

He left Grish behind, taking me to the closest hospital, where a trauma doctor was able to fix me up as well as he could. Now I owe that fucker my life.

According to DJ, I was saying Giana's name the whole time, so Franco ordered a private jet and had him take me to Italy. I think Franco thought I was dying, too, and didn't want my dying wish to be on his head. He's superstitious that way. Like I would waste my afterlife haunting his Cuban ass.

I'm not pissed at any of them. I'm opening my eyes in Santa Croce, in Gia's bed with the sea breeze drifting around me and my beautiful girl asleep at my side.

She's fully clothed and her back is turned, but her dark hair spreads over the pillow, and honeysuckle touches my nose. I have everything in the world I want to live for right here in my grasp with nothing standing in my way…

Except all that shit I said to her in Palm Beach.

Fuck, I was a bastard.

I had to lay it on thick so she wouldn't argue, so she'd be upset enough to go all the way across the ocean, back here, to her home. I had to make her believe I was a cold-hearted snake to save her life. I've got a lot of making up to do, but I'll do it. I'll do anything—

"You're awake?" A crisp, male voice snatches my attention from gazing at Gia's beautiful back to seeing Michele the drag queen standing over the bed, frowning fiercely.

"Yeah." I slide my hands down beside me and attempt to push myself into a sitting position. Nothing happens. "Sorry. I guess my arms aren't cooperating right now."

"The doctor said it would take some time for you to get your strength back." He leans down and grabs me around the torso, pulling me into a sitting position. "Lucky for you, or I would never allow you to sleep in this bed with her."

"Shit." I hold his shoulders, feeling incredibly awkward. "Thanks for helping me out. Were you a nurse?"

"No." His tone is clipped, and he walks over to where a pot of coffee is brewing. "Do you want coffee or vodka?"

"Kind of early for vodka."

"Not from what I've been told." He pours a cup of coffee and carries it to where I'm stuck, weak and useless.

"Thanks again." I take a sip, nodding at the flavor. "This is good."

He returns to the kitchen, where he toasts bread and spreads it with butter and jam, eating and not offering me anything more. I'm not particularly hungry, but I can tell something's on this guy's mind.

I'm not much for beating around the bush. "You want to tell me now, or should we wait?"

Lowering his hand with a thud, his eyes flash. "I don't like you. I don't know what you're doing here or what you hope is going to happen, but I'm not letting you hurt Gia again. If you think you'll come back here and play the sympathy card and get between her thighs, you're wrong. I'm not letting that happen, pal."

He's breathing fast, and I blink down to my hands in my lap. Gia told me about this guy. I know they grew up together, they were engaged, and he feels protective of her. I know I fucked up royally with Gia.

But I had my reasons, and he doesn't know me.

"I'm not your pal." Speaking slowly, I have fire in my own eyes. "And I'm not looking to get back in Gia's good graces, I'm looking to get back into her heart. I hurt her because it was the only way I could protect her from my world. Now my world has essentially imploded, and even if it hadn't, I was doing everything in my power to get out of it."

"That doesn't change what you did, and it doesn't change the fact that I love Gia. I intend to protect her from you."

I'm probably not supposed to get overly excited, but I can't help it. I'm here, and my lady is in my grasp. This guy had better get used to it.

"I love Gia, and I plan to spend the rest of my life making up for what I did to her. I want to make her happy if she'll give me one more chance. If I do hurt her, you have my permission to hunt me down and make me pay however you see fit."

That shuts his mouth. He crosses his arms, leaning back in his chair at the table. His eyes are narrowed on me, and my eyes are narrowed on him—until I hear the softest sigh from the bed beside me. It's a sound that melts the fist of iron in my chest. My beautiful girl.

"Whoa, sorry." She sits up on the opposite side of the bed, her back to me. "You were already asleep, so I couldn't explain the sleeping arrangements last night."

"I don't mind sharing a bed with you." My voice is warm, inviting, and I'm gratified to see a hint of pink coloring her cheeks.

"It's just this apartment is so small, it only has room for one bed, and Michele is already on the sofa." She goes to the kitchen, where she pours a cup of coffee.

She's wearing sea-green pajama pants with little mermaids on them and a purple tank top that barely contains her full breasts. My dick stiffens, and I'm glad to know it's still working after all that's happened, not that I have the strength to do anything about it.

Or permission.

"No apologies necessary. Thanks for taking me in like this."

"I figured if I'm fully clothed and you're still recovering, we can keep it platonic."

"I'm happy to trade places if you're uncomfortable," Michele tells her, giving me a death glare.

Her back is turned, and I realize my eyes have drifted to her round ass in those thin cotton pants. I'm wounded, but I'm not blind.

"You don't have to worry about me touching you." Yes, I get the irony of that statement, considering how this all started. "Not that it's on the table. I know it's off the table."

"It's *far* off the table." Gia's glares at me, and she holds up a hand. "I'm sorry. I can make a pallet on the floor if this is too confusing for anyone."

"Hey." My voice is level, calming. "It's not confusing. I understand the arrangements here completely."

She nods, returning to where I'm lying on my back. "Are

you sure you don't need any pain medication?" She pushes a long, dark curl behind her ear. "You've got to be hurting."

Does she not realize how fucking gorgeous she is with her sexy curves on full display, her long hair falling around her shoulders, and her feet bare? Closing my eyes, I meditate on cold showers, baseball, crying infants, and every other boner killer I can conjure. Last thing I need is an erection when I just assured her I wouldn't touch her.

"I'm good, thanks."

"You do need to take your antibiotic." She reads the instructions on the bottle, and I gaze at her beauty.

Has it been six weeks since I've seen her? My eyes drink her in like water in the desert. How could I let those assholes spook me? I should've holed up in my apartment with a gun to protect her like a cowboy in the old west. Let them shoot us out.

No one's ever separating me from my woman again... that is, if she'll have me again.

"It says you should take one a day... Have you taken any yet?"

"I don't remember. Just give me one." I want to get better now.

Everything in me strains for health, for the ability to take her in my arms and prove to her how I'll love her so well. I'll never let her down again.

"I've got to go into town." Michele is still frowning at me. "Text me if you need anything."

He leaves, and Gia goes to the kitchen, digging around in the refrigerator. "Are you hungry? I have yogurt, eggs, toast..."

"I'm sorry to make you wait on me."

"Nonsense, you're injured. You'd do the same if it were me." She has no idea. "What can I make for you?"

"Something easy. Yogurt?"

She glances at me, wrinkling her nose. "It's probably better for you since you've had a shock, and you're taking antibiotics.

You'll need something more substantial if you're going to get your strength back."

No shit.

She opens a small container of yogurt and carries it to me with a spoon. While I'm eating, she goes to the balcony, taking what looks like sewing materials and a shiny rainbow bundle.

"Is that what you're doing now?" I'm sitting up in bed watching her. "Sewing?"

She nods, a little smile touching her full, kissable lips. "Before I started dancing, I used to dream of making and designing clothes."

"Why didn't you?"

"I don't know." She shrugs. "I don't have any connections. My aunt said my designs were too daring."

"Is that the same aunt who used to cut you down all the time?"

She blinks down to her lap, seeming embarrassed. "I told you about that?"

"You did." Looking around the small apartment, I piece the clues together. "This must be your mother's old place. What made you come here? You should have had enough money to go anywhere, start a whole new life."

"I could've." Her voice grows softer. "I wasn't thinking that way at the time. I only wanted comfort. Memories of my mother were the only thing I had."

Her words twist pain in my chest. "I'm sorry, Gia."

She shakes her head firmly, turning to the bundle in her lap. "I don't want to talk about it."

Silence falls between us. I look towards the open window, but from where I'm lying in the bed, I can't see the ocean. Still, I can hear it. I can smell the fresh scent of the water and hear the seagulls crying.

I understand why she would love this little place, filled with the only happy memories she has of her childhood. My insides burn with longing for her, this beautiful girl who gave me everything. That surge of possessiveness is still so strong inside me, even now with her holding me at arm's length, refusing to look at me, her pretty gaze focused on the item in her lap.

"Is that one of your daring designs?" I nod to the colorful bundle.

She holds up a rainbow pantsuit with two long strips of fabric extending from the waist. "It's for Michele. He wants to wear it in his show in Florida."

"A Giana Rossi original?"

"I prefer the House of Rossi." Her smile is cautiously proud. "He described the concept. I found the fabric, then I sketched out a pattern. It kind of… comes up the sides like this and crisscrosses at the neck. It's not really daring."

"I like it. I'm sure when he wears it, you'll get more commissions."

"I designed all my costumes at The Rhino." She turns the fabric, stitching a Velcro closure along the back. "A few of Shula's, too."

"It sounds to me like costuming is your gift."

She shrugs. "Maybe, but I don't know how I'd get my foot in the door. Once Michele goes back to Florida, I'll be far away."

"Lately, I've noticed how life has a funny way of circling around if you work hard and keep trying." I stretch my back against the headboard. "For instance, I actually think I'm going to survive this, and here I am… with you."

Large brown eyes blink up to mine, then she quickly looks away. "I'm glad you're feeling better. You're too young to die."

Exhaling a sharp pain, I shake my head. "It's a wonder I've survived this long."

"How did it happen?"

It takes me a minute to think about it, to remember how that night played out. "This was actually an accident. I got in between two friends who were fighting."

"What kind of friends fight with guns?"

That makes me laugh, which again shoots pain through

my injury. Closing my eyes, I lean my head back, waiting for it to pass.

She's at my side so fast, placing her cool hand against my forehead. "Are you okay?" Fear is in her voice, and when I open my eyes, hers are softer. "Please let me give you something."

Only one thing I want from her…

"I'm okay." I do my best to breathe through the pain, to force a chuckle. "I guess I have nine lives." She's so close, I have to take a chance. "I hope I'm able to spend one of them with you."

It's too fast.

The momentary warmth in her eyes shutters, as if she just remembered something. Something like I hurt her.

She stands, pulling on invisible armor. "I'll let you stay until your strength is back, but don't get confused. We're not going down that road again."

Nodding, I rest my head against the wall. I have no one to blame but myself for her defensiveness. "I understand."

CHAPTER 30

Gia

A WEEK PASSES, AND TRIP CONTINUES TO HEAL. I CONTINUE TO sleep every night in the bed with him beside me. I keep my back turned, but I feel his breath against my skin. His scent is all over my sheets, citrus and suede, heating my body and weakening my resistance.

The place between my thighs remembers how it felt to be touched by him, and I grow wet. When I finally sleep, I make love to him in my dreams. His mouth is on my breasts, kissing and sucking. His mouth is between my thighs, licking and thrusting. I wake with my heart beating and my body surging with need. I long to slide my hand between my thighs and soothe that ache, but this bed is too small. He's too close. It's torture.

DJ stops by every day to check on him and help him shower and change his bandages. I'm grateful he's around, because I'm not sure how I would respond to being so close to Trip naked. I'm not sure I could handle seeing his injury.

When he arrived here in so much pain, my heart literally

ached. As much as he hurt me, I couldn't bear the sight of him suffering, much less the thought he might die. I had to fight the tears, fight the urge to hold him, especially when he looked at me with so much longing.

His strength increases daily. He's able to sit up on his own. He's even able to take a few steps, but it saps his energy. He sleeps a lot, and when he's awake, we talk.

He told me more about his father, how he grew up watching him belittle his mother and bully everyone else, including him. He told me about the massive apartment overlooking Central Park, and the friends he made there, the two sisters who lived above him and how they played in the courtyard as children. I imagine him as a little boy, his hair lighter, his cheeks chubby, climbing on the fountain and hiding in the passageways.

Our relationship is growing deeper than what we had in Florida, and the walls I've erected to keep him out start to crack. He swallowed so much pain in his early life. I want to smooth my hand over his forehead, make him explain why he said those cruel words to me. Why would he throw away what we had that way?

When it's time for his antibiotic, I sit on the side of the bed, holding a glass of water.

His hazel eyes move like a caress over my fingers wrapped around the cool drink dotted with condensation, to my exposed arm, to my neck, my lips…

"It's so warm today." My voice is breathless when he takes the glass from my hand.

I lift my long hair off my skin to tie it up on my head, and his eyes fall to my breasts, bound by the V in my lavender wrap dress.

The hunger in his gaze is as hot as my insides every night, and if he said we were going to have sex right now, I would likely stand and take off my clothes.

Instead, he grins. "Why are you so sweet to me?"

"I don't know." I shrug, doing my best to act as casual as

he always does. "You set me up in a fabulous condo. You gave me a job when I had none."

"Am I allowed to take credit for that? I didn't even know you."

"You were a good boss. You cared about your employees, and I did jeopardize your business."

He groans, dropping his head back. "None of that mattered to me."

"You threatened to have me deported." Heat rises in my throat, and it's good. It reminds me why I have to keep my guard up around him.

His lips tighten, and he lifts his chin. "It's time I tell you everything."

"Okay." I'm quiet. "I'd like to hear everything."

Our eyes meet, and his are deadly serious. "I told you I'm a bad man. I've done things I never want you to know." Exhaling heavily, he studies his hands. "Fuck, I don't even know what I can tell you now without putting your life in danger."

I sit back and wait, preparing myself for the worst.

He continues. "I work with very rich, very powerful men. I don't mean just in America. These men are powerful on a global scale and richer than you could imagine. They'll do anything to protect their power and money, but above all, to keep their identities secret."

"Why secret? Most people like to show off."

"Not these guys. They're deadly quiet, because much, if not all, of their work—well, it bends the law."

My brow furrows, and I remember my unexpected visitor. "One of them came to see me."

"Who was it?" His eyes flash, and the muscle in his jaw flexes.

It's such an intense show of anger, I'm afraid. "He was my Number 1 fan. Andre Bertonelli."

"What did he say to you?"

Shaking my head, I cut to the main points. "He wanted

money. He said he didn't want to hurt me, but he said you would force his hand."

Trip's eyes close, with an exhale. He rests his head against the headboard, and his tone is flat. "Andre Bertonelli is dead."

"Oh!" My throat tightens as I remember the desperate man in my room. "Is that how you were shot? Did you kill him?"

"No." His tone turns deadly. "I wish I'd killed him. I was trying to get answers from the criminal who gave me the news when I was shot."

I'm strangely relieved Trip isn't a murderer, despite what he keeps saying, he's not a bad man. Still, "Why do you work with men like that?"

Shaking his head, his green eyes meet mine. "It was a short-cut to wealth and power. I was arrogant. I wanted to be inde-pendent… I didn't know there are no shortcuts, and in the end, it cost me more than I wanted to pay."

"Are you in danger now?"

"I don't know." He looks down. "I quietly began divesting my interests in Manhattan, in south Florida, cashing in my chips and moving my money into offshore accounts. I don't know why they were watching me, but I'm not looking to go back and ask."

A loud knock on the door startles me. "Hold that thought."

I skip over to answer, feeling a little nervous now, after our conversation, but when I open the wooden barrier, a woman is there. She's about my height wearing oversized dark sun-glasses, and her red-velvet mouth is curved in a fierce scowl.

"Are you Giana Rossi?" Her voice is sharp, all business, and she removes her sunglasses to glare at me with ice-blue eagle eyes.

"I'm sorry. Do I know you?" I feel like I'm in trouble with the school principal, which in my case would be Mother Superior.

"You do not know me." She strides into the room, dressed in a sleek black shift dress with a small triangle Prada logo at the shoulder. Her dark hair is bobbed at her ears, and her bangs are cut in a straight line. "My name is Anabella Vitolo, and it seems you are in possession of a dress that belongs to me. I'm on my way back to Milan this afternoon, and I have no more time to wait for you to return it."

"What dress?" My brow furrows, and I try to think.

"Don't play stupid with me, young lady. It's a couture Prada from the Fall ready to wear collection. That dress is worth five thousand dollars, and if you think—"

"The Prada!" I shriek. "Oh my goodness, I'm so sorry! I was working on it and my friend here was injured. I put it aside to take care of him, and I guess I forgot."

"I have no interest in your personal life." She crosses her arms, glaring at me. "Give me the dress."

"Of course!" I quickly dash to the large armoire, removing the dress. "I was so close to being finished. Look…" I go to where she's standing. "Only a few stitches left. If you have five minutes, I can whip it up real quick. No charge."

Her eyes narrow. "I wasn't planning to pay."

"It truly is my fault." Trip is on the bed, looking so handsome in spite of himself. His hair is a little messy, and the scruff has returned to his cheeks. Michele loaned him a white button-up shirt, and it's open to reveal the white bandage stretched around his athletic build. "I burst in without a warning, turned everything to complete chaos, and I've taken up all her time for the last week."

She studies him. "You're American."

"I live in New York, and you're from Milan?"

"Yes." Her answer is clipped, and she glances at the dress I'm holding. "I'll give you five minutes."

Grabbing my kit, I quickly remove the needle I'd placed in the skirt when I pricked my finger and step out to the balcony where I left my chair. I can work better without the pressure of them watching me.

"What do you do in Milan, Ms. Vitolo?" Trip's voice has a touch of business in it.

Our unexpected visitor hesitates, but she answers him with an air of entitlement. "I'm the outreach coordinator at the House of Prada. I report directly to the creative director."

Swallowing hard, I try not to faint. *The House of Prada?*

"Outreach coordinator…" Trip continues unaffected. "That sounds like marketing. You might know my friend Blake van Hamilton. She modeled for Prada in the last September issue of *Vogue*. Jacque Carlisle shot it?"

"Your friend modeled our clothes for Jacque Carlisle?" Her tone changes, and I lean closer, listening as I finish my stitching.

"For American *Vogue*." Now Trip's tone is entitled, and a grin wrinkles my nose. "My friend here, Giana Rossi is an aspiring designer. You should take a look at her sketches."

"Hmm… What fashion school did she attend?"

Cold flushes my skin. I only graduated high school, and I've never had a day in any sort of design school or formal training.

Trip doesn't hesitate. "The same fashion school as Karl Lagerfeld, Coco Chanel, Jean Paul Gaultier."

Blinking hard, I swallow the sob in my throat. He's fighting for me. Why is he doing this?

"I see. So no design school?"

"But she has experience." He's so confident. "She designed the dance costumes for several of my employees in south Florida. Ask her to show you what she's done when she comes back. Or better yet, check out her newest sketches on that table there. I'm sure Prada wants to cultivate talented, young Italian designers. She could be the next Gianni Versace, and if you don't watch it, I'll steal her away to Miami."

I blink hard against the tears. Anabella doesn't reply, but I hear her moving around the room. I'm finished with my work, and I tie it off, cutting the thread with my teeth like my mother taught me.

Hesitating, I step inside, carrying the dress to where she's standing beside the dining table, looking down at my sketches.

"Again, I'm so sorry this was lost in the confusion." I hand the beautiful dress to her. "I hope you'll forgive me. I'm usually very organized."

She takes the dress, scanning my face before inspecting the repair. "This is good stitching, neat and small. Your friend here claims you're an aspiring designer."

"It's been my dream since I was a girl. My mother taught me to sew like they do in the fashion houses in Milan."

"Do you have anything you've created here you could show me?"

I can barely breathe. "I have this." Going to the armoire, I open the double doors and take out the rainbow pantsuit I made for Michele. "I know it's unusual, but my friend is a drag queen. He wanted something to make a statement." She takes it from my hand, inspecting the fabric, the stitching.

Digging deeper, I find the magenta-pink feathered costume I never wore as Glitter Girl. "I designed this to match a pair of platform Valentino Mary Janes."

"From the fall collection?" Her voice has changed to interest, and I nod. "I know the ones you're referencing. The Barbie pink palate."

"Yes." It's like I'm having an out of body experience.

I'm showing my designs, my sketches, and my craftsmanship to a woman from Prada. How is this happening?

Anabella Vitolo crosses her arms. "I'm on my way to Milan, but I'd like to take these sketches." I can't nod fast enough. "We actually lost one of our interns last week, so there's an opening. Can you come for an interview in the next few days?"

"Yes!" I want to ask if tomorrow is too soon.

"I'll show these to the creative director. The design intern position is not easy. It's long hours and doesn't pay much. You're basically an errand girl, but it'll get your foot in the door." Reaching into her small bag, she takes out a card and hands it to me. "This is my contact information. If I don't hear from you by the end of next week, I'll assume you aren't interested."

I take the card, and she takes the dress, turning on her heel and leaving the room. The door clicks closed, and I can't move. I'm standing in the same place, staring at the small piece of beige cardstock with her name printed on it, trying to remember how to breathe.

"What just happened?" My voice is barely a whisper. "What did you do?"

Trip's deep laugh breaks the spell, and he carefully slides from the bed, walking slowly to where I stand dumbfounded. "I only helped get the door open." He puts both hands on my shoulders, smiling down at me. "You have to walk through it."

Stepping forward, I wrap my arms around his waist—so tightly, he exhales a gasp of pain. My eyes are squeezed shut, and I have to hold onto him or I'll faint. I'm already crying. It's all too much.

"I can't believe it."

Placing his fingers beneath my chin, he lifts my face. "Believe it, beautiful girl. You deserve this."

I want to rise onto my toes and kiss him. I want to tell him all is forgiven, and I'll believe anything he tells me from now until the end of time.

Gazing into his eyes, I infuse my voice with all the emotion I'm feeling. "You are not a bad man. You are a good man. *Molto gentile da parte tua.*"

"What does that mean?" Intense emotion reflects in his eyes.

He has no idea, and I have to swallow my heart. "It means thank you."

It means much more, but I remember the strength I've gained over the last year, how I've learned to rely on myself. So I force myself to release him, to go to where I left my sketch pad and pick it up. I've got work to do.

Sleeping in the same bed with Trip and not touching him after what he did for me was excruciating. Anabella Vitolo was the first visitor we'd had since he arrived, and her intensity left him exhausted and me flying.

Tonight, my back is not turned. As he sleeps, I gaze at his elegant face, so relaxed. He's so handsome. He's making my dreams come true. He's helping me find my way.

Is it enough to make up for what he did? My brain still says no, but my heart is screaming yes. My hormones were screaming yes the first time I saw him, even pale and on the edge of death, I loved him so much.

He did apologize. I retrace his words from that very first night when he thought he was dying. *You deserve to be cherished… I'm so sorry.*

Tucking my hand under my chin, I squeeze my fist tighter so I don't reach out and touch him. I want to press my lips to his and slide our tongues together. I want to thread my fingers in his hair and show him my gratitude the way our bodies do so well.

But I hold myself in check. I promised Michele, I promised me, I wouldn't let him in again. Still, I can't forget what he's done for me. Is it enough?

I don't even realize I've slept until the light shines on my face. Squinting, I sit up in the bed, inhaling deeply the rich coffee Michele has brewed for us.

"You're up early," I groan, rubbing my eyes.

"It's after nine, *farfalle.*" It's the first time he's called me *butterfly* since he's been here. It feels right with this new opportunity in front of me.

"I can't believe I slept so late." I scoot higher in the bed, taking the cup.

"We need to celebrate. My work visa came, which means

I'm heading back to Florida… *soon*." He slides his eyes in Trip's direction.

I take a sip of my coffee. "You're waiting for him to leave?"

Trip rouses beside me, rubbing his eyes and looking around. "Good morning."

Michele puts a cup of coffee under Trip's nose. "Time to rise and shine."

"Why yes, I've had enough sleep." Trip squeezes his eyes again before opening them, and I snort a laugh.

"I need to know when you're planning to go home. You're well, and I got my work visa. I want to go back to Florida, but I'm not leaving you here with Gia."

Way to lay it all out there, I think. "Misha's worried about your intentions."

"He hasn't heard about Prada." Trip tilts his head like we're sharing a secret, which I guess we are.

I quickly fill my ex-fiancé-guard-dog in on what happened yesterday, and he hops off the bed. "Gia! That's fantastic. You'll go to Milan, and he'll go… wherever."

Michle waves his fingers towards the door.

"Misha!" I laugh. "That's not very grateful."

"It's what will happen." He lowers his brow, glaring at Trip. "Helping her is the least you can do."

"He's right." Trip's voice is even. "It's the very least. You get ready to fly, to chase your dreams. Don't worry about me."

He's letting me go, and it twists in my stomach. "Is that what you want?"

I look up at him, and he returns my gaze with so much affection, my eyes heat.

"I want everything good for you in the world."

CHAPTER 31

Trip

THIS MORNING, GIA CAUGHT THE TRAIN TO MILAN FOR HER interview, and now Michele stands at the door with his suitcase in hand, headed to the airport.

"What you did for Giana was very good." He nods, then he cuts his dark eyes up at me. "But our agreement still stands. You hurt her, and I have your permission to make you pay however I see fit."

As if I would ever hurt her again. It's ridiculous to think. "Does this mean I have your blessing?"

"It means she can decide what she wants, and if you hurt her again, you'll have to deal with me."

Good enough. "I wouldn't fight you."

Saying goodbye to her was harder than I expected. Her eyes were so bright with hope. She was practically floating out the door.

I watched as she carefully packed all her sketches and the costumes she designed. Over the past two days, she worked on a new sketch for a dress based on a Prada design from the 2000s, and I marveled at her creativity.

When she took my hand and thanked me, I imagined how parents must feel sending their children to school—not my parents, of course. Still, a fierce protectiveness rose in my chest, and I almost asked if I could go with her, to shield her from any criticism or office politics.

I didn't, and she left.

And my heart went with her.

With Michele gone, I'm alone in this small apartment where she grew up, where she came for comfort after I threw her out. It is a warm place to heal with the view and the scents and the sounds.

After all that went down, I'm not ready to return to the states. Franco said I could crash with him if I needed a place, but I declined.

Our family has a villa in the south of France, but I decide to steer clear of any obvious places like family property.

Hell, staying here was a gamble, but I took the chance since Andre was dead—not to mention, I thought I was soon to follow.

DJ shows up after lunch to hang out as I shower. These days, I can change my own bandage, and I don't really need him anymore.

I glance over the door at his thick, bald head. "You know, you could head back to New York whenever you're ready."

"What about you?" His husky voice is concerned.

"I'll stay until she comes back, then I'll go somewhere." He doesn't answer, and I quickly add, "I owe you my life, friend. I'll never forget it."

"Just doing my job. Glad I was there to save you." He looks at his watch. "I figure I'll stick around til Franco gives me the all-clear."

Shaking my head, I'm hit with a surge of gratitude for

this guy who saved my life, who brought me here for a second chance and waited as I recovered.

He leaves me to pass the afternoon alone, and I spend most of it searching for places to rent in Milan—just out of curiosity—and petting the black-and-white village cat I named Figaro, from the movie *Pinocchio*.

He started snooping around a few days ago, and Gia threatened me with my life if I fed him. How could I resist this guy? He's a charmer like me with a black handlebar mustache on his white nose, so I slipped him a few pieces of tuna. Now he's my friend for life, or until the food runs out. Pretty much like most of my friends.

Walking slowly to the window sill, I scratch his neck. He responds by jumping onto the bed where I'm spending less and less time and curls up beside me. Stroking his black and white head, I miss her with an intensity I've never felt for anyone, not family or friends… What is left for me to do to prove myself?

"If she tells me to go, I'll have to go, Fig." I slide my thumb along the markings on his muzzle. "But I really hope she doesn't."

Later that night, when I climb into the bed alone, I look over at her side, thinking how accustomed I've become to seeing her there. Even if she's fully clothed with her back to me, knowing I could reach out and feel her warmth brought me comfort.

Of course, I would fantasize about all the things I wanted to do with her, but none of it felt right without her invitation. I longed for things to be the way they were before with us— excited, eager, hungry, trusting.

Taking out my phone, I send her a text. ***Did you have a good first day?***

Gray dots float, and I'm happy she's there. I'm waiting for a text when the screen changes to the picture of us in bed from her Instagram. I told her she couldn't tag me in it, but I also saved it to my phone, making it her contact photo.

Now she's calling me.

"Hey, how'd it go today?" I can hear the change in my voice.

I'm not casual. I'm not indifferent. I'm eager to hear her words.

I'm in love.

"It was amazing!" Her cute little accent has grown thicker, and she sounds so good. "I got inspired on the train ride, so I sketched out two more dresses and a pantsuit. I wanted to show them I could do more than just costumes."

"I'd like to see them. Can you send me photos?"

"They kept all my sketches, but I'll take pictures tomorrow. They want to give me a tour of the studio, then I'm done. I'll be home tomorrow night."

Her words squeeze my chest, and I can't wait to see her again. We end the call, and I'm already planning. It's my last chance, and I'm making the most of it.

Bouquets of fresh peonies are in crystal vases around the room. I think about the night she had planned for me, the night I nearly destroyed us both.

She had made her signature spaghetti, which I can't possibly replicate. I bought spaghetti and marinara sauce from a restaurant down the street. I grabbed a bottle of Barolo, flowers for every corner of the room, and a bottle of champagne to celebrate.

If they don't offer her the position, they're idiots, and I'll personally invest in the debut House of Rossi and position it directly across the street from Prada in Milan.

Looking down, I'm in the pink linen shirt Michele loaned me, with the sleeves rolled up to my elbows. I've never thought of myself as a man who wears pink, but it's clean, and beggars can't be choosers.

I've been checking the clock constantly. She should be home any moment, when a brief knock precedes the door opening. It's a short, round woman with her hair in a gray bun and tiny, squinty black eyes.

"*Vero.*" She scowls, and I smile, unsure how to proceed.

"I'm sorry," I reply in English. "My Italian is not good."

She switches to English, and as she speaks, I realize who she is. "I heard there were men sleeping here with my niece, many men. I couldn't believe it, but now I see it's true."

"Are you Aunt Gratziela?" I have to be sure, since we do have a language barrier.

"I am. Her poor father was my brother, rest his soul. He had no idea what the woman he married was really like or how she would raise his daughter."

Anger flashes in my throat, and I don't care if she's an old woman, I step to her. "How did she raise her daughter?" The woman's face only comes up to my chest, so I bend lower, meeting her judgmental glare. "Choose your words wisely."

"Have you been sleeping here? In this room with one bed?"

"I was injured, and Gia took me in. She nursed me back to health."

"She *nursed* you?" She barks a laugh, unintimidated. "How much are you paying for this *nursing*? Is that how she was able to buy this house?"

"I bought this house with my own money." Gia's voice slices through our argument. "That's all you need to know."

Stepping back, I see her walking up the stairs with fire in her eyes. She's gorgeous in a sleeveless black shift dress with her dark hair brushed smooth. She's professional and brave and ready to fight for herself—only if I'm around, she'll never fight alone.

"The money you earned taking in these men. Everyone in town is talking, and you thought you could hide it."

"I never tried to hide anything." Gia is the same height as her aunt, and the two are nose to nose. "What do you want to know? I'll tell you everything."

I stand tall behind her, crossing my arms.

The old woman glances at me. "Who is this man? Why is he here?"

"He's my friend. He's staying with me."

"Are you sleeping in the same bed?"

"Yes."

The old woman shakes her head. "Just like your mother."

"What do you mean? You said I was nothing like my mother." Gia's eyes flash, protective anger in her voice.

"Your mother was a *porca troia*, a *prostituta*. She sold her body for money."

My girl staggers as if she's been hit, but I'm at her back, holding her up. "That's not true," Gia hisses. "My mother was not that."

"How do you think she afforded this place? She was a wicked woman, and she raised you to be wicked just like her." Her aunt punctuates her words with a pointed finger. "I tried to take you to church. I tried to teach you better, but your wicked blood won out."

Taking Gia's arm, I move her to my side, wrapping my fist around the old woman's pointing finger.

"Don't do that." My jaw is clenched, and she jerks her finger from my hand.

"What do you know? *Sfigato!*"

"He is not *sfigato*." Gia's eyes are blazing, and I hold her waist. "He helped me."

"I know how your business works." Her aunt moves her hands like she's washing them. "I am done with you. You are *verme*."

My Italian sucks, but I know what *verme* means. "Look at me, old woman." I'm thinly veiled rage at this point, and her eyes widen. "I don't know Gia's mother, but I know Gia. She's a *good* girl. She's always been good. In fact, she's better than you because she doesn't make assumptions and pass judgment on things she knows nothing about. Ever. She's kind and loving. She helps her friends, and she took me in when I almost died—even when I didn't deserve it. Even when I hurt her."

The old woman blows air through her lips and shakes her head like she's unimpressed. I'm ready to make an impression.

"You called me stupid? Perhaps you'd better learn who I am. I could buy this village and throw you out. I love your niece, and I'll do anything to protect her. That includes getting rid of you. So you'd better watch your step, and if you know what's good for you, you'd better watch your mouth."

"How dare you threaten me?" Her eyes widen.

"It's not a threat." I get right in her face. "It's a promise. Now get out of here." My voice rises louder. "I said GO!"

The old woman lets out a little noise as she holds her skirt, scampering down the stone steps to the door leading out to the street.

Just before she closes, I yell, "Don't come back!"

Shutting the door slowly, I turn to my beauty, feeling pretty proud—until I see her expression. Her eyes are sad, her shoulders drooped.

"Hey." I hurry to where she stands, doing my best to sound encouraging. "Don't let that old bitch get you down. We've got her on the run."

"My mother was a prostitute?" She puts her small suitcase on the bed and her portfolio of sketches on a chair.

"Your mother isn't here to speak for herself." I reach out, curling my fingers, wanting to touch her so much. "Maybe she had to do things, make certain choices, to pay the bills. Maybe she didn't want you to know. From all you've told me, she loved you very much. God knows I'd never judge her."

"I've done things for money…" Her voice trails off, then she looks up and her expression changes. Her eyes blink wide, and she turns, taking in the flowers and the wine and the food simmering on the stove.

"What is all this?" She looks up at me, confused.

I slide my hands in the pockets of my chino pants and shrug. "I thought we should celebrate. I took a chance they offered you the job?"

Her lips press together, and her cute nose crinkles. She cups her hands over her mouth and nods quickly. "They did!"

A *whoop!* escapes my lips, and she runs to me, jumping into my arms, and *fuck,* that hurts. Still, I wouldn't let her go for the world. I squeeze her tighter. Her arms are around my neck, her face is buried in my shoulder, and I lean back against the counter and close my eyes. My wound is screaming, but God, it feels so damn good to hold her again.

Her legs slide down my waist, and she steps back quickly, eyes wide. "I'm so sorry! Did I hurt you? I wasn't thinking—"

"You did not hurt me." Reaching out, I grab her again, pulling her into my arms again. "I've wanted to hold you for so long."

Her shoulder rises, and her body stiffens. *Fuck,* I release my hold, reading her body language. **No touching...**

She goes to the table where the bottle of Barolo is waiting. "Why don't we have some wine? Would you like a glass?"

"Of course." I turn, lifting the lid off the saucepan and giving the contents a stir. "I thought you might be hungry, so I bought this in the village."

She walks to me, handing me a glass of wine and peeking at the sauce. "It smells amazing. And you bought flowers?"

"To celebrate." Taking my glass, I give hers a little clink. "I even got champagne."

"It's all so beautiful." She takes a sip of the wine, looking around the small space.

"You're so beautiful. I missed you."

She nods, her wide eyes scanning me. "You're better."

"Getting there, and I've been looking for places to stay. It's time for me to go." I smile warmly. "Time for your second act."

"My second act." Her full lips press together, making me so hungry for her kiss. "I remember having you in the audience. How it made me confident. I felt like I could do anything for your eyes. Like now."

"I want to support you. I'll always cheer for you." I look down at my wine. "But you don't need me."

"I'm not sure that's true."

Our eyes meet, and hope surges to life in my chest. "What are you saying, Gia?"

She inhales deeply, taking measured steps. "After what happened… I swore I'd never let you near me again. I was determined to get over you and learn from my mistakes."

Her words hurt, but there's less conviction in her tone.

"You're a smart girl, a survivor." I speak carefully. "You deserve only good things, and I'll understand if you decide you can't be with me."

"I never made that decision." She glances up at me, fire in her pretty brown eyes. "*You* made that decision. You told me to go. You said it was only about Glitter Girl."

Wincing, I would give my left arm to take back those words. *As it is…*

"It was a lie." I speak like I'm approaching a wounded animal. "I loved you before I ever knew you were her. After our dinner, I had no interest in Glitter Girl. Don't you remember?"

"I remember…" She takes a breath. "But I'm afraid."

"Of what, beautiful girl?"

"I'm afraid to trust you. I'm afraid to lose control again."

"You have total control now. Don't be afraid."

"I am afraid, though. I'm afraid of how much I feel for you. I love you, and you have the power to hurt me so easily." Tears are in her voice, and it guts me.

"I did hurt you, but don't you *ever* for one second think it was easy." My fist closes on the countertop, regret aching inside me. "If I'd had time to plan, maybe… I don't know. All I know was my friend had been murdered, and everything was happening fast. I couldn't risk you being next. I forced myself to say those words, Gia, but they almost killed me. When you left, I bled out every day remembering your tears."

She's blinking fast, and salty drops hit her cheeks. I close the space between us, lifting my hand, holding it so close, longing to touch her, to wipe those tears away.

My voice is husky with my own emotion. "If you ever decide to forgive me, to trust me again, I swear on my life… *Dammit*, I swear, I'll dedicate however many days I have left to making it up to you, to protecting you. I'll never make you cry again."

She sniffs, a sob wobbling from her throat. "You're making me cry now."

Exhaling a groan, heat is in my eyes. "Do I have permission to touch you?"

"Yes."

She's in my arms before the word passes through her lips. Cupping her face, I lean down to capture her mouth with mine, sliding my lips across hers, slipping my tongue inside to taste hers. She's fine wine and pure decadence. She's my heart and my soul.

Before her, I didn't care if I lived or died, but she gives my selfish existence meaning. Her hands clutch my shoulders, and strength surges through my limbs. She threads her fingers in my hair, and I groan.

"My love," she moans, kissing my cheeks, my lips. "I only want you to touch me. I only want your eyes on me. Ever."

"Beautiful girl." I kiss her again, sliding my tongue with hers as my hands slide around her waist, down to cup her luscious ass. "I'll never let you go. I want to give you thousands of beautiful things. I love you."

"And I'll give them all back to you." Our eyes meet, and she's smiling.

She's so damn beautiful.

"I'd like to make love to you now… unless you're too hungry?"

"I thought you'd never ask!" She grips the collar of my shirt in her fists, jerking me to her, across the short distance until we fall together on the bed.

We laugh, and she's on top of me, straddling my waist and unbuttoning my shirt, tracing her progress with kisses against my skin. My dick is so hard, and I grip her thighs, pushing up her skirt and tearing at her thong underwear.

"I need to taste you." My voice is hoarse, ravenous.

"Get this off me before I rip it!" She's as frantic as I am, grasping at her back, and I chuckle as I toss my shirt aside.

I slide the zipper down, and she shoves her arms out of the dress, quickly removing her bra. I groan when her gorgeous tits bounce out, and I slide my palms up to cup them, squeeze them, tweak her hard nipples with my fingers. We climb to the center of the bed on our knees, and I go behind her.

"God, you are so fucking hot." My mouth is on her neck, and she moans, writhing against me. "Sleeping in this bed with you night after night was fucking torture."

"I almost died every time," she gasps. "I don't think I can wait. I'm going to come."

"Not without me." Reaching between us, I grasp my erection, sliding it between her legs until I find her slippery core and thrust deeply.

"Oh, fuck!" We both groan, and I rock my hips, driving in and out of her divine depths.

She moves with me, meeting my thrusts, holding the back of my neck with her hand. Reaching between her thighs, I slide my fingers up and down, searching until I find that little spot.

Fever swirls around us. I'm circling my fingers over her clit, thrusting my cock in her hot, wet pussy, and she's grasping at my hair, my neck, moaning. We don't last long before I feel her break into spasms. Her body stiffens in my arms, and I can't hold out anymore. I let go of the need driving me wild, pulsing in my veins and driving through my pelvis, spilling into her.

We hold each other as we consummate the promises we've made, as white-hot reunion solders us together into one.

When I can breathe, I slide my arms around her body, one around her waist and the other over her shoulders. My face is at her ear, and I kiss her.

"I love you so much." I'm not even ashamed of the emotion so thick in my voice.

We lie back on the bed, and I pull her into my embrace. Her body is flush with mine, soft breasts against my chest, soft hips against mine. I slide my hand along her cheek, smoothing back her dark curls. She gazes at me with glowing, beautiful eyes. She's stolen my heart and my soul.

"Thank you for forgiving me, my beautiful Gia." I kiss her forehead. "You saved my life."

Her eyes close, and tears sparkle in her lashes. Sliding my thumb over her cheek, I kiss her closed lids.

She touches my cheek, and when our eyes meet again, she smiles. "Thank you for fighting for me."

"I will always fight for you. I love you."

"I love you." She stretches in my arms, kissing me firmly on the lips.

We're surrounded by flowers and warmth and healing, the beautiful scent of the ocean laced with the fresh flowers and the food. It's something I didn't think was possible in my old life. It's something I didn't expect to have until I met this beautiful girl with her pure heart.

She truly has saved me, and together, we can rise above the evil. She's my butterfly, and together we can fly.

EPILOGUE

Gia

"WE'RE LEAVING FOR DUOMO IN A HALF-HOUR." ANABELLA'S assistant Mira grins as she peeks her head inside the door of the design studio. "Don't forget your kit."

I nearly choke on my coffee. "I get to go this time?"

"Yes." She walks over to where I stand at a sketch table, working on my latest creation. "I told them I needed help with so many outfits to fit and makeup to check…"

Mira is my age, but stick-thin with pale skin and heavy brows. Her look is very Audrey Hepburn in *Funny Face,* with her light brown hair styled in a ponytail with bangs. She wears black pants and black turtlenecks with penny loafers and no socks every day.

When I was hired as second assistant (the very bottom of the ladder), she was promoted, and she has become one of my closest friends in the office—possibly because she has a vested interest in keeping me onboard. Second assistant is basically a glorified gofer.

Leaning closer, she inspects the sketch I've been working

on for ten minutes, during a rare break in my routine of fetching coffee and checking emails and listening to voicemails and delivering swatches and being insulted by Pietro, the head designer.

It's a collarless, black suede jacket with waist-length fringe extending from the shoulders on the front and back, creating the effect of a flowy cape.

"I like this." She lifts my hasty pen-and-ink drawing. "You should show it to Pietro."

"Sure," I exhale a frustrated groan. "I'll show him my new favorite sketch so he can dump on it."

"Pietro is a jerk, but he has this wrong idea that's how the lead designer is supposed to act. He can help you. Keep at him."

"Maybe." I shuffle my sketch into my portfolio. "After a while, you start to believe his insults."

Not having any design school background has given me a major case of imposter syndrome.

"Show him that sketch." She flicks her wrist. "He's really into fringe right now. Edgy rock-n-roll is the theme of his show in September. He's pushing back on all the Barbie pink."

"He is?" I slide my hand over the ink drawing I finished yesterday. "I have another sketch of a black dress with strappy ties over the bust and around the neck. I paired it with a black leather biker jacket. Should I show him that too?"

"Sure! Bring them all. I wouldn't encourage you if I didn't think you had talent." Her red lips curl into a smile. "You're a comer, Gia."

Butterflies are in my stomach at her compliment. I've been working on transforming my dance costumes into edgy, sexy streetwear. Trip actually gave me the idea.

He told me the first costume I wore as Glitter Girl—the one that kept him in his seat instead of walking out the door— was the one with green-fringed, assless chaps. Apparently the *assless* part got him. Or my ass.

Who knew my boyfriend avoided strip shows until he saw

me dance? He said strippers made him sad because he'd think about all the circumstances that had brought the girls there.

It was unexpectedly sweet, but I had to push back. "Not all strippers come from bad circumstances, you know. Some of them choose the profession, and they do very well at it."

"You're saying it was your childhood dream?" His eyebrow arched along with those sexy lips.

"No, but the joke is on you," I teased. "I actually did turn to dancing out of desperation, and you couldn't get enough of me."

"Mm, you can say that again." He laughed, smoothing my hair off my cheeks and kissing my lips. "You were hot as fuck, and those assless chaps made my dick very, very happy."

Naturally, that led to a pretty intense round of lovemaking.

We've been in Milan together a month, and my personal life is fabulous beyond my wildest dreams. I insisted he come with me, even though we're still working out the details of *us*.

Milan is landlocked, which made me a little sad, having always lived near the sea. So he rented a house overlooking the canal with a view of the mountains in the distance and flowering shrubs climbing the walls.

We open the French doors each morning, and the cool breeze sweeps inside, carrying the scent of coffee and fresh baked sweets from the cafés below. It's like Santa Croce, and I love him for working so hard to make my transition easier. He spoils me like crazy.

I love my job with Prada, but it's been tough. Trip was ready to go down and punch Pietro in the nose for all his insults and move me to Armani or Versace, but I want to pay my dues. If I'm going to work in the design field, I want to earn my place here—just like I did when I was a dancer.

Collecting my things, I follow Mira out to the tiny, beige Fiat we'll take to the iconic temple in the center of Milan. Mira is beside herself because the famous Jacque Carlisle is photographing the campaign for the September issue of American *Vogue*.

"He's one of the greatest fashion photographers—right up there with Annie Leibovitz and Helmut Newton."

Annie Leibovitz is the only photographer whose work I've seen, but I remembered Trip talking about Carlisle to Anabella. "That's incredible. He'll get to see Pietro treat me like shit all day."

"Just stay cool and keep out of sight. Be invisible."

Glancing down at my white blouse and full black skirt, I'm not sure if I can. I've been trying to dress more like the girls in the office, but with my curves and my hair, it's tough not to stand out. They're all stick figures, and my figure is the opposite of *stick*.

Lucky for me, Trip loves every inch.

Exhaling a sigh, I follow Mira across the expansive court-yard, carrying a case of water and a giant bag of makeup, pins, clips, and a myriad of brushes. A small tent has been erected off to the side where the models will change and have their hair and makeup done.

Hesitating, I can't resist gazing up at the massive medieval church with its pointed spires and stunning façade. It's the first time I've been to Duomo since we moved to Milan. I've been working so much, we haven't had time to be tourists.

"It's so beautiful." The words slip past my lips before I can stop them.

"One must imagine the peasants approaching this house of God for the very first time." Turning, I cautiously meet the crinkled blue eyes of an older man with white hair and a gray beard. "It must've seemed like entering the Celestial City."

Dropping my chin, I do my best to follow Mira's instructions. "I wouldn't know, sir."

"What's your name?" He studies me, arching an eyebrow. "You have the body of a young Sofia Loren."

"Thank you…" *I guess?* Is this allowed?

"Yes, thank you, Giana." Pietro puts a finger on my shoulder, turning me towards the makeup tent. "Mira needs your help, and I'm sure the models are parched."

"Of course. I'm sorry."

The older man watches me scurry away with the case of water, while Pietro rolls his eyes as if I'm the most annoying insect on the planet. "Our new second assistant is always bumbling where she's not supposed to be."

His comment stings, but I remind myself I'm paying my dues. Ducking into the tent, I go to where Mira is blotting a model's finished face with a giant setting sponge.

"Water, thank you!" She takes one for her and one for the model, who's, like, a foot taller than me and half my weight.

She's wearing a long, black dress with tiny red flowers dotted sparsely throughout the fabric. The quarter-length sleeves fall in voluminous puffs at her forearms, and the skirt is a high-low design. Her hair is braided right at the top and frizzed out big to her shoulders, and black Birkenstock sandals are on her feet.

"Did you show him your sketches?" Mira leans over, whispering.

"He turned me away with his finger like I was a stray dog."

"So I take that as a no."

Rolling my eyes, I shake my head. "Who's the old man with him?"

Mira frowns at me. "Jacque Carlisle. I thought you knew him."

"I never said I knew him."

Brianna, the photographer's assistant, bursts into the tent. "Okay, Giana, Mr. Carlisle wants to use you in the editorial. Let's get moving."

"What?" Shaking my head, I look from her to Mira.

"Let's move it, people, we don't have all day!" Briana orders. "We need makeup and hair here… I don't know what we have that'll fit you."

A flurry of assistants surrounds me, removing the pins from my hair and taking my portfolio bag off my shoulder. Before I can argue, a black denim jacket is draped over my white blouse, and a guy applies heavy black eyeliner to my eyes.

Mira whips out a pair of black jeggings. "These will stretch!"

I pull them on, and when she sees my red toenails, she claps. "Excellent! Shoe problem solved. He'll love your feet."

Nerves jangle in my chest as I walk out from behind the black canvas changing area to where the platforms and lights are set up in the square.

I know what I look like, and I know what the models look like. I expect he'll use me as a prop somehow. I'll be the girl holding flowers or the street vendor selling fruit or the assistant carrying her little dog. I'm not expecting to be the focus of the shoot.

"Yes!" Jacque strides to where I'm standing, catching me by the wrist and leading me to the center of the stage. "You're perfect. How do you feel?"

"Like I have no idea what's happening." Wide-eyed, I look around at the models on the sidelines with their arms crossed. "Like a fish out of water."

"You are not a fish." Jacques fixes his smiling blue eyes on me. "You are a mermaid, a magical creature. I want you to imagine you're on a holiday. You're in this beautiful new city, seeing the sights for the first time. I want wonder, excitement, playful energy. Okay?"

I swallow the dryness in my throat. "Okay."

It's not difficult to do what he asks, since it *is* the first time I've visited Duomo. I look around, feeling very awkward, especially when I see Pietro beside the other models glaring at me.

Jacque goes to a small table and picks up a giant camera, then he presses a button and energetic, sexy music begins to play. It's a song I don't know, "Want Me" by Jodi Whatley, he says.

He returns, giving me a wink. "You are the woman in this song. Now make us want you. Seduce the camera."

Taking a deep breath, I channel muscle memory, listening to the music and taking on a character the way I would do when I danced. Picturing Trip in the audience, I bat my eyes, throw my hair, and become the woman he desires, the woman I want him to want.

For the next two hours, I'm posed and arranged in a tiny metal chair. I recline on the side of the fountain, stand with my back to an enormous Corinthian column, bend one leg and allow my shirt to fall off my shoulder.

My white blouse is unbuttoned dangerously low. My curls are brushed into dramatic waves over my eyes, down my back, and my lips are painted glossy nude.

Jacque is thrilled with my black lace bra, my curves, my "bedroom eyes." By the time we're finished, he declares me his "new muse" to a disgusted Pietro. "I must work with you again. Do you have representation?"

"Um… my boyfriend might help me." Wrinkling my nose, I'm not sure if Trip knows about modeling, but he seems to know a little about everything.

Jacque smiles, tapping my chin. "My assistant will call you. All you have to do is say yes. I'll guide you through the rest."

"Thank you."

"How amazing was that?" Mira is bouncing in the driver's seat as we head back to the studio. "It was like watching Beth Boldt finding Naomi Campbell. You're a natural, and I get to tell the story. I can say I knew you when you were a mere second assistant."

I don't know what she's talking about—probably because I never went to design school. "I didn't show him my sketches."

Mira squeezes my shoulder. "I have a feeling before long, you'll be able to show anybody anything, and they'll be begging for more."

With all that happened today, my head is spinning when I arrive back at the apartment. I'm dying to tell Trip everything, particularly the part where I said he was my agent, but when I walk in the door, I can't find him.

Food is simmering on the stove, and a bottle of wine is on the table. I smile at the crystal vase of peonies. He's always buying me flowers, but where is he?

I cross the living room to the balcony calling his name, but he's not there.

I'm in our master suite before I notice the sound of the shower running. Pressing my lips together, I have an idea. All the sexy music and channeling my inner dancer got me a little heated up.

Placing my hand on the door, I gently guide it open, hoping to surprise him. His face is under the spray, one hand braced against the wall, and his head is bowed as the water washes his dark hair forward.

My eyes travel down the lines of muscle in his back. He has the physique of an athlete—long, lean muscles, narrow waist, solid legs. My stomach tingles, and I quickly unbutton my white shirt, unzipping my skirt and discarding my bra and panties on the small chair at my vanity.

He lifts his chin, looking over his shoulder as I open the door. Hazel eyes smolder, gliding from my eyes to my lips, to my bare breasts, to my stomach, finally to my pussy, which is slick and needy for his touch.

"You're home." Desire thickens his voice, but before he can turn I go to him, wrapping my arms around him and pressing my soft parts against his hard ones.

"I'm home." Stretching higher, I slide my tongue along his shoulder, fresh water filling my mouth. "I have so much to tell you, but first, I missed you."

My hand is against his stomach, and I slide it lower,

smoothing it over the erection rising to meet my grasp. The muscles in his arms flex, and his fingers curl on the wall.

"I missed you." The strain in his tone lights my core.

Rising on my toes, I kiss the back of his neck, behind his ear. "I imagined you in here thinking of me, stroking your cock."

"I'm always thinking of you." He turns his face, capturing my mouth. "But I save my cock for you."

"Such a good boy." I grin, biting his ear, and he groans.

"I'll show you a good boy." He turns, and I lose my grip on the iron rod between his thighs.

With a growl, he switches our positions so I'm facing the shower, and his hands are on my body, sliding between my thighs as he massages my clit, slipping a finger into me.

"Already so wet?" He groans as his other hand cups my breasts, tweaking and pulling my nipples. Pleasure floods my veins with heat, and I drop my head back against his shoulder. "What does my bad girl want?"

"I want your cock." I answer fast, already so close to the edge, getting closer from his aggressive touches. "Give it to me."

"Hm… Do I need to remind you who's boss?" He bites the side of my neck, and I moan, remembering our edging session and how my brain nearly exploded.

"Yes…" I gasp, rubbing my ass against his erection, bracing one hand against the shower, and reaching behind me for his cock. "Spank me."

Gripping my hip, he drives roughly into me, holding me steady as he thrusts hard and fast.

"Oh, God…" My palms flatten against the wall, and I'm moaning, meeting his vigorous fucking with my own.

His hand is between my thighs, massaging my clit as the streaks of orgasm flood my veins, as fire burns beneath my skin. I'm moaning and writhing as I start to come with his cock so deep in me, hitting me harder, finding the place where my mind begins to fry.

"Oh, shit, there… right there!" My voice rises to a scream as he groans, thrusting harder.

My legs break into trembles as I orgasm, and I'm afraid I might lose my footing. His arm wraps around my waist, holding me up, and the hand massaging my clit begins to slap. The sharp slaps make me scream, and I'm pulling him deeper into my hungry core.

"Fuck," he groans deeply, and I feel him pulsing, hot jets filling me. "Fuck, yes."

Our bodies stiffen, and we collapse forward against the wall, fusing together in ecstasy. The hand between my thighs now smoothing me, bringing me down, and I reach back to scratch my fingers in his hair, to seal my mouth to his as our tongues lick and curl and consume.

When we're once again able to breathe, I turn in his arms. He smiles down at me, eyes brimming with possession and warmth and all the feelings surging in my belly.

"I love you, Giana Rossi." It's a thrill straight to my heart, and I rise on my toes to kiss him again.

"I love you so much, and I've got so much to tell you."

Stepping back, he switches off the shower, reaching for a thick towel to dry us off and two plush, white terry robes to wrap around our bodies.

"Let's have some wine, and you can tell me everything."

Following him to the kitchen, I thread my fingers in his as I rest my head on his shoulder. He goes to where he reheated my signature spaghetti from last night and prepares us both a bowl, sprinkling freshly grated parmesan cheese on top.

"Mira invited me to help her on a photo shoot today." I take a sip of red wine. "The photographer was that man you knew."

"Jacque Carlisle?" He follows me as we carry our dishes to the table. "He's a big deal in the fashion world."

"He asked me to model for him." We take our seats, and I

shake my head, waving my hands. "It all happened so fast. He restructured the entire shoot around me, said I'm his muse… Pietro was furious, but Mira was thrilled. Anabella, too."

Trip's smile is calm, warm. He has that easy confidence I love so much about him as he reaches across the table to hold my hand. "Jacque has a type—real women. I don't blame him for wanting to work with you."

Getting out of my seat, I round the table to sit in his lap. He scoots back so I can straddle him, wrapping my arms around his neck and resting my head on his shoulder. Strong arms surround me, and I allow the warmth of him to flood into me, easing my fears and boosting my confidence.

"I was so overwhelmed." My voice is quiet, and his strong hand slides up and down my back. "I might've told him you were my agent."

"I can be your agent—if you really want that."

My head pops up. "You would?"

"I'll do anything for you, my love, but you might prefer someone who actually knows about the modeling business. I can make some calls and find the best person for you."

Chewing my lip, my chest is so tight. "None of this would've happened if you hadn't believed in me and made Anabella believe in me."

"I only gave you a helpful nudge."

I meet his eyes again, and I don't know how to say what I'm feeling. "I want all these things, but more than anything, I want you with me. I want us to be together… in all of it."

A different smile curves his lips this time, not casual or aloof, but serious. "My beautiful Gia, I had a plan in mind for tonight, but I don't want to steal your thunder."

"What was your plan?"

He pats my side, and I climb out of his lap so he can go to his coat, hanging by the door. "As I told you, I've cashed out all my holdings in Florida. Franco has taken over those businesses, and Bianca and the girls are with him now."

"She told me what happened after you sent me away."

He nods, turning to me, his pretty eyes so earnest. "I've done everything I can to ensure our safety here—your safety in particular. From what I've been able to learn, no one is searching for me. I'll always monitor that situation, but I'm not going back to the states."

My lips part in surprise. "What about your family? Your friends?"

A sad little smile curls his lips. "They'll be fine without me. If I miss them, maybe I'll visit, but I have everything I could ever want right here." He returns to where I'm standing in my plush robe, revealing a small, robins-egg blue velvet box in his hand. "Just one thing remains."

"Trip?" Happiness rises in my chest as tears flood my eyes. I cover my mouth as he lowers to one knee, holding my left hand. "What is this?"

"I told you once before I wanted to stay with you, to protect you." He opens the box, and I can't breathe. "I tried to send you away, and it nearly killed me. I can't survive without you, Gia. I love you with everything I am. Will you be my wife? Will you stay with me and know I'll lay down my life for you?"

Tears stream down my face before I can even speak the word *Yes*.

The Tiffany engagement ring is a thick platinum band with a two-carat diamond in the center. It's breathtaking and one of a kind and absolutely what my man would choose.

"You've only ever loved me for who I am." I slide my hands down his cheeks, to his neck, dropping to my knees so our faces can be close together. "We're wild and unpredictable. We break the rules, and touch what we shouldn't."

His brow furrows, and he hesitates. "Are you saying—"

"I'm saying there's no one else I want to spend my life with. I want all my adventures to begin and end with you. I want to come to you when I'm afraid or overwhelmed. I want your eyes to be the only ones watching over me."

He smiles, kissing my brow, my cheek, my lips. "My eyes are only for you."

"I love you, William Alexander the third. I will be your wife. I will have your babies. We'll create the new life we both deserve."

The ring is on my finger, and his expression melts into pure love. Our mouths meet once more, and it seals a promise for forever. It's a seal that will bind us through eternity.

It's the transformation that makes us one forever.

Thank you for reading *For Your Eyes Only!*

Complete the series: READ FORBIDDEN NOW…

Dirk's book is a *spicy* **professor-student romance** in which characters are not who they appear and situations turn on a dime. It's thrilling and kinky and brings the series to a shocking, exciting conclusion!
Keep clicking for a short sneak peek…

Also available on Audio.

FORBIDDEN

I have one job: Get close and take him out. The only problem is, I want him more.

I was barely five when I lost my brother; seven when my father was murdered.
Overnight, I was taken by my mysterious uncle, grafted into a world of crime I didn't understand and couldn't escape.

The first ten years, I did my best to blend in.
The next four, I reinvented myself, growing stronger, searching for answers.
Now I have one assignment—take down the man who knows our secrets.

Professor Dirk Winston is my target, and I'm expected to be a good soldier, disguised as a good student.
Only he's not the passive bookworm I expect.
He's ripped muscles, bedroom eyes, dirty mouth, and ready for a fight.

But I've got my plans of my own, and this hot teacher is going to do more than give me grades and take my panties.
He's going to help me get revenge.

(FORBIDDEN is a five-alarm-spicy age-gap, student-professor romance with secrets, lies, and answers to all your questions. No cheating. No cliffhanger.)

CHAPTER 1

Dirk

"I HAVE A BAD FEELING ABOUT THIS." MY OLDER BROTHER WATCHES me, hands on his hips.

Standing in front of the half-renovated warehouse I call home, all my belongings fitting neatly in a large duffel bag, I've never felt more off-course.

"Who are you, Han Solo?" I drop the bag in the back of my Jeep beside a smaller case.

"Sure, if that's the analogy, and you're leaving the field in the middle of a battle."

"That would make *me* Han Solo." I exhale a bitter laugh, turning to face him, pushing too-long brown hair off my forehead. "There's no battle, Hutch. It's been four years. The case is closed. Hell, even Hugh says it's over."

"You know we can't trust what Hugh says," he growls, refusing to let it go.

Hutch is an intimidating guy—former Marine, too many

muscles, too many tattoos. We're three years apart in age, but he's always had my back.

It was easy to say yes to joining his private investigation firm eight years ago. He's the muscle, Oskar Lourde, or Scar as we call him, is Hutch's former military guide, scary as hell and an expert tracker. I'm the tech guy, tracking messages across the dark web, hacking into street cams and security networks to follow suspects throughout the city, often throughout the night. My hours are insane, but I've never been a nine-to-five guy.

All that changed after our last case.

"I won't argue with you, but he paid his bill. We have no reason to keep pursuing it—whatever it would be now."

Hugh van Hamilton is our richest client, and he has a bad habit of withholding vital information from the team he's supposed to trust, a.k.a., us. When he hired us to protect his nieces, we discovered their safety was only the tip of the iceberg.

We spent the next year tracking down blackmailers, exposing a money laundering ring, dodging a Russian oligarch, and escaping a murder charge that almost sent Scar away for life.

I won't lie—it was fun. The challenge, the excitement, the cat-and-mouse, we don't get a lot of that in our tiny town, and now that it's done, I've emerged from my tech-cave to discover I'm the only one waking up every morning alone.

"We have plenty of reasons to keep going." Hutch shakes his head. "Their network is still in place. It's only a matter of time before a new leader emerges, and it'll probably be the guy who murdered Simon Petrovich."

"Simon was the head. We cut off the head, and the body died."

"We didn't cut off the head, and whoever did is going to come back."

That makes me laugh, and I football-charge him with my shoulder. "You're like a bull on red. They're not coming back."

He easily blocks me, pulling me in for a brief hug. "Watch yourself. I don't want to have to kick your ass again."

"Like you ever kicked my ass."

"Only because it would've broken Mom's heart. You were her favorite son."

"Whatever." If that's true, it's because I acted like a son.

Hutch was born to play the dad role, unlike our real dad, who checked out when we were only kids. Our mom leaned on my brother for everything, all the way until she died.

Shaking away that dark memory, I grip his shoulder. "I haven't seen any rumors of a resurgence on any of the chat boards. It's time to let it go. You're married, Scar has a baby on the way…"

My voice trails off as I consider our broody Viking of a partner settled with a wife and baby. Hana's pregnancy was the final straw that made me realize I had to make a change.

"It's time for me to get on with my life." Stepping back, I straighten my jacket, ready to get on the road.

"When we started the firm, we said we'd be partners until retirement."

"I'm still your partner." I push back on the guilt his words trigger, icy tendrils creeping across my chest. "But I've been talking about doing this for years. You thought it was a good idea at one point."

"When you wanted to teach one class at the community college in town. Now you're moving to Miranda Bay, joining the faculty at Thornton." He glances at my belongings crammed in the back of my vehicle, sounding for all it's worth like a parent sending his only child off to college. "This is completely different."

"I'm an hour down the road. I can keep up with anything that pops up, and if I need to come back, it's an easy drive."

"So stay in Hamiltown and commute the days you teach. You could keep your office hours here instead of breaking up the team."

"I'm a faculty member. I don't want to half-ass it. I want to be active in the department. This is the right choice for me,

Hutch. I've spent too many nights chasing bad guys. It's time for me to develop human habits, before I wake up at sixty and realize I'm alone."

"Ah, fuck that. You're nowhere near sixty."

"Maybe not, but the last four years went by faster than I like."

My brother runs a hand over his dark scruff. He's quiet, which means he's thinking. Hutch is stubborn, but he's not inflexible.

Finally, he relents. "Just don't get too comfortable around all those kids running around in wool blazers with their scarves flying over their shoulders."

"It's not Hogwarts," I chuckle, gesturing to the warehouse looming behind us. "Anyway, I've still got to finish this dump. You think I'd let all my hard work go to waste?"

I bought the abandoned garment factory on the edge of town when I graduated from Columbia, and I've been slowly renovating, turning it into an open-floor-plan residence ever since. So far, I've got the upper level completely livable. That just leaves the rest.

Hutch squints up at the massive structure. "You should just hire someone to finish it while you're gone. We have the money."

"Where's the fun in that?" It's slow going, but I enjoy working with my hands. It's a nice balance to being in front of a screen.

"So how long is this teaching thing going to last?"

I slide my backpack off my shoulder as we climb into my Jeep. I'll drive him back to our office in town before I hit the road. "I'm an adjunct professor, so for now it's only a semester to semester gig. If they don't like me, it could be a one and done deal."

"They'll like you."

We drive for a few minutes in silence, and it bothers me that he could be angry at my decision. "I need to do this, Hutch."

He blinks over at me, and the tension in his jaw relaxes. "I know."

A few more minutes of silence, and we're entering town. I parallel park on Main Street in front of our glass door reading *Winston and Lourde* in gold lettering. "You take care of yourself and Blake. Let me know when you've got a baby on the way."

"Not sure Blake's ready for motherhood." A sly grin curls his lips, and my eyes narrow.

"I'm not sure if that look means you're wanting to change her mind or you're still enjoying being on your honeymoon."

"Nothing wrong with an extended honeymoon." He holds the door open for me. "And if we have any accidents, that's okay, too."

A pang of something like jealousy twists in my stomach. It's ridiculous, and I dismiss it. I'm happy for my brother, and I'm equally happy returning to campus life, hitting the books, learning what's new and breaking in the world of academia.

"Hey, handsome." A high, sweet voice greets me as I enter our office building.

"Hana." I catch her in a side hug, her hand resting on the baby belly lifting the front of her black, knee-length dress.

It's short with spaghetti straps, and her pale, blonde spiral curls are gathered up on her head in a messy way, leaving tendrils falling around her cheeks. She's really cute pregnant, and Scar is beaming like I've never seen—he almost looks approachable.

"Professor Winston." Her small nose wrinkles. "I thought you were already on the road. I'm glad I get to tell you goodbye."

"I'm heading out now. Hutch needed a ride to town, and I'm on my way."

Scar walks up to where we're standing. His long hair is pulled back in a samurai bun, and his inked arms extend from his short-sleeved black tee. He slips one around his wife, covering her rounded belly with a large hand.

His torso and arms were severely burned in a fire when he and Hutch were serving together overseas. Elaborate tattoos now cover those scars, and combined with his piercings and wolf eyes, he's an intimidating presence. Hana isn't fazed.

She covers his large hand with her small one, exhaling a light laugh. "Can you believe how fat I am? Just look at me!"

Joy beams in her eyes, but I push back. "You're not fat, you're pregnant."

"But just look how chubby my cheeks are!"

If I didn't know Hana better, I'd think she was shaming herself, but she's not. Hana has struggled with addiction and disordered eating all stemming from the abuse she suffered as a child. She's actually happy.

Scar's eyes smolder with love, and he speaks in a soft growl. "You're beautiful."

She beams up at him, and the heat between them tightens the skin on the back of my neck. I'm not jealous of them…

Okay, fuck it. Maybe I'm a little jealous—of all of them. I'm glad these two wounded souls have found each other. Hell, even Blake and Hutch are pretty incredible together.

Blake is Hana's older sister, and she's fiercely protective of her family, much like my brother. She and Hutch are iron sharpening iron, two powerful forces making each other stronger.

It's all great and happily ever after, the fairytale ending they all deserve, and I'm fucking completely out of the loop. Heat is in my throat, and I force a smile. This is why I need to get out of here, why I need a break.

"Professor." Scar shakes his head with a chuckle. "I don't know how you're going to handle all those teenagers."

"It's a three-hundred level course, so they'll be a little older."

"Just don't do anything stupid. I won't be there to bail you out."

"Got it. No punching the students." I glance around our small office at the computer system I installed, the server and firewall, all the tech I maintain. "Think you can handle all this while I'm gone? I am taking the brains with me."

"Last I checked, your brains were in your briefs."

"That does it—" I lunge at him, driving a shoulder into his abdomen.

He grabs my arms, taking a step back, and for a minute, we push against each other like two rams locking horns over the high ground.

"Good lord, don't break the office." Blake scolds as she enters the glass door.

"He couldn't leave without a fight." Hutch puts his hands on our shoulders, parting us.

We're both red faced, breathing hard, and grinning. "You've been working out." Scar nods at me.

"More like you're getting soft in your old age, Pops."

He makes a move like he might come at me again, but Hutch steps between us, giving Hana a hug. "Hey, sis, you look good."

"Is that what I have to look forward to if it's a boy?" Hana returns his hug, arching an eyebrow at us. "Remind me not to buy anything breakable."

"I'm pretty sure everything in our house was glued together." I laugh, taking my laptop off my desk and slipping it in my backpack. "I've got to hit the road. Let me know if anything comes up. I'll be busy, but not too busy to work remotely."

Scar's lips tighten, and he nods, a hint of a smile telling me he knows why I'm doing this, even if I won't say it out loud.

My brother's send-off is more ominous. "Stay close to your phone. My gut says this is the calm before the storm."

Another tight smile, and I head out, climbing into my Jeep and slamming the door. It's not the first time I've said goodbye to Hamiltown, South Carolina, but it's the first time I've felt like I'm starting something new outside it. It's an unusual feeling, a mixture of excitement and dread, like anything could happen.

Turning the wheel, my mind drifts to what's coming. I'm

starting a new road, forging a new path. After a tense, stressful, dangerous few years, I'm ready to see if I can make a life for myself.

My brother's anticipating a storm, but I'm looking for a silver lining in those clouds.

Read FORBIDDEN Now!

Also available on Audio.

BOOKS BY TIA LOUISE
ROMANCE IN KINDLE UNLIMITED

THE BRADFORD BOYS
*The Way We Touch, 2024**
*The Way We Play, 2024**
*The Way We Score, 2025**
*The Way We Run, 2025**
*The Way We Win, 2025**
(*Available on Audiobook.)

THE BE STILL SERIES
*A Little Taste, 2023**
*A Little Twist, 2023**
*A Little Luck, 2023**
*A Little Naughty, 2024**
(*Available on Audiobook.)

THE HAMILTOWN HEAT SERIES
*Fearless, 2022**
*Filthy, 2022**
For Your Eyes Only, 2022
*Forbidden, 2023**
(*Available on Audiobook.)

THE TAKING CHANCES SERIES
*This Much is True**
*Twist of Fate**
*Trouble**
(*Available on Audiobook.)

FIGHT FOR LOVE SERIES
Wait for Me★
Boss of Me★
Here with Me★
Reckless Kiss★
(★Available on Audiobook.)

BELIEVE IN LOVE SERIES
Make You Mine
Make Me Yours★
Stay★
(★Available on Audiobook.)

SOUTHERN HEAT SERIES
When We Touch
When We Kiss

THE ONE TO HOLD SERIES
One to Hold (#1 - Derek & Melissa)★
One to Keep (#2 - Patrick & Elaine)★
One to Protect (#3 - Derek & Melissa)★
One to Love (#4 - Kenny & Slayde)
One to Leave (#5 - Stuart & Mariska)
One to Save (#6 - Derek & Melissa)★
One to Chase (#7 - Marcus & Amy)★
One to Take (#8 - Stuart & Mariska)
(★Available on Audiobook.)

THE DIRTY PLAYERS SERIES
PRINCE (#1)*
PLAYER (#2)*
DEALER (#3)
THIEF (#4)
(*Available on Audiobook.)

THE BRIGHT LIGHTS SERIES
Under the Lights (#1)
Under the Stars (#2)
Hit Girl (#3)

COLLABORATIONS
*The Last Guy**
The Right Stud
Tangled Up

ACKNOWLEDGMENTS

Readers like you are the reason this book even exists.

I wasn't planning to write a story for Trip when I launched this world, but I wanted to stay in the *Fearless-Filthy-Forbidden* (Jan. 12) realm with this special contribution to the "Blurred Lines" collection.

Kerissa S. is a reader just like you who asked if I might ever consider writing a book for Trip, and here it is. So for everyone who messages me asking if there will be a book for Leon or Marley or Henry and Courtney (and Ollie!), in case you think I'm putting you off, I'm really not! (lol!) You never know.

THANK YOU for loving my books so much, you want one for every single character you love. I'm incredibly blessed to have so many amazing, enthusiastic, *supportive* readers and friends cheering me on and anxiously awaiting each new adventure.

I'm so thankful for my husband "Mr. TL" for his encouragement, for helping me brainstorm, and for always wanting to read my books.

Thank you to my beautiful daughters who have left the nest but still believe in me, make me laugh, and support me from afar. I love you ladies!

Thanks so much to my alpha readers Renee McCleary, Maria Black, and Ilona Townsel for your encouragement and feedback in the early stages. You guys are The. Best.

Huge thanks to my awesome betas, Jennifer Christy, Amy Reierson, Courtney Anderson, and Amanda Shepard for your enthusiasm and fantastic notes, and to my special guest betas Corinne Akers and Jennifer Kreinbring for your excellent feedback!

Thanks to Jaime Ryter for your eagle-eyed notes (*made you cry again!*) and to Lori Jackson and Emily Wittig for the gorgeous cover designs. As always, thanks to the amazing Stacy Blake, who helps me make my gorgeous paperback interiors!

Thanks to my dear Starfish, to my Mermaids, and to my Veeps for keeping me sane and motivated while I'm in the cave.

I can't begin to put into words how much I appreciate the love and support of all the book-bloggers/tokers/gramers, of my author-buds, and of my readers and friends. I love you guys!

I hope you all devour this new story and come back begging for MORE!

Stay sexy,

<3 Tia

ABOUT THE AUTHOR

Tia Louise is the *USA Today* best-selling, award-winning author of super-hot and sexy romances. She'll steal your heart, make you laugh, melt your kindle... *and have you begging for more!*

Signed Copies of all books online at:
http://smarturl.it/SignedPBs

Connect with Tia:
Website
Instagram (@AuthorTLouise)
TikTok (@TheTiaLouise)
Pinterest
Bookbub Author Page
Amazon Author Page
Goodreads
Snapchat

**** On Facebook? ****

Be a Mermaid! Join Tia's Reader Group at
"Tia's Books, Babes & Mermaids"!

www.AuthorTiaLouise.com
allnightreads@gmail.com